"Featuring one of the most original magic systems ever devised and a pair of likable, layered protagonists, *Flex* is a fast-paced, imaginative, and emotionally engaging adventure. The developing friendships and rapport among the characters are portrayed with sensitivity and avoids cliches, and the magical battle sequences are rigorous and filled with ingenious touches that will make gamers and tax lawyers alike grin with joy."

Ken Liu, winner of the Nebula, Hugo, and World Fantasy Awards

"*Flex* is a real gem sharp, weird, and wildly innovative. It zigs when you think it'll zag, then tricks you into screaming when you're ready to laugh out loud. So drop everything and settle in for the night because once you open this one, you're not going anywhere."

Cherie Priest, author of Boneshaker, *winner of the Locus Award for Best Novel and the PNBA Award*

"Do you like magic? Do you like drugs? Donut-based psychological theories? Video games? Do you like *paperwork*!? Read this book!"

Ann Leckie, author of Ancillary Justice *and winner of the Hugo, Nebula and Arthur C Clarke Awards*

"Amazing. I have literally never read a book like this. Read this NOW, if only to be forced to turn the page wondering what the hell Steinmetz is going to come up with next."

Mur Lafferty, Campbell award-winning "Best New Writer 2013" and author of The Shambling Guide to New York

"Big ideas, epic thrills, and an unlikely paper-pushing hero you'll never forget. Just when you think you know what's next, the book levels up spectacularly."

John Scott T

"*Flex* is hot, inventive, and exciting. A real joyride of a story... a whole new kind of magic and a whole new ballgame. Totally recommended."

Seanan McGuire, winner of the John W Campbell Award and Hugo-nominated author

"Not since Philip K Dick started toying with reality for fun and profit has there been a novel so enjoyably hallucinatory as *Flex*. A heady mix of the surreal and the mundane, it will appeal to fans of video games, donuts, insurance, bureaucracy and crime families. Oh, and modern day mage wars. Yet for all of its wild plot, this is a story about the tender bond between parents and children, the loyalty of friends and how the odd among us find their places in the world. Ferrett Steinmetz has written a page turner!"

James Patrick Kelly, winner of the Hugo, Nebula and Locus Awards

"*Flex* is a breath of magical, drug-addled, emotionally tortured fresh air, with one of the most unique and fascinating main characters I've read in ages. In an urban fantasy genre filled with handsome vampires and sassy witches, Ferrett presents us with Paul Tsabo, a Greek insurance adjuster with a prosthetic foot, forced into the half-mad underworld of a reality-bending narcotic to save his daughter from a devastating house fire. With great characters, evocative writing, and boundless creativity, *Flex* is one of the strongest debut novels I've ever seen, and one of my favorite novels of the year."

Dan Wells, author of I Am Not a Serial Killer

"*Flex* was an absolute delight to read, and my only real lament is that I can't cast some bureaucromancy of my own to conjure up the sequel right friggin' now".

Michael Patrick Hicks, author of Convergence

"A well-paced, sometimes serious, sometimes zany mission to save the world from a mass murderer, with some moral dilemmas mixed in for spice, *Flex* was an enjoyable read that ended up somewhere close to *Breaking Bad* by way of *Scott Pilgrim versus the World*."
Speculative Post

"Half part *Breaking Bad* and half part urban fantasy, *Flex* is an enthusiastic romp through a world of ingenious magic accessed by geeky, obsessive projection. Tremendously entertaining rule-tinkering and loophole-hunts abound. A terrific read."
Robert Jackson Bennett, author of American Elsewhere

"This world is amazing just the idea that an obsession can bend reality enough to create magic is a brilliant one. The idea on its own brings something fresh to urban fantasy, and was enough on its own to draw me into the book. Steinmetz brings something new and fresh to the genre."
Stephanie Gunn, writer for ASIF and judge of the Australian Shadows Awards

"When we think of magic users in fiction, we tend to think of magicians like Dumbledore or Gandalf: wise, old graybeards whose professorial robes invoke their deep education into occult arcana. They are cool, collected practitioners of their arts. Even less establishment sorcerers tend to have a sheen of coolness about them; think of Kate Daniels or Harry Dresden, swathed in black, working as mercenaries or detectives, out in the thick of it. Which is why it is so utterly charming to meet Paul Tsabo in *Flex*, the debut novel from Ferrett Steinmetz".
B&N Sci-Fi & Fantasy Blog

FERRETT STEINMETZ

THE UPLOADED

ANGRY
ROBOT

ANGRY ROBOT
An imprint of Watkins Media Lt

20 Fletcher Gate,
Nottingham,
NG1 2FZ
UK

angryrobotbooks.com
twitter.com/angryrobotbooks
Is this the Upterlife

An Angry Robot paperback original 2017
1

I'm not Jewish. But for years, my Jewish friends have generously invited me to their houses to share Seder with them.

This book's dedicated to anyone who shelters friends during their special times.

PART I: COMPLIANCE

PROLOGUE

It was six weeks after my parents' funeral before I realized they were never going to call me again.

"This is normal dead people behavior," my sister Izzy reassured me, brushing my hair aside to blot away my tears. "It takes the newly deceased a while before they get bored enough to call home."

I didn't like the idea of being boring. But then again, everyone living had become seriously uncool ever since Walter Wickliffe had invented Heaven.

"We're not *boring!*" I protested. "We're their *children*, Izzy. The landlord's trying to kick us out, Child Protective Services wants to split us apart, and Mom and Dad won't check their email?"

Izzy went very still, then. She wasn't much older than I was; twelve to my nine years old. And at the time, I thought her calmness meant she was bored by me too, that she was ready to die – ready to upload her consciousness to the Upterlife and leave me behind just like Mom and Dad had.

But now, years later, I see what that stillness meant: even though Izzy had spent her life cleaning up Mom and Dad's messes, this was a special hell for her. She didn't know a thing about rental contracts or wills or social workers, but now she had to learn and learn quickly or else the last of her family would be torn from her forever.

And *she* had to comfort *me*.

"They love us," she said, and then whispered it again as if she took strength from the thought: "Yes. They love us. But Amichai, the Upterlife – it's designed to be the most fun game anyone's ever played. It's got to be so fun that you don't mind leaving your body behind. And... I guess it's normal to forget the real world exists for a week or two after you pass on."

"That's one week! It's been *six weeks*, Izzy! They *should* have called!"

"I know that."

"It can't be *that* good, can it? The Upterlife?"

She closed her eyes; a crease appeared in the middle of her forehead. And I got angry because I thought she was preparing new excuses for Mom and Dad, *again*, and that she was going to remind me how much I liked playing the sample Upterlife games on the touchpads, *again*, even though they were crappy sample zones that weren't nearly as good as the Upterlife itself. The Upterlife trial zones were populated with stammering AI constructs; the full Upterlife was staffed with psychologically realistic NPCs who were as skilled as human actors. You could create mouthwatering ice cream cones in the trial zones – but locked in this meat-world, the best you could do was lick the screen. The dead could lick the simulated cone with simulated bodies, and the experience was supposedly better than anything we could get in *this* life.

I thought Izzy was going to defend the Upterlife to me – again. But years later, I realize Izzy was swallowing back sickness – because now that she'd finally had a taste of the financial pressures Mom and Dad dealt with, she understood why our parents might want to scurry away into an eternal reality where every virtual luxury was kept free to keep fourteen generations of dead voters happy.

"It's – not that the Upterlife is that good, Amichai," she stammered, "It's–"

The monitor on the wall rang. Izzy flinched; the only people who called us nowadays were either our dead landlord to demand rent, or dead social workers calling to tell us Izzy had filled out the wrong form, but–

It was Mom and Dad.

I leapt out of Izzy's lap to thumb the "answer" button.

And though the screen was as grimy and cracked as anything in this rundown world, the video irised open like a window to paradise. The camera soared across verdant green hills, showing off lush vegetation healthier than anything I'd seen in our polluted town.

Then it swirled in like a hero shot to focus in on Mom and Dad, looking happier than they'd looked in those last few months before the Bubbler plague had caused their skin to slide off. Dad rested his hands on a glowing scimitar, clad in shining dragonskin armor; Mom held a staff that rooted itself into the earth like a tree.

I'd only ever seen them dressed in woolen suits.

I barely recognized Dad with his new luxurious long hair, all his worrylines erased; Mom had plumped up from her emaciated food-ration figure, her once-scurvied teeth now a dazzling white. They both looked like movie stars.

"Amichai!" Dad waved. "Izzy! *Hail and well met, friends!*"

It was kind of cool that they were already talking to us like we were questgivers.

"Mom! Dad!" I cried. "Are you OK?"

"Oh, Amichai, things couldn't be better for us," Mom said. "The Upterlife's the best time a girl could ask for."

"But don't kill yourself," Dad said seriously. "I mean, suffering the plague was so *worth* getting all of this, but... suicide's against the law."

I was so glad to see them again that all my anger fizzed out of me like a soda, replaced with relief. "So you're all right?"

"Absolutely!" Mom said. "We're leveling up fast, Amichai. There's so much to learn, it's the most endless game, we can't wait for you to join us..."

And Izzy sat still for an hour as Mom and Dad regaled me with the tales of questing deep into the Underworld, finding the Springseed that grim Hades had guarded, all to end winter forever in their personal domains. And I was mesmerized, because they didn't talk about it like it was a game – this was *life* to them, sipping faerie wine on their endless, endless vacation.

I curled up in front of the television, listening with the dim envy of someone who didn't get to go on vacation but got nice postcards.

And finally, when Izzy realized that Mom and Dad would talk all day about how they'd become the ambassadors to the black-flame firbolgs, she cut in: "So... the landlord says we can't afford to stay here?"

They sighed, looked offscreen. "Well, Izzy..."

"Yes?"

"The landlord's right."

They had explanations, of course. Rent was too expensive when Walter Wickliffe – bless his soul – made sure the state-run orphanages were practically as good as our apartment. And maybe Izzy and I would be separated physically, but everything's digital now, you can do just as well with videoconferences and texts, and they were *sure* the orphanages would do their best to assign us to the same labor projects.

I remember Izzy clenching and unclenching her fists, trying not to scream at Mom and Dad – because if she started screaming, then she'd be the least fun part of this new game that was Mom and Dad's life and they'd choose not to come back. I remember Mom and Dad beaming commercial smiles at us, telling us this would all be for the best.

But most of all, I remember that sick horror as I realized Mom and Dad would spend weeks on a quest to rescue the Springseed, but not their actual children.

I remember the day I came to hate the Upterlife.

1: SIX YEARS LATER

"So why *are* we smuggling a pony into this hospital, Amichai?" Dare asked.

We had not, I should stress, done anything illegal yet.

The pony had been legally purchased, albeit at a ruinous price that only Dare could afford, from a rapid-grow breeder in Central Park. And despite the fact that the rotting alleyway walls glistened firefly green with a hundred embedded cameras, there were no laws against using carrots to entice a Sleipnir-class pony into an alleyway *near* the hospital's service elevator.

Yet after what the courts had done to poor Izzy, I was listing the crimes I planned to commit tonight. Breaking into the elevator? Illegal. Neutralizing the dead's security cameras to sneak a pony in to cheer up my plague-stricken sister? *Super* illegal.

Visiting after hours? OK, *technically* illegal, but they'd probably let that one slide.

"We are going to remind my sister that there are things worth living for," I told him. I swept a carrot around dramatically to point at the elevator doors. "Trapped in that house of ailments lies a girl who *thought* she would be gloriously killed in action, working as a soldier for the LifeGuard! And now, thanks to scandalously unjust courts and a bodywarping plague, she will spend her days in agony and–"

It would have been a pretty good speech, if the pony had played along. As it was, it dashed ahead to snatch the carrot from my fingers and then rubbed up against me in affectionate triumph, crushing me against the wall.

Sheepish, I scratched her sandy fur – I guess it's called fur – and slipped away so she wouldn't nosh on the rest of the carrots in my woolen jacket. The beast's compliance seemed entirely carrot-based, and our supplies were running low.

Dare grasped his hands together so he didn't fidget, bowing instinctively so his straight black hair tumbled forward to cover his eyes. Even though he had the money to dress in sharp clothes that would have broken any man's heart, he dressed like a schlub in ill-fitting woolen coats.

He muttered quickly, like he was trying to get all his thoughts out before angry voices shouted him down.

"Amichai," Dare mumbled. "Me and Peaches were tuned into the courtroom when the judge ruled Izzy insufficiently disabled for euthanasia, remember? I know Izzy's depressed. I know she's going to spend the rest of her life with her arms… distorted… like that. But, you know, maaaaaaybe before you ruin your life with some mad equine reverse heist, well… I mean, you didn't explain to me why you wanted to fill the sprinkler system with colored paint, either, and I could have told you why *that* art project wouldn't have worked out the way you thought if, you know, you'd asked me before you pulled the fire alarm, so maybe… I dunno…"

He dribbled, embarrassed, to a stop. "Maybe you might run by me what you hope to accomplish?"

I snapped my fingers three times by his left ear. He flinched, like he did whenever someone made a sudden noise.

"I'm up here, Dare." I bent down to brush his hair away, bringing his chin up so he'd make eye contact. "First: I'm your friend, not your family, remember? It's OK to disagree with me."

Dare… had issues with conflict. I kept forgetting that, because my family had fought like banshees ever since Mom and Dad had died.

Dare had the opposite problem. His extended family, every last one of them dead, was desperate to ensure he and his sister Peaches kept the Khan-Tien family mausoleum running according to the family standards. So if he screwed up, his dad yelled at him – then his granddad, then his great-granddad, and so on to fourteen generations of cranky, cranky Khan-Tiens micromanaging him out of existence.

All that perfection had kinda knocked the wind from his sails. I'd taken it upon myself to give the kid a breeze. (Though I shouldn't call him a kid, he was technically fifteen, same as me.)

"I'm sorry, Amichai." His light brown cheeks flushed darker. "I didn't mean to…"

"*Ut!*" I put my finger over his lips. "What's our rule?"

"No apologies."

"Good. So on to the second point: you snuck out in the middle of the night to buy me a pony on the off chance it *might* make me feel better?"

His tan skin flushed, that shy grin peeking out from beneath his hair like the sun emerging from behind a cloud. I lived for that goofy grin some days.

"You arc such a *mensch*," I said, grabbing his shoulders and kissing the top of his head.

"…I don't even know what that means."

The pony – a Sleipnir-class top-of-the-line breed, genegineered for maximum intelligence, compact muscles to carry tons of server parts, and apparently heartmelting amounts of adorable fuzziness – tilted her head as if she hoped I too would explain all this to her.

"It means a good friend like you deserves an explanation," I said magnanimously. "And Izzy… she thought she'd be killed in the line of duty before her twenty-first birthday. Now the judges say she's got to live out her natural life, in a body where she can barely pick up a glass of water, for the next seventy years."

"That's bad, Amichai, but it's not like she's Shriving Mortal. Sure, the LifeGuard kicked her out, but she's still got the Upterlife in her future. She can't be *that* depressed…"

"She hasn't called in three days."

Dare froze. He was my roommate at the Walter Wickliffe 82nd Street Orphanage. He knew how Izzy and I called each other every night, no matter what happened, just to check in.

"She's giving up hope," I continued. "Without me, those next seventy years will kill her in ways the Upterlife will never give back. But when she sees that her brother can smuggle a pony into her hospital room to take her for a wild ride down the hallways…" I held my fingers out to frame the imaginary scene, drawing Dare's attention over to the elevators. "Then Izzy will know there's still good things to be found here. In the meat-world. And that wonder will sustain her."

He swallowed. "That… that sounds like an Upterlife quest."

I crossed my arms, preening. "Doesn't it?"

"No! That's bad. You can't compete with the Upterlife, Amichai. You can't make real life into videogames."

"You'd do it if it was *your* sister, man."

"Amichai." Dare turned me around in a slow circle to show me the constellations of cameras blink-flickering brokenly at us from the alleyway's walls. They looked like eyes, peering out from the shadows. They pretty much *were* eyes, networked into the messy, force-grown coral.

It's two o'clock in the morning, I thought, shivering. *This alleyway's a snooze. Probably nobody's tuned in.* And of course, Dare and I had both chosen a meandering pathway that kept us in the sights of the broken cameras – there weren't enough living left to do maintenance, which meant you could steal some much-needed privacy in the dark zones.

But the dead could look through any working camera. Most of them were playing their brains out in the Upterlife, of course – but fourteen generations of people have been stored in the servers since Walter Wickliffe perfected brain-transference software. That's a hundred and twenty *billion* postmortemed. And even if only one out of a thousand people refuses to play in the Upterlife's reindeer games, that still leaves a hundred and twenty million dead folks poking around in the meat-world.

Lots of those dull fumblers peered through obscure cameras, hoping to find the living doing wacky things so they could sell the footage to *Sins of the Flesh* for fabulous Upterlife prizes.

(Yes, some people die and go to heaven to watch reality television. Don't ask me, *I* don't understand them.)

But his point was made: I might cheer Izzy up. I might also Shrive Mortal before this was done. And if I died before I could play nice long enough to lower my Shrive-status back to Venal, that meant permanent meat-death – my brain's last save point deleted, my body rotting, my consciousness barred from the Upterlife...

"This all assumes they actually catch me doing the deed," I said.

"You're smuggling a half-ton pony into an intensive care ward, Amichai! Of *course* you're going to get caught."

"No!" I whipped out the IceBreaker and waved it back and forth before Dare's eyes, hoping the majestic glory of my technology might persuade him. And the IceBreaker was glorious – fourteen inches of the best hacking technology Mama Alex had to offer, a crystalline hologram projector mounted on a cylindrical black broadcast amplifier. "Dare, come on, you think I'd smuggle a pony into a hospital without an ace up my sleeve?"

Dare tried hard not to be impressed – but he'd seen me soldering and debugging the IceBreaker for the past few weeks, swearing as I tried to get the software drivers on the various parts working without conflicts. He'd made a few snarky comments about whether I'd ever succeed in assembling it – which is why I didn't mention how I'd called Mama Alex a few times for troubleshooting advice.

But with the IceBreaker, I had a chance of pulling this escapade off.

He squinted, afraid to get near it; his dead family had drummed a fear of programmers into him. "Is that legal technology?"

"...all the *parts* are legal..."

"And if Gumdrool caught you with those parts hooked together, how much trouble would you be in?"

Technically, programming was knowledge forbidden to the living – you could theoretically hack the dead's servers. "Orphanage rules are different. According the law, this fine device contains nothing that I have programmed personally."

"So it does nothing that could get you arrested?"

"So many questions! And no! I've merely piped together a bunch of perfectly legal, dead-written programs until their chained output did things their creators never would have intended."

Dare was skeptical... but one of the benefits of having a reputation as a performance artist was that people will follow you around to see what trouble you get into. "So walk me through this not-illegal plan."

I lured the pony over to the elevator with another carrot, then fired up the IceBreaker. The alleyway glowed a CRT green as flows of output streamed up a holographic projection on the wall. "I'm not breaking in to the elevator," I assured him, quietly cracking open the hospital's wifi network. "This is like... it's like turning a house's doorknob to check if it's unlocked."

"Uh-huh."

"And then rattling the windows."

"Sure."

"And then maybe fitting five hundred thousand of the most commonly used keys into the front door's lock."

The elevator's bells dinged as it rattle-and-creaked its way down to ground level. The pony danced backwards, snuffling warily at the rusted gate, and I couldn't blame her; that creaky transport looked like it'd been built back in the days of gas-powered cars.

I stroked my pony's hair, whispering sweet nothings in her ear: "Nothing to fear, mon amour. Amichai has your safety well in mind."

Dare cleared his throat. "You don't. That elevator has security cameras, and everyone knows *Sins of the Flesh* gets their best footage from security cameras – they'll see you, and report you, and–"

I shushed Dare, then whisked him aside, tasking him with keeping the pony hidden from view.

"I'm in," I told Dare, tapping in a series of new commands to the IceBreaker. "And now I'm recording the footage these cameras are taking of this empty elevator. And now... I'm broadcasting the looped footage back into the cameras." I snapped my fingers. "The dead are now watching reruns–"

Dare started hyperventilating so hard the pony licked him on the face.

"Amichai!" he spluttered, pushing the pony's head away. "You just blinded the dead! There's no way that's legal!"

"I never said it was legal! I just said they wouldn't *catch* me."

"Sweet void."

" – and all I have to do is creep through the hospital, taking footage and feeding blank loops back to them – they'll never see me coming –"

"I know you don't care about *your* future, Amichai, but Career Day's coming up soon. This is the sort of thing that gets you a black mark forever. Shit, I could get in trouble just for buying you the pony. And I *need* my career, I can't get blackballed, you know I–"

I grabbed him by the shoulders again. "You want out, don't you?"

He squinched one eye shut, grimacing up at me. "...not if you're going to guilt me into staying..."

"Nah. This one could turn foul. The pony, the keeping me company – you can exit now and you've *still* done more than enough to be a top-notch friend."

Though honestly, I *had* hoped for a partner-in-crime – but if Dare wasn't into it, I wasn't going to force the issue.

He pulled me into a hug, and we did that man-thing where we thumped each other on the back because you know, you couldn't just enjoy a hug from your best friend. Especially not when your best friend happens to be gay, and your orphanage is filled with gossipy jerks whispering your platonic friendship must be something way more.

"All right." Dare squinted up at the building's outline. "I'd guess that elevator opens into a storage room behind a nursing station, so watch yourself. If you get into trouble, make alternating lefts and rights to head towards the exit."

I didn't question, even though Dare had never visited Izzy in the hospital. The boy had a sixth sense for buildings. He spent all his Upterlife trial time creating the most amazing architectural plans – his biggest dream was that one day, he'd make a building that actually got *built*.

"And you gotta keep that pony in line, Amichai." I looked down; I had four carrots left. "Because remember: the nurses are legally obligated to keep their patients alive. Every patient in there is desperate for a ticket to the Upterlife, and they're hungry for fatal accidents they can blame on anyone else. One dies on your watch? That's a straight ticket to the void. Careful they don't fling themselves underfoot."

"They will voiding not," I told him. "This is an Upterlife quest, Dare. I'm gonna ride her through there like it was a parade. Start a party."

Dare shook his head, chuckling. "What's your Shrive-rank these days, Amichai? What are the dead judging you as? Venal? Mortal? Criminal?"

"Liminal," I lied. He laughed.

"I'd like to see your parade, Amichai, but it'll be a miracle if you make it up there without getting caught. But if anyone can make miracles happen… it's you."

I went for another manly hug – but Dare was already darting between the dead cameras, racing back to the orphanage.

I coaxed the pony into the elevator, then thumbed the button. The elevator showered us in rust and mouse crap as it juddered to life. This was doubtlessly its first use since the Bubbler plague six years back.

"Easy, beautiful," I said. The pony nickered nervously, leaning against me and pinning me to the wall. She was maybe four feet tall, but that four feet was solid muscle, genetically engineered for superhuman (and superpony) feats. Whereas I have arms like pipe cleaners and flap like a flag in a breeze. Most Sleipnir ponies had autobridles installed, electronic gadgets in their skulls that induced sleep-seizures when they got too frisky, but I'd demanded a pony that was completely free.

I thought about what Dare had said. Maybe I was too rebellious for my own good. Maybe trying to outdo the Upterlife to cheer up my sister was a fool's game.

I could still call this off. I could bring the pony back to Central Farm, then visit my sister tomorrow with a bouquet of daisies. Something, you know, normal.

But if I did normal things, then my sister would be scared instead of telling everyone stories about her crazy brother.

After they'd vanished into the Upterlife, my parents had taught me all sorts of dippy lessons about being brave and staying true to yourself. But their most lasting lesson came when they died and found cooler things to do:

People leave you if you don't have anything interesting to offer them.

So when the elevator shuddered to a halt, my hands shook as I unlatched the door. I knew I could get caught. I knew the consequences. But I also knew the truth:

Far better to die a legendary meat-death than to be forgotten.

I stepped into the hospital.

2: PONY CONGA LINES IN THE VIRULENCE WARD

It had been six years since the Bubbler had killed 94 percent of New York City, and the hospital's hallways still stank of rotting meat. The nurses had buried the stench under lemon-scented cleanser – but the stink seeped up from the tiles, a sour reek that made the pony whinny and retreat back into the elevator.

That smell brought back memories of my parents' skin sliding off their bodies. They'd screamed for help until their tongues fell out. And yet instead of giving them painkillers, their dead doctors gave them cheerful lectures about how stupid meat-bodies were. You couldn't shut off the pain response! Not like in the Upterlife, where filtering out unwanted responses from your electronic body was as simple as changing a setting! No worries, you'll be dead and happy soon.

The dead doctors were why I'd thought it would be easy to slip in. There wasn't one living doctor walking the halls of Lenox Hill hospital; you had to do a century's worth of residency training before anyone would let you work on the living. Izzy kept telling me how lucky she was to have dead professionals looking after her, but me?

I wondered how much these "experienced" doctors had

forgotten about mortal discomforts.

The elevator opened up into a nurse's station, just as Dare had predicted. But I checked the cameras and confirmed there were no physical attendants around. All the living were good for was hauling equipment; most of the work here was done by sensors the dead monitored, surgical bots the dead controlled, computer-controlled IVs the dead dispensed drugs through.

I lured the pony out with my carrot, holding the IceBreaker in front of me like a magic wand, carefully ensuring every camera before me was hacked before creeping into the next safe zone.

My skin crawled as I inched forward into the next camera's field of vision. I couldn't stop thinking about Dare's warning: *everyone knows* Sins of the Flesh *gets their best footage from security cameras – they'll see you, and report you.*

I wondered if playing the "I'm just a dumb kid" card would get me out of trouble. It had before. The dead viewed the living as naive idiots.

Then again, most dumb kids hadn't set a record for "most days in the Time-Out Chamber."

"Don't get caught, Amichai," I whispered to myself. "Don't get caught."

The pony licked my face encouragingly.

Lenox Hill was cold, dim, and shabby, with gray unpainted coral walls featuring TV monitors embedded every few feet – the same as every other building in New York. When I'd watched Dare create his artificial buildings in the Upterlife trial zones, he'd showed me all the ways people used to pretty up their living quarters – paint, wallpaper, molded wood. Ever since he'd showed me his designs, I couldn't stop thinking how beautiful this world could be if we cared about it. I imagined buildings filled with sunlamps, comfortable beds, portraits and paintings. Instead, all we got were the same dreary cut-and-copied hallways.

They'd dimmed the lights to save on electricity, but the patients never slept. They hunched over their glowing computer tablets, dorking around in the Upterlife trial zones.

The pony poked her head into a patient's room, snuffled around curiously. A dull-eyed middle-aged woman looked up.

I waggled my eyebrows at her: *hey, lady, want a pony?*

She cocked her gaunt head, slightly irritated as she focused in on us – as if rogue pony-vendors were continually bursting into her ward to promise wild adventures–

And then her tablet beeped, colors reflecting off her face as her game rewarded her with some new dazzling digital sight.

She returned to playing.

I'd seen that look before. Everyone at the orphanage got an hour's worth of Upterlife trial time a day, and you could get away with murder while everyone was glued to their screens. Game designers had spent centuries perfecting the art of doling out rewards to create addictions.

And while the hospitals wouldn't give you painkillers, they *would* give you 24/7 access to the Upterlife trial zones. Since the doctors would only admit you when you had one foot in the grave and the other on a banana peel, the trial zones were considered to be a way of transitioning to a postmortemed existence.

I walked the pony by a few other rooms, knocking on the doorframes, quietly offering ponycentric mischief to the young and the old alike. But usually, a half hour of Upterlife sample play was your reward at the end of a backbreaking day of labor. Now they could get all they wanted for free, the patients guzzled deep on an unlimited supply. They were too busy to even call an orderly in.

Too bad. They were missing an awesome miniparade. If I was in charge of this hospital, I'd bring in cool surprises every day. So the patients would be alert and asking questions like, "Yesterday, Amichai held an impromptu dance-off among the nurses. What'll he do today?"

"You're a killer pony," I said, ruffling her mane to make up for the fact that nobody was paying attention to her. She whinnied appreciatively.

We crept down the hallways. There were blinking eyelights embedded in each wall, floor, and ceiling – so the dead could see you from every angle.

The pony clopped ahead, about to walk right into some live, unhacked cameras.

"Whoa!" I yelled, hauling her to a stop. She looked back in confusion: *weren't you trying to get me in here a moment ago?*

I checked my pockets. Two carrots left.

I sure hoped someone was serving carrots for dinner tonight.

Thankfully, there were no living nurses within earshot to hear the clop of her hooves. Plagues regularly swept through New York's close-packed population, ever since the supergerms had evolved past our antibacterials. But the Bubbler'd been particularly vicious, slaughtering nine out of ten living people before we'd developed gene-treatments to fight it. Six years later, the dead were still struggling to fill meat-jobs with living bodies.

And it's not like the skeleton crew of nurses cared enough to investigate weird noises. Like all living workers, they were overworked and underenthused, doing their job just well enough to slog into old age and slump wearily into the Upterlife's wonders.

It would take a ruckus to rouse the living from their stupors. Unfortunately, the pony was an imminent ruckus.

Then I saw Izzy – and suddenly, all of this horsing around seemed natural.

She was wide awake in a small bed, kept sterile within

an oval vacuum-curtain of airjets. She stared longingly at an Upterlife tablet.

Even though her skin had pulled taut over her shrunken muscles, like a shirt shrunk in the wash, she still sat up straight with the rigid posture they'd drilled into her at the LifeGuard academy. Her shoulders hunched painfully as she waved in commands. They'd paralyzed her for two weeks while the new gene-treatments reknitted her skin to her muscles – but despite their best efforts, her epidermis had reattached in weird places.

She frowned as she stared down at her game tablet, her cheeks reddened with broken blisters – and my heart lifted to see that peevish scowl. Whenever Frank Beldon had filed new paperwork to restrict our visiting hours, Izzy'd give a tiny sigh and frown as though she knew she *could* fix this problem, she just didn't know *how*.

Right now, her problem was leading her army of virtual ponies to victory.

I couldn't hear what she was playing, not over the low *whoosh* of the aircurtain that kept her germs separated from the rest of the ward – but I knew *Pony Police Action* was her favorite game.

I began IceBreaking her surveillance cameras so we could talk privately.

The LifeGuard had tons of recruitment videogames to encourage people to join the cops. If you were into first-person shooters, they'd fling you into messy combat so you'd think every LifeGuard member died in action. If you were into simulations, they'd give you control of artificial cities and reward those who expanded their Upterlife server banks the fastest.

But if you identified as femme and were into strategy games, like Izzy, they gave you a pony farm to breed the most adorable LifeGuard horses, then sent you out on missions to stamp out NeoChristian resistance enclaves.

She scowled down at the screen. Dare could afford the neural-interface modules where you thought commands into the computer, but our family had to make do with antiquated hand gestures.

Izzy's hands spasmed as she tried to move her ponies into strategic positions and failed. She waved away another failure, relentlessly trying to get her gnarled fingers to obey her, then clumsily flipped the tablet face down on the thin bedsheets. She flopped backwards, staring in despair at the ceiling...

"Hey," I said, leading the pony in. "There's *one* pony who'll do what you ask."

The dazed, happy look on her face was worth all this effort.

Her mouth hung open. "... Is that a Sleipnir-class pony?"

I grinned. "Only the best ponies visit the best sisters."

It would have been a magical moment, except the pony chose that moment to poop.

"You're full of horseshit as usual," Izzy laughed, greeting her pony with open arms. The pony stepped into the whooshing aircurtain between them, then pranced back in surprise as the wind ruffled her ears – but pushed through to the other side.

It would have been heartwarming had the pony nuzzled my sister, but instead she ate the daisies off Izzy's bedstand.

Izzy hugged the pony awkwardly, struggling with her newly twisted arms. She buried her face in the pony's mane, hiding her tears.

My stomach sank as I realized there was no way I could take Izzy for a pony ride; I hadn't brought rope, and her legs were too weak for her to stay on the pony's back. Maybe all I'd done was to remind her of the things she couldn't do any more...

"It's OK," I told her. "We'll get a retrial. They'd have

fasttracked you to the Upterlife six years ago. It's the voiding Bubbler – there's so few living people left, they won't let anyone die until they've squeezed the last of the life out of us. But we'll get a new judge, new doctors to look you over, we'll convince them you can't hold down a job based on physical tasks…"

That frown was suddenly aimed at me, and I realized:

I was her problem.

"We can't afford a retrial, Amichai," she said lifelessly. And she was right. A retrial would require money we didn't have. Maybe it would have worked if Mom and Dad were willing to fight the courts, but they'd gone on a deep quest to fight the Dark Elves and we hadn't heard from them for months.

"I'll talk to Peaches – she has to know somebody…"

"You've done enough already, Amichai." She patted the pony. "You spent hours nagging doctors to testify I was unfit for manual labor. I should be helping you…"

"You're in trouble. I'm getting you out. That's what family does for each other."

"I'm *fine*. The physical therapy, it's not fun, but… well, they say the chip factories aren't heavy work. It's just quality-testing circuitry."

She was trying so hard to convince herself that factory work wouldn't be too bad. Seventy years slaving at unfulfilling work in a body she hated would leave scars that ran deep – too deep. Watch the newsfeeds closely, and you'd find hints of people who'd lived in the Upterlife for three hundred years and still hadn't recovered from their abusive meat-lives.

And her life *would* be nothing but abuse, because the dead thought the living were only good for their bodies. If the LifeGuard had found a job for a woman with poor motor control, Izzy would have been fine. But if Izzy couldn't kick in a door and tackle a NeoChristian, the dead had no need for her. They scorned the living's suggestions, because the dead had centuries of experience – they didn't want some wet-behind-the-ears meat-kid to weigh in on tactics, they wanted raw physical force to aim at their enemies.

Izzy was already starting to measure herself by those sad standards. Her dead supervisors at the chip reclamation factories would write her up as incompetent for every clumsy twitch, and Izzy would slowly come to believe *she* was incompetent because she couldn't do the things *they* wanted.

But she was more than that. *So* much more. She was smart, and clever – she needed to get to the Upterlife where brains were all that mattered...

"I know you think I should just nip off to the Upterlife," Izzy said. "But... maybe it's better if I pay the long way there. I was all hot to defend the servers through glorious LifeGuard missions – maybe I'll find there's just as much dignity in keeping the Upterlife's hard drives defect-free..."

"If you really believed that bullshit, then why are you playing *Pony Police Action* instead of chip-testing games?"

"Because I don't have a choice, Amichai!"

I stood, stunned; even the pony pranced back a guilty step, daisy petals still on its lips. I stepped forward to hug her, but she batted me away, her blows terrifyingly weak.

"I am *not*," she said tautly, "bankrupting this family in some longshot attempt to get into the Upterlife. No, Amichai, this is *not* my ideal career choice. But *I work with what I have.* And unlike you, I don't fight when it's unfair – I fight when I can *win*. So maybe it is unfair I have to put in seventy years of hard labor without... without even being able to play Upterlife games – but if it is, well, I guess I'll have a really sweet reward awaiting me when I finally die. *OK?*"

She glared at me, daring me to contradict her. I couldn't. I'd come here to make her feel better, and instead I'd made her feel worse.

"All right." I held my hands up in surrender. "No more

trials. But… I'll help you with your physical therapy, all right?" And while I helped her, I could remind her that her value to me was not measured by how many steps she could walk that day.

She huffed. "We both know Mr Beldon doesn't like you visiting. He thinks your attachment to me is influencing you in negative ways." Her hazel eyes pointedly flicked over to the pony.

"But that pony's your reward," I told her. "Maybe you can't herd virtual ponies. But if you work real hard at your physical therapy, and get better, I'll take you out for a glorious ride on her back."

"She's beautiful, Amichai." But she hid her disappointment: cool as the meat-pony was, it couldn't cast spells or fly or evolve into another pony breed.

I wondered, as I always did, whether Izzy would have appreciated the meat-world more if the government hadn't thrown her in that voiding orphanage. Her supervisors had made sure all the physical labor was dull and all the interesting things came from watching a screen. I'd organized cooking classes at the 82nd Street Orphanage; Frank Beldon had shut it down because food was for nutrition, not pleasure. Not that there'd been a lot of interest; most of the kids were ashamed to have bodies. Focusing on physical, messy eating was so uncool – and physical therapy was the lowliest of punishments…

"That's her name, then," I said. "Therapy."

"…what?"

"Therapy. Therapy the pony. Whenever someone asks, 'How's your therapy going?', you think of this adorable little moppet." I patted Therapy's flank. "When they say, 'You have to go to therapy,' you don't think of whatever muscle-stretching hell they put you through – you think of this beautiful microhorse licking your face."

"That is the stupidest thing I have ever heard," she said flatly.

She managed to keep a straight face for about twenty seconds, and then we both burst into laughter.

"OK." She wiped away bloodstreaked tears of laughter. "OK, I will accept your pony, you hardheaded ludicrous *eyngeshparter*–"

"Good."

"– if *you* start thinking about your career."

"Bad."

"Career Day is just two months away, Amichai. You want me to relax? Convince me you have a career. After all, it's the biggest choice in your life!"

"I'd be happy if they *gave* me choices," I muttered. Izzy had always been too gung ho about Career Day. All the jobs that involved making interesting decisions – artists and lawyers and scientists and mathematicians – were taken by dead people. We living got the leftovers.

"I was thinking tech services." I twirled the IceBreaker. "You know, maintaining the Upterlife servers."

"What you're doing isn't tech, Amichai." She cringed from the IceBreaker just like Dare had, clutching Therapy as if to shield her pony from my toxic technology.

"It isn't?"

"That's... close to programming."

"So? When I get in, they'll teach me programming."

"You have to wait until they teach you, Amichai! It's illegal!"

"Mama Alex teaches me fine."

She frowned. "Mama Alex Shrives Criminal, Amichai. She smuggles equipment – no, don't tell me she's never been caught, I heard the rumors at the LifeGuard academy. I know you want to make your life interesting, but... if you keep spending time with criminals, then you might not get a job at all..."

I didn't tell her Mama Alex had implied she'd find work for me if I washed out on Career Day.

"They don't let you Shrive unless you have a job," she said urgently. "No Shrive, no Upterlife. If I got to the Upterlife and found you did something... stupid..."

She let that silence draw out. Every day, the radio announced the names of the criminals who'd died and not had their brainscans uploaded to the servers.

"...I'd be heartbroken," Izzy finished. "So please. Put in your applications."

"Great. I can haul equipment, or I can dig ditches."

"Three centuries from now, when we're sipping champagne in our Upterlife mansion, what will it matter what job you had?"

"This life matters, Izzy. It does."

She reached out her hands to me. It hurt her to move.

The doctors said she was noninfectious, I thought. This aircurtain was so she wouldn't catch anything from the other patients. Still, I shivered, remembering how my parents had Bubbled away.

Then I suppressed the shiver and stepped through the aircurtain to let Izzy wrap her sore-covered fingers around mine.

"Amichai, I know you're mad at Mom and Dad–"

"I'm sorry, I don't know this 'Mom' or 'Dad' you speak of. When I call them, I don't seem to get an answer."

"– but you have to understand: that's how awesome the Upterlife is. But the servers won't be any fun for me without my little brother there. So please? Take care of yourself?"

Her earnest eyes were the only untouched feature in her lumpen face.

And she was right. I needed a job. If I got a good job, I could take care of her. If I got something that made enough money,

I could save up to afford a neural interface connection so she wouldn't have to rely on her hands for gaming. I could pay the exemption taxes to get her out of working, maybe even hire a better lawyer for a retrial.

I could take care of her, instead of her taking care of me.

"I promise you I'll get a good job," I told her.

"OK." Her trust was heartrending. "I just want what's best for you, Ami."

"I never doubt your intentions, sis." I chucked her on the chin, feeling overwhelmed; my record was spottier than a Dalmatian. Frank Beldon, that gray rag of an orphanage principal, had dutifully catalogued my every transgression. What employer would take me?

"Good," she said. "I know it'll be boring for a while–"

"Decades."

"– but when it's all done, your reward will be *perfect*."

I walked out of the room, lost in thought.

"Uh – Amichai?"

"Yeah?"

"I… I love the pony, but they won't let me keep her…"

If I got a good job, I could also pay Dare back for the pony. Not that Dare ever worried about money, not with the Khan-Tien Mortuaries backing him, but nobody wants a mooch for a best friend.

I led Therapy back to the elevator, pondering my options. The LifeGuard? Nah. I was weak as a boneless kitten, and the LifeGuard needed muscle – they had dead veterans to handle the tacticals.

Actually, all the interesting careers were taken by dead people. Brain jobs to the brains, meat jobs to the meat. Why train a new engineer when you could find a bored dead dude looking for a challenge?

The irony was that those who craved mental challenges kept returning to the world of the living. Whereas the living were desperate to get into the Upterlife. It was a crazy reversal…

"Mister Damrosch." The voice was dry and dour.

Therapy whinnied as the lights flickered on. Televisions embedded in the hospital hallways clicked on, revealing a sallow balding man with a bad tie, a graying combover hairdo, and a perpetually peeved expression:

Frank Beldon.

What's he doing here? I wondered, reflecting for the ten millionth time that he could choose to have any body he liked in the Upterlife, and he still chose that unflatteringly bushy mustache.

Then I realized: if my orphanage's principal was here at the hospital, I was caught.

Lost in thoughts of my future, I'd forgotten to recheck the once-hacked cameras with the IceBreaker. And with that went my last shot at a good career – and my last chance at helping Izzy.

3: TRAPPED IN A HUNDRED BELDONS

Frank glared at me from a hundred different monitors. Brawny nurses stepped in front of the freight elevator, blocking our exit. They touched the computers studded in their ear cartilage, listening for orders.

"Congratulations," said Beldon, chuckling. "In two centuries of managing orphanages, I thought I'd never see anyone top your trick with the paint in the fire sprinklers. Yet here you are!" He gave me a slow clap.

Frank Beldon held seven degrees in adolescent psychology, and yet was perpetually baffled by actual teenagers. Rumor was, he only kept a real-life job because he hoped that some day he could get us to prove his crackpot theories on childhood development.

"You never proved that fire sprinkler trick was me," I said, planning to make my next trick a disappearing one – but two refrigerator-sized men behind me put the damper on that. Beldon must have called every nurse working the night shift, putting them just where he'd wanted them before getting my attention.

Standard procedure: the dead made the plans, the living carried them out.

"Perhaps." Beldon licked dry lips. "But you've given me such copious physical evidence this time. A clever prank, or a cry for help? Your future depends on how you got past the cameras, Mister Damrosch. If you programmed that device, I can't stop my brethren from voiding you..."

"These are all canned routines, silly ghost." I waggled the IceBreaker at him. "Each approved for living usage. Not a scrap of new code."

"Irregardless," he said. "These cameras are our eyes to the world. Hand over your device and the pony, and I'll make a note you were cooperative."

"What's cooperating get me?"

"Viewed in the correct manner," he purred, "this violation could be a beneficial note on your Career Day application. You're young. Rebellious. But clever. *If* the right words were dropped in the right ears, and *if* the inventor explained how to close such security gaps in the future... Why, perhaps, there might even be a career in Maintenance for you."

"Why do you need the pony?"

Therapy pranced in circles, hoping the nurses were here to play with her. The nurses circled us, arms extended, trying various poses as they doped out how to wrestle a pony into submission.

"You brought an animal into a hot zone, Mister Damrosch. Your sister *is* infected, after all. Dr Greywoode informs me that as a potential plague carrier, the beast will have to be put down."

Izzy's doctor flashed across the screens, nodding solemnly. And I might have believed her...

If the nurses had been wearing protective gear to shield them from plague.

The truth was simpler: I'd pissed off the dead, and crossing them had a price.

Therapy looked at me with trusting brown eyes. Animal deaths weren't like real deaths. Once their hearts stopped, they were gone forever.

My career could *also* be gone forever.

"I need a job." I extended the IceBreaker towards Beldon's nearest viewscreen, as if he could pluck it from my hands. "You think Maintenance will take me? I Shrive Venal, you know."

"Well, I can't promise you anything…"

Of course you can't, I thought.

But even if he could, I couldn't condemn a living creature to the void. Not even for Izzy.

I thumbed the selfdestruct button and hurled the IceBreaker into the storage room.

"Get that device!" Beldon shouted. The nurses in front knocked heads, grabbing the IceBreaker just as it burst into smoldering circuit boards.

Two other nurses lurched towards me – so I slapped Therapy on the butt. She galloped forward with a surprised whinny, bowling them over. I whooped in delight at Frank's outraged expression, then charged after Therapy. *No ponies for you, Beldon.*

I'm not strong, but years of dodging Gumdrool's orphanage patrols have lent me the gift of speed. I flailed my arms, trying to spook Therapy into turning down the right hallways, remembering Dare's words: *if you get into trouble, make alternating lefts and rights.*

By the time I caught up with her, she was pressed against the door to an exit stairwell. Score one point for Dare.

Therapy hung her head low, terrified. I approached carefully, making eye contact so she wouldn't pay attention to the nurses running up behind me.

"It's OK," I wheezed, trying to catch my breath.

She allowed me to approach, and I pushed open the door. And I swear, Therapy gave me an almost human look as she glanced down the stairwell.

It was a look that asked: *is this really necessary?*

In response, I pushed her in. She clopped nimbly down

the coral stairs. I hopped over guard rails, trying to keep up as Therapy trotted in wide spirals, story after story, until she hit the ground floor.

I shoved open the door. The fire alarm went off. Therapy took off like a shot, sparing a single glance behind before leaping effortlessly over an eight-foot fence and vanishing into Central Farm's mazelike gardens.

I turned to the angry nurses descending the staircase.

"Sure, you're mad now," I said, holding out my wrists to be cuffed. "But you'll be telling this story for *centuries*."

4: NOWHERE

The feeling of freedom is an escape artist. You can feel gloriously liberated for a while – but the sensation wriggles away, leaving you with fistfuls of regret.

When I set Therapy loose, it felt like I could do anything. My future was mine – not my sister's, or Beldon's, or the dead's, but a blank canvas for me to paint. Everyone was wrong to tell me how to live, because my way was not just pure, but *righteous*.

Then the orderlies threw me in a cop cart. The LifeGuard told me how serious this was. The Wickliffe teachers shook their heads with regret. Everyone treated me like I was an unShriven body at a funeral.

I thought about Izzy.

Maybe I *had* been too crazy. I could have brought flowers. Instead, I'd put an innocent animal in danger, then chosen a pony's life over my sister's future.

The line between "rebel" and "screw-up" is a fine one.

By the time they threw me into Wickliffe's Time-Out Chamber, I was sick, confused, regretful. All that wild freedom felt like a drunken frenzy, and I felt stupid for buying into it.

But not regretful enough to apologize to Gumdrool.

No, never enough for that.

5: THE TORMENTS OF THE TIME-OUT CHAMBER

Here's a fun fact: when you're locked in a room with an endlessly repeated half-hour TV drama, a show you can't shut off or turn down, waiting for your hearing in a Time-Out Chamber that offers no other distractions aside from peering through the hole in the metal door they shove your lunch tray through, well...

...you go through several stages of regret.

The first stage is watching the show. Fortunately, this Walter Wickliffe biography had a cool title – *The Man Who Conquered Death*.

It was pure propaganda, of course. But the dead directors had spent centuries blurring the lines between brainwashing and entertainment.

The ghost they got to play Walter Wickliffe did a great job. In the Upterlife you can copy anyone's body if they authorize the use of their personal image – and this guy had licensed Walter's slicked-back hair, his kind gray eyes, even the ratty tuxedo. They say Walter was considered old-fashioned back in his day. Yet that outfit was so unmistakably Walter, it might as well have been his superhero uniform.

Which makes sense, because Walter Wickliffe was kind of a superhero. He even had an origin story. The film did a good job showing Young Walter recoiling in horror as his dad strangled Walter's mom in an alcoholic rage, then got shot dead by the cops.

Every film had The Moment when tiny Walter laid a bouquet of dandelions on his mother's grave – the only flowers he could afford – and young Walter shook his fists at the heavens, proclaiming, "From now on, death will never again take anyone I love!"

The actor playing Walter was good. Most actors ham it up. This guy whispered. He slipped into Wickliffe's square-shouldered look, a clear-eyed gaze that said, *This will not stop me*.

Which was cool the first six or seven times.

After that, you start yanking on the doorknob to get out. You know they're playing this to soften you up before your trial, to get you feeling bad about betraying the system. And I did. I mean, Walter had saved the world. I couldn't even save my sister.

So I started mocking the show.

There was a lot to mock; post-origin, *The Man Who Conquered Death* was all downhill. How could it not be? There's only so many ways you can show a guy perfecting consciousness uploading in a lab. So I started catcalling Walter. "Oh! Yes, Walter, spend some more time sitting at a keyboard, looking intense! Surely *that* will solve death!"

With nobody else to hear, razzing Walter Wickliffe just felt lame. I wished I had more friends at the orphanage. Why were all my friends online and far away? And shouldn't someone have come to visit by now? The Time-Out Chamber wasn't meant to be solitary confinement.

…how badly had I screwed up?

The next stage is a depressive funk where you tune out the show except for the coolest bits. For me, that was always Walter's showdown with Congress. Even the actor knew better than to try repeating *those* words. He let the archived recordings roll as Walter testified, telling the world if the United States didn't acknowledge uploading as a fundamental human right, then he would dismantle his technology:

America thinks that life, liberty, and the pursuit of happiness are fundamental human rights. Well, the Upterlife offers eternal life, boundless liberty, and infinite happiness. Black or white, rich or poor, zealot or atheist; all should pass through, but for the lowliest of criminals. And if you do not allow this, then this country is not free, and these servers are not paradise.

I pumped the fist. Void yeah, Walter. You show 'em.

How many times had I seen this show now? Ten? Twenty? I'd been here for half a day with no food. They should have hauled me before the orphanage board of directors already. I knew the drill, and the fact that it was taking this long to get a hearing meant I was deep in the soup.

I should have let them kill Therapy. She was just a pony. People sacrificed animals for good fortune, right?

How could they look them in those big brown eyes and *do* that?

A quiet rap at the door.

"Don't react," Nadi whispered through the lunch-hole. I didn't, of course. The ghosts were *always* watching cells. Cells were where the living did their craziest things – escape attempts, black-market transactions, smearing shit on the walls – which made it prime footage to harvest for *Sins of the Flesh*.

I was glad to hear a friendly voice, but also disappointed; Nadi was barely ten. Which made sense. The older kids had refused to talk to me ever since the sprinkler incident.

"The cameras out here are still clogged," she said. The tie dye paint spraying out of every fire sprinkler had turned the walls glorious colors, as I had planned – but they also blotted most of the cameras. The hours my fellow orphans spent being forced to scrub camera lenses with toothbrushes had *not* improved my standing at the Wickliffe Orphanage.

"Yeah, well, I probably should have done a better job with the pony," I whispered. I slumped in mock despair by the door, burying my head in my hands so the cameras couldn't see my lips move.

"Are you as bored as I think?"

"If Beldon came on to give me a lecture, I would listen with rapt attention."

"Going crazy," she said. "Got it. Anything I can do?"

"Entertain me?"

"I can't slip you an earputer; Gumdrool's watching the feeds."

Gumdrool was a living kid my age, and Beldon had given him *camera access?* Letting him view the world through the eyes of the dead? Crazy. Then again, Beldon always had used Gumdrool as his meat-world enforcer.

That explained Dare's absence, though. If Gumdrool caught Dare trying to talk to me, he'd revoke Dare's Upterlife trial time – and then Dare couldn't access his online architecture projects. And Dare needed to prep his building schematics so he'd be ready to audition on Career Day.

"Then do something else," I begged Nadi. "I'm going crazy in here."

"Like what?"

"Anything."

"OK. We'll think of something."

She vanished. I trembled; this was the longest I'd ever been without Shriving. What if I died? Everything I'd experienced in the last day – meeting Therapy, the hospital chase, my promise to my sister – would vanish like a corrupted file.

What made it into the Upterlife wouldn't be me.

A stupid fear, I know. Humans forget things all the time.

We forget names, the last place we put our wallets, the facts on the test we've studied for – and yet we never worry that scoring 86 percent on a test means we've become someone 14 percent different. You can't Shrive at the moment of death – that's when your brain's already turning to mush – so you're always missing a few hours when you arrive. But that's still *you* in there.

Worrying about whether the me that uploaded would somehow be different from the me in this cell was one of those dumb moldy-oldie philosophy questions – "What if the color yellow I see isn't the same color that you see?" We all had moments fretting about that discrepancy – but if my parents' irresponsibility had taught me anything, it was that you became *more* you in the Upterlife.

Still, there was a reason the first thing couples did after they got married was to get Shrived. You'd be incomplete without some memories. And what if I lost all of these recent experiences of pony-based excitement and my promises to Izzy? I wouldn't be me then, would I?

I itched to save my brain to the servers.

Then it occurred to me: maybe they weren't letting me Shrive because the orphanage was preparing a criminal trial.

I was going to disappear into the void.

Just as I was about to hammer on the door and beg to be uploaded, Nadi whispered: "Think outside the box."

What the void did *that* mean? I peered through the lunch-hole, trying to see where Nadi had gone to…

…and the entire wall facing the Time-Out Chamber's door had been transformed into a penciled mural.

"You kids," I said, realizing Nadi and her friends must have been up all night while I dozed off in exhaustion. They weren't good drawings; without computerized curve-correctors and autofills, the best they could do was crooked stick figures. It was the sweetest thing I'd ever seen.

It was also a rerun.

They'd drawn last week's *Transformers* episode. Which was, in turn, a remake of an old *Transformers* I'd watched as a kid. You could expect a remake of your favorite series about every eight years; why should the dead devise new ideas when there were classic episodes waiting to be mined, remixed, and graphically updated?

Someone else shoved a bowl of gruel through the lunch-hole. Good; they didn't intend to starve me. But I wondered how Izzy was dealing with things, whether Therapy was safe somewhere. I hoped I hadn't completely fucked my future.

…all should pass through, but for the lowliest of criminals…

And there was Walter, saving the world again. Shut up, Walter.

When I was on the verge of breaking down, I'd peer out the lunch-hole to look at the mural. It made me happy and uncomfortable all at once. Later, one of Gumdrool's Junior LifeGuard painted it over.

Hours later, Nadi crept out again. "You're *still* here?" she asked.

"They're really trying to break me this time."

"It's not you – some NeoChristian crazy broke into the school. Took like seven guys to tackle her. They're trying to figure out what to do with her, and until then we're all on lockdown. Where'd my mural go?"

"They painted it over."

"Weird. You mean it didn't autosave?"

I hid my smile from the cameras. "That's the real world for you."

"You want another one? Nora found some pencils in an abandoned building. It's pretty messed up, drawing on real things. You know how hard it is to draw a straight line when the computer's not helping?"

"I do, I do. But listen. That picture was… great, but it… it wasn't you. Can you draw something I've never seen?"

"Sure. What shows do you watch?"

"No, no." I turned around to face her through the lunch-hole, hoping nobody was watching me through the cameras at that moment. "Look, the Transformers are something that other people made. And that's cool, but it's not nearly as cool as the things only you can make. So can you show me something only *you* could think of?"

"Like what?"

"I dunno. How about… someone having an adventure? Not in the Upterlife. In real life. Where they… have to fight a mean guy."

"Like Gumdrool? He took Sarah's candy once. Said the temptation of hunger made her unfit to serve."

"Yeah. Have them fighting Gumdrool." I thought how Gumdrool would react when he saw himself as the enemy in a mural. "But don't call him Gumdrool. I don't want you to get into trouble."

She pursed her lips. "But how…" She sized up the wall like it was a cliff to be climbed. "All right. Only 'cuz the school looked so pretty when the fire alarm went off. It was like splattery rainbows everywhere."

I smiled. I'd wanted to do something that made people here pay attention to the real world… and I'd done it.

I fell asleep – or tried to. But I heard Nadi and Nora muttering in hushed excitement, trying new things, crossing out stuff and starting over again. Their eagerness fed mine.

"All right." Nadi's voice trembled. "I think we're ready." A brief debate, then agreement. "OK. Now."

I looked through the lunch-hole, and saw the majesty of Woman-Pony.

Woman-Pony was a crazy snarl of illegible stick-figures – but that was OK, because Nadi and Nora started explaining it from start to finish, talking over each other's sentences in their eagerness to explain it all.

Woman-Pony was having a grand adventure in Little Venice, searching for a mean musclebuilder (whatever that was) who'd stolen her candy. Along the way they fought off what were either mutant batflies or tiny dragons – Nadi argued they were batflies, while Nora staunchly insisted upon dragons.

Regardless, they fought either dragons or bats, found a mystical land of orange groves in the sewers and sold the oranges to a snakeman, who gave them a magic sword, which they used to threaten to cut the mean musclebuilder away from the Upterlife and he gave them back their candy.

"The end," they said. They bowed, then looked shyly to me for approval.

The door smashed me in the face.

"Amichai Damrosch," said Gumdrool, shaking his head as if he expected better. Behind him, his Junior LifeGuard members – *really* junior, not a one over thirteen – sniggered and seized the girls.

Gumdrool sighed dramatically as he turned to look at the mural. He was one handsome sonuvabitch, all chiseled chin and piercing blue eyes. He wore a spotless white Junior LifeGuard uniform, a harsh blond buzzcut, and a chest full of medals Beldon had given him. Rumor was, he wore that uniform to bed.

He looked magnificently sorrowful, noble, like a painting.

"Amichai, Amichai," he muttered, massaging the bridge of his nose. "You're encouraging young girls to break curfew, risking their Upterlives for... *this*?" He waved one beefy hand at the mural, wrinkling his nose.

The girls shivered as the younger LifeGuards laughed. "Y'can't even see what it's s'posed to be," one said. The rest tried to pose like the ludicrously unanatomical stick-figures, exchanging dumb guffaws.

"Drawing murals won't make them Shrive Criminal," I shot back. "It'll make them *artists.*"

He whirled on me, furious. "How *dare* you take a chance with these girls' eternal lives, Damrosch? I suppose it's all fun and games to you. You hang out with Mama Alex, you're used to the idea of meat-death–"

"– don't you shit-talk Mama Alex–"

"– but I've seen people die unShriven, Amichai. I've seen the terror in their eyes as they realize their brain's dying and nothing will survive them. Gone, like the moldy oldies..."

The girls looked at each other, terrified.

"You keep thinking if you act up enough, you'll find someone who loves you in this world – but your family will leave, your friends will leave, and by the time you realize you can't join them in the Upterlife because you're trying to impress these pathetic meat-sacks, it'll be too late."

My cheeks flushed with a shame I should not feel. "They're not doing anything illegal, Gumdrool! They're just... drawing! Drawing awesome things!"

The junior LifeGuard tried to restrain their laughter. Gumdrool shushed them with a hand, looking at the girls with deep concern.

"So," he said quietly to me. "You think this is... awesome."

"Yes."

"This crudely drawn collection of figures."

"Yes."

"Good. Boys, quiet the girls." Gumdrool's Junior LifeGuard clapped their hands over their mouths.

"Now, Amichai." Gumdrool rested his index finger on a penciled snarl. "Tell me what's happening here."

I tried to remember what they'd said. But they'd been so eager to show off their ideas, stepping on each other's sentences in their haste to finish, that I couldn't keep track.

And without their excited explanations, well... the

drawings weren't very good.

This is why I hate you, I thought.

"That's the, uh… the snake-vendor, right?"

The girls slumped, disheartened.

"There's your lesson, girls." Gumdrool knelt to dab their cheeks with a handkerchief. "You're terrible at drawing. But feel no shame! The dead have been writing and drawing for centuries. That's what they're good at. And you, with your strong bodies? You're good at moving things."

"Of course they're not good artists *now!*" The girls flinched; I felt horrible. "But once their talent matches their ambition, they'll be magnificent!"

The girls looked to Gumdrool, who shook his head. "You might make something OK, given a lifetime's effort – but why bother when your lives are better spent protecting the Upterlife?"

Gumdrool shoved me back into the cell, casually, as if to remind me how many years he'd spent studying martial arts.

"Girls," he said, "There's a neural network in the Upterlife devoted to analyzing every desire you've ever had. It's picking apart your last Shrive right now, making sure your postmortal existence will satisfy your wildest dreams.

"The servers will love you forever… If you work to protect them." Gumdrool bared his teeth at the coral walls as though he wanted to chew through them. "Here, in this rotting meat-world, where everything decays, we've built one perfect thing. The only important thing is to maintain the servers for the next generation, for as long as your body will last. *Then* you may pass into a well-deserved eternity."

"And if they're bored now?" I asked.

"I guess I could bore them," Gumdrool allowed. "Maybe if I asked Mr Beldon to take away their trial-Upterlife for, I don't know… a month…?"

"A *month?*" They danced like they had to go to the

bathroom. They begged Gumdrool not to do it, don't take their trial-Upterlife away, they were almost all the way through the Licorice Forests…

"You see?" Gumdrool spread his hands. "Nobody wants to spend time in this stupid world, Amichai."

He slammed the cell door shut.

"Don't worry, girls," he assured them. "I wouldn't actually take your trial time away. Boys, on the way back to their rooms, ask Mr Beldon if they can have some extra trial time for being such obedient citizens."

They left.

Gumdrool hauled out a can of white paint and painted over the mural.

6: THE WALTER WICKLIFFE ORPHANAGE HEARING ROOM (AGAIN)

In theory, Dr Beldon ran the Walter Wickliffe 82nd Street Orphanage with an iron fist. But while the living kids under his roof had no rights, their dead parents could still intervene for them.

Some kids wheedled their dead dads into letting them stay up late at night, watching slasher flicks while Frank steamed about the inappropriateness of it all. Whereas my parents showed up twice a year, made a mild fuss about how Mr Beldon should allow Izzy and me more visits, and then vanished – allowing a smirking Frank to force me to bed at 8pm nightly.

But I was *really* hoping Mom and Dad would show up for my trial.

I watched the clock on the gray coral wall. It was screwed in above the video monitors, and I watched in anguish as the seconds ticked down. Mom and Dad *had* to come – I'd emailed them, Izzy had bombarded them with emails…

The clock read 2:57 – three minutes to go. The two video monitors marked "GUARDIANS" stayed blank.

The monitor inscribed "ORPHANAGE ADMIN" had Frank giving me one of his watery, compassionate glances – the busybody dead were sticklers for punctuality. But what made me nervous was Dr Greywoode, a stern black woman glaring at me from a monitor marked "WITNESS."

As a minor, my punishment should have been an in-house matter.

Maybe this *was* a criminal trial.

"Let's make a bet, Amichai," said Gumdrool in his best let's-be-reasonable tone. "If your parents show up, I'll give you a fine reference to the LifeGuard. Assuming you're still employable when this is over."

He looked grim. Even I had to admit that if there was one thing Gumdrool hated, it was seeing a citizen void themselves.

"And if they *don't* show up?" I asked.

"You must finally admit your parents don't love you. They love the Upterlife."

I wanted to punch that sympathetic smile… But Gumdrool's arms were like banded cables. I'd watched him twist kids into pretzels.

I glared at the monitors as though I could will my parents into attending.

"They'll be here, Gumdrool."

"That's *Drumgoole*." He elbowed me in the back of the head, a Gumdrool special; quick enough to be overlooked by the camera, on the scalp where it hurt the most, under the hair where the bruise wouldn't show. "Ian Montgomery Drumgoole. Show some respect, Amichai. I'm trying to be your friend."

"Real friends don't hurt you."

"Real friends question you," he whispered. "Why is it you only seek out people who'll encourage your self-destruction?"

He straightened. "I mark the time as 3:00. This means Amichai's parents have waived their right to appear, has it not?"

"It does," Dr Greywoode agreed from her videoscreen, clucking her tongue. "A shame. When a boy's Upterlife is at stake, you'd think his parents would at least send an email."

"Correction, Doctor," Beldon said, cheerfully. "His Upterlife is not at stake."

"It is if I can help it. That's why I called a full hearing. I want him blacklisted from Career Day."

I broke out in a cold sweat. How could I help Izzy without a job?

"A case could be made to expel him," Beldon agreed, polishing his virtual pince-nez glasses. "But the truth is, society is better served by healing this poor boy's ills. Amichai is a textbook case of incoherent rebellion, one we see all too often – in the absence of a firm parental hand, he seeks attention through increasingly outrageous antics. It's merely a stage of growth. Note how all his friends are online – scattered dysfunctionals like himself. Once he's been convinced of the uselessness of his rebellious shenanigans, he'll mature into a productive citizen."

Fun fact: when you're in trouble, everyone has a pet theory as to why you're such a screw-up. They trade theories like baseball cards.

"I'm not going through a *stage*," I protested. "I just don't like what you're offering."

"Amichai, Amichai." Beldon's chuckle was like a newspaper whapped lovingly upon a puppy's nose. "You think you're so unique. Have you ever wondered why I haven't expelled you? Despite the pigs set loose in the school, the endless flashmobs, the paintbombs in the sprinklers…"

"You never proved that was me."

"Point is, Amichai, I used to hate the dead, before I transitioned. I remember the things I did to *my* poor orphanage…"

"You never had a rebellious thought in your life, Frankie."

"My supervisors could tell you the legend of Fraggin' Frank Beldon." He smoothed back his combover. "The point is, Amichai, no matter how we rage, eventually we must earn our living. So we settle down."

"I won't."

"Then we take everything away. Until you learn that rebelling against society means you die a meat-death."

He flashed a photograph of mangled bodies from a Criminal enclave. I broke into a panicked sweat.

"That's not fair!"

"It's more than fair, Amichai," he replied. "If you keep headed down this path, you'll never reach the Upterlife. You don't want to leave your sister alone the way your parents did, do you?"

It was a cheap shot. But could I leave Izzy behind with no one to help her? Leaving her feeling that she was just some handicapped waste of flesh?

"See?" Beldon exchanged a knowing glance with Dr Greywoode. "He'll cave. They all do."

"Excellent work, Doctor Beldon," said Greywoode. "Before we deal with the errant equine, let us first attend to the matter of this unauthorized video jamming device – which, as far as our analysis of the remains can discern, had no traces of newly written code, making it technically legal. I believe you implied Mr Damrosch's technical skills might be rewarded, Dr Beldon?"

"*If* he'd cooperated," Beldon replied.

"A shame."

"A shame. Now let's dispense the punishment."

7: UNDER THE HOOD OF A SHRIVE MACHINE

Beldon told me that my first Shrive after the hearing would determine my punishment – and I didn't want to Shrive alone. So I slouched down the paint-spattered hallways to Dare's room.

President Wickliffe was an orphan himself, so the state orphanages were always well-funded. The 82nd Street Orphanage had rows of featureless gray doors leading to identical gray rooms, where each ward of the state was given a government-supplied bed surrounded by government-supplied eye-cameras, a government-supplied Shrive Point, and a government-supplied earputer loaded with spyware. (I'd jailbroken it as soon as possible – which wasn't illegal, just tricky.)

The orphanage was still recovering from the Bubbler. The influx of kids six years back meant they'd had to split normal rooms into twos and threes, sometimes replacing beds with sleeping bags and stuffing kids into supply closets. We made do.

The one human touch – *my* touch, I thought proudly – was that all those once-gray walls were now splattered with watery dayglo paint. But nobody had done anything to add to my art.

My earputer sent out social broadcasts mentioning I was in the area, in case anyone wanted to come out and say hello. The doors stayed shut. The social maps showed me people clustered in their rooms, playing videogames together, ignoring me.

I had fans. But as Beldon had said, my friends were online, scattered across the city. I only got to be a real-life star when I showed up at the Blackout Parties. Here in the orphanage, I was an outcast.

An outcast who hadn't Shrived in two days. *Nobody* went that long without making a backup copy of their brain. And if this Shrive went Criminal, well, I might never Shrive again.

I needed to be with a friend when I got the news.

Dare's room had a heavy-duty computerized lock on the door. Dare had been heartbroken when Gumdrool's thugs kept breaking in to "confiscate" his stuff. They said his luxuries created a distraction from the Upterlife's goals.

So he'd bought the lock. I'd installed it. Ever since then, Dare's room had been our safe haven. It raised some eyebrows, since we spent hours together alone – but let 'em talk.

Dare was checked in as "alone and available."

Yet I heard him having an argument with *someone*.

Confused, I leaned in to speak a passphrase into the lock's microphone: "The burly broccoli strides across the blasted heath," I replied. A brief buzz of complaint: *Incorrect*.

"Someone's *said* that?" I muttered in disbelief.

"Look, I have to answer this!" Dare yelled, then: "Sorry, Chai, the readout says three people have used that phrase. But I can't–"

I drew a deep breath, determined to make this impressive. "How about… My coral skyscraper flies on wings of soystrami?"

A chime rang, and a tired Dare let me in.

"Ooo, good one." His exhausted grin sagged at the edges.

"'Wings of soystrami.' It rolls off the tongue."

"Thank you. But it's getting harder, man." The passphrase wasn't really a phrase, of course; I'd rigged the lock so it was connected to a public search of every written word over the past three centuries. It only opened if you spoke an eight-word sentence that had never before been expressed by a human being. Gumdrool's thuglets weren't that creative.

"But you shouldn't be here," Dare said. "My relatives, they're–"

"You're still talking to that deadbeat?" a grandmotherly voice shrieked.

"*That's the Amichai scum you betrayed us for?*" an outraged old man shouted loud enough that I had to clap my hands over my ears.

Great. I'd been hoping maybe Dare could get me a job if my Shrive failed, but *that* idea just flew out the window.

"He's bad publicity!" yelled a gruff woman. "A criminal and a malingerer! And you aided him!"

"Dr Greywoode's a client of ours! Did your addled brain forget that, Dare? Do you know what she'd do if she discovered you bought that pony for this hooligan?"

"She'd–" Dare said.

"She'd tell our customers our physical employees had become unreliable! And that would be the end of us all!" a fifth voice barked, followed by a hue and cry of agreement from generations of Khan-Tiens.

"It wouldn't be the end," Dare protested weakly. "It'd hurt the business a little…"

"Our business is our existence, you stupid boy!" a cacophony of voices shouted through the speakers, so many they struggled to be heard. "We've had no new customers for centuries! The Khan-Tien Mortuaries cannot afford to lose a single client! How selfish you are, risking our business for a boy who's not even family! Why can't you be like your sister Peaches?"

Dare had stuffed a pillow over the wall-monitor in a vain attempt to muffle his relatives. I tapped a few commands into the control panel on the walls, activating the temporary mute; you couldn't shut the dead out forever, but you could get a two-hour privacy respite. Dare's great-great-great-great-great-grandparents protested as the speakers hissed into silence.

"Thanks, man," Dare said. His hands trembled. He shivered for hours after a visit from his greats; they knew all his vulnerabilities, and always went for the sucker punch.

"I could teach you. It's not programming. It's just reading manuals."

"Too close for my comfort."

I squeezed myself into a corner. Dare's place was cramped with *stuff*. As a ward of the state, I arrived with next to nothing, all my possessions reclaimed. But Dare had disowned his family voluntarily, paying rent to live here, and so had brought unthinkable luxuries with him – down quilts, nylon jackets, a refrigerator. Even the orphanage's kitchen didn't have a fridge – the "Live Local, Die Global" taxes had made them ridiculously expensive.

"I guess the friggin' ghosts are getting everyone down today…"

"I told you, Amichai, don't call them 'ghosts'. It's a slur, and…" Then he noticed the look on my face. "Oh, crap – your hearing! How'd it go?"

"I won't know until I Shrive." I glanced at his Shrive Point's scarred alloy hood. "If I Shrive Mortal, Dr Greywoode will throw me in jail. And then what the void happens to Izzy?"

I sniffled, trying not to cry. Dare, bless his soul, gave me a thumpy man-hug. "My Shrive Point's your Shrive Point, man."

I blushed. "So if you see tears, you'll realize it's not terror, but rather that I'm so full of testosterone it leaks from my eyes?"

"Stop it." He waved me off. "I grew up with fourteen generations of Khan-Tiens watching whenever I took a dump… And then they'd yell at me for not wiping properly. Trust me, there is *no* way to embarrass me."

"Did they really yell at you for…?"

"Toilet training is a group event in the Khan-Tien family," he said, stonefaced. "Point is, if you need to Shrive out, Shrive out. And if you need to cry, you go right the void ahead."

I felt a deep gratitude. "Thanks, man."

He gestured; his earputer projected a beautiful spiral staircase of golden wires onto the wall. "I'll just work on The Recursive Staircase while you Shrive…"

Dare was working in Earth environments now – since the Upterlife was computer-generated, the laws of physics could be changed at will. Many of the dead resided in low-gravity environments or places with even odder rules. After an experimental period of alternate-physics mansions, Dare'd begun working in the Earth zones again.

I should have Shrived, but I loved watching him create.

Dare frowned and shifted some cables in that effortless way he always did. He always added things in real time; if he'd misjudged the physics, the entire thing would have collapsed in a tangled heap. But no. The structure swayed precariously for a minute – and then reshaped itself into a spiraling funnel that somehow looped in on itself like a mobius strip. A beautiful, shell-like stairway.

Dare had a unique vision: he saw not just what was there, but what *could* be. Dare was always quietly pondering ways to improve things – a talent most of the living had forgotten.

"Is that your Career Day application?" I admired the way light glittered off the cables.

"This or the oakwood mansion." He shifted the light to sunset, and the whole thing glimmered like a fiery spiderweb. "This one's more technical, but it's… you know… unusual."

"Pretty as void, though."

He sighed and closed the project window. "I gotta go with what people want."

And by "people," he meant "dead people." The dead had their own ideas about virtual architecture – finicky rules about what constituted grace and a pleasing form. A good home consisted of a subtle mutation of something they'd seen a thousand times before.

"What if you could make them appreciate the unusual, though?" I leaned over to pull the project back onscreen. "You could make something so unique, even those gummed-up stiffminds *have* to acknowledge how great it is."

"I'm not that good." His shy grin told me he thought he might be.

"You do great work. You ever notice how Gumdrool never docks your Upterlife time?"

"…really?"

"Even he doesn't wanna mess with your talent."

"Oh." Dare considered this. "That's nice of him, I guess. He's… got issues, but he's trying to get us to the right place."

I frowned. I hadn't wanted to make Gumdrool out to be a good guy.

"I dunno, man," I said. "It's like Gumdrools thinks it's a privilege to work. If he got a job breaking rocks in a mine, Gumdrool would spend his free time thinking up more efficient sledgehammers."

"It's not the worst way of looking at things, Amichai. Put in the effort, you'll get rewarded. That's the way things work."

Easy for you to say, I thought bitterly. Dare'd been gifted with a natural talent for architecture. And even if Dare didn't get an architecture career slot, his family would still hand him a job at the Khan-Tien Mortuaries. Not one, but *two* lucrative careers – an easy life for Dare.

Whereas my whole life rested on this next Shrive.

I lay down on his bed and picked up his Shrive Point.

He crossed his fingers. "I'll bet you're still Venal."

I looked at the five glowing icons that ringed the Shrive Point in a halo – the five rankings the dead's collective unconscious could give you. Then I pulled the Shrive Point's battered hood over my head.

Shriving served two purposes: first, it took a full scan reading of your brain to save a copy of your consciousness into storage. When your meat-body died, your last brain-snapshot would be uploaded into the Upterlife, where you could run and frolic with all the other deadbeat parents.

The second purpose of Shriving was to determine if you were *worthy* of the Upterlife.

The Shrive Point hummed as a gentle female voice started asking questions, each designed to highlight a new section of your brain to be scanned:

"What is your favorite pavement?" it asked. "When were you burned? What is colorful clothing?"

Ultrasound beams poked through my brain to prod the answers into full-blown memories. In real life, I was twitching on the bed – but in my mind I was touching Broadway's cracked pavement, I was yanking my hand off a gas burner as blisters puffed up on my finger, I was wrapped in Mom's woolen dresses as she hugged me. All those feelings were sucked up and catalogued, along with a thousand related memories.

Fifteen minutes later, it was time for the dead to vote. I stared at the five icons. Dare sat behind me, squeezing my shoulder reassuringly.

See, once you've stored your memories, every Upterlife inhabitant gets a subconscious vote as to whether your memories say you're the sort of person who deserves entrance to the Upterlife. They don't know they're doing it, but I'm told a happy side-effect is that everyone in the Upterlife feels like they know the new arrivals already. No wonder they're all so chummy.

If the vote fails, you die forever.

Fortunately, the dead's standards were pretty loose. As President Wickliffe hammered home during every election campaign: "Black or white, rich or poor, zealot or atheist; all should pass through, but for the lowliest of criminals."

But those lowliest criminals got filtered out. When folks judge you based on what *you* know you've done, there's no escaping your punishment.

Technically speaking, the dead's vote only mattered when you died. But with each backup copy you made of your consciousness, they sifted through your memories to tell you how likely you were to make it into the Upterlife if you died that day. That was your Shrive ranking.

Dare encouragingly placed his finger on the darkened Venal icon, second over from the right. Venal was represented by a cartoon icon of an angel with clipped wings. Venal meant you had done a few things the dead didn't care for, but who's perfect?

Next to it, on the far right, indicating the best possible reading, was a stick-figure angel, complete with halo. That icon represented Liminal: the perfect state between living and dead, a guaranteed Upterlife admittance.

…I hadn't Shrived Liminal since my parents died.

Resting in the center of the five icons, deceptively average-looking, was a stick figure of a man. That was Mortal. By the time you got to Mortal, the dead were split 50/50 on your entrance.

Kids who Shrived Mortal were shunned, viewed as a corrupting influence – which was usually enough to encourage Mortal kids to get their acts together and shift back towards more Liminal behavior.

"Does the result normally take this long for you?" Dare's

voice was hushed with terror.

"They've got a lot to think over," I said, feeling sick.

Two more statuses hovered to the left of Mortal: Criminal, depicted by a bent-backed stick figure, and the Terminal tombstone. Terminal, it was rumored, glowed fire-alarm red if you ever managed to piss off the dead that badly... But I'd never known anyone who had.

Criminal, on the other hand, meant you'd done something the dead couldn't forgive: a planned suicide, murder, programming. That knowledge couldn't be used to arrest you – some old statute said you couldn't be forced to testify against yourself – but the LifeGuard *would* be notified, and they'd come sniffing around to dig up evidence on whatever it was you'd done.

I wasn't going to Shrive Criminal over a pony, was I?

Venal's silver light flickered, like a roulette wheel spinning to a stop, then finally glowed steady. I let loose a breath I hadn't realized I was holding.

"Now I'm only mostly screwed." I thumbed the button to send my Shrive results to Dr Greywoode.

"Sorry, man," Dare said. "If it's any consolation, I didn't get away with my crime either."

But you just get yelled at, I thought, uncharitably. "What happened?"

"Peaches, that's what happened. She saw the charge on our bank account, and told Mom."

"Like Peaches is a saint!" I protested. "I don't know why you don't rat her out. She goes to more Blackout Parties than you do..."

"She looks better," he sighed. "You've never seen her when she's in business mode, all work clothes and innocence. You only see her in her clubbing gear. And you know, maybe you watch her a little too hard."

I flinched. Peaches was *insanely* hot. And fun to talk to.

And fun to dance with.

She never danced with me alone – Peaches played the field, holding impromptu contests to see what boy won the right to buy her a drink – but we'd had a couple of late-night talks up on rooftops, where she'd hugged her knees and talked about how she was just playing along with her family until they trusted her with the money. Then she was going to create a place for living rebels like us, a safe haven where we could live and dance.

I'd told her that was a beautiful dream.

She'd kissed me.

Dare would kill me if he knew. Peaches and Dare had such a rivalry that talking to one of them was like crossing a picket line, even though they always went to the same parties and Peaches always dropped by the orphanage to check in on him, and Dare stopped by the Mortuaries to check in on her. They cared about each other – but in the Khan-Tien family tradition, they mostly showed that love by constantly whittling each other down.

None of that stopped me from thinking about how sweet Peaches' kiss had been.

It wasn't a crush, OK? Peaches kissed everyone. For her, a liplock was like a moister handshake. Some thought she was callous.

I knew better. Peaches had survived the Bubbler back when it was still considered a death sentence… so when Izzy had come down with it, Peaches had spent hours by Izzy's side, lifting up her long black hair to show Izzy her own scars. Reassuring her there was life after the plague.

"Any news on Therapy?" I asked, changing the subject. "Did you find her?"

"I had Omar and Cerise scanning Central Farm's feeds last night. Nothing. Face it, Chai: you set free a Sleipnir-class pony – that's money on the hoof. Someone's snagged her by now."

I thought about Therapy in the hands of some mean-spirited farmer. I'd have let Therapy run unmodified, but her new owner would install an autobridle in Therapy's head to induce seizures whenever she got too frisky.

"I'm not giving up hope, Dare, I'm... Why are you sniffing like that?"

"Do you smell smoke?"

That's when the fire alarms went off. And the screaming started.

8: THE WICKLIFFE FOOD STORAGE FACILITY, COMPLETE WITH PSYCHO

"Why aren't the fire sprinklers working?" Dare frowned at the ceiling, then squinted at the choked dribbles of water falling through the darkening smoke. The paint packets I'd put inside must have done a number on the sprinklers – and though Beldon had ordered them repaired, the living technicians hadn't doublechecked their work.

Dare flung open the door to the hallway. Some of the sprinklers were working as advertised, but probably three out of five were still gunked up.

I shouldn't have been surprised. Living technicians were overworked and undermotivated to fix problems that affected the living. Beldon'd had every kid in the orphanage scrubbing the paint-spattered cameras clean because that affected his dead ass. But a malfunctioning fire sprinkler system? He hadn't held a fire drill in years.

The dead didn't have the physical resources to maintain the living's safety, and the living all wanted to die. The combination made for sketchy repair work.

Dare's eyes went wide. "Amichai, if the school burns down because your prank gummed up the sprinklers – that can't be good for your Shrive–"

"I didn't know there'd be a fire!" But I wondered: *had*

Gumdrool set me up? It sounded too paranoid to say out loud, but–

More screaming from the pantry. A girl's voice. She shrieked defiance, though she sounded furious and scared – yet so vital and alive she lit up the halls of the orphanage.

If the technicians who'd fixed the sprinklers had cared half as much about whatever this girl was yelling about, this school would be *fireproofed.*

The Junior LifeGuard members ignored the shouts as they jogged down the hallway, opening each door with skeleton passkeys. Each room revealed young kids sprawled on their beds, eyes shut and tongues lolling out, seemingly overcome by smoke – even though the dark smoke, barely worse than what you'd get from a pan of burnt sausages, was up drifting by the ceiling.

"Come on," said the LifeGuard, not unkindly, grabbing the kids by their ears. The kids rose to their feet, embarrassed by how easily their suicide attempt had been seen through. "Now we all hope to burn to death, but the fire's broken out all the way back in the pantry. It won't get fatal here for another five minutes. Now get outside to safety, or get voided."

Shamed and shepherded, my fellow orphans trudged towards the exit. The girl screamed louder.

"That poor woman," I said. You couldn't make out *what* she was bellowing, not through the murmured hustle of the evacuation, but… there was a lust for life in that cry I hadn't heard in, well, ever. People had howled in pain during the plagues, but it had been a resigned frustration that their stupid body was still functioning.

This girl may have been burning to death, but she was fighting for what was left of her life with such passion that I needed to see her. "She sounds livid…"

Dare grabbed my shirt and hauled me backwards. I hadn't realized I'd turned to face the girl's voice.

"She's burning to death," he said. "Good for her! But right now, if the school burns down and you die in some stupid rescue attempt, you think the dead will overlook your property damage? You can't get voided now. You gotta give yourself time to get back into favor, do good work until you Shrive Liminal – if you die right after an orphanage fire you contributed to, you'll get voided for sure. *Think*, man."

The hallways were crowding up as people filed out, checking their earputers for news updates. The smoke burned my eyes as the air grew hotter. Everyone was coughing.

"She sounds like she's in a lot of pain."

"She won't *remember* that part!" Dare snapped. "You *never* remember your own death! Pain doesn't matter!"

Except he'd never watched his own parents die, or been old enough to remember when his sister got the plague. That pain had seemed significant to me. "Aren't we supposed to help each other?"

"We're supposed to help each other *to the Upterlife*." He said it softly, with strained embarrassment, like he was telling me I couldn't wear diapers to school anymore.

Her voice shrieked over the crowd's murmurs: "...JESUS!"

"If she was into it, I'd let her burn. She's not." I slipped out of Dare's grip, struggling upstream through the exiting crowd. I held my breath as I dashed through clouds of soot, navigating by memory–

And entered the pantry, which had no fire in it whatsoever.

Wickliffe's pantry had been an auditorium back before the "Live Local, Die Global" initiatives. Now, come summer's end, we were expected to spend our days harvesting food from Central Farm's crops. We'd gather in the pantry to dry, pickle, salt, and can enough food to last us through winter.

A handful of parents had complained we spent more time canning than learning. But what did we need to learn? Reading, writing, maybe a trade or two. No math or science;

the dead had that handled.

Come mid-June, the pantry was mostly empty – as usual, the students had done a halfassed job putting things away, the auditorium stairs filled with cracked jars and bags of old potatoes.

But down on stage, next to the sinks and chopping trays, was a stocky red-haired girl surrounded by Gumdrool's thuglets.

"STOP TELLING ME THEY'VE GONE TO JESUS!" the girl yelled. "They're *not* in His arms! Do you think you can change *my* mind?"

She was backed up against a castiron wood stove, a carving knife in her hand. She shifted stances as three uniformed boys worked out which way to come at her through the piles of heaped onions. She moved effortlessly to meet their attack, like a warrior-maiden from a fantasy show.

She was the most beautiful living girl I'd ever seen.

The remains of one of the Time-Out Chamber's restraint jackets dangled around her waist; underneath, her traditional white woolen robe was torn down to expose her freckled shoulders in a way that made me blush. Her body was beautiful, her movements were graceful, and it was probably a bad idea to be smitten by a girl so willing to stab people.

"We didn't say they went to Jeeza," Gumdrool's thugs leered. "We said your parents were *wormfood! Brains rotting! Bodies slack! And now you have to live here. It's the *law!*"

"In an institution designed to alter my behavior? You will put no yoke of iron upon me. You might cut open my parents' brains, but I will *not* give way before the wicked!"

She weaved the knife in a careful figure-eight pattern – and that's when I noticed the cross tattooed at the hollow of her throat.

A NeoChristian.

Great. Beautiful *and* crazy. Always my weak spot.

"Depart from me, workers of lawlessness." She brought her voice under control; her hand trembled only a little. "Or else I'll be forced to condemn you to Hell."

The thuglets smiled. This is what they'd been hoping for. They geared up to rush her, happy to have an excuse to fall upon the knife.

Could this girl be *that* naïve, to not know death was what we all wanted?

"No," I said loudly, taking a step forward. "She won't *kill* you…"

Her green eyes held disbelief. "I will," she insisted. "I do not fear death; I will live, even as I die." Her free hand drifted up to touch her cross tattoo.

"Look at her grip," I snorted. "No, what's going to happen is that she's going to stab someone in the gut inexpertly. Who wants a colostomy bag? Who wants a lifetime working with my sister down at the chip reclamation plant?"

Gumdrool's boys backed away. They were maybe thirteen years old tops, for which I was grateful – more experienced recruits might have noticed how carefully she tracked their movements. The NeoChristians believed in God and good combat training; she could have slaughtered us all without breaking a sweat.

Still, murdering someone got you a Shriveless jail cell for life. Not that NeoChristians cared about Shrives, of course, but this girl deserved something better than life in prison.

One thug eyed me sullenly. "We're tasked to bring her back to processing."

I looked at the stacks of cans. "And clearly, by 'processing,' you thought 'food processing.' Were you planning on pickling her?"

"She escaped." He sneered at me. "Aren't you on trial, Damrosch?"

"I smuggled a pony into a hospital. This proves my skill at

moving recalcitrant beauties. Clear out, kiddies, I'll take the heat."

"If you don't get her to the processing center, we'll tell Gumdrool. This is on you." They skedaddled up the aisles, grateful not to have to deal with a lunatic skybeard-worshipper.

I sat on a counter, well out of her reach. She lowered her knife with an effort; they'd goaded her hard. I realized how much she'd wanted to stab someone.

"I take it you set the fire?" I asked.

"A trash bin outside the door." She smirked in satisfaction as she picked up a burlap sack. "Sends up gouts of smoke, sends people running, fogs the cameras. A good distraction when surrounded by computer programs."

I was relieved; she wasn't a killer. Otherwise she'd have set the place ablaze.

"What's your name?"

"Evangeline." She stuffed dried apples into the sack. I tried not to stare at her underwear.

"Nice to meet you, Evangeline." I didn't offer to shake hands. "I'm Amichai. Amichai Damrosch."

Her eyes narrowed. "That a Jewish name?"

Uh-oh, I thought. I'd heard some of the NeoChristians had problems with the Jews, though I'd never believed it. In the past, Judaism had been linked to religion and years of persecution – but religion had pretty much evaporated after the Upterlife had been invented, leaving Jewishness as just another ethnicity. At my house, all being Jewish had meant was that Mom and Dad threw holiday parties on different days.

"In name only," I said, running my hand nervously through my Jewfro. "Well, and the hair. My family hasn't worshipped in centuries."

"I suppose you think that's a point in your favor. Still, you

did shoo those boys away before I had to dispatch them, so…
I owe you a favor, Amichai Damrosch."

I watched as she tossed aside a leaking jar of beets. "What
are you trying to *do*?"

"My parents have been kidnapped across the country,
just like Joseph, and it's my duty to bring them back. It's a
lot harder, getting by in the city; more cameras to dodge.
And I didn't stock up on enough food for the final push
into Manhattan, no wise virgin I, so I had to break into a
store. That's when your LifeGuard caught me. They want to
refashion me into one of you."

She spoke quickly. I could barely make sense of her words.
"How *old* are you?"

"Sixteen."

A year older than me? I'd heard the NeoChristians put
their kids through a constant diet of combat training, but I'd
never seen up-close evidence before. She could have passed
for twenty-five. A pretty twenty-five.

The dirt ground into her palms and her sunken cheeks told
me she'd been on her own for a while, too. She looked like a
wild raccoon – kinda cute, but able to bite your face off.

Maybe she was crazy. Like, "searching for delusions" crazy.
Watching people go through meat-death did weird things to
survivors.

"But… they said your parents were dead," I stammered. "I
mean *dead* dead. This place is made for orphans. I mean, isn't
it better to have *someplace* to live?"

Her knuckles went white around the knife handle. "I told
you, they're *not dead*. I'd rejoice if they put on the crown of
righteousness. As it is, it's the iron yoke."

"What iron yoke?"

She sighed, as if talking to someone unbearably slow.
"Your government has kidnapped my parents. They're being
reprogrammed to believe in your culture right now."

"*Brainwashed?* Why would anyone want to brainwash you?"

She snorted in disdain. "This isn't mere brainwashing. I've spent hours on the waterboard, training to endure physical torture. You're shoving needles into our heads to make us sin. Reprogramming us. Like computers."

"Don't be ridiculous," I snapped. "Organic tissue is all bunched up; our memories are mangled together. That's why the Upterlife is a one-way trip; once they've extracted all your thoughts, they can't stuff them back into your jumbled wetbrain again."

"I didn't say you were successful. Yet." She examined a rack of goat jerky I'd smoked last year, threw hunks into the sack.

"Stop saying it's me. I don't have anything to do with it."

"Your people, then."

"No! My people aren't putting an... an iron yoke on anyone! Even if they *could* flip neurons around like computer settings, which is unlikely because the brain is a messy stew of cells, you think the dead would let anyone get away with that? If someone had the power to rewire organic tissue, then reprogramming the dead's memories would be trivial. That knowledge would get anyone Terminal status – the LifeGuard would be on them like gold on wheat."

"That's assuming the men who did this care about Shriving."

"You told me they're my people. We're *all* obsessed with Shriving. Your story makes *zero sense*."

Even though I'd shredded her story, she refused to budge. No surprises there. She already believed in an invisible superbeing who automatically Shrived the brains of each human, dog, and cockroach.

"OK." I showed her my palms. "Your parents are kidnapped. But if you murder someone, the LifeGuard will throw you in jail. How will you save them then?"

She gave me an exhausted look, as though my kindness was a drink offered at the wrong time. "Your concern is commendable, Amichai. But my parents did not love their lives so much as to shrink from death. Neither shall I."

"See, that's why nobody *likes* you people!" I cried. "Not only do you spend your days quoting some crazy old text file, but *nobody's out to exterminate you.* You think we want to kill you, but you've got it backwards. You spend your days yelling that the Upterlife is a crime against some imaginary guy and then try to blow our servers up! We don't want *you* dead – you want *us* to die!"

"Clearly this isn't a productive avenue of discourse." She fished a pickle out of a barrel, took an experimental bite, tossed a few into her sack before slinging it over her shoulder. "Still, I should thank you for staying my hand. I'd prefer not to kill those with stained souls."

Doesn't anyone care about this world? I wondered.

"Look, I have to bring you to the processing center – I'm already in a lot of trouble–"

She jabbed the tip of the knife into my belly.

"Thanks for teaching me a valuable lesson." Her smile was irritatingly gorgeous, given how she was a wrist-twist away from gutting me. "If you interfere, I will not kill you; rather, I will slice open your bowels inexpertly."

"I stood up for you," I said bitterly – but even the touch of her knife was weirdly seductive.

"You were kind." She kissed me gently on the forehead, a look of regret crossing her face. "But I thought you of all people would understand that not every act is rewarded in *this* lifetime."

She sucked in a deep breath, then pushed open the door to the hallway.

Gumdrool tased her.

"Gotcha!" He fired again as Evangeline fell, twitching. "That trashcan trick is straight out of the NeoChristian playbook. We just needed to make sure you couldn't hurt anyone… you server-bombing *bitch*."

He kicked her in the ribs three times, pausing in between each blow, as if each kick was a special treat he allowed himself. When he finished, he sniffed a deep breath through his nostrils, shuddering with pleasure.

Then he bowed to me. "Well done, Damrosch," he said with a note of admiration. "You did your duty."

I looked at Evangeline, shuddering. He'd smacked me around… but I'd never seen him go after a noncitizen before. I got the impression that if he didn't want to capture her alive, he'd have stomped her skull in with no more emotion than he'd show crushing a cockroach.

The three boys who'd taunted Evangeline wrestled a new restraint jacket onto her.

"And *you* fools!" he shouted, advancing towards them. "Practically throwing yourself on her knife! Remember, the dead are always watching. You're lucky Damrosch saved your ass – if she'd killed you, you would have been judged a suicide!"

Shocked, they dropped the restraint jacket as they realized what they'd avoided. Suicide was a sure ticket to the void.

"That's right," Gumdrool spat. "You almost voided yourself. You think about that."

Gumdrool tied the new restraint vest around Evangeline, clucking his tongue. "She wouldn't have slipped out, either, if your knot skills hadn't been so weak. Improve your physical skills! Don't be as poor stewards of this world as the sprinkler repairmen! We all aim to get to the Upterlife, boys, but this world counts… for now."

With Evangeline restrained, he turned to me.

"You rescued these three idiots from the void, and kept

this terrorist scum busy until reinforcements arrived. Commendable. I shall put a note in your file."

"No need," said Frank, his voice crackling to life over the speakers. "Dr Greywoode and I have agreed on a suitable punishment. Amichai will spend the next three months shaping coral."

I had to grab a table to keep myself upright.

"Three *months*?" I protested. "In *coral*? What about Career Day? What about... What about Izzy?"

"Come Career Day, you'll be eight weeks into your apprenticeship for your new lifetime job. Welcome to the construction industry, Mr Damrosch."

9: CORAL-SNIFFING AT THE KIRZNER BUILDING

When I was nine, I'd dreamed of being a coral shaper. I'd bugged Mom until she took me to the toy store to buy an aircoral kit.

I stood before the three sample models, wringing my hands: did I want to grow a seven-foot replica of the lush Kirzner Apartment Complex? Would I grow a patriotic copy of the World Trade Center III, the first successfully bioengineered building? Would the Drummond Basilica, the tallest organic skyscraper in the world, even fit in my bedroom?

The Kirzner was the prettiest.

Real coral buildings were fed by seeding clouds with vitamin mixtures, but my kit came with a tin watering can and a bucket of growth mix. I remember pouring mix on until the building-bed was sopping wet, thinking if I fed it a lot it'd grow superfast.

Alas, aircoral doesn't work that way. It grew sixteen inches a week, no matter how much I fed it. It *was* kinda neat, seeing the pink skeleton interlacing in genetically programmed patterns, forming tiny windows and crenellations. My aircoral somehow managed to be both drab and ugly, but you could see why it had revolutionized the construction industry – no labor necessary, no equipment, just time and food.

Mostly, however, the coral was dull. You sprayed it once a week. It grew. There were warnings in the booklet about fungal bloom and cancerous outgrowths, along with explanations of what to do if such excitement ever happened, but it never did.

I got bored, stuck it in the back of my closet.

It starved to death.

I remembered my first coral as I trudged up the staircases of the real Kirzner. The Kirzner Complex was meant to impress, the hallways lined with dusty oriental rugs and mahogany tables, lit by tastefully recessed lighting.

It might have been pretty if anyone lived here.

My coral-testing kit grew heavier with each floor; each apartment had seven access panels to collect coral samples, each of which were needed to verify the health of the building, each of which involved squirming my scrawny frame into stinking hatches to chip out a sample. I hauled eight hundred test tubes, and had to fill all of them before day's end.

It was pointless. A monkey could have done this job. They could engineer coral, why couldn't they engineer a coral-chipping monkey?

Because hiring me was cheaper, that's why.

At least this job let me save up money for Izzy.

My earputer's music switched to its hourly newscast – the latest trends in the Upterlife. The hottest postmortemed body designer had designed a new nose more sensitive than a bloodhound's; she was petitioning President Wickliffe to seed all the Upterlife's zones with upgraded scent imagery. Sure, the Upterlife parks smelled fine to humans, but why not add the data to make the odors more realistic to those with doglike hypersensitivity?

Sure, that upgrade would drain living resources – yet another hardship the living would endure to make our future lives more awesome.

Then the announcer – postmortemed himself, natch – listed the people who'd voided themselves today. The announcer took time to gravely examine the sins that had barred each person from the Upterlife, thundering in ominous tones how this could be *you* if you weren't careful!

Then back to the mandatory work music: uptempo, so forgettable it bordered on the subliminal, designed by muzakians to prod us into working quickly and efficiently.

Yet with each floor I thought, I'll get Izzy into one of these apartments.

I pictured Izzy's smile as I unlatched the door and the apartment's motion-activated lights flickered on. "This," I muttered, "is all yours." She'd ask why it was covered in dusty tarps, and the real answer was that the apartment's inhabitants had died six years ago... But in my fantasy, it was so I could sweep the tarps off as she squeed happily.

I could see my sister's smile as I revealed each miracle that came standard with a Kirzner residence – neuroscanning televisions that played whatever story you were most in the mood for! Drink dispensers that read your tastebuds to concoct infinitely delicious beverages! Massage-chairs that triangulated your tensest muscles to squeeze away your tension! No more Bubbler-cramps, Izzy!

Then I had that other fantasy, the one where I set it all on fire and danced through the flames.

Sadly, the best toys are kept under tarps for all but the most kissass of the living. Nobody alive can afford to stay here unless the dead subsidize them. Even though the Bubbler had devastated New York, the ghosts would rather keep their apartments empty than let the wrong people in.

Me, I'd been looking at the places I could afford to move to after Career Day. Places with sick coral, all crumbling walls and dead-fish smells. Rent and food would consume 80 percent of my salary. The remaining 20 percent, if I saved up for a decade without any emergency expenses, might buy Izzy a neural adapter so she wouldn't have to use her hands to play *Pony Police Action*.

Test tube in hand, I wedged myself headfirst behind another TV, opening an access hatch and gagging at the lowtide stink of coral.

"Is there a problem, officer?" said a musical voice. I banged my head in surprise.

Peaches stood in the apartment doorway, flashing me a wicked smile.

You've never seen her in front of Mom and Dad, Dare had told me. *All work clothes and innocence.* The transformation was astounding. She'd pulled her long black hair into a tight bun. She'd hidden the gnarled Bubbler scars on her arms and shoulders underneath a demure, full-sleeved business suit. Her lush curves were neutralized beneath that stylish dress – but her hornrimmed glasses couldn't hide the glimmer of mischief in her eyes.

"What are you doing all the way over here?" I asked, a goofy grin spreading across my face. The Kirzner buildings were forty blocks away from the orphanage – Beldon made sure getting to my job took an hour's walk. They wanted to wear me down.

Yet here was my favorite Blackout Party dance partner, meeting me on the far side of New York. It was a pleasant surprise...

...or would have been, if I wasn't in these filthy overalls.

She sashayed into the room – Peaches always glided from place to place like a ballet dancer, sometimes doing twirls along the way. She lifted the tarps to peek underneath as she spun through the apartment.

"I was looking for a LifeGuard," she said. "Izzy tells me you've been spamming everyone with job applications."

"I need better prospects," I muttered. "Listen, could you stop touching the tarps? I'm not supposed to disturb anything…"

"No problems… *officer.*" She raised her hands as if offering to be handcuffed, which sent naughty thoughts cascading through my mind. Then she pulled her glasses down over the tip of her nose to look me over. "Stylish dress choice, by the way. It's *you.*"

I ran my fingers through my Jewfro to smooth it; my hand came out speckled with coral crap.

"Coral crap's an aphrodisiac." I dabbed a little behind my ear. "Drives the ladies wild."

She wrinkled her nose. "Izzy's right. You *do* look sick. Thinner. Paler. I keep telling her this is what hard labor does to people, but she doesn't believe me. But even accounting for your employment's exertions… you *have* lost some of your charm."

I felt decrepit when she looked at me. "I didn't know you guys were still talking to each other."

Peaches tugged a tarp off a chair. "We both survived the Bubbler, Amichai. That's a bond. And you know me – I check in on people."

"That you do." Maybe it was New York's reduced population, but it seemed like Peaches knew everyone. She chatted people up at her job at the Khan-Tien Mortuaries, she made pals down at the Blackout Parties.

She sank into the livefoam seat; its cushioned arms massage-hugged her. "So why have you been avoiding me?"

"Seriously, Peaches, that chair's for people who live here–"

She giggled. "*I* live here, silly."

"…you're that rich?"

"Well, I don't live *here*," she clarified, flashing me a daypass. "Not yet. But all us Khan-Tien employees get to live at the Kirzner, once you've perpetrated enough drudgery to prove you harbor no interesting aspirations. If I work thirty incident-free years, I'll get to live here fulltime. But sometimes they give me weekend passes. They want to give me a taste. To keep me hungry."

"And are you? Hungry, I mean?"

She shook her head, stepping close enough for me to smell her perfume. "Not for what they're offering," she whispered. "But they don't know that. Yet."

"Well, *I'm* starving." I goggled at all this gadgetry. "Dare must be serious about disowning the Khan-Tiens, if he's giving all this up."

"This? This is nothing," she demurred, throwing the tarp back over the seat. "Scraps. It's all the dead will offer."

"I dunno. You're rich. To a poor kid like me, man... This is heaven."

Peaches' exasperation made my stomach churn.

"This is nothing compared to what we *could* have." She held a glass underneath the taste-dispenser, filling it, conspicuously not offering me a cup. "Haven't you noticed all the technological advancements of the last three centuries have benefited the dead?"

"That's because we stripped the planet bare. There's not enough rare metals left to serve the living."

Peaches swept the curtain open on the apartment's picture window, directing my gaze across Central Farm's patchwork gardens. I noticed how all the apple trees were lit by the golden glow of the Upterlife's servers. Each skyscraper-sized computing cluster was fed by thick cables that pumped in geothermally-generated electricity. New York was crammed with hundreds of Upterlife servers, each year's new databanks squeezing out old apartment complexes.

The dead never had a problem taking from our world to improve theirs.

"You don't believe there's a shortage, do you?" she said, and I realized I didn't. "This world would be a wonderland, if that was their priority. All the rare earth metals they can mine from asteroids go to new servers. Our remaining gas fuels their mining spaceships. They give us ponies instead of cars.

"I mean, crap, we're still *gesturing* at computers, Amichai! Why doesn't Izzy's earputer read her mind? Why wasn't she genegineered like your pony to be muscular and plague-resistant? Because the dead want all the good things kept in the Upterlife!

"Only the living can help the living." She sipped something milky that smelled of roasted almonds. Our hips were close enough to touch. "You call the dead 'ghosts,' Amichai. That's no accident; the living *exorcise* ghosts. If we could get rid of them, we could shape our own futures…"

I'd like to tell you how I envisioned ways to improve our political and technological situations. But all I could think was, *she's so close. Does she want me to put my arm around her?*

That was the thing about Peaches. She was flirtatious if you didn't flirt back. But the minute you reached for her, she was smoke.

"…we could make this world a paradise," I admitted. "But what am I gonna do? I can't leave Izzy behind."

My arm hung, pathetically, by my side. I consoled myself with the knowledge I would have just smeared her in coral crap anyway.

She scowled, draining her glass. "Seriously, Amichai, have you stopped attending the Blackout Parties altogether?"

"I'm only sleeping five hours a night. Twelve hours chipping coral, then I have to visit Izzy…" I didn't add, *and I take the long walk back through Central Farm, looking for a lost pony.* "I just haven't had time."

"You need to come tonight."

"I can't afford to lose this job. In fact, I have to get back to–"

She placed one manicured finger over my lips. Her cool touch shut my whole body down.

"The dead want you beaten down, Amichai. But you have impressed certain flesh-and-blood parties."

"Really?" She smirked. "Those who don't know who *really* came up with the IceBreaker, anyway," she teased.

"I came up with the idea of looping camera feeds," I insisted. "I just asked Mama Alex how to *do* it..."

"Doesn't matter. The point is, you've got me to help you, but instead you're filling out forms. Why didn't you ask me? I could have pulled some strings for you."

Because I hate asking for help, I thought. Because Izzy's been carrying me my whole life, and my parents aren't reliable, and now I'm too embarrassed to ask anyone.

"Because I've *got* this, Peaches."

She blew a stray strand of hair out of her eyes, exasperated. "What if I told you I could get you a job in the LifeGuard?"

The *LifeGuard?* Where'd *that* come from? But I felt a shock of hope. "I... I'm not really LifeGuard material..."

"LifeGuards make mad cash, with top-level benefits. If you get in, Izzy's set. Isn't that worth the price?"

"Why... Why would you do that?"

"Why look a gift horse in the mouth, Amichai?"

"...Because it's a pretty mouth?"

She chuckled. "You're so sweet when you're awkward." She tapped me on the chin with one finger. "But you need a job. I know someone who needs someone with your skillsets. Whereas *I* need someone I trust placed deep inside the LifeGuard. Call it... a lively expectation of future favors."

Izzy had been hot to join the LifeGuard, but I'd never fallen for their propa-game-da. As a LifeGuard, I'd be busting up Blackout Parties, plotting to catch Mama Alex–

But a career in the LifeGuard would save my sister.

Peaches rested her hand on my shoulder. "Just come to the party tonight. Please. And if you don't come tonight, well... I'll find someone else to dance with."

"You never dance with just one boy anyway."

"Some of them, I dance with longer." She kissed me on the cheek. "Don't keep me waiting, Amichai. This is a one-night-only opportunity, and you'll never have a shot at something this good ever again. And besides, you…"

She frowned, all of her carefully studied poise dropping away to express a genuine concern.

"You need to relax. This job's eating you alive."

Embarrassed, she smoothed the hem of her dress; when she looked up again, she was all business.

"Catch you later tonight, Mr Damrosch." She gave me a mischievous wink, and pirouetted out.

10: LENOX HILL HOSPITAL, PLUS TWO INTRUDERS

My arms ached after a hard day of chipping coral, and my legs were rubber. I could hitch a ride back on a salesman's ponycart for a buck, stashed in with some beer barrels or a pile of old clothes. It was slower, since the vendors made stops along the way to sell their wares – but I'd trade a two-hour ride for an hour's walk any day.

But then I thought, *that's a buck I could give to Izzy.* So I lugged those heavy test tubes until my hands blistered, and thought about saving up for a pushcart to stow my sample case in. It seemed like a crazy luxury after only three voiding weeks.

Shouldn't there be public carts waiting to carry people across town? Why shouldn't the government encourage us to travel, instead of keeping us at home to save energy?

And why did Peaches think she could get me into the LifeGuard with *my* record? You had to Shrive a perfect Liminal just to take the entrance exam. Peaches could pull strings, but… strings *that* big?

And why did she think I'd make a decent LifeGuard? They were all muscles and violence. In the unlikely event I made it through boot camp, did she think I'd be happy spending my days singing patriotic songs and shooting people in the head?

The LifeGuard were supposedly here to protect us, but everyone remembered what they'd done to Boston. Boston had rioted when Wickliffe had shut down public transit to encourage the new locavore gardening initiatives. Wickliffe had negotiated with Boston for weeks before he'd finally given the orders, even crying on camera to beg the rebels to stop –

– but once he'd declared Boston voided, it was the LifeGuard who'd walled Boston off. They'd cut supply lines, kept anyone from escaping, trapped Boston's citizens until they ate each other alive. Half a million ugly meat-deaths.

They replayed the footage every year, on the anniversary. Ostensibly we were supposed to mourn for the City Shrived Criminal, but realistically it was a reminder of what the LifeGuard would do to you if you stepped out of line.

Could *I* shoot a starving mother trying to get some food for her kid? Just because she'd crossed the quarantine border?

What if that meant Izzy got to live a good life?

Normally, I'd walk through Central Farm, hunting for Therapy. Today, I had to see Izzy.

The nurses at the hospital desk frisked me nowadays, like I kept ponies in my pocket – so I'd filled my pockets with rotting coral to discourage them from sticking their hands in. They frogmarched me all the way to Izzy's room.

I needed to hear what Izzy thought. She'd had physical therapy today, so she'd be wiped out – but we'd always made time to talk to each other at the end of the day.

Except she was talking to someone already. And I tensed as the nurse shoved me through the doorway, because I already knew who:

Mom and Dad.

"...this poor, dragon-ravaged town," Mom said, with the hushed air of a camp counselor telling stories around a campfire. "Everyone was starving, since all their crops had been devoured. And you *know* those cowardly Firbolg traders wouldn't help…"

"Those *bastards*." Izzy sat painfully crosslegged in front of their screens. She clenched her fists in rage.

"Why, you can't expect *other* people to be brave," Dad chuckled. "Only you can test your own mettle. And so we ventured there, thinking our Vorpal Vortexes would do the job. But we soon found *this* dragon couldn't be slain by steel."

"I assume silver blades were its weakness?" Izzy's forehead was creased with that little frown as she worked out how to slay an imaginary dragon.

"No! No mortal weapon would suffice!" Mom said, low and urgent. "This dragon fed on *despair*."

"Then… how did you defeat it?"

"We had to give each townsperson hope. It took a hundred quests – bringing starcrossed lovers together, hunting down lost treasures, convincing poor, clumsy Snozzel that he was worthy to be a knight–"

"Is Snozzel a…?" Izzy asked.

"He's an AI," Mom admitted. "But honey, you just don't ask if people are artificial. It's terribly rude."

"Sorry." Izzy hung her head, suppressing a wince; normally she couldn't get out of bed on therapy days. But she hid her pain from Mom and Dad so they wouldn't feel bad.

"So we had a town *full* of hopeless townspeople. It took us months to find out what each of them needed…"

"…but when we finally convinced Snozzel to slay the dragon, the dragon starved on the spot!" Dad interjected.

Izzy applauded. "No wonder you were too busy to check in with us! What an amazing adventure! What heroism!"

Dad tipped his cap to her, blushing. "Now, sweetie," he demurred. "It's nothing you won't do when you get here with us…"

"Oh, for void's sake!" I said. "You disappear for months to

cheer up some stupid AI, but you can't even show up for your daughter's *hearing?*"

"…what hearing?" Mom asked.

They looked startled, confused… and completely innocent.

I shot Izzy a glance: did you even bring up your trial with them? Izzy made a shushing gesture: don't make a fuss, Amichai, they don't need to know –

"I left you a thousand messages!" I yelled. "Izzy was on trial for her life! Maybe if you'd shown up to testify, but no, you ghosted away – *again* –"

"Amichai!" Izzy snapped. "I get so little time to hear what they're up to, don't you spoil it–"

"You can't keep making excuses for them! They need to–"

"*Amichai Warren Damrosch!*" A stern Mom-voice, even carried through speakers, could still silence me.

"Look, Amichai," Dad said. "We're sorry we didn't check our voicemails."

"Checking voicemails is just so character-breaking when you're adventuring," Mom sighed.

"But the moment poor Snozzel could get by on his own, we checked in on you. And everything's fine, isn't it? You've got a steady job, Izzy's recovering…"

"Have you even *looked* at Izzy?" I snapped.

Dad shook his head, as if he just wasn't up to the task of getting through to me.

"Oh, Amichai," Mom sighed, pressing her palm to the screen. Izzy nudged me; I trudged over obligingly to touch my palm to Mom's, but all I felt was cold plastic. "I know you're angry. But life's short, and then you die."

The old platitude failed to comfort.

"I'm not saying life's not a bitch," Dad chuckled. "Believe me, I know! I remember being so worried about scraping up enough money to feed us – but I never forgot a birthday party, did I? I always surprised you with something.

Remember the fire-balloons?"

Dad always made a huge fuss over our birthdays, devising new surprises. But he never asked whether I *wanted* the surprises.

"Then we died," Mom said softly. "It was awful. Izzy, don't think just because we didn't say anything doesn't mean we don't notice how badly you're doing."

"There's just nothing to be said. Life is terrible."

"We're so grateful to have left all that awfulness behind. But once you straighten up and die right, we've got a section of Wingbright Pass we can't wait to show you. We'll adventure as a family–"

"Except for, uh, certain grownup areas," Dad coughed.

"–well, maybe not Wingbright Pass. We'll find somewhere. It's a big Upterlife, sweetie."

They beamed, as if that had solved everything.

"...and when Izzy spends the next sixty years locked into an agonizing job?" I asked. "What if her employers scar her so deeply, she'll forget how to be happy? What'll her Upterlife be like then?"

Mom stammered. "Well... we... we've met a couple of survivors like that, but they managed, to... to shake that off in a century or two..."

"That's your solution to everything, isn't it? Give it time."

"Sweetie, time is our gift to you–"

"That's not *your* gift. *You* didn't do a voiding thing except die young. And then you left us to go on stupid adventures that mean *nothing*!"

"Like *you're* any better?"

I turned, stunned by my sister's accusation. She rolled her eyes, looking up to the heavens as if hoping someone would knock sense into me – and then slapped her palms on her thighs, wiping the sweat off as if she was getting around to a job long overdue.

"Look, Amichai – you've *tried* to take care of me. And I appreciate that. But you also..."

"I also what?"

She swallowed, hesitant to speak. Tears stung my eyes: angry as she was, she still didn't want to hurt her baby brother.

"You can't yell at Mom and Dad for being irresponsible when you're the one pulling the crazy pranks," she said. "You think I don't know how close you came to Shriving Criminal, after the pony stunt? At least Mom and Dad's adventures aren't putting them in real danger. You don't want to admit how much you have in common with them, but... you almost *left* me, Amichai. Alone."

Left unsaid, because she couldn't say it out loud: *You almost got yourself voided.*

I could barely breathe.

Dad cleared his throat, annoyed. "Amichai's not your legal guardian, Izzy. I am. And I assure you from this moment on, if it's that serious, we'll take care of you. We can file paperwork just as well as Amichai, can't we, darling? We can get a new hearing, I'm sure."

"Oh yes," Mom said, confident as always. "This time we'll do better."

Izzy squeezed my hand, her grip still far too weak. And I wanted to believe Mom and Dad. I wanted them to tell me their stories, to feel their heroic battles meant something.

But their promises were as empty as their adventures. All their good intentions were dreams. Emptiness.

Ghost stories.

"Look, I gotta go," I said, giving Izzy a goodbye hug.

"You just got here!"

"I've got a job to take," thinking that yeah, I could join the LifeGuard.

Because I had to do better than my parents.

11: SUBWAY TUNNELS REPURPOSED INTO PARTIES

Blackout Parties, it must be stressed, are also not illegal. There is absolutely *nothing wrong* in discovering a dead spot in an abandoned building. There is *no law* that says every inch of New York must be surveilled by cameras. And if the cameras in the vicinity of a Blackout Party fail mysteriously in the hours before the event, well, who's to say it's not providence?

Perhaps the LifeGuard sits far back, eyeing the party with binoculars (since their more complicated surveillance equipment tends to short out once the counterinsurgent hackers set up shop).

The LifeGuard keeps their distance, though they want to interfere so much their fillings ache. Yet their dead superiors give the orders to hold back: certain segments of New York must be allowed to let off steam. The truncheon-strokers are informed, by those who lived through it, that the last time the LifeGuard *really* clamped down on Blackout Parties it led to a Boston-sized rebellion.

This is one of the few benefits of having all-dead politicians; the Boston riots were fifty years ago, but they remember them as though the slaughter was yesterday. Walter Wickliffe and his cabinet will reign eternal, never resigning due to sickness or death – and the missteps that led to the massacre will not be reduced to a historical lesson, but will remain real and emotional memories.

Even ghosts feel guilty about what happened to Boston.

I felt guilty, too. I was headed to my last Blackout Party to join an organization that wanted to exterminate Blackout Parties. This would be my last dance to organic music, the last laugh with my friends, the last drink with people who wanted to be alive.

I was doing the responsible thing by joining the LifeGuard.

So why did it feel like dying?

36th Avenue, at least, was well lit; the streetlights had been shut down, replaced by the golden glow of Upterlife servers. I nodded to my fellow travelers as they passed by; the shepherds guiding their lambs back from the shearing stations, the repairmen with their pushwagons of welding kits, grimy sweatshop workers trudging home from the clothing mills. They all had the characteristic self-loathing of physical producers. Who wanted to make anything for the real world? Clothes tore, wagon wheels rotted, coral crumbled.

Only the Upterlife lasted forever.

I was blasted out of my reverie by the howl of a magnetorail whizzing overhead at 300 mph, delivering circuitboards.

My legs ached. I'd walked thirty blocks to City Hall from Lenox Hill. This was why everyone wanted ponies. With a pony, you could haul goods across the city with ease.

I hoped Therapy was OK. Once I got into the LifeGuard, I wouldn't have time to search for her.

I ran my hands along a long wall, looking for the bricked-up entryway with a narrow hole knocked in it. It wasn't easy, but that was part of the fun.

See, *finding* a Blackout Party is a trick in and of itself. All invitations are passed on through the curl of a fleshy tongue – no electronic invitations, only the exhalation of living lungs.

Blackout Parties allow no cameras, no recordings, no

blogging – it's a celebration as transient as our bodies.

And like life, each party is distinct. Which is why I wandered in darkness down the abandoned access tunnel, uncertain what I'd find. I muttered to myself, rehearsing what I'd bellow once I got in:

"Calm yourself, citizens," I muttered. "Amichai is here. Let the rumpus commence."

I smacked my lips, trying to swallow back the taste of lame.

I used to be special. Once, I'd shown up with twenty friends and a PA system, and we'd conga-lined our way in. Another time the party had filled with white smoke, and when the smoke cleared, wham! There Dare and I crouched, clad in badass ninja outfits.

But I hadn't had time to prepare. For the first time, I understood why older people were so scarce at the Blackout Parties. I'd only been working for three weeks – and I was so exhausted, I was ready to call it a night before I even *got* to the party.

As I found the firefly-bioluminescence streaming foggily towards the music, my hips began to sway.

I grinned. I wasn't ghosted yet.

I followed the biofog. As it grew brighter, I saw its glow reflecting off polished gold-and-black tiles. The walls curved upwards towards a vaulted cathedral ceiling, the tiles crisscrossing inwards to focus upon stained-glass windows. The golden glow of the Upterlife shone through them like diamonds.

It was glorious.

Then I realized, as Mama Alex must have intended:

This place had been built by the dead. The *real* dead. The moldy oldies, who'd died before the Upterlife had been invented.

How old were these walls? Three hundred years? Four hundred? No matter. This had been made back when

electricity itself was new, when magnets and turning gears promised a future that rattled and clanked. Each tile had been placed by a now-dead hand, this art their sole legacy.

Mama Alex had repurposed this, refashioned a desolated tomb into a vibrant party, thrumming with music designed to resurrect the spirit of these dearly departed artists.

It would be a crime not to party here.

I moved deeper into the chamber, where the walls had been scrubbed and lit with floodlights – though all the fans in the world couldn't quite push away Little Venice's moldy death-scent wafting down the tunnels. Rusted tracks curved in and out, winding their way past polished wood-and-brass ticket stations, each staffed with smiling old women serving drinks.

I squeezed my eyes shut as I approached the main entrance.

"CALM YOURSELF, CITIZENS," I bellowed, my voice swallowed up by the thrumming beat. "AMI–"

Someone shoved his fingers in my mouth to examine my gums.

I coughed, smelling Halitosis Harry's sewery reek.

"Three weeks since I seen you. Bold Amichai musta gotten a job," Harry said, peeling open cracked lips to expose grass-green rotted teeth. He wore a wooden clapboard. It read: "WHY WORK TILL YOU'RE NINETY? LET US TEACH YOU THE MYSTERIES OF PASSIVE RESISTANCE!" And then, in smaller letters: "Venality guaranteed! Will Shrive upon request!"

I spat, clearing the taste from my mouth. "Harry! You're looking well."

Harry gave me a peeved look.

"Sorry," I apologized. "Terrible. You look terrible."

"You think?" he asked hopefully. He palpated my thighs before giving me a look of disappointment.

"You're doing it wrong, my friend." He extracted two cigars

from a filthy pocket. "Your legs are stronger. Gotta counteract that, to confound the corpses." He jammed the cigar in my mouth, lit it. "Suck deep, my friend. Get those lungs filled with tumors the size of babies' fists. As long as smoking's legal, let's *use* it."

The cigar tasted even worse than his fingers. "What's in this?" I choked.

"Haven't a clue." He tapped his temple in a just-between-us gesture. "If I knew how bad t'was, it might be suicide."

"I'll save it for later," I told him. I extinguished the cigar, then tucked it into my pocket so as to not hurt Harry's feelings. He was a nice guy for a Degenerate – but even though the Degenerates generally made it to the Upterlife, sickening myself in protest held no appeal.

"I've seen how this goes, Amichai. You mean to show up for the party, but first you need to unwind. So you play an Upterlife game. Chat with a friend. And then it's too late to go out, and you've passed another day like it was a bowel movement..."

"Gotta go, Harry."

"You're working too hard!" he called after me. "When you're too tired to party, the corpsicles are stealing your life!"

The exhaustion in my bones told me he had a point.

Partygoers danced up and down the tracks. Most of the attendees were within about ten years of Career Day graduation, yet there was a scattering of older people in their thirties and forties. The elder party people grinned as they headbanged to the music, but they stayed off to one side of the dance floor in a segregation I'd never noticed before today.

Back before my Career Day, the partying elders had seemed a little too frazzled for my tastes. They didn't make an effort to gussy up in good clothes – these forty-something enthusiasts showed up in their sweaty work outfits and danced like they longed to forget. That strained desperation to relax had always subliminally put me off, even though everyone was friendly; I'd dance with them if they asked, but I never asked any of them *to* dance.

But now that I had my own crappy career to exhaust me? Those grownups seemed like heroes. That strained desperation was them fighting the weariness of a twelve-hour shift to shout, "I am going to go out after work and *dance more.*"

I'd never appreciated their valor before – and yet, even though I had shown up in my stinking work clothes, I still was reluctant to drift over to that side of the party.

I stepped onto the dance floor, sucking in breath to bellow my arrival a second time, hoping to be so cool that all sides would embrace me – but a thin hand grabbed my shoulder.

"So you *didn't* sell me out," a friendly voice said.

"They haven't got a bribe big enough, Mama." I flung myself past her bodyguards and into Mama Alex's arms. She rubbed her wrinkled brown cheeks against mine, her beaded gray dreadlocks rattling on my shoulders.

Technically, everyone at the Blackout Parties was equal – the oldest living person was still treated like a baby by the dead, so age wasn't supposed to matter. But experience *did* matter, and so in practice the younger folks deferred to the ones who'd held parties without being arrested.

The teaching elders were somehow different than the elders on the dance floor. When someone with years of experience took you by the hand and treated you like you were ready to be taught, the responsibility was flattering. And they stepped aside quickly, applauding at your successes, because the truth was that age *didn't* matter: what mattered was holding the most awesome parties possible.

And nobody held cooler parties than Mama Alex.

"Oh, Amichai, I have *missed* you." Then she held me at arm's length, frowning. "But if you *ever* stay away from my parties for this long again, I'm gonna disown you. Disrespect the party, you disrespect me."

I blushed. It was like she knew I intended to join the LifeGuard. Her guards, five burly women, scowled in disapproval.

"No disrespect, no disrespect," I said.

She poked me in the chest. "You get in trouble using one of *my* inventions, and don't even send an encrypted mail to tell me I'm in the clear? Not fair, Amichai. Not fair at all."

"My sister's in the hospital, Mama," I apologized. "I have to look after her. But you? I keep forgetting anyone *can* get you in trouble…"

"People get me in trouble, all right," she said. "I just have the experience to wriggle *out*."

"So it's said." Mama Alex, it was rumored, Shrived Criminal – and given how many LifeGuards she'd pissed off, I believed it. Everyone knew *her* Career Day choice: maintenance. Sixty years ago, she'd won the right to be taught the mysteries of programming – and, after Boston, she'd quit.

She had work for anyone who wanted it, as long as you didn't ask questions. She'd give you good cash if you could find her a camera-free place to set up her labs. Rumor was she paid top dollar for smugglers and geneticists.

She'd teach you anything you wanted to know… Although when she talked tech, most people clapped their hands over their ears, lest they be tainted with Programming.

Still, Mama Alex never seemed nervous. She lived as gridless as a NeoChristian; no job, no bank account. Rumor was she'd hotwired a backdoor Shrive Point, one that circumvented the usual voting process. I thought that was bullcrap – partially because the kind of processing power you'd need to crack the dead's codes were way above what any one woman could scavenge, but mostly because Mama Alex didn't seem to care all that much about the Upterlife.

She whapped me on the head. "And what's this I hear about you wanting to join the LifeGuard? You never wanted to hear about *my* jobs."

Because what you do is dangerous.

"I… just didn't need the money that badly."

"And now you do? Why didn't you come to me?"

"It upsets Izzy."

She sucked air between her teeth. "If your sister's so convinced my work's bad, maybe she should slave for a while in the factories. Find out the downside of her precious Upterlife."

"My sister is *not* a tool in your revolution. She is *my sister*. If she spends her life ignorant and happy, then I have done my voiding job."

Her guards tensed.

Mama Alex burst into laughter.

"Peaches can put you in the uniform, but you'll never be a LifeGuard." She thumped my shoulder. "You're a pain in my ass, Amichai, but I always know where you stand. I like that. So where's my IceBreaker?"

"Technically speaking, it's not *yours*. I mean, *I* built it."

She glared at me. I'd come up with the idea of looping video, and I had *assembled* it, but she'd sourced the parts for me and given me black-market tutorials.

"…and," I added, after she'd stared me down to size, "It kinda broke when I thumbed the selfdestruct."

"How broke?"

"Pieces."

"*Recoverable* pieces?"

"Depends," I said. "Who's analyzing the evidence? You, or Wickliffe's clowns?"

"Fearless boy." She clasped my hand in her bony fingers. When she removed it, a shiny new IceBreaker rested in my palm.

I marveled at it; the old one had been a little bigger than a screwdriver, but this one was Thermos-sized, bristling with black microfiber antennae.

"Oh, this is Christmas in my hand," I murmured, punching up its stats – three times the range, a hundred times the recording capacity. It even came with a waterproof plastic case – who could afford plastic these days?

"Don't forget who you're really working for on this mission," she said. My heart skipped a beat: *Will I be a LifeGuard spy for Mama?* "If Peaches says she can get you in to the LifeGuard, that means you can do us all favors later on. Still, I wouldn't trust that boy farther than my gals could throw him."

"Trust who?"

She wrinkled her nose. "That–" Someone tapped her on the shoulder, whispering about an urgent matter that demanded her attention.

"Just be careful." She kneeled down to whisper in my ear. "*I* don't know about this Server. That makes it dangerous. It also makes you my eyes. Report back."

"I will." *What server?* I wondered.

I holstered the IceBreaker – it had a holster! – and headed towards the dance floor. A cheer went up as people noticed me making my way into the crowd. *"Calm yourself, citizens,"* I said–

"Wooo, *Pony Boy!*" A girl in neon dancer-garb whirled me about in a big hug. A geriatric dancer pumped my hand, grinning like a mudshark, saying, "You – are – *famous!*"

"For what?"

"You crazy son-of-a-bitch, you made *Sins of the Flesh*!" Dare yelled in my ear, booze on his breath. "The whole Upterlife knows your name now!"

Dare was effervescent, but my blood iced in my veins. *Sins of the Flesh* was heavyduty PR – the most popular show in the Upterlife. Despite Dare's assurances, I wasn't sure I wanted the dead to know my name.

"How? We haven't made a video in weeks–"

"The dead made it for us!" Dare said. People whooped. "DJ! *Show us the pony again*!"

A holographic screen flickered to life above us. There I was, leading Therapy through the hospital, there were the nurses sneaking up on me – and as Therapy charged past the panicked staff, the video doubled in speed. We zipped around the corridors to the tune of "Yakety Sax."

The crowd doubled over with laughter.

"Relax." Dare squeezed my shoulder. "They slotted you into the 'On the Lighter Side' segment. The announcers said you were trying to cheer up your sister. The dead love it, man – you've gone viral."

He paused, then muttered: "Listen, if they interview you, could you mention my architecture plans?"

"Let's start the pony!" someone cried. A cheer went up: "Let's pony it for Amichai!" Everyone put their right hand out as though they held a bridle and clipclopped their feet on the floor.

The beat changed from a techno rhythm to an off-kilter salsa. Hundreds of bodysensors monitored the dancers, noted their speed and position, then dynamically generated music according to what they were collectively doing. Want a heavy metal riff? Bang your head. A slow dance? Grab a partner and grind sensually, and hope enough other people do the same.

The pony clipclopping created this bizarrely intertwined riff, a hypnotic steeldrum rumba.

"You even got your own dance, Amichai," Dare said. "It's *freaktastic*."

Then a hot boy started making out with Dare, and a cute girl grabbed me, and soon we all pranced in circles to this crazy beat, whinnying and snorting, some even jumping on each others' backs to ride lasciviously.

They must have been doing this all night, because people ran up with bowls of sugar cubes – transporting cane sugar this far north was hella expensive, who'd paid for that? – and started handing them out. I didn't know why, until two girls I didn't know pressed up against me, begging me to feed them.

That's when I saw Peaches, surrounded by four boytoys, grabbing each of them by the back of their hair like it was a mane. They sucked her fingers as she fed them sugarlumps.

I looked away, sick with jealousy. I had pretty girls begging for my sugar, but seeing Peaches feeding someone else made me feel like a loser. That was crazy – this was *my* dance, wasn't it?

Dare's head whipped to one side. Someone was yelling.

Now, arguments weren't unusual at Blackout Parties; the living were a scrappy bunch, and if you weren't dancing then you were debating politics. But Dare waved his arms in the danger gesture, gesticulating over –

– at Gumdrool.

He was pressed up against a wall by Halitosis Harry, his face wrinkled in revulsion. Harry was bumping his clapboard up against Gumdrool's chest like a baseball manager taunting an umpire, outraged by Gumdrool's brawny body and Junior LifeGuard outfit.

"All the dead do is bleed us dry!" Harry screamed. "They enslave us!"

"You 'slaves' *become* the masters!" Gumdrool yelled back. "You think it's *coincidence* there hasn't been a war between Upterlife-enabled countries in two centuries?"

"Slave-owners have no need to fight."

"*Look* at your flesh," Gumdrool said, flicking a louse off Harry's forehead. "You're an insult to all those who ever voided for the Upterlife. Why, I should void you right now…"

Harry lunged for Gumdrool. Gumdrool shoved Harry backwards with a contemptuous sneer, sending Harry crashing into a table full of drinks.

The music crumbled into an atonal squawk as people stopped dancing. Gumdrool took a step forward. *"Had enough, bag-of-bones?"*

I tackled him.

I got lucky; he didn't see me coming. Even so, he twisted as I caught him around the waist, his knee slamming into my ribs. I clawed at his eyes, hoping someone would help before Gumdrool cleaned my clock.

Instead, someone hauled me off him. It took the remaining four of Mama's guards to subdue Gumdrool.

"All right," Mama Alex said, waving the crowd back. "Keep dancing. We'll handle this."

The dance lurched uncertainly back to life as Mama Alex knelt before me, making *tsk*ing noises.

"You should know better, Amichai. First rule of Blackout Party: no violence."

"I was defending Harry!"

"You were defending the man who swung first?" She jerked her chin towards Harry, who was being escorted out of the party. "Still I can't deny Harry was provoked. Peaches, does Junior Fascist here have the pull he claims?"

"If he doesn't, nobody does," Peaches said.

Mama nodded, and an aide uncuffed Gumdrool. He rubbed his wrists, looking furious – but not furious enough to swing at anyone.

I, on the other hand, couldn't stop staring at Peaches. "Why in the void did you let Gumdrool in *here*?"

"Ian Drumgoole," Peaches said, putting her arm around both our shoulders. "Meet your infiltration expert. Amichai, meet your ticket into the LifeGuard."

12: THE BRUTAL NEGOTIATION TECHNIQUES OF PEACHES KHAN-TIEN

There are some sentences you don't expect to hear, like *Your left kidney has turned into a fish*, or *Everyone loves weasels in their butt*.

So when Peaches said, *You'll be working with Drumgoole*, I had to unpack the sentence to sort the words into the proper order.

Gumdrool just laughed.

"*Damrosch?*" he chuckled, incredulous. "Of course. He got a taste of the void, now he's a model citizen. Mr Beldon was right: everyone caves."

"I didn't *cave*," I spat back. "I'm—"

Peaches' nails dug into the scruff of my neck. "No insults, boys. Negotiation."

She hauled us down a tunnel to where an abandoned subway car, half off the tracks, lay against a wall. She wrenched open the doors; ancient lights flickered on, revealing a table propped mostly level that held three cups of steaming tea. She shoved us into the cracked bucket seats.

I had Peaches whiplash. Five minutes ago, she'd been drunk and dancing. Now she was tucking her hair back into a sharp business 'do, eyeing us both like we were chess pieces.

"Some people might see two enemies here." Peaches

gestured for us to pick up our tea. "*I* see two people whose futures depend upon each other. But should this turn into a dick-measuring contest, I'll walk."

"I need people who'll do the right thing," Gumdrool said calmly.

"And is showing up at a *Blackout Party* in your Junior LifeGuard uniform the" – she made the quote-bunny-ears with her fingers – "'right thing'?"

"I'm proud of what I do. I'm not going to hide it."

"Yes, a man on a stealth mission certainly doesn't want to *hide*." She rolled her eyes. "How about you, Amichai? Can you negotiate?"

Her coldness made me feel small. Did our friendship matter?

"Tell me what I'm here for," I said.

"A fine starting point." She drummed her fingers on the table absently to the memory of the Blackout Party's music. "Now. Amichai. You wanted someone with an in to the LifeGuard. Ian's *so* in, I had to negotiate a special release from Mama Alex to allow him down here. Tell Ian why you want in."

"That's none of his business," I said.

"This is *all* business, you idiot. Put your cards on the table."

I sighed. "My sister needs me to get a good job so I can help her. The LifeGuard is the best job."

Gumdrool leaned forward, examining me more closely. "Why, Amichai Damrosch. Are you telling me the boy who's practically made a career out of luring people into sin will toe the line to preserve someone *else's* Upterlife?"

"I haven't *lured*–"

Peaches kicked me in the shin before I could start up another argument. "Yes, Amichai needs some guidance to calm his *impulsiveness*," she said pointedly. "But you need someone stealthy – did you find evidence of any of his pranks? I know you've looked. And he broke all the way into the hospital, and would have broken all the way *out* again if he hadn't blanked. He's flexible, tenacious – visionary, even. Isn't that potential why you've been trying to reform him?"

He rubbed the back of his neck. "I... can't deny your talent, Damrosch. But are you potential for a good LifeGuard... or a Criminal Shrive in the making? We don't want any more Mama Alexes, do we?"

He gave me a smirk that dared me to contradict him.

"... and?" Peaches urged.

"I'm willing to acknowledge his usefulness," Gumdrool allowed. "He *did* talk that Christian bitch down – even if she escaped later on..."

"She *escaped?*" I squeed in total fanboy bliss. "Her breakout must have been legendary..."

"So you admit Amichai can help you," Peaches said. "Now tell him what your mission is."

He swallowed tea, considering. "I was hunting through New York's camerafeeds for dark zones–"

"Hang on, hang on," I said, making the "time-out" sign with my hands. "You can view New York's feeds? Not just in the orphanages, but everywhere in the *city?*"

He blushed. "Mr Beldon lends me his access. Don't worry, I can't see anything untoward – modesty routines blur the indecent areas..."

"Which means you've *tried* to look."

"I didn't set out to. It happens when you're camera-patrolling Wickliffe, though–"

"Especially in the girls' dormitories, I'd imagine–"

"Boys, *boys*," Peaches said, raising her voice. "You can either forget past sins, or you can forget my help."

Gumdrool sucked in a long breath, exhaled patiently. "In any case, I was scanning the street feeds for dark zones. Cameras die all the time: equipment failure, lens grime, rats in the wires. We've had problems replacing our street eyes, after the Bubbler's manpower shortages. Still, one of the quickest ways to pinpoint criminal activity is to look for places where dead cameras overlap."

In other words, you were looking for our next Blackout Party, I thought. But I thought of Izzy, and said nothing.

"This dead zone was in Little Venice – a two-day slog through flooded wreckage. But you know the black markets; they'll set up shop in the least expected places. So I set out to see what was there."

"Was it a black market?"

"No. It's a server. A *new* server."

"...An Upterlife server?"

"Yes," Gumdrool said, concerned. "And it's not ours."

I gave Peaches a wary glance; she sat stonefaced.

"That doesn't make sense," I said. "Building servers in a flood zone? The *existing* Little Venice skyscrapers are toppling."

"That's where they've hidden it," Gumdrool urged me, as if he knew how crazy he sounded. "The server's hidden in the intersection of four collapsed buildings; you have to crawl through an abandoned apartment complex before you can even see it.

"But it's there," he assured me. "Shiny new. Fully powered. Heavily guarded. By... by NeoChristians."

"That's crazy," I said. "NeoChristians hate technology. They don't Shrive. They certainly don't *branch*. And not in New York."

Branches were a way of life back when the Upterlife started. People decided they didn't want a Walter Wickliffe-designed heaven and created their own servers, using Wickliffe's reverse-engineered code. It was chaotic at first, because not only were there tons of businesses with second-rate consciousness-saving servers, but *governments* ran their own as well.

That all died off. Sure, you could set up your own network of branched Upterlife code. But Wickliffe had every incentive to make the Upterlife as secure, pleasant, and redundant as possible – after all, he lived there. He had the best hardware, the smartest brains, the best funding.

He made a lot of concessions to France, and Japan, and Africa in patient efforts to get other countries to use his brainstoring technology. When China converted to Upterlife servers, it looked like world peace was on the way.

Then some rogue nation weaponized a branch.

Remember how the dead's unconscious thought patterns get utilized to judge the living's Shrives? Well, if you tweak the settings to set your inhabitants' spare brainpower to "searching for weaknesses in the Upterlife servers around them" instead...

I'd say you can find a lot of exploits, but that's not true. Wickliffe is a paranoid man who's been patching holes for centuries. Yet even one new exploit can destroy lives. You can burn out servers, corrupt consciousnesses, turn the dead into living viruses.

So programming became outlawed. That leaves some folks in the Kentucky backwoods who've been quietly tending to their homegrown servers for generations, carrying their families in old RVs, wanting nothing to do with the "official" code. They take deep pride in their heritage. The authorities usually overlook them.

Terrorists, however, *love* branch servers. The Upterlife's too spread out at this point to damage it physically... But they're all hoping to find the big exploit that drops the Upterlife in one shot.

"If the NeoChristians have built a branch server, it's out of our league," I said. "This is a terrorist attack on the Upterlife, man. Call the LifeGuard."

"*No.*" Gumdrool grabbed my wrist. "We need to find out for ourselves."

"Why?"

"Because we can use this to guarantee our jobs in the LifeGuard. Look, New York just endured a population collapse. Cameras are burning out because there's no one to replace them – imagine what the LifeGuard is struggling with as they fight to maintain order! For the first time in generations, there's the opportunity to rise to the top *while we're alive.*"

Gumdrool's glazed emphasis on *opportunity* surprised me.

"If we can tell them not just 'There's something there' but 'Here's the details of this NeoChristian threat,' then we've shown our *value*. The fact that the NeoChristians built a branch server in New York shows how understaffed the LifeGuard are. If we prove ourselves, they'll even give *you* a job. And even I have to admit the only person I know who can get me close enough without tripping their alarms is *you*."

"So why so eager, Ian?" I asked. "Aren't you as good as in the LifeGuard already?"

Gumdrool's stiff little smile meant I'd scored a hit.

"All your cards on the table, Ian," Peaches warned him.

He looked wounded. "It's... it's not enough to get into the Upterlife. I need Walter Wickliffe to welcome me to the Upterlife personally. To say, 'Well done, Ian, you're a man I can trust.'"

Is everything we do a reaction to the ways our parents screwed us over? I wondered. Gumdrool's parents had left him, and he'd fixated on impressing Walter Wickliffe instead.

It was pathetic. But we had that much in common.

"All right, I'm in." I reached out to shake his hand.

"Not so fast," Gumdrool said. "Before I bring you along, I want to see your latest Shrive. Even I can't get you into the LifeGuard if you're Mortal. And I want you to sneak me into someplace new, as a test. Not the orphanage; a secure location you haven't broken into before."

"That's fine," I replied. "I have one condition of my own."

13: THE KHAN-TIEN ~~PARKING GARAGE~~ MORTUARY

"Peaches, you can't be serious," Dare said, hopping from foot to foot like he had to pee. "Breaking into our parents' mortuary? What if we get caught?"

"*We* do not have to get caught," Peaches replied, staring up at the stained walls of the Khan-Tien Mortuaries. The Khan-Tiens were notoriously cheap, so you could still see the centuries-old, faded 24 HOUR PARKING signs attached to what had once been a parking garage, with a flapping tarp that said KHAN-TIEN MORTAL REMAINS STORAGE tied over it. "*We* didn't ask you here. *You* just want in because Amichai's involved."

"Someone's gotta talk him out of your crazy schemes," Dare muttered.

"Quiet," I shushed them, staring at readouts on my IceBreaker. My upgraded IceBreaker put intimidatingly effective technology at my disposal, but it wasn't a magic wand. The Khan-Tiens were cheap but paranoid – they needed good security, because the pray-and-stay Christians stored plastic cups, rare metals, all sorts of pre-crash valuables inside their portacrypts.

I scanned the locks. My preliminary analysis showed they used no obvious passwords, and had lockout protocols. If

I flooded them with attempts, I'd trip alarms. There were
finicky workarounds I could use to mask the number of
attempts, but those could take hours to fire off...

Gumdrool watched with interest. I hunched over to hide
the controls; I didn't want him to figure out how to do this
on his own. Still, it was a good sign that he hadn't slugged me
and hauled the IceBreaker back to Beldon.

"What if he fails?" Dare whispered.

"Then I tell our family this was a security analysis to test our
defenses," Peaches sighed. "I swear, have you *no* imagination,
Dare?"

"'Imagination's for when brute force fails,'" I said, quoting
Mama Alex, then slapped my forehead when I saw the
solution. "Wait! I've got it. Peaches, open this door."

"I can't." She gave me an *are you nuts?* eyeroll. "The point
is, *you* have to break in, Amichai."

"Let's try that again: open this door, or I'll drop all my
camerashields, trigger the alarms, and tell your parents how
you encouraged me to steal from your business in an attempt
to get me into the LifeGuard. They hated it when Dare bought
me a pony – imagine how they'd react when they discovered
you were helping me out! What was it they called me again,
Dare?"

Dare chuckled, shooting me that shy smile. "A criminal
and a malingerer."

"What d'you say, Peaches? How would you feel about me
ratting you out to your family?"

Peaches grinned, reaching up to touch her earputer for the
access code. "Oh, my. I guess I have no choice but to open the
doors for you under the leverage of such a *scurrilous* threat."

Gumdrool grabbed her wrist. "That's cheating!"

"That's social engineering," I told him. "Why waste time
cracking networks when you can blackmail the people who
own the codes?"

"I suppose that's how you got access to the sprinkler system."

"I neither confirm nor deny your colorful sprinklers. But I *will* say that if you tell a senior you can troubleshoot a malfunctioning fire alarm for them, you get all sorts of interesting passwords."

"Clever," Gumdrool said appreciatively. "It's good to have you using your tricks for my benefit, Amichai."

My feeling of triumph wilted. Gumdrool as my boss? But that's the job I was auditioning for.

We walked onto the mortuary's cracked asphalt – one big road sloping up around the corner, enclosed in old concrete vaults held up with rusted beams. You could see yellowed paint outlining the old parking spaces – but squeezed into every two slots was a slanted Rose Cottage, which looked neither like a rose or a cottage.

The Rose Cottages were, in fact, squashed replicas of oldtime New York apartment living rooms.

The Khan-Tien Mortuaries used to be the Khan-Tien Parking Garages, back when cars were cheap and life was cheaper. Then the Peak Oil crash hit just as the Upterlife was causing theological havoc. If you were a Christian, wasn't the Upterlife the new Tower of Babel – an attempt to outdo God? Was the Upterlife-you a soulless replica, or your soul distilled? What if the Rapture came, and your soul was trapped in the Upterlife?

The Khan-Tiens, left with all this empty real estate, made a compromise: you're not *really* dead. Your brain's just externalized. We'll store your body until Jesus returns… At very reasonable prices.

The NeoChristians rejected this idea violently, splintering off into a terrorist sect. The pray-and-stay Christians ate it up. And the upper-class pray-and-stays wanted their body kept in a nice, pleasant place – hence, the Rose Cottages.

Dare stopped, looking at the rows of drab, locked doors.

"They look awful from the outside, I know. But inside, each one's a unique capsule of past beauty. They really knew how to make things back then – tiny churches, jazz clubs, arcades…"

"No wonder you're in love with architecture," I said. "You repaired a different home every day."

He gave me a wistful grin. "If it wasn't for my relatives, I could have happily spent my life maintaining these old rooms."

"Charming. Shouldn't you be breaking into a place with a computer terminal and a Shrive Point?" Gumdrool asked.

"That'd be space #137," Dare replied. "Mr Fiore was a landlord. He lost faith after a decade in the Upterlife, so he won't check in…"

"Sounds excellent," Gumdrool said.

We crammed into the room. Mr Fiore must have spent his whole life collecting crucifixes: stained-glass crosses over the windows, bronze crosses on the walls, ceramic standup Jesuses lining the coffee tables. He'd even carved a cross into the hood of his Shrive Point.

It made me sad, seeing a lifetime of faith abandoned. Mr Fiore's freeze-dried body knelt by the bed, forever praying, a useless stub he'd saved on the offchance he might be wrong about heaven.

"All right," Gumdrool said, edging respectfully around the Shriveled body. "How do we log in?"

"They used keyboards," I told him. "You know how to type?" A subtle insult; only hackers typed these days. Everyone else just pointed at screens and subvocalized.

"I'll dope it out."

Dare paced. "That's not programming, is it, Amichai? My architecture applications are in for Career Day – a scandal could destroy my chances…"

"You're such a waste!" Peaches blew a lock of hair out of her eyes. "No *wonder* you always get caught. If you're going to do something sketchy, commit."

"Like those four boys you were kissing earlier tonight?" Dare asked. "They looked sketchy, but you were doing *them* like you meant it..."

Peaches lunged for Dare. Gumdrool stopped her.

"The new population- rebuild laws say she's mandated to have a child by twenty-one anyway," said Gumdrool. "Viewed in that light, her amorous antics are simply... patriotic."

Gumdrool hunt-and-pecked in his login credentials; Peaches unconsciously tapped her feet along with his rhythm, spurred into minidances by the slightest sound. When he was done, he squeezed my shoulder hard enough to leave bruises. "Don't use my account for anything illegal," he warned, clearing a space for me by the keyboard.

"You think I want to get caught before we start?" I replied.

Though I *might* have videotaped his painfully slow typing with my earputer to harvest his keystrokes for later.

I shoved him aside, typing with one hand and mousing my way through dialog prompts with the other. A frozen snapshot of Therapy, taken from the *Sins of the Flesh* video, stayed constant in the lower right corner – but the rest was a sea of menus and checkboxes. The dead had so many more controls than the living had access to. But I pulled up tutorials, walking through the advanced settings.

He peered in closer. "I've never seen those control panels before."

"That's because you never *looked*." Put the living in front of a screen and they froze, choosing the simplest options lest they get themselves into trouble.

I cackled in triumph. Buried under hundreds of administrative controls, I'd found the setting I'd hoped for: *visual expression match*. I circled Therapy's image with a lasso tool, clarified the image to widen the range of matches I could find, then dumped the cleaned-up vidclip into the search trap.

"What are you doing?" Gumdrool's chin was almost on my shoulder.

"Doing a global search for something that looks like *that.*" I pointed at Therapy.

"Searching where?"

"*Everywhere.*" I rested my finger against the blue progress bar inching towards completion. "Every living feed in New York."

Gumdrool rubbed his eyes. "That's crazy. We don't have that kind of processing power."

"The screen begs to differ, my friend."

"If you can do that, then why is the LifeGuard asking us to scan for dark zones? If it can find a single pony in New York, then it must be trivial to develop a formula that finds inoperative cameras and triangulates the most vulnerable blank spots…"

I blinked. Given one sample of the cameras' capacities, he'd extrapolated other logical uses.

"They used to do that," Peaches said. "Before Boston, all the cameras were monitored by AIs. Then President Wickliffe started making noises that the dead had lost touch with the living. Too many people were dorking around in the Upterlife without a clue what the living needed; they were voting in brutal laws that caused meat-world riots.

"So Wickliffe rammed through a legislative act that switched off the automated scanners in favor of a crowd-sourced solution. How did he put it? 'A window to the world, a reminder of your duty.'"

"Wow. He got the dead to change their minds?" Dare said, both skeptical and awed.

"He burned a lot of political power to do it. The dead hated working for the living's benefit, and the living despised him for how many people he'd voided putting down Boston. It was a landmark moment in history, if any of you lot bothered to pay attention to politics: it was the first election where practically everyone living voted against Wickliffe, but a narrow tie among the dead was still enough to get him elected. It was the day we living realized our votes had become statistically insignificant."

Gumdrool traced his finger along the monitor, lost in thought. "So only the dead watch the feeds?"

"That's when he created *Sins of the Flesh*," Peaches shrugged. "He had to offer Upterlife prizes to encourage them to monitor the meat-world. I mean, what else can they use?"

"Doesn't sound too efficient," Dare groused. "A handful of corpsicles watching the feeds?"

"It's not a 'handful' of dead," Peaches explained, treating her brother to yet another gaze from her vast selection of disappointed looks. "Even if only one out of a thousand watches, that's still millions of snoopers."

"...but it's desegmented," Gumdrool concluded. "You'll catch the little crimes, but the big picture stuff suffers. Because none of those millions are talking to each other."

"Right."

"I'll fix that." Gumdrool straightened the medals on his Junior LifeGuard uniform, and in that moment I could imagine him changing the world into something darker.

I had to help him. LifeGuards had pull. The pull to make Izzy's life easier.

"You won't fix anything, you idiot," Dare said. "He made our lives less safe, so it'd be more interesting for his people to *watch*. That's the way Wickliffe *wants* it."

"That's why I need to talk to him." Gumdrool's voice was curiously distant. "He needs to understand how badly things are decaying in the physical sphere..."

The monitor beeped, showing several locations timeplotted

across a narrow arc.

"We have achieved pony!" I said.

"I can't believe you did all this to search for a stupid *horse*," Gumdrool said.

"I didn't. She's a pony. And that was my condition before taking this mission." I clicked through to some grainy videos of Therapy. It was hard to make her out – most of the clips were from a distance, as if the people involved were dodging cameras – but in the clearest clip, she was being surrounded by a bunch of black market vendors with electrified nets.

They flung the nets over Therapy. She lashed out with her hind legs, catching a vendor in the chest hard enough that he crunched into a coral wall.

Then there was the sparkle of a net-taser and Therapy fell to the floor, twitching. They closed in on her – one vendor took out an autobridle, its drill whirring, ready to install itself in Therapy's brain...

"Greenwich Village," I said, headed for the door. "We'll break her out and then head for the branch."

Gumdrool blocked my way.

"We head for the branch now," he insisted. "It'll take us two days to get there, and void knows what those NeoChristians will do before then."

"But Therapy–"

Peaches cut me off. "Amichai, your pony's not time-sensitive. This is. Ian, will you let him use the cameras again once we get the branch info?"

"As long as he shows me how he did that it."

"Then don't argue, Amichai. If you want to break into the black market, do it on your own time."

"Whose side are you on?" I grumbled.

"The smart side."

I missed the old Peaches, the one who cuddled with me on darkened rooftops. But I finally saw Peaches through Dare's eyes: was she the crazy rave-dancer, the business broker, or the uncertain girl who sometimes shared secrets?

I wanted to believe the quiet, meaningful girl who'd kissed me was the real Peaches. But I couldn't shake the feeling that the quiet girl was a luxury Peaches allowed herself once business was done – like a single chocolate at the end of a meal.

"You still haven't Shrived for me, Damrosch," Gumdrool said, shoving me ass-backwards onto the Shrive Point. "I need to ensure you're clean enough for the LifeGuard to take you."

Resigned, I put on the hood. From the inside, I could see the knife marks where Mr Fiore had carved a cross – presumably to make his Shriving more acceptable to Jesus.

I pushed the button. What is the longest your fingernails have been? What is the smell of rubbing alcohol? How many birds have you seen flying?

When the scan completed, we watched the five icons.

"It's taking a long time," Gumdrool said.

"That's how long it always takes for him," Dare replied. I whispered a silent thanks for covering for me – this was longer than even my last Shrive. "But Amichai always comes up Venal."

The machine dinged, as if to contradict him. Dim amber illuminated a straight stick figure. *Mortal.*

I knew why. "*Sins of the* goddamned *Flesh,*" I muttered.

14: CONVERSATIONS WITH CRIMINALS

Dare and Peaches backed away from me.

"It's a, a temporary thing." Dare wiped his palms on his jeans. "Some folks, you know, have a Mortal stage. Like, uh, Great-Grandma Mi-Yong..."

"Who got kicked out of the family business," Peaches said, giving me a look that said, *I care for you, but I don't think I can help you now.*

"I'm still *here*, guys," I said. They flinched. "I haven't changed. It's the voiding *show*, is all. The dead now associate me with a show about criminals. I'm subliminally *tainted*..."

Would that taint fade, in time? Even the hoariest swindlers at the Blackout Parties Shrived Venal. It took a lot to Shrive Mortal.

How will you help Izzy now? I thought.

"Aw, *void* it!" Gumdrool ripped the Shrive Point off the wall, aimed it at me – and then smashed it on the floor instead. The hood shattered, the scratched cross breaking apart.

"What the void?" Dare shrieked. "You're damaging Mr Fiore's property! We're contractually obligated to keep everything functioning!"

"This is *useless!* How can I get into the LifeGuard if I'm–"

Then he seemed to think better of speaking plainly in front of someone Mortal.

"Wait, wait." Peaches' fingers clutched the air as if she could gather the shards of this plan back together. "It's salvageable."

"Mortals can't get into the LifeGuard," Gumdrool said, slumping onto the plastic couch. "It's useless – useless..."

I sat down numbly. I'd just ruined Izzy's whole life.

No, that's Mom and Dad, I thought. They screwed her over by being too self-absorbed.

And you didn't? a tiny voice shot back.

"Here's how we fix it." Peaches held up her hands, did a small pirouette to gather her thoughts. "You're not just using Amichai as a security expert, Ian. You're *redeeming* him."

"Redeeming how?"

"I mean, isn't that what you've been doing all along? Hunting for threats to the Upterlife. Your Junior LifeGuard experience is just the starting point – you've been secretly assembling a squadron of loyal citizens. And when you found this... this NeoChristian branch, you told Amichai this was his chance to turn his life around."

"I told you," Gumdrool wailed. "Mortals can't get into the LifeGuard!"

"It's a PR problem," she said. "Amichai's bad Shrive is about perception, so... we change the perception."

"How?"

Her eyes clocked overtime as she got into the story. "A Mortal, using formerly illicit videomasking technology to hunt down Upterlife-hating terrorists! Led by... by... one of the best and brightest Junior members of the LifeGuard! You're not just two boys, but a movement to redeem the lowliest of criminals! Drumgoole's Squadron!"

"That's the kind of story Mr Wickliffe *would* love..." Gumdrool said hesitantly.

"I've got connections in SEO news-seeders. The automated pickups love tales like this. Once this permeates the deadosphere, you'll both be heroes."

"But..." I said, knowing there was always a catch.

"You can't call the the dead 'ghosts,' Amichai. Ever. That slur's a soundbite disaster waiting to happen."

"...And?"

"We have to get the LifeGuard actionable information, now," she said, chewing her hair thoughtfully. "You guys have to be big damn heroes – otherwise, the story risks spinning as two kids stumbling across a terrorist cell. And we need more people involved, to feed the idea of this being a movement."

"Great," I said.

"Before Amichai's Shrive, you could have gotten away with a couple of blurry video feeds. But now? You'll need sentry locations. Maps. Blueprints."

I followed her gaze over to Dare.

Dare was too busy picking pieces of broken Shrive hood off the floor. When the silence caught his attention, he dropped them, holding his hands in a timeout "T."

"No." Dare backed away. "No, no, *no*."

"She's right, dude," I said. "We need blueprints. You can look at a building and intuit its layout."

"Look, Amichai, it's been fun helping you film stunts. But branch servers? That's *real* danger."

"We map and withdraw," I protested. "I need to get there for Izzy, I'm not going to do anything crazy–"

"You know what branch zealots do when they get ahold of you, Chai? They torture you. For *months*. And once your brain's reduced to a gibbering, unreliable wreck, *that's* when they upload you."

"That's an urban legend," Peaches said.

"And you –" Dare leveled a finger at his sister "– are *not* as smart as you think. I know my sister. She's always overreaching, Amichai. You don't want to be there when her plans collapse."

"Dare," I said, "Do it for Izzy. You just have to scout the perimeter, tell us where to send the troops in…"

He shook his head. "She'll be fine, Amichai. Izzy's always made you paranoid–"

"Paranoid?"

"Look, I get your parents left. It sucks. But just 'cause *you* need a guardian angel to keep you in line doesn't mean... I mean, life'll suck for Izzy, sure, but it sucks for everyone. I know you're convinced she can't get by without you, but...

"But you're the one who's broken, man. You got into this whole mess because you need to make Big Statements. Drop the histrionics. Carve coral for sixty years. Life's for checking in and checking out."

"And Izzy?" I asked. "Sixty years of self-hatred?"

He rolled his eyes. "She does her job, she'll be OK. A couple hundred years in the Upterlife, that shit rolls right off."

I wanted to slap Dare. He crapped his pants whenever his relatives rang. How dare he lecture *me*?

Peaches patted Dare on the shoulder. "When you're right, you're right. I'll get you some plaster. Start fixing that wall."

"I was just tidying up," he said. "I don't work here any more."

"Sure you don't." Peaches gave him a good-natured eye roll. "You said it: we check in and check out. You're Mortuary for life, kid. Did you really think you'd escape our relatives?"

Dare looked shocked. "What? You know I've got my architect application in."

"...sixty long years getting nagged by our aunts and uncles, never sleeping because they're waking you at three in the morning to fix the mortuary, wishing you could do anything they'd approve of..."

"I just *told* you, I've got my application in–"

"Get real, kid," she snapped. "Half the world just died. Who the void needs *new* buildings?"

"But I'm talented. I do great work." The words sounded plaintive, as if he was reciting someone else's words from rote memory –

– and then I realized he was reciting *me*.

"Yeah," she scoffed. "Let's assume they want to train living kids to do something that nobody needs and the dead can do. That leaves, what... maybe three architecture slots a generation? If you had that kind of talent, don't you think one of our grand-aunts would have encouraged you?"

"I've been making money selling my plans..."

"To nouveau-dead, still in love with the living. Once that fad passes, you're back in the hands of our great-grandparents."

"No. *No*. I'm better than that. I can get out of here!"

"I thought you were eager to live your boring life out to its end, brother. So what happens when *you're* not special?"

He turned to me, lost. "Amichai. You've seen my plans. You told me they were beautiful..."

Peaches had set him up... leaving me to knock him down. And I'd like to tell you I did the right thing.

But he'd just told me to condemn Izzy to sixty years of hell.

"Dude." I shook my head, pretending to be diplomatic. "You do good stuff... for a kid your age."

Dare looked like I'd punched him. I'd always been the one who'd boosted him, and now I'd yanked him down. I felt sick.

I cleared my throat, starting to tell him that no, I'd lied, he was brilliant...

But if I reassured him, I'd lose Izzy. I needed this to work so I could protect Izzy, both here and in the Upterlife. And...

And wouldn't the PR help Dare? He'd even asked me to plug him! The amateur architect who helped bust open a NeoChristian branch... that'd get customers lining up to buy his plans. This was a win-win for everyone.

So why did I feel sick?

"Come with us," Peaches said, slipping her arm around her brother's shoulder. "We'll make you a hero."

"We're your only hope, Dare." I crossed my arms and turned away – as if he needed me more than I needed him.

Gumdrool gave me an admiring nod. That was the worst.

"...all right," Dare said. His shoulders slumped inwards, like a collapsing building. "Tell me what I need to do."

"Come with us." I took Dare's hand, already trying to think up ways to make up for what I'd just done. But it was too late.

15: FEEDING MY SISTER'S LAST HOPE

I brought Izzy some plums from Central Farm. She bit into one hungrily. "Why does fresh food always taste so good in the hospital?" she asked, wiping the juice off her chin.

"If they made hospital food taste good, everyone would stay."

She polished off the plum. They'd worked her so hard in physical therapy today that she barely had the strength left to hold the fruit, so she dropped the pit onto the bedsheet and then craned her neck around to lick the juice off her fingers like a cat.

"So, uh, I guess Mom and Dad went back to adventuring," I finally said.

"It was good to catch up with them. And they promised they'd check in more often." She shrugged, exhausted. "We'll see."

"How can you..." I swallowed, not knowing who I was angrier at, them or her. "How can you stand their bullshit, Izzy? They always say they'll be here for us, and they never are—"

"I don't expect much from my family, Amichai. I just appreciate them when they're around."

She reached for another plum.

"...listen, Izzy," I said. "I'm gonna be... out of town for a few days. I'll be fine, but I've... I've got a lead on something that could really help us both."

"Is it related to fixing your problems with *Sins of the Flesh*?"

Crap. "…maybe."

"My superiors asked about you when I was in the LifeGuard academy, you know."

I hadn't known. I shrunk back into my chair in embarrassed silence. Izzy kept eating the plum carefully, chewing slowly as she considered her words.

"Yeah. My drill sergeant brought in the updates that Mr Beldon had sent her. They called me in for meetings, showed me videos. They asked me what I thought your punishment should be."

"What'd you tell them?"

"I said that it wasn't the living's job to decide." She finished off the plum, let that pit tumble out of her palm. "And that the dead were a far better judge of when you got out of control."

"Oh, for…" I realized what she was getting at. "I didn't Shrive *Criminal*, Izzy. I'd never have screwed up so badly that they'd send you in to investigate me…"

She scooped the pits up, dropped them into an overflowing trashcan. "Mortal is bad enough."

"I wouldn't normally *be* Mortal! It's just, you appear on TV before billions, and it contaminates the dead's opinions…"

"But you're not stopping there, are you?"

Her clear gaze was filled with the worst kind of disappointment: the kind that had never been steeped in hope. She'd just quietly assumed I'd keep stepping out of line – and of course she'd been right.

"It's a mission for the LifeGuard," I said carefully. "If it goes well, they'll give me a job."

Izzy had memorized all the ways someone could get into the LifeGuard. "Spontaneous promotion from civilian" wasn't on the list.

She shook her head slowly, the same soft shake of denial

she gave Mom and Dad whenever they promised they'd talk to the judges tomorrow...

"It's not Criminal," I assured her. "It's dangerous, but it's not Criminal. And Peaches thinks it can work."

"Peaches says that?" It was galling to see that Peaches had more credibility than I did around here, but at least it bought me some breathing room.

"OK. Cards on the table." I hunched forward on the bed, moving so close she had no choice but to look at me. "I don't want to do this. You know I never wanted to be in the LifeGuard. And this... adventure... will have me going up against some nasty people."

They torture you, Dare had said. For months.

"Then *why*, Amichai?" She ran her hands through her thatchy hair. "Just calm down and let this blow over. The dead will forgive you in time, I'm sure of it..."

"I will stop." I cupped her cheek. "I'll give all this up and tend coral for the rest of my days. All *you* have to do is look me in the eye and tell me you'll be all right if I do nothing to help you."

She squared her shoulders as best she could, considering her shoulderblades were now lopsided. She sucked in a deep breath, quivering with terror, considering sixty years of painful labor without an escape.

And I realized that, despite the trouble my misadventures had gotten me into, they'd given my big sister some weirdass form of hope. I'd tie dyed the orphanage, I'd smuggled ponies into her room – and even though she hated the way I fought the system, she secretly loved the way I got away with things she'd never thought I could pull off.

I was her magic in the world. And if I stopped fighting, something terrible within her would collapse.

She scrubbed tears from her cheeks with her wrists. "I don't *want* to need your help."

"It's OK," I told her. "It's OK. You want another plum?"

She nodded slowly. "Yeah. Yeah, I do."

I put the fruit into her hands, feeding her. We talked about small stuff, exchanging old family jokes and harmless gossip. I held her hand until she fell asleep.

Then I left for Little Venice.

16: THE CITY THAT REFUSED TO DROWN

Little Venice was where New York had drowned five years ago, and the waters still stank of dead bodies.

We would have drowned, too, if Gumdrool hadn't been there to save us. Owing my career to that sonuvabitch was hard enough, but owing him my life? I gained respect with each block, because he guarded our passage.

Little Venice's streets were hip-deep in spillover from the Atlantic Ocean, a thick muck choked with the Bubbler's stink and liquefied corpses and rotting seaweed – a dead town that swallowed bodies and vomited out glutinous sickness. You could see dead men's bones fused to old shop windows, all engulfed in creeping mutant coral like yellowed sharks' teeth.

Yet Gumdrool scouted ahead through the ruins. He'd procured thick neoprene hip-waders and elbow-length gloves so we wouldn't die of infected cuts. He taught us the landscape, explaining each danger, helping us recognize the safe paths among the teetering skyscrapers.

If my attention wandered, he'd whack me on the head. "Watch!" he'd say, with the air of a man training a dog.

And lo, turns out I'd nearly stepped into a flooded manhole lined with razor-sharp coral.

I hated looking dumb in front of Peaches, but seeming

foolish in front of Gumdrool? Agony. But he was right to hit. My gall drove me to learn faster, which meant Gumdrool's whap-an-Amichai techniques were effective.

That made me despise him even more.

He whapped Peaches, too, told her to stop dancing her way through the water. The only one he hadn't clouted was Dare, who walked numbly in whatever direction Gumdrool pointed.

"Aren't you worried about your brother?" I asked Peaches, as Dare lowered himself unquestioningly into an alley brimming with slimy water. "You were pretty harsh."

"He's always been a drama queen." She swigged from her canteen, rinsing Little Venice's taste from her mouth. "He'll thank us when this is done."

I wasn't sure. Dare looked heartbroken. But she was his sister, and who knew him better?

The terrain wasn't too bad back when we'd climbed over the levees. Those relatively clean waters streamed straight from the churn of Lexington Avenue – sorry, the Lexington River – where the old bodegas and tech shops had been picked over.

But after an hour's slog, we hit the deeper waters – the ones where the Roosevelt River had spilled into the apartment complexes. The streets had buckled and filled with water, then collapsed the buildings, then the dead had spilled into the rivers to eddy up and rot. Five years later, you could still find cold limbs bobbing in stagnant waters.

Overhead, the remaining apartment buildings rocked, shifting in the wind. The muck-water had sluiced out their foundations – but the aircoral had mutated, grown aggressive, spreading out in huge, skin-ripping encrustations.

"Everything's unstable here," Gumdrool warned us. "Coral collapses, sinkholes open up, buildings topple. Watch each step and you'll stay alive."

"Gee, Ian," I shot back. "Keep this up, and I might even think you care."

He blinked. "I *do* care. President Wickliffe told us how to live: 'all should pass through, but for the lowliest criminals.' You, Amichai, were in danger of becoming a lowly criminal."

"*Hey.*"

He held his hands up. "I understand the temptations. If you knew all the things I've done, I..." He blushed, then looked away. "If I was certain of my chances in the LifeGuard, I wouldn't be here."

"Have you considered the LifeGuard might not want a mean sonuvabitch like you?"

He shrugged. "That's living-talk. If I do my job right, you have hundreds of years to forgive me. But if I mess up, you void. Haven't you felt the need for the servers yet?"

I had. Little Venice made us exquisitely aware of our mortality. Every time I slipped on a scree of loosened coral, my body shrieked, *This is the end!*

I'd never realized how good immortality felt until someone took it away.

But despite the crunch of human ribcages underfoot, I was *excited*. This was my last vacation. After this, my life would consist of nothing but LifeGuard missions; I would relish this freedom while I had it.

So we climbed a creaking staircase up to an old brownstone to rest briefly in an abandoned apartment, the coral walls bulging cancerous. We stripped out of the thick wetsuits, poured our pooled sweat out of the boots. Peaches combed muck from her hair while I chomped on a wrinkled apple.

Back in the days when the living had outnumbered the dead, they'd shipped all sorts of foods halfway across the world – oranges, coffee, chocolate – squirting them full of preservatives. Such a waste. All that energy could be better spent on new servers and magnetorails to deliver circuit boards, so people ate local foods. Which supposedly tasted way better than chemical-stuffed crap.

Still, how great would a can of tuna have been right then?

Dare slumped down next to me, and we both stared out over the collapsed apartment buildings.

"Ew," said Peaches, opening the door to the bedroom. "More bodies."

"I'll get it," Gumdrool said, opening up his Limbo Bag. To avoid twinning, you couldn't get into the Upterlife without a DNA sample from a corpse to prove your death. Until then, the ones who'd died here were stuck in a Limbo server, neither alive nor Upterlifed.

Gumdrool photographed the remains before extracting tiny scrapes of jerky-like flesh, but his Limbo Bag sagged with the weight of a thousand specimens. It slowed him down, but Gumdrool stressed it was important to get as many lost souls into the Upterlife as possible.

"We've got a lot of ground to cover before dark," Gumdrool said. "Don't abandon your duty to yourself, Dare. Eat something."

Gumdrool pressed a pear into his hands. Dare chewed it mechanically.

Our GPS maps hadn't been updated with Little Venice's current layout – who'd bother? It had flooded five years ago, when the guys who manned the pumps that kept this section of New York afloat had died. Maybe men more devoted to their jobs might have fought their way to the pumps and pulled off a miracle, but nobody was that inspired these days.

And once it was clear the underground flooding was sluicing holes in the substrata, causing skyscrapers to topple, the rescue effort began. It drew few volunteers, though. Rescuing was dangerous work, normally a plus, but there was a chance your body might be swept away. So millions died, too sick to get to the rescue spirocopters.

Yet even if someone had bothered to update the GPS maps, our batteries were low. Back at the orphanage, we were surrounded by electrical broadcast signals that recharged low-wattage devices. Only a handful of working charge stations remained in Little Venice.

Last time, Gumdrool had told us, his batteries had died before he got to the branch server, forcing him to return without evidence. So we kept our cameras off. And respected Gumdrool because he'd forged this path alone.

We covered a mere ten blocks the first day. When the sun set, we took shelter in what had once been a performance hall. It was an empty space that opened up to the sky, with ruins that sloped down towards a fetid pond. Dare hung up our suits to dry – my feet already crawled with fungus – while Gumdrool boiled and filtered water for tomorrow's trip.

"My legs ache," I told Peaches.

"Well, there's one solution for that." She rose to her feet, graceful as a dead ballerina, and offered me her hand. "Let us dance."

"What? You're crazy. There's no music…"

She tugged me up to place my left hand at the small of her back, taking my right hand in hers. "We can hum our own rhythm. And dancing always comforts me."

Peaches took the lead, counting an oldfashioned "one-two-three, *one*-two-three" rhythm, until I figured out where my feet should go. We spun in time, sweeping across the sunset's dwindling light. Cobbling together beauty from whatever we had on hand.

I felt alive.

Peaches kissed me on the cheek. "Told you," she said, walking me through a twirl.

"Usually you rave-dance. You pirouette sometimes when you're distracted – I thought that was just a quirk…"

"No," she laughed. "I dance whenever I can. It centers me.

And I mean, I *was* classically trained."

"Who trained you?"

"My family, who else?" She shook her head fondly. "At first I thought it was torture. Who wanted to learn how to use their stupid meat-bodies? 'When I'm in the Upterlife, I'll program perfect dance routines for myself,' I told them. They insisted a proper lady knew ballet. It taught character. Obedience."

I knew that wasn't the whole truth. "...and?"

"...and I was still knotted with Bubbler scars," she admitted, pulling her arms in; she wore long-sleeved shirts to cover her pockmarked skin. "They said dancing would unstick my fused muscles."

"Did it?"

"Not at first," she allowed. "I was as stiff as steel. Once I loosened up, the other girls made fun of my toned body – they said I was too into my meat-body, that ugly weightlifters didn't make the Upterlife..."

"Girls *said* that?"

She chuckled at my naivete, still dancing. "Amichai, teenaged girls cut other girls open and dump in salt. They're the most vicious creatures in the world."

"You're not vicious."

"I look harmless," she snapped absently. "That's something I cultivate. Don't idolize me, Amichai."

She walked me through another set of steps in silence.

"Anyway, after a while, I started to, you know, crave the dance," she continued. "That motion. That promise the next time will be the perfect movement. I began practicing in secret."

"Why would you do that?"

"Because the great-relatives watched all my classes. They told me I was too fat, that I moved like a cow. I know you get lonely sometimes, Amichai, but... having parents who care too much isn't all that great, either."

She laid her head on my shoulder, drawing me into a hug. "So I found places without cameras," she said. "I made my own moves. And I never let anyone see them."

I slid my arms around her neck. She was strong enough to carefully reveal this fragility.

"And that's…" I swallowed. "That's why you went to the Blackout Parties, wasn't it? You heard about a place with no cameras where people danced…"

"I was so *scared*, Amichai." She shivered. "I'd always been such a good girl. I couldn't imagine what it would mean if I got caught sneaking out. I was only twelve. But… I would have died if I didn't."

"And?"

She stepped away from me, spreading her arms wide to show herself off.

I shook my head in admiration. "You must have been the most beautiful thing on the dance floor."

I'd never seen Peaches blush before. "I–"

"I'll take first watch," Gumdrool interrupted, hauling the fresh canteens back. "Two-hour shifts. Who wants second shift?"

I'd never found it easier to hate Gumdrool.

"…We're sleeping now?" Peaches asked.

"Big day tomorrow. We need rest. You can support the population rebuilding efforts later, but tonight you get some shuteye."

"What do we need to watch for?" I asked, looking around at the empty buildings and dead water.

"You don't…?" He swallowed. "Those things *patrolled*."

"The NeoChristians?"

"…yes."

Gumdrool had clutched his truncheon all day, which surprised me – he was a match for any NeoChristian. I guess a group of them might have scared him.

I lay down on the broken rubble, sure I'd never sleep with Peaches so close. Then Gumdrool shook me awake.

I opened my eyes onto the deepest blackness I'd ever seen; there were no Upterlife servers glowing, no firefly-green cameras staring at us.

"It's your watch," whispered Gumdrool. "But don't rely on your eyes. They can hide in the darkness... but they can't be quiet. Don't fall asleep."

"They're not *things*," I corrected him, remembering Evangeline. "They're NeoChristians."

He shuddered. "Whatever they are, they're... not subtle. You'll hear them coming."

"And if they come?"

"We run." He shut down his earputer. "Good night."

He rolled over and started snoring.

I listened to the wind whistling through broken windows, the creak and teeter of unstable skyscrapers. A clatter, and something splashed into into the water; I nearly grabbed at Gumdrool before realizing it was just debris falling into the river.

After a while, I heard something slurping down where the water sloshed against the building's foundations. A gurgle. A choke. Muffled tears.

I almost yelled "Run!" Then I remembered how I'd almost panicked over the debris. Yeah, that'd impress Peaches, rousing her from a dead sleep to flee from a stray dog.

More slurping. More muffled retching.

I thought about waking Gumdrool, but I just couldn't. I could yell loud enough to wake people, if I had to. And the shore wasn't *that* far away.

This wasn't nearly as stupid as the pony.

I crept up on the water. My shoes crunched on coral, but whatever it was didn't seem to notice. I saw a hunched figure, lit by smog-choked starlight, crouched over the water...

...Dare.

He brought up mouthfuls of gummy water in cupped hands, slurping it down. Then he gagged, swallowing back vomit.

"What are you *doing?*" I whispered. "That water's full of germs."

His eyes glittered. "It's my key to the Upterlife." He gulped down another mouthful.

Uh-oh, I thought.

"Dare, you can't... can't suicide." Even the word sounded Criminal in my mouth. "That's a straight ticket to the void."

He laughed. "You were right, Amichai; I can't make it in this world. I'll never get that architect slot."

"So you work at the family Mortuaries. That's not so bad..."

A bitter chuckle. "You think I renounced my family and moved into an orphanage on a *lark*? You should see my grandparents. They can't think for themselves. All they can do is echo my ancestors' decisions. They quiver like custard when you ask them for an opinion. After twenty years, I'll be sucked so dry I won't be worth Shriving.

"I need to die now." He gulped more water. I slapped his hands away.

"You can't start a career as a dead man!"

"Why not? I'm young. Someone will take me on as an apprentice. When I'm dead, I'll be able to walk through my plans, touch them, see the flaws as the dead do. Don't you see, Ami? The only way I can make this work is to transition *now*."

His logic was sickeningly accurate.

"Everyone has a baby suicide attempt, Dare," I told him. "I drank a bottle of floor cleaner when I was eight. But that's childish fantasy. You can't get into the Upterlife that way..."

"Oh, I will. I didn't Shrive before I left – the only me the

Upterlife has access to is yesterday's happy Dare, the Dare who was positive he'd get his slot as an architect. *That* Dare's sure to get in."

"But the cameras – they watch everything – they'll know you–"

He gestured at the lightless sky. "Who's watching now? If I die of dysentery, who's to say it wasn't something I caught in the water? A sad end, they'll say – but no. I beat them."

He lifted water reverently in cupped hands. "This is the sacrifice I make for future Dare. He'll never even know I did it."

It should have been a triumph. He'd beaten the system.

"*I'll* tell them," I said, trying to control the shivering in my voice.

He laughed bitterly. "Will you, Amichai? Will you tell the truth and kill me forever?"

My skin pimpled with goosebumps as I realized he'd backed me into a corner. If I told, I'd void him. If I didn't tell, he'd die. Either way was my fault.

Dare shook his head. "You won't tell."

"Dare, I *lied*. You *are* that good. I was just protecting Izzy–"

He snorted in disbelief. "After your parents left, you'd say anything to keep me around. It's sweet, Amichai. But I'll see you in the Upterlife–"

Gumdrool kicked Dare square in the stomach.

Dare doubled over, choking, vomiting water. I stood shocked by Gumdrool's sudden appearance as he booted Dare in the gut again, shouting, "Spit it out! Spit it out, you traitor!"

I lunged for him. He backhanded me so hard my ears rang.

He knelt on Dare's spine; Dare moaned in protest. "Look here, you little runt – you do *not* sneak into the Upterlife before you've given every last ounce of your life. Cheats like you are the whole reason the Upterlife's lost its way. Maybe

Damrosch doesn't have the guts to get you voided, but I do. I'll bar you from those servers forever."

He bent Dare's fingers back until Dare screamed. "And if I catch you 'slipping' off an outcropping, or anything that even *looks* like it's intentional, I will blind you. Think you could be an architect then?"

I rushed at Gumdrool. He shoved me back contemptuously.

"We're both trying to keep him here," Gumdrool told me. "Except *my* techniques work."

"I hate you!" Dare shrieked, writhing in his own sick. "I fucking *hate* you!"

"You'll forgive me," Gumdrool said serenely. "In a century or two."

He walked back to go to sleep, leaving us to explain everything to a furious Peaches.

17: IN THE ROOM OF ROTTING PIGEONS

"You guys ready?" Gumdrool asked the next morning. He tapped his truncheon against his thigh in warning.

"Lead the way," Dare said, picking up his backpack. His stomach must have hurt like void – I'd seen the bruises – but he hissed through his teeth, refusing to give Gumdrool the satisfaction.

Gumdrool looked surprised. "No debates?"

"That would imply we had better choices," Peaches snapped.

We'd stayed up all night, discussing whether we could leave Gumdrool. We couldn't. Even if you took me out of the equation – I *had* quit my job, after all, leaving me voided unless we pulled off something big – it was still a day's hike across treacherous ground to return home. We'd barely made it this far *with* Gumdrool.

Gumdrool nodded approvingly.

"It'll all work out in the end. Remember: half a millennium from now, you'll thank me for hauling your sorry asses into the Upterlife."

He clambered over a heap of coral-crusted wreckage. We followed.

As we headed deeper into Little Venice, we saw more toppled-over buildings. I could see how you could lose four collapsed skyscrapers in this mess.

We stayed out of the dangerous street-tides whenever possible, which meant forging our way through mazes of apartment complexes. The coral had metastasized; some colonies had swollen to close off hallways, while others had devoured each other to leave nothing but crumbling skeletal lace. We kicked in doors, tiptoed across bulging floors that flexed dangerously underfoot.

Gumdrool hounded Dare, forcing him to take point on anything that looked dangerous. "You go first." He pointed out a path towards a kitchen window. "Then I'll follow."

It was cruel. Dare winced when he walked. Peaches and I wondered whether his ribs were broken. Yet Gumdrool never stopped.

"It's all about revenge with you, isn't it?" Dare whispered.

Gumdrool looked hurt.

It *wasn't* about revenge, not for him. Gumdrool's whole world had crystallized around one goal: *get everyone into the Upterlife*. Nothing else mattered: not remorse, not apologies, not humanity.

That flinty faith allowed him to assume any damage he did in this life would fade. It allowed Gumdrool to justify anything as long as it kept the servers running. He had a shark's instincts: his first thought was always his first action, ready to react to any threat with instant, unblunted force.

I was so busy fretting over Gumdrool that I overlooked the danger Dare was in.

The kitchen floor was little more than cracked tile resting across desiccated coral beams. It already sagged beneath an antique steel icebox, a cast iron stove, a wooden table – and Dare's added weight was too much.

The floor sank underneath Dare's feet.

The icebox tipped over.

Dare was too busy concentrating on his footing to notice the icebox about to crush him.

"Dare!" I shrieked, diving forward to push him towards the window. Peaches lurched behind me–

And the good news is, we both succeeded. I shoved him against a windowsill before the icebox hit him. Peaches dragged me back before the icebox fell on me.

As the icebox crashed through the brittle coral beams, the kitchen floor collapsed.

I shrieked in a quite unmanful panic as I plunged to my death. I wondered if that's why your life passes before your eyes when you die – it's your brain's last, futile attempt to upload itself...

Thankfully, the basement was flooded. I tumbled backward into waist-deep water, sending a huge slosh that rattled old furniture around me. Something splashed down – Peaches, spluttering and coughing–

I shoved her aside as the cast iron stove tumbled in. The table crashed down, showering us in a rain of rusted cutlery.

The water was frigid; I flailed. Peaches surfaced, gagging.

We couldn't see anything. The ragged hole in the ceiling strangled the light.

"Are you all right?" Gumdrool had the nerve to sound concerned. The bastard.

"Fine, I think." I shivered with shock. "Peaches?"

"I'm fine. Void, it smells like death in here..."

"Don't try to climb up," Gumdrool said. "You might pull the whole apartment down on you. We'll go outside, find a safe way in."

"I don't see any windows here," I said. "Or doors. Why's it so voiding dark?"

"Whoever lived here must have barricaded themselves inside towards the end," Peaches said.

"One way to find out." I tapped my earputer into flashlight mode–

— an old dresser with a cracked mirror, a muddy T smeared across its reflective surface, the drawers overflowing with rotting pigeons –

Peaches whacked my ear. "You want to run out of power before we get to the branch?"

She was right. My energy display was down to two meager red bars. I shut it off.

"No big loss," I said. "You've seen one rotting pigeon room, you've seen 'em all." Which was a lie – I wanted another look at that mirror, which reminded me of something – but Peaches was right. We couldn't waste energy.

"Don't touch anything," Gumdrool called down. "We'll come get you. It's OK, we're almost to the branch server."

"Thank heavens," I said. "Sweet void, it's chilly in here."

A clatter and thunk as they moved away. Then the gentle sound of water sloshing against walls. Peaches and I, breathing hard.

We felt around, hunting for a dry spot. There wasn't much. We found a bed, its mattress slick with rot – and opted to prop the kitchen table in a shallow area before we clambered up onto it.

"We should cuddle up," Peaches volunteered. "You know, for warmth."

"I could stand the heat."

She pressed her soft body against mine. I felt every inch of her sliding against me.

"You know what's silly?" she asked.

"A rubber chicken that doubles as a whoopee cushion?"

She smacked me. "Amichai, I was *that close* to getting uploaded. So why am I trembling?"

I shrugged. "Evolution's spent millions of years ensuring death is the worst thing that could happen to us... Because until Wickliffe, it kinda was. It's a good instinct, I guess – keeps us from leaping off cliffs..."

"Nobody knows what it's like to die." Peaches shivered. "There's always *some* gap between Shrive and transition. And as I fell, I thought, all this hatred I've picked up for Drumgoole

– that'll be erased. Like a program your DVR forgot to record."

"That is kinda scary," I reassured her.

"No. It's *stupid*." She shook her head. "It's the dumb arguments the moldy oldies had. Maybe that gap makes a difference out in the Balkan provinces, where the government hauls a Shrive Point around to your village every three months, but a day's loss? Even if I forget a little, it's still *me*, right?"

"Hey, at least you have a ticket in," I laughed. "I'm kinda living the moldy oldie experience here."

"Void, Amichai. I'm so *selfish*. I didn't even think about what it's like for you now. Is that why you screamed?"

"I was kind of hoping you hadn't noticed."

"They probably heard you back at the orphanage." She squeezed my hand.

"I don't like being trapped here." I pressed her fingertips to my forehead so she understood what I meant; trapped within this body.

"People lived like this for millennia," she murmured, kissing my fingers.

"By hallucinating a big beard in the sky that watched everything they did."

"Mmm." She moved closer. "They also had other methods of distraction…"

"…in *here?*"

"We'll hear them coming long in advance. And a little snuggling would take my mind off everything that's happening now…"

She put her hand on the back of my neck, pulling me against her, her hips moving like they did on the dance floor. She breathed in my ear, warm and wet, rubbing her soft cheek against mine, her hand sliding down my thigh…

"Hey," I said. "A little too much."

She pulled away. "Too *much?*"

"We're just scared, is all. We almost died, so we're doing what biology encourages."

"So?"

"…so you shouldn't be putting the moves on me just out of relief."

Peaches' silence held the quiet of a bomb about to explode.

"Have I ever," she asked, "questioned *your* motivations?"

"All the time."

"Because despite what you may think, there were a *lot* of other people I could have brought on this mission. People who," she said, thumping me on the chest, "wouldn't clash with Drumgoole all the time–"

"Tell me he doesn't deserve it!"

"People who didn't Shrive voiding Mortal, so *I* had to come along on this stupid expedition to save their hash–"

"– I would have been all right if it wasn't for *Sins of the Flesh*–"

"People who would have known how to cross a stupid floor without pulling an icebox down on themselves–"

"– you didn't have to save me–"

"I was saving you because I *liked* you, you moron!"

In the darkness, I heard a sound I'd never heard before, nor expected to – Peaches crying.

I reached out to hug her; she slapped me away.

"I have *plans*, you dolt!" She sniffled back tears. "I'm going to steal technology from the dead. I'm going to make this world *better* than theirs. I've got the money – or I will, in thirty years.

"But I'll need influence. And there were tons of competent people I could have tasked to this, people with ambition and good judgment and talent… but I chose *you* because you were my friend, and you were in trouble.

"And after all I have sacrificed to help you," she finished, shoving me off the table, "you think I want to curl up with you because I'm *scared?*"

I sat, dumbstruck, in the icy water. Then I heard the scrape of coral against coral.

"Oh, thank the stars," I whispered. Who'd have thought I'd have been happy to see Gumdrool?

The slab kept moving. But Gumdrool wasn't using his hands to shift it; he nudged it to one side with his head. And though I was still dark-blinded, the man's silhouette was far too gaunt to be Gumdrool. Far too naked.

And carrying far too many dead pigeons in his mouth.

Peaches let out a hiss, too shocked to scream. The thing let out a quavery roar, like a beast trying to cram a howl through a man's throat, then crawled on all fours onto a slippery crest of coral.

He was human; crawling clearly pained him. He kept his hands balled into loose fists, resting all his weight upon his knuckles, which were crusted with scabs. Yet he moved with the spidery nimbleness of a man who'd compensated for his handicap.

He sniffed the air, not noticing us in the shadowy back of the room. Then he shambled to the dresser piled high with dead birds. He scrabbled with numb fingers at a drawer, opening his jaws to drop in his pigeons. He stared in the mirror, looking oddly satisfied.

"*Yuck*," Peaches muttered.

Naked Crazy whipped around and pounced. He rushed over me to get to Peaches – I thought he might push me underwater and drown me, but he battered me with his forearms as though he didn't understand the use of hands. I shoved back as he clambered on Peaches–

That's when I noticed the cross tattooed at the hollow of his throat.

Whatever they are, they're… not subtle, Gumdrool had said.

"Dude," I whispered. "What *happened* to you?"

He ignored me, chomping into Peaches.

She screamed, yanking at his hair. Naked Crazy tipped his head back to swallow something. Blood poured down Peaches' neck.

I grabbed him, trying to haul him off her, but his naked skin was slippery. Plus, Naked Crazy was well, crazy. We were still stunned with shock – but like Gumdrool, Naked Crazy had zero barriers between plan and execution.

Still, I pulled back as he went for Peaches, yanking him away before he snapped her nose off. He whirled on me, going for my neck – had he torn Peaches' throat out?

I slammed my palm into his jaw. He snapped at my fingers.

Peaches thrashed up through the water. Naked Crazy shoved her against the dresser.

Dead birds tumbled from the drawers as the dresser lurched forward. I caught it in both hands, looking straight into the cracked mirror, seeing the muddy T scrawled across its face…

And I knew where I'd seen that "T": the Shrive Point in the landlord's office.

Pigeons bobbed around my waist as I realized that these weren't dead birds.

They were *offerings*.

Peaches cursed me, yelling to get him off her, but instead I fumbled at my earputer:

"Cross! Golden!"

A holographic light shot out. A three-foot-high filigreed golden cross revolved in the air over the makeshift dresser-altar.

Naked Crazy leapt away as though he'd been burned – and then cocked his head, whimpering, looking at the cross as though he couldn't quite make sense of it. He shifted back from his four-legged stance to sit ass-to-heels, making tortured noises in the back of his throat.

Peaches hit him with a rock.

Naked Crazy lurched woozily towards her. Peaches clocked

him again. He fell face first into the water.

"Come on, let's go." Peaches tugged me away.

I stopped long enough to pull our Naked Crazy out of the water.

"Let him drown," Peaches said, pressing her hand to her shredded ear. "He tried to eat us."

"Death's different for him."

She scowled, but helped me shove him up onto the bed. Then we hauled ass out of the basement, scrambling up a pile of rocks to the half-flooded street outside.

Gumdrool stood on a ridge of rubble, three limp Naked Crazies at his feet. He flicked blood off his truncheon.

Dare clutched his arm, groaning; the Naked Crazies had clearly bitten him badly before Gumdrool had pounded their assailants into unconsciousness. But when he saw his sister, they ran to each other, touching each other's wounds, asking, "Are you all right?"

"We heard you screaming and followed the sound, but so did these guys," Gumdrool said. "They attacked us the moment they saw us–"

Howls echoed across the rubble.

Gumdrool pulled us close to him, trying to shield us – but as he turned in a slow circle, we all saw ragged, skeletal men and women emerging from their hidden shrines. They crawled out from crumbling entryways on every side of us, blinking at the sunlight, faces smeared with blood and carrion.

They lifted their heads, sniffing the air, inadvertently baring their cross tattoos at us as they tried to scent our trail–

Then one of them spotted us, and let out a gargling bark. They jerked themselves up awkwardly off their all-fours stance to hunch forward, loping towards us with a terrifying speed.

We fled.

18: INSIDE A MAZE OF TWISTY LITTLE COLLAPSED PASSAGES, ALL ALIKE

"In here!" Gumdrool waved us into a slanted doorway. We hid inside a group of apartment buildings that had collapsed onto each other and stabilized. The buildings leaned on each other for support like drunkards, their rooms mashed together.

Behind us, the Naked Crazy Pack howled, calling like to like.

Peaches slammed the warped wooden door shut. I looked around for something heavy to lean against it, but Gumdrool shoved us into a darkened hallway.

"There are a hundred other ways to get in here," he said, flicking on his earputer light. "We can't wall them out. We need to go deep, lose ourselves in the building."

The corridors twisted away, crumpling into dead ends. Their ceilings sagged low enough that some had dropped onto the rotted carpet, creating an unstable ramp up into the pancaked second floor. Gumdrool yanked me up the ramp, took a sharp left onto a mashed staircase.

"They don't live in here, do they?" Peaches yelled, pressing a cloth against her mangled ear.

"They didn't last time," he said. He ran up the staircase and kicked in a door, revealing a rubble-filled hallway. He squirmed through a hole in the rubble to pull us into a room of shattered mirrors. I stared at twisted steel hunks before realizing they were dumbbells; an exercise room. Gumdrool dragged us into another sloping corridor.

"Why didn't you warn us about the Naked Crazies?" I asked.

"Because I thought you were an infiltration expert! I didn't think famed sneak thief Amichai Damrosch would collapse a voiding *floor* and alert the whole voiding *neighborhood*."

"Climbing through condemned buildings is a different skill than stealth, and you know it," Peaches shot back. "Besides, if you'd told Amichai these were *feral* NeoChristians, he might have been more careful."

"Damn straight," I agreed, grateful for her forgiveness.

"I'm defending you in the abstract. Real-life you is still an idiot."

"I'm a… wait. Where's Dare?"

We turned to see Dare trailing behind, clutching his bleeding arm. "I got lost…" he apologized.

"You never get lost," I said accusingly.

"Keep up," said Gumdrool, wedging himself into a narrow gap between two crushed walls. The Naked Crazies barked, indicating they'd made it into the building. We squeezed through, trying to put some space between us – but the crawlspace dead ended and we had to double back to tumble into another lobby, the ceiling sagging ominously.

"The building's settled. That's changed the layout." Gumdrool tapped his earputer, causing a woefully incomplete map of the apartment complex to flicker in midair. He jabbed at a jiggling X. "That's the exit to the branch server."

"Heading this way will dead end, judging from the way these floors have collapsed," Dare said, tracing the maps. "Lemme find a new path."

"Wait, this is the way to the branch server?" Peaches squinted at Gumdrool. "And you led those psychos *in* here?"

"Like I had a choice!"

"We could have hidden until they gave up searching! You think a horde of crazies won't put the branch staff on high alert?"

"I didn't know where else to hide," Gumdrool shot back. "I made the best of a bad situation *your boyfriend* handed me."

"He's not my only boyfriend."

"Wait a minute," I said. "You think I'm your–"

The ceiling collapsed, dumping a pack of feral NeoChristians on our heads.

Two of them dropped onto Gumdrool, snapping and snarling. His truncheon flew from his hand, rolling erratically across the warped floor; I snatched it up as a naked old woman loped towards me on all fours.

Another Naked Crazy fell on its ass to Peaches' left; the last landed with a thump on a desk next to Dare, catching its spine on the corner.

At least Dare gets the injured one, I thought.

Then killer gramma was on me.

I'd like to say I wouldn't hit a lady... But Killer Naked Crazy Grammas are fair game, in my book. I swung with the truncheon as hard as I could, apologizing as I caught her just below the ear. She fell to the ground, keening.

Peaches muttered something in her earputer; a silver cross shimmered into existence. Her Naked Crazy blinked in surprise, then lunged for Peaches.

I broke his nose.

They're being reprogrammed to believe in your culture right now, Evangeline had said. Or to believe in something, anyway.

"They're not *vampires*, Peaches," I told her. "It worked on that one guy 'cause we were at his, what do you call it, altar. He had memories of crosses there. The rest of them–"

There was a *zzzap* from Gumdrool's taser.

"– something's stirred their brains."

Naked Gramma bit my leg. I screamed in pain, whacking her with the truncheon – then felt guilty. Her angry animal scowl looked out of place – if it hadn't been for the cross tattoo marking her as a NeoChristian, I could imagine her baking cookies for her grandchildren. Instead, a crazy Jew was pounding her spine.

Zzzap. The other one on Gumdrool twitched, though his taser's charge was weakening.

Gumdrool could handle himself, though. I turned to check on Dare, expecting to see him standing over his wounded Naked Crazy. Instead, the Naked Crazy held him down, snarling and biting.

What the… I thought. Then I realized: Dare was only pretending to fight. No one would blame him if the Naked Crazies ate him alive. Dare gritted his teeth as the thing chewed his shoulder, his mouth set in a bitter smile.

Peaches snatched my truncheon, going to town on her brother's assailant. They spent their days trading insults… but when Dare was in danger, Peaches went berserk.

"Void it, Dare," I hissed. "You *fight*."

A bloodsoaked grin. "Can't make a man live."

Gumdrool's remaining Naked Crazy gurgled as Gumdrool wrapped his hands around her throat. He bore down, choking her.

I tugged his arm. "No."

"Not your call, Amichai." He squeezed her throat tighter, casual as a man trying to get the last of the toothpaste out. "Anyone we leave behind will be a threat later."

I shook my IceBreaker at him. "It's my call as long as I have this."

He looked baffled. "Amichai, don't you understand? Neo-Christians aren't human. Human beings Shrive. Anyone who doesn't Shrive is a threat to our existence. Did you learn nothing in Little Venice about how badly humans need the Upterlife?"

"You let go, or I walk. This–" I waved at their nakedness "–isn't their fault. Somebody *did* this to them."

"The NeoChristians must have tortured their rebels," Peaches said. "Tortured them until they forgot how to be human…" She shot Dare a guilty glance; Dare had warned us that branch programmers did things like this.

I, however, was pretty sure our enemy wasn't NeoChristian branch programmers.

Gumdrool reluctantly loosened his grip. "Your compassion's commendable. But if this mission fails, I will void you personally."

I thought Dare might refuse to navigate, letting the NeoChristians surround us – but though he wanted to die, he'd never endanger his sister. He rotated the map, triangulating the best route to the branch server.

More howls. From one direction now: behind us.

"They're clustering back into a pack," Gumdrool said. "Converging on us."

Dare led us through distorted hallways that fed into a single crumpled corridor – a hallway that exited into a shadowed courtyard. The hallway was lined with doors, popped open by the weight of the buildings overhead, leading into crushed apartments.

Gumdrool pulled us back. "No," he said, pointing. I saw the firefly gleam of two security cameras mounted over the exit.

"On it." I got out the IceBreaker, which churned as it struggled to map the crumpled hallway interior. I thumbed the script-kiddie "Capture!" button, flooding the cameras with password attempts.

It failed.

"What's happening?" Gumdrool piston-squeezed the handle of his taser, recharging the flywheel battery.

"Shoulda figured," I grumbled, bringing up the antisecurity and decryption menus. "These are harder to crack than your standard streetcams."

I flooded the air with queries, mapping their broadcast keys and security protocols. I grinned; I'd read the documentation on these break-in programs before, but I'd never had a chance to use them. Now it was my hacking skills against a bunch of techheads. *Evil* techheads.

"You sure that's not programming?" Dare asked, more terrified of the IceBreaker than the Naked Crazies. I laughed despite myself.

Rumor was, the guys who'd created these programs had Shrived Criminal. Me? I combined their collective efforts in new ways, layering module on top of module in fashions they'd never intended. It was like focusing sunlight through magnifying lens after magnifying lens until those cameras were under a white-hot laser.

The Naked Crazy howls echoed through the corridors, coming closer.

"Hurry, Amichai," Gumdrool said, cuffing me. "If that's what the NeoChristians did to their friends, imagine what they'll do to us."

I relaxed as the camera icons turned emerald. I recorded intruder-free space to loop-broadcast back at them.

"We're good." I looked at the IceBreaker's display, which was now configured to pick out new cameras as we got within range. "Advance slowly, and stay out of the sunlight."

We gasped as we saw the branch server.

Now, when Gumdrool had said "a server," I thought he'd meant the branch servers you saw on the newsfeeds when they busted some poor rural branch: small enough to be towed behind a truck, big enough to house a cluster of optical RAID drives and a family who didn't mind roughing it.

This, however, was a filigreed skyscraper: a golden obelisk of circuitry thrusting up towards the sky. Python-thick power cables fed into it from all directions; you could *hear* it sucking up electricity.

It stood in a shadowed space that had once been a courtyard shared between the four buildings. The apartment complexes had crumbled into each other in a precarious square, hiding the server from street view.

But the courtyard was freshly paved. And the gleaming tower was surrounded by razorwire prison fences and palmprint gatelocks.

"That's bigger than I'd thought," Peaches said.

"That's what she said."

Peaches whirled upon me, disappointed. "Really, Amichai? Centuries of jokes to choose from, and *that's* the dusty nugget you unearth?"

"Sorry."

"Seriously, though," Dare murmured, impressed. "That's big enough for government work."

Peaches whistled. "How do they miss *that* on the satellite photos?"

"The better question is, how do they mask the spirocopter traffic?" Dare raised a bloodied arm to point at a helicopter pad on top of the building. On it sat a military spirocopter, a fat green spider bristling with narrow vortex-tubes to help it negotiate the trickiest of winds.

Then he gestured out over the courtyard. "See how they've bulldozed the ground there? They had to replace all this wreckage with a stable, flood-resistant foundation. That's a lot of materiel, manpower, electricity."

"What are those in the back?" Peaches asked, pointing towards a series of small buildings nested in a tangle of barbed wire. Bored prisoners in orange outfits shuffled about. Each of them had a cross tattooed at the hollow of their throat.

"Prisoners' quarters," Dare said. "I think. Mama Alex used to have me analyze server schematics–"

I looked at Dare, astonished. "You worked for Mama Alex?"

"You think I bought you a Sleipnir with handouts from my family? Anyway, it looks like a pretty stock Upterlife server configuration. There's room inside for a security staff of twenty LifeGuards, plus a host of fulltime scientists to maintain it. Though you wouldn't want to lock prisoners inside – not with multiple hardwired terminals in every room..."

"Imagine all that power," Gumdrool said, awed.

"So the outdoor prison complex to hold the NeoChristians there must be an afterthought. And shoddy work at that." Dare sniffed as though he would have done better. "But I don't recognize the tripod-guns around the perimeter. They're not bullet-guns..."

"Dazers," I said. "Anyone in there steps a millimeter beyond the painted borders, and their eyes get targeted with high-powered lasers oscillating at frequencies designed to stun the human brain. They developed those after Boston."

"Doesn't seem like a deterrent," Gumdrool said. "Just close your eyes."

"You'll get sunburned eyelids on top of a seizure," I shot back. "And if you hold your hands over your eyes, they'll fry your hands."

My IceBreaker beeped. Good news: it was powerful enough to find all cameras within a city block. Bad news: the courtyard held hundreds of cameras, covering every square foot. The wireframe map was festooned with Christmas lights.

"Uh, they're serious about security here," I said, bringing up my heavy-duty secpass routines. "*Much* more paranoid than the Khan-Tiens."

"So hack it."

"Breaking security isn't magic – I have to crack each camera's security code individually. That's gonna take time." More ragged howls, growing louder. "Is there a room to hide in?"

"Not well enough to be concealed," Gumdrool said, looking back at the crushed apartments lining the corridor. "Shove open a door, and there we'll be."

"Just cover us from casual observers."

We crouched in a smashed kitchen. The Naked Crazies thundered closer.

I commandeered the cameras one by one – but there were

too many. And I had to wait for the right footage, or I'd capture a loop with a moonwalking NeoChristian.

This setup was too paranoid. Who could watch that many cameras? You wouldn't have the dead monitoring it, like they did back home...

Before Boston, all the cameras were monitored by AIs, Peaches had said.

My arms goosebumped as I realized my standard solutions wouldn't work. The hallway, a mostly-static area, was one thing – but the tents, with the wandering prisoners? Any computerized security scan would instantly notice a switch from a live feed to a recorded one.

"Amichai." Peaches fought to keep the trembling from her voice. "They're getting closer."

"I know, I know," I said, furiously trying to think up a solution. I pulled up menus on some compromised cameras and started sorting through the options. These cameras had everything, from infrared to facial recognition software to brainwave-encoded security tunneling, though precious few of those features had been enabled.

If they'd configured all the advanced security options, I'd never have gotten in. Who'd buy this many expensive cameras and leave them configured out of the box?

Footsteps, thumping down nearby hallways. Once they swarmed down here, we'd be trapped in this kitchen.

"Shut them down," Gumdrool said. "Do it *now!*"

"Shut it down and everyone in that branch will be alerted that we're here," I said. "You want to wind up naked and barking?"

"No."

"Then shut up and let me *think!*"

"Maybe if you'd thought in the first place," Dare hissed, "we wouldn't *be* voiding here!"

Could I shut down the automated scanners? No. A quick scan showed the alarms weren't triggered at the camera level.

Somewhere within that server, there was an AI scanning all incoming feeds...

The incoming feeds. I could alter them.

"Amichai..." Peaches said, wrapping her arms around me.

I shrugged her off. If the cameras could find patterns like I'd used to search for Therapy, then it could *exclude* them. I uploaded an image of myself from my earputer, assigned it to an autofilter, set the filter to not send anything matching that pattern to the central alarm processor. Replace it with cloned background noise. Now repeat for Gumdrool, then Dare, then Peaches...

"*Amichai.*" Peaches was more insistent.

I wrote a macro to replicate that change across hundreds of cameras.

Thump. Shrieks of triumph. The Naked Crazies' footsteps echoed down the corridor.

"Amichai!" Peaches yelled.

I lowered the IceBreaker, realizing I couldn't install the filters in time. We either ran out into the courtyard to be captured, or got eaten alive.

Peaches cut off my apology with a kiss. She cupped my face in her hands.

"Make your life worthwhile," she said.

She dashed into the hallway, slamming the door behind her.

"*Look here, you crazies!*" She pounded the walls, drawing their attention. The pitch of the howls rose triumphantly.

Dare and I bolted for her. Gumdrool dragged us back.

"She's *saving* us, you idiots," he whispered. "Quiet, or you'll undo everything."

He was right. But I'd never hated him more.

I tuned in the camera feeds to watch Peaches; she fled into the courtyard. The Naked Crazies boiled down the corridor, elbowing each other aside.

"Help!" She flailed her arms in an exaggeratedly girlish

manner. "*Heeeeeellllllllp!*"

I watched as the camera alarms sounded. But would the people inside even care about a teenaged girl?

Then I thought of the prisons outside, and recognized Peaches' gamble. They'd want to know how she'd found them, and she had proof the owners of this complex took prisoners. And now that I looked down, I felt her earputer pressed into my palm.

Most of the Naked Crazies charged across the pavement towards her. A handful broke off towards the prisoners' camp, teeth bared.

The prisoners lined up at the moat to watch, grim, mournful. The dazers strobed. Those Naked Crazies fell twitching.

A murderous handful still headed for Peaches, though. The gate remained closed.

"Come on, come *on*," I whispered. Dare and Gumdrool squeezed my shoulders. Which was stupid; them tearing Peaches' throat open, I realized, was the *good* scenario. The *Upterlife* scenario.

Yet there we were, white-knuckled, Dare begging the server techs to let his sister in…

…which they did. The gate clacked open. Peaches rushed inside, fell to her knees in gratitude. Three soldiers in nondescript uniforms charged out the front door, firing over the heads of the Naked Crazies. The Naked Crazies scattered, racing across the concrete to dive through the warrens' crooked doors.

The soldiers didn't seem happy to see Peaches, though. They dragged her to her feet, barking questions as to how she got here. She did the perfect lost little girl act, blubbering how her friends had dared her to go into Little Venice and then those *things* had started chasing her…

The guards were skeptical. "You telling me it's coincidence you show up on the day Big Kahuna arrives?" one asked.

"Scans don't lie," another told him. "Let's copy her brain

and sift through her memories."

They dragged her inside. I tried to track Peaches on the internal cameras, but the IceBreaker couldn't penetrate the walls from this distance.

"Scan her?" Dare said, furious. "They can't do that. Our brain patterns are our own – we can't testify against ourselves!"

"These are NeoChristians," Gumdrool said. "They can do whatever they voiding well please. Once they know everything she knows, they'll come for us."

"Not if we rescue her first."

Gumdrool spluttered. "*Rescue* her? She's guarded by a military force inside a branch server. This mission's FUBAR. We've got photos, camera locations, security scans. If we get back in time, we can get the LifeGuard here before the NeoChristians pull up stakes."

"You're right," I said. "Someone needs to get this information back home. We'd just slow you down."

"*No*, Amichai," Dare said. "We don't have a chance without him." He pronounced the word "him" as though his mouth were filled with cockroaches.

"*We're* not leaving Peaches behind," I assured him. "But someone has to alert the LifeGuard. So get moving, Gumdrool! When we get Peaches out–"

"– if –" Dare contradicted me.

"– we'll catch up."

Gumdrool appraised me, looking for the angle. I kept my face neutral, ignoring Dare's withering scowl.

"All right," Gumdrool said, hoisting his backpack. "I'll go."

"You know they'll destroy her," Dare said.

Gumdrool hesitated.

"They'll turn her into… into one of those," Dare continued. "You beat the shit out of me because I was going to sneak into the Upterlife without your say-so – and now that someone's in danger of getting voided, you just *walk*?"

"*Dare!*" I yelled. "We can't risk this. Someone has to get the word out…"

"Shut *up*, Amichai!" He was so furious, I cringed. "*You* got us into this! If you'd Shrived Venal, Peaches wouldn't have had to come along! And now my sister's in danger, and you're talking our best hope of saving her into *leaving*?"

"It's not like that…" I protested. But yeah, it looked bad. I'd been Dare's best friend ever since he'd come to the orphanage, but I could see the doubt in his eyes: *I left my family. Maybe it's time to leave my friends.*

"We can do it, Dare…"

"All *you* ever do is get in trouble," Dare spat. "We need someone who can get us both in *and* out.

"Ian," he pled. "We don't have a hope in void of saving Peaches without you. If all your stupid blather about the lowliest of criminals meant anything, then nothing would stop you from helping her."

Gumdrool stood in the doorway, his back to us. His shoulders shook.

"Remember the mission, Ian," I pled.

"No. He's right." Gumdrool squeezed Dare's shoulder. "We have to get Peaches out."

Dare shot me a triumphant look. But I couldn't tell him what I had learned while I was hip-deep in camera protocols:

This technology was pure LifeGuard.

We were breaking into a branch server created by the highest levels of the United States Government.

That was why I'd been trying to ditch Gumdrool. Alone, Dare and I might have had a chance to sneak in undetected. Now, it was a matter of time until Gumdrool discovered who was behind this.

And what would he do when he realized this was bought and paid for by the people he practically worshipped?

PART II: RESCUE

19: CONVERSATIONS WITH CRIMINALS II

"Gimme your earputers," I said.

Dare handed his over without hesitation. Gumdrool balked. "Why?"

"Because we may get separated in there, and communicating over an open network is suicide. We gotta encrypt."

He gave me a curt nod, then tossed his towards me. I tweaked settings as fast as I could. I wished I could send a secret message to Dare, but Gumdrool watched my every move.

"So what's the plan?" I asked, glancing towards the server's golden tower. Fortunately, all the conscious Naked Crazies had fled. The prisoners, dressed in orange jumpsuits, stood at the border of the tripod-dazers, calling out names.

The names of the unconscious Naked Crazies.

Their hope broke my heart.

I'd thought of the Naked Crazies as, well, naked crazies. But they'd been beloved back before someone had driven them mad; you could see the devotion on the prisoners' resigned faces as they tried to get their sons and mothers to remember them. The NeoChristians pressed their hands against their tattoos as they called out for Elijah or Abishai or Japtheth, their voices wavering but never breaking. They lifted their voices high, like a lifeline thrown out to an empty sea.

"You're the infiltrator," Gumdrool said. "Where's your plan?"

"I've had enough of following Amichai's plans," Dare said. "We should follow yours."

"If he had any plans, he'd be barking orders already." I tossed Gumdrool's earputer back before he could see what I'd done. I wished I could covertly text Dare a message, but Dare's poker face was awful. "Is there a back entrance?"

"A freight entrance. Huge hydraulic doors. It'd make a lot of noise."

"Front door it is, then."

We crept out into the courtyard. The air had the chill of a place in endless shadow; nestled in between the four apartment buildings, the only time this courtyard saw sunlight was a few minutes on either side of noon. Our shoes scuffed on the concrete, echoing off the branch server's copper walls. The surface bristled with inset cameras.

If I'd been wrong about the screening filter I'd just applied, the cameras would see us. Then the front door would fly open and guards would come running out.

They didn't. I began bypassing the palmprint locks on the fences.

The prisoners turned to stare at us. They looked gaunt but unbroken, standing stiffly in the courtyard, strangely dignified.

They looked like all the old workers on New York streets, brewing beer or sewing dresses to kill time until they died, hopelessness graven into every wrinkle.

Had the living always looked so much like prisoners?

Except we, at least, got rewarded in the end. The NeoChristians got the void. I mean, they had their primitive belief that some beard in the sky automatically Shrived their souls, but...

Nobody deserved the void.

I wanted to believe the dead drew a distinction between me and these NeoChristians. And if they did: I might, one day, get uploaded.

Until then, both of us were disposable bodies.

I'd closed my fingers into fists so tight, I'd drawn blood. The dead had robbed the NeoChristians, robbed Izzy, robbed the living of ambition and pride... while I'd played pranks. Dare had helped me understand that the world could be different, but that was not enough:

You have to be willing to give up your life to make the future happen.

A voice inside whispered: *Burn it all down.*

Yes. Before the sun set, this server would burn.

As I walked out into the courtyard, Gumdrool nudged me. "Looks like we have an old friend."

I followed his gaze towards a familiar shock of red hair. Back at Wickliffe, she'd looked like a fantasy warrior – now she looked like the last woman in some postapocalyptic vidshow, a deep bruise under her left eye, cradling an injured arm. But she stood as though she owned the courtyard, unbowed, unbroken.

Beautiful.

Evangeline's eyes widened as she recognized me... And then narrowed as she recognized Gumdrool.

I jerked my head towards Gumdrool, then made a disgusted face to indicate I wasn't with him, I was just *with* him.

"Ah, the irony." Gumdrool spoke as though the sight of Evangeline in prison was a fine summer sunset. "Escaping us, only to be captured by her own kind."

"That's not her kind," Dare said. "Why would they imprison each other?"

Gumdrool rolled his eyes. "Read your history, kid. Every religion warred – Protestants hated Catholics hated Jews. If your skybeard hated shrimp and your friend's skybeard loved it, the daggers came out *so* much faster."

Evangeline jerked her thumb towards her chest, then pointed outward. Her meaning was clear: *Will you free us?*

Gumdrool gave her a thumbs-up. Evangeline seemed startled, but I confirmed our intent with a nod.

Why would Gumdrool want them out?

Evangeline coughed conspicuously. The prisoners, who had turned to watch us, wandered off. Evangeline alone stared after me, as if her faith in me was binding.

We got to the door, keeping a careful distance from the still-unconscious Naked Crazies – but now I wondered what their names had been. The server had an access panel attached to the wall.

In a secure site, wireless was only good for hard-to-reach devices, like wall-mounted cameras. Smart secops procedures had you lock each access point within a titanium case, then have the cases trigger an alarm if anyone attempted to tamper with them.

But here? The access panel was padlocked. One simple tumbler lock was all that stood between me and direct access. And I'd figured out how to break into *those* in my first week at the orphanage.

"You surprised me back there," I whispered to Gumdrool as I got my lockpicks out. "I thought you'd let those NeoChristians rot."

"They would have raised the alarm otherwise," he shrugged. "No harm in *telling* them we'll free them."

Dare wrinkled his nose in disgust.

"Hurry up," he whispered. "We need to get Peaches out before they Crazy her up."

"I'm on it like Izzy was in there."

"Yeah, well – *your* sister would have said goodbye."

His anger made me realize: Peaches had kissed me farewell,

but left Dare without a word.

Then I thought of poor Izzy. I'd get voided if they caught us... but would the dead punish her for my crimes? *My superiors asked about you when I was in the LifeGuard academy*, she'd told me.

That tiny voice: *burn it all down*.

I popped the padlock open. Some careful wiresplicing gave me limited access to the network, which got me access to the local cameras. I infected them with my image-snipping macro, then verified the hallway was empty before opening the door.

The hallways were white, spotless, well-lit – unlike anything I'd ever seen before. Centuries of treating the physical world as an afterthought made peeling paint, flickering lights, and scuffed floors the best I could expect to see.

We heard Peaches screaming – not in pain, but in protest.

The building was large, making it hard to pinpoint Peaches' location – but as always, Dare maneuvered his way through the branch like he'd lived there.

We ducked guard patrols – who heard us approaching, looked at the blank videos I fed them, and trusted images over ears. Puzzlingly, the guard's quarters were stuffed with boxes full of heavy-duty security hardware, all the latest biosensors and heat-scanners – but they lay on the floor, half-assembled. Someone had made casual efforts to put them together before giving up.

My palms prickled with sweat. This place had been designed to be impossible to infiltrate. But the builders had gotten lazy.

We should have been in custody by now.

"We're approaching the labs," Dare whispered. "Be careful."

We crept down a long hallway, with a lab full of barking dogs on one side and a kitchenette on the other.

"No! Fuck it! I'm *done!*"

We dashed into the kitchen just as a harried-looking man in a lab coat stormed, shouting, out of the laboratory. An older scientist ran up, caught the younger one by the sleeve.

Dare and I stared. These were *living* scientists.

"Get back in there," said the older man, scowling. "Their brains are still workable. There's plenty of intact pathways left."

I could peer into the lab through the kitchen door, watching the two Rottweilers strapped to a table. Their paws had been clamped into netted restraints, the tops of their skulls sawn off and replaced with a clear plastic covering. Gold filaments were embedded into their brains, trailing up to sockets in the ceiling.

And I thought those were the brains he was referring to – until I looked beyond the dogs...

Behind them, six twitching NeoChristians were strapped to a glowing wall, gold filaments jammed into shaved scalps. They groaned, begging for mercy with the wrong words – "Tractor, slacken window," they slurred. "Ocean expose."

The younger scientist punched a wall. "Are you kidding? Their brains are Swiss cheese! They can't remember their *names*, let alone their opinions on underwear! We should overwrite all their thought patterns with dog brains, set them loose, and bring in a fresh batch we can *work* with!"

"He's soft-hearted. He won't round them *all* up," the older scientist said. "So we have to make each test subject last."

"If He wants results, maybe He should get His ass down here! This work's impossible! *You* know how hard it is to change someone's mind on something! It's not like their beliefs on God, or good clothing, or the most reliable guns are bound in one place – they're scattered throughout their cortexes, intertwined with a thousand memories. Yet he wants us to alter their most deeply rooted opinions? Without the subject even noticing? On these stupid, used-up test subjects where we've already plumbed their heads so hard they've forgotten how to form *sentences*?"

"Watch what you're saying, Phil," the older scientist said urgently, looking from side to side. "The guards might hear you…"

"Those zealous thugs don't hear anything He doesn't broadcast directly to them. This is *bullshit*. I'm gonna talk to Him, tell Him we need more test subjects, or I'll quit."

"Quit? You think you can–"

"Besides, the more subjects we doggify, the safer we are! You'd think He'd *want* more feral guards roaming Little Venice to eat intruders! If He can't see what a waste this is, recycling these–"

The older scientist slammed Phil against the wall.

"Look, you moron. I had a younger partner before. She tried to quit."

He let the silence hang ominously.

Phil went pale. "He wouldn't – would He?"

"You've never seen Him drunk and screaming. He *loathes* us."

He released Phil. Phil rubbed his throat.

"You're new here, Phil, so I'll cut you a break. Our job is to give Him some small sign of progress every week. And we *are* getting closer, despite this scarcity of test subjects and the ridiculous constraints He's put us under. But you give Him excuses, you *will* get voided."

Phil considered this.

"…all right," he said sullenly. "Let's get it done." He walked back into the lab, where he stopped at a glowing wall with rotating images of six brains. He traced rings around the fuzzy electrical pathways that shimmered through the brain images, then tapped a green button.

"I *said*," he asked, in the patient tone you'd use to speak to a slow child, "Do – you – like – silken – robes?"

The NeoChristians' tongues flopped like dying fish. Their faces contorted with effort as they tried to form words; a few bobbed their heads. The gold filaments shook.

"Galvanic responses show they're still lying," sighed the older scientist. "They can't remember what a robe is at this point. They'd say anything to make it stop."

"Yeah, looks like those pathways are fried," Phil admitted. "Heck, this one's so crosswired every time she tries to remember her daughter, all she can bring to mind is chainlink fences… Doesn't stop her from trying, though. She remembers loving a fence, and doesn't know why."

"Seems cruel."

"Hey, what's it matter? These are NeoChristians! You guys are all going to Heaven, right?" The NeoChristians writhed in anguish, straining at their bonds. "Oh, I forgot; Heaven was the first memory we crossconnected. What do they associate Heaven with now?"

"Shoeboxes." The NeoChristians wailed.

"Well, it's shoebox heaven for you guys, then."

They busied themselves resetting their equipment. Dare and I shivered with fury.

"We had a *deal*," I muttered. "We spend our lives in slavery, and as a reward we get the Upterlife. But that's not enough. No, they want to reshape our thoughts while we live…"

"To make us better slaves," Dare whispered.

"Gear it down, guys," Gumdrool said. "This isn't the Upterlife. These are the guys out to *destroy* the Upterlife, remember?"

He might have been right. Mama Alex herself couldn't sneak into Upterlife servers – so why was *this* government facility vulnerable to a smart hack? Who'd handed them all this money and no expertise?

We slipped past that lab, following Peaches' yells – and saw two guards dragging her into a small antechamber.

They'd shaved her beautiful black locks off to stab a golden crown into her scalp.

"Please, sir!" she shrieked. "I told, you, I got lost…"

Peaches was sticking to character, forcing them to scan her to get the full truth. Buying us time.

They dragged her in and slammed the door.

I pulled up an internal camera feed; Gumdrool looked on, plotting tactics.

Two guards strapped Peaches into a black leather chair under the supervision of a gray-haired Asian woman. Peaches was bathed in the glow of a wall monitor – someone dead, supervising the supervisor.

Peaches pulled at her restraints – then froze, looking up at the screen.

"You," she whispered. "How can *you*…"

A guard punched her in the gut. "He'll tell you when to speak."

"That's good, that's good," the Asian woman muttered. "Restrict your blows to the stomach. We need her conscious."

She spoke mildly and looked milder, wearing a plain white lab coat over a thin frame. Her face was expressionless as a doll, an unappealing mole on her upper lip her only memorable feature.

She flicked her fingers across a keyboard; a Shrive Point hummed to life above Peaches. This Shrive Point bristled with circuits and probes, crackling ominously – a Shrive designed to rip secrets from your mind.

Dare lunged for the door. Gumdrool yanked him back.

"Wait till the guards leave," Gumdrool hissed. "I can't take on two men by myself without triggering alarms."

"I don't like coming here in the first place, Dr Hsiang," said another voice – a deeper, more resonant one, with a familiar well-worn authority. "And someone slips past our feral Christian packs to show up here? Now? It's no coincidence."

"Who *is* that?" Dare muttered.

"I know that voice," Gumdrool murmured. "I *know* it."

I knew it, too – but it seemed out of place in a torture chamber.

"It's not as though anyone tracks your movements," said the doctor, continuing to tap in commands.

"Don't backtalk me." The guards glanced at the speakers, fidgeting, eager to leave. "Remember, I'm far from thrilled about the necessity for this research... And you promised you'd be implanting new opinions within three years. Don't think I'll hesitate to call in my erasure team if this place is compromised..."

Dr Hsiang gave the slightest of shrugs. "Your threats are noted as always. Yet I work with what you give me, sir. Organic neurology is a complex area. Given time and better resources, I can–"

"I've given you plenty of time. I made faster progress than you have – and with the money I've committed here, obscurity is getting harder to guarantee..."

"– with all due respect sir, the best you could do was *translate* a brain, not copy it. You had forty years to study without interference – and you could design custom hardware. In twenty years, shuffled from hidden location to hidden location, I've accomplished more than you had."

"On the back of *my* studies!"

"You had better help available," she retorted, that smooth face never changing expression. "If anyone here had the intellect to understand the ramifications of our research..." Hsiang gestured at the guards, who were as frightened as puppies in a thunderstorm.

"You know I don't dare send actual researchers here."

"Then you acknowledge I am your best hope. Unless you feel like stepping down to tend to this full time, of course."

"...stepping down?" Gumdrool muttered, brow furrowing.

"Hit 'em now!" I said. "Give me your taser, I'll take one out, you hit the other, Dare will handle the doctor..."

Gumdrool shrugged me off. "I know that voice..."

The voice chuckled. "Clever, Hsiang. Don't think I can't. I could split my consciousness off – if I devoted my full willpower to this, I'd crack it in under a year."

"You're one of the greatest consciousness-scanning masters in existence," Hsiang said, placing a faint but unmistakable emphasis on *one of.* "But surreptitiously altering opinions is magnitudes more complex than recording them..."

"Ian! Get in *now!*"

He kicked in the door. Dare and I ran in behind him –

– Gumdrool smashed his truncheon into my throat.

I fell to my knees as Gumdrool rammed his nightstick into Dare's solar plexus. The guards stood, stunned, as Gumdrool knelt to hold out his truncheon to them, like a knight presenting a sword to his king.

Except he wasn't presenting it to them. Gumdrool offered the truncheon to the screen.

I looked up to see a familiar face – perhaps *the* most familiar face. Except the kind gray eyes I'd seen all my life were cold and flinty, and the beatific smile had been replaced by a tight-lipped businessman's scrutiny:

President Walter Wickliffe. Creator of the Upterlife.

"Greetings, sir," Gumdrool said, keeping his head bowed. "Please accept this gift of two intruders, as recompense for all the sins I have committed against you."

"You don't sin against me, son. You sin against society. What is it you've done?"

"I have Shrived Mortal since my eleventh birthday, sir," Gumdrool replied. "But now I can make it up to you."

20: TRAPPED IN A GOLDEN TOWER, WITH A MAN I NEVER HOPED TO SEE

President Wickliffe's computerized eyes fuzzed with static.

"Ian Montgomery Drumgoole," Wickliffe recited, a moue of distaste crinkling his pencil mustache. "Applied to, and rejected by, the Junior LifeGuard sixteen times. Wore the uniform anyway. Dr Frank Beldon, the barely competent head of the 82nd Street Orphanage, claimed the unauthorized uniform was therapeutic, despite several complaints of impersonating an officer. Your… disciples… have been written up several times for exceeding their authority."

Gumdrool was a reject? I thought. The only reason he'd gotten to lord it over me was because Beldon had taken a *liking* to him? I thought of all the punishments he'd handed down to me, realizing all the pain Dare and I had endured at his hands had been off the books…

But if I was angry, Peaches lunged at her restraints hard enough to rattle the equipment.

"You *lied* to me, you scumsucker!" she cried, fingers crooked to claw Gumdrool's eyes out. "You told me you were a lock for the LifeGuard!"

"And now, I am." Gumdrool had the lazy smile of a cat who'd caught a pigeon. "Sir, I respectfully submit my only sin has been an excess of devotion. And, frankly speaking, you need me."

"*Need* you?" Wickliffe spluttered. "Why, you're a symptom of the very thing I'm fighting *against*. In my day, thugs like you would have Shrived Criminal."

Gumdrool chuckled under his breath, as if Mr Wickliffe was just kidding.

"I'm no criminal, sir. I'm just a humble servant who wants to keep your servers running. And my arrival proves just how off track the Upterlife's gotten."

"I don't debate philosophy with murderers."

…suddenly, I realized how lucky I'd been that Gumdrool had only chosen to put me in the Time-Out Chamber.

"Oh, sir, it was never murder," Gumdrool explained. "I just… gave fate a chance to step in, is all. A pot of boiling oil a little closer to the edge of the stove. A skateboard balanced at the top of the stairs. And never for anyone Shriving Venal – Mortal kids only."

Which I would have been, had I simply returned to the orphanage. Would I have survived the year if Gumdrool hadn't needed an infiltration expert?

"They were young." Wickliffe shivered with rage. "I would have caught and condemned you *personally* if I'd examined the orphanage's death records before now! Those boys could have changed!"

"No, sir," Gumdrool raised a finger. "They couldn't. They wouldn't. That's the *point*. Your compassion's commendable – don't think I don't want everyone in. I do. But you see what's happening, don't you?"

Wickliffe scowled… But didn't tell Gumdrool to stop.

"Little Venice drowned because the living failed in their duty," Gumdrool continued earnestly. "Your guards are careless, your technicians so by-the-book they leave doors wide open for hackers. The living need to be whipped into shape."

Wickliffe gave Gumdrool a disdainful look. Majestically, he

recited his most famous philosophy: *"All should pass through, but for the lowliest of criminals."*

I shivered when he said it. Those words still held power.

"Words for a different world," Gumdrool said, unmoved. "Yes, I barred a few unworthies from passing through – you should thank me! Because your error is handing the Upterlife out too freely. Entry must be *earned*. You must redefine what a criminal is, sir. Not just to bar entrance for suicide, murder, and programming – but also dereliction of duty!"

Wickliffe snorted. "And what will *you* be in this new regime?"

"Smart. Flexible. I snuck in – allow me to serve, and I will show you the truth through sheer devotion. I'll master the technology, ensure your guards rely upon their eyes. I'll remind you of the performance the living *should* deliver."

I tried to wheeze out a protest through my bruised larynx.

Dr Hsiang stepped before Gumdrool, a smooth lawyer ready to plead a case. "He's correct, sir," she said. "I've tried managing security in my spare time – it's a distraction. You need a competent fulltime security manager."

Wickliffe snorted again, as if he was too genteel to say what he really thought. Even in the torture chamber, he radiated a paternal charm.

"Your entry was indeed a clever subterfuge," he allowed. "Getting past our perimeter displayed an impressive synergy of skills – stealth and quickness to get past the ferals, social engineering, network-sniffing. That's the kind of hack I would have been proud to pull off back in my salad days."

"That's right," Gumdrool said. "I can help you."

"Except *you're* not holding the hacking device, boy," Wickliffe replied loftily. "So, Amichai – what do you have to say?"

The two guards shook me like a rug.

"Brow–" I gargled.

"Brow what?"

"Brown note."

All hell broke loose.

I should add, of course, that the "brown note" is a myth...
Mostly.

In case you don't know, the brown note is a rumored
infrasonic frequency that, once broadcast, creates a cascading
resonance that causes everyone within range to lose control
of their bowels.

Naturally, this is nonsense. Sound waves are a weak
medium, literally light as air. You'd need something as solid
as fists to cause someone to squirt.

There are, naturally, two corollaries to this thought: the
first is that while there is no brown note *per se*, there are
frequencies that will cause instant migraine headaches. Think
of it as weaponized fingernails on a chalkboard.

The second is that while air is a terrible medium to conduct
low-frequency vibrations, this can be gotten around if you
have a speaker in direct contact with someone's skin. Like,
say, someone's hacked earputer.

Which explains why, while the guards and Dr Hsiang
bent over in agony as the IceBreaker broadcast its piercing
note, Gumdrool's earputer did indeed help him discover the
fullness of the brown note.

Right in his underwear.

21: A DIFFERENT MAZE OF TWISTY PASSAGES, SLICK WITH FIRE RETARDANT

Of course the alarms went off.

"Amichai, wait," Wickliffe said. "You must trust me. I'm on your side, I'm trying to fix things..."

I thought of the NeoChristians. "Get stuffed."

We tugged the Velcro straps off and propped Peaches on her feet. She still wobbled from the audial assault. I kissed her on the forehead, then loaded a Peaches-image-removing macro across the cameras.

"Run." I handed Gumdrool's taser to Dare. "I'll distract the guards."

"All of them?"

I brandished the IceBreaker. "This'll help. Peaches sacrificed herself for me. Now I'll help her get the message out. Once you tell the living what Wickliffe's planning, it'll be the final straw. They'll *have* to revolt.

"And don't..." I swallowed, wondering whether I had to say it. "Don't you dare die."

If you looked up "Duh" in Wikipedia, a photograph of Dare's face would be all you needed.

"I came here to save Peaches," he said, followed by a palpable pause that might as well have said... *not you*.

He gave me one handshake, a businesslike farewell. To

Dare, this was simply what I owed him after I'd lied to help my sister.

And honestly?

He was right.

He fled, hauling Peaches behind.

I grabbed Gumdrool's truncheon. It felt like claiming a prize.

Wickliffe's mouth moved soundlessly as he tried to find the right words. He looked lost.

"I thought you were a superhero," I said, disgusted. "Fighting death, making the world better…"

"I still *am*, Amichai." His voice was tense with desperation. "Things get complex once you're balancing the world on your shoulders. It's not what you think…"

"Are you destroying those NeoChristians' brains?"

"Yes."

"Will you let them go?"

"I can't!"

"Then we have nothing to talk about."

I dashed into the hallway. With luck, I was still camera-invisible.

Truncheon in one hand, IceBreaker in the other, I fled deeper into the building, dodging into an office. Wickliffe was on to me – he was doubtlessly scanning the cameras for my infection. I couldn't be subtle.

Dare had said there were two exits and twenty guards. Wickliffe would have them block the gates, then execute a room-by-room search. I had to cover their escape–

A keening noise vibrated my fillings. It stabbed into my brain like a maniac with an icepick, shredding my concentration.

Wickliffe. Using my tricks against me.

I kicked the faceplate off a terminal and wired in the IceBreaker – but Wickliffe had locked the speaker access up tight. My eyes watered, the readouts blurring as the room blared migraine at me...

Fortunately, the IceBreaker was programmed to autoscan for weak points. The fire-prevention systems still had their default password. I convinced them the server was ablaze, which caused the speakers to blare fire alarms instead; as an added bonus, it filled the hallways with slippery fire-suppressant gel.

That wouldn't be enough. I wrote a new camera macro that placed fake Amichais, Dares, and Peaches throughout the complex, triggering cascades of alarms. I unlocked all the animal cages, unleashing dogs and chimpanzees. I infected computers with a virus that yelled "They're over here!" at random intervals.

I looked for other ways to disrupt the system – but Wickliffe raced ahead of me, locking everything down. It was time to make my escape...

But I thought of those prisoners, watching their loved ones get brainburned, then seeing their fellow worshippers released into the wild as naked crazies.

My clothes were damp with sweat. My head ached. Yet beneath that terror lay a fierce pride. I'd scared Walter Wickliffe. Even if I died, I'd still be in Wickliffe's Upterlife – he'd remember this moment of vulnerability, the feeling that some living *kid* had cracked him, for the rest of his existence.

This was the only immortality available to Shakespeare, Einstein, Jobs – and to Hitler, Stalin, and Bin Laden. I realized why they'd been so desperate for fame and power: when your life had an end point, you grabbed whatever you could take.

There hadn't been a war between Upterlife-enabled nations in years. Were today's potential tyrants patiently waiting to reenact their bloody fantasies in the Upterlife? I'd never thought of the living's sluggishness as a positive.

Time was running out. Even if I could free the prisoners, I doubted I could get out of the server.

I wondered if Mom and Dad would miss me.

I wondered if Izzy would forgive me.

I wondered if the people I'd saved would thank me.

I found a back channel to the dazers surrounding the prisoners' camp – then flashed their laser-sights in tune to "Yakety Sax" before I shut them down. With any luck, their escape would cause more chaos to cover Dare and Peaches' retreat…

…but my bag of tricks was bare.

I crept out into the hallway, which was slick with foam and echoed with gunfire. Was that Dare and Peaches being shot?

If Dare and Peaches were still around, they were voided for sure. Still, "voided" was better than "doggification." Which was I intended to do for the last of the poor prisoners.

The dogs barked as I entered the lab. The wired NeoChristians looked up at me, begging for death.

"It's OK," I said. "I'm here to free you."

"Freeze."

Gumdrool stood in the doorway, aiming a rifle. "I told you he'd come back here, Mister President. I *know* him. I know all his kind."

Wickliffe's face swam onto the monitors around me. "Maybe you *can* fill a gap in my organizational structure." He spoke with the air of a man with a plate of rotten meat shoved under his nose.

"That's your downfall, Damrosch," Gumdrool said. "You never think anyone's as clever as you are."

"Hair fire," I said to my earputer. That should have triggered the next batch of anti-Gumdrool measures–

"I turned mine off." Gumdrool tapped his earputer knowingly. "You don't get *me* the same way twice."

He smashed his rifle across the bridge of my nose. I'd like to tell you I took it stoically, but I fell to the ground crying.

"That's enough," Wickliffe said. "No violence."

"No more's necessary, sir." Gumdrool knelt down, looking remorseful. "I'm sorry, Amichai. I *told* you I'd seen people die unShriven. And I tried so hard to keep you from that fate... But with luck, you'll be so brainburned by the end you won't understand what's happening." He glanced over at the NeoChristians shivering on the wall. "You renounced any claim to the Upterlife the moment you sided with those stupid terrorists."

"The terrorists are smarter than you think," said a voice.

Gumdrool whirled, almost quick enough – but the air filled with the pop-and-crackle of a taser hitting flesh. Gumdrool collapsed, spasming.

Evangeline strode through the doorway, a stolen rifle strapped over her shoulder, wearing a scavenged bulletproof vest two sizes too big. Even dressed in mismatched clothing, she was the most beautiful sight I'd ever seen.

She shook out her tangled red hair and tossed me the second vest – then tugged a flechette pistol from her waist and shot all the monitors in the room. Wickliffe's images shattered. The dogs howled in fear.

When she'd shot the last of the cameras, she turned to me.

"Put the vest on, you fool," she said. "Do you think we can wait forever?"

22: THE EXITS OF GRINNING DEAD MEN

Evangeline watched Gumdrool while I slipped the heavy jacket over my shoulders.

"I should have locked you up myself," he told her. "You'd never have escaped then."

Evangeline's boot lashed out, catching Gumdrool neatly in the ribs. She kicked once, twice, three times, her blows lifting him off the tile floor. The blunt efficiency carried in her tiny frame was terrifying.

She noticed my stare. Her lips pursed in disapproval. "They say revenge is unworthy," she said. "But some sins deserve to be repaid, each for each."

"I *freed* you," I said, flabbergasted. "You should be running for the hills."

"Which now of these three, thinkest thou, was neighbor unto him that fell among the thieves?"

I gave her a blank look.

"It means you did me a good favor," she sighed. "Most wouldn't have, including many of my brethren. Only a handful volunteered to distract the guards while I searched for… survivors. Come on, let's go."

I staggered to my feet – between the truncheon to the throat and the gun butt to the face, I was still pretty woozy. Evangeline, however, finally noticed the six NeoChristians. She crossed herself, falling to her knees…

She unsheathed a knife. Her hands trembled as she hugged a woman to her breast, kissing her on the forehead.

"Muh f- fence..." said the woman meaningfully. "Fence."

"Turpentine highway," urged one of the men, his words sagging in the middle. "Turpentine *key.*"

"Sssh," said Evangeline, cradling the woman's head. The woman cried, weeping onto Evangeline's bulletproof vest.

Evangeline stabbed her in the heart. The pain in the woman's eyes melted into relief as she died.

Evangeline closed her eyes and crossed herself. She moved to the man, stabbing him, then stroking his hair while he bled out. Then the next, crossing and killing, crossing and killing.

Her knife never faltered.

When she finished she whirled upon Gumdrool, yanking him up by the hair, pressing her bloodied blade to his throat.

Wordlessly, Gumdrool pressed his jugular into the edge, confident in his immortality.

I reached out to stop her – even Gumdrool deserved better than the finality of meat-death. Didn't he?

Evangeline glared at the dead bodies slumped in their harnesses... Then screamed, smashing Gumdrool's face into the floor. She spun on one heel and marched out.

I struggled to keep up. My feet slipped on the foamed hallways; her footing was sure and precise. She bit her plump lips, licking back blood.

"You... probably could have done it," I told her. "He's Shriving Mortal. I don't think Wickliffe would have saved him. Or is that a – what do you call them – I mean, do *you* call them sins, too?"

She kept moving.

"I'm sorry about your friends," I offered, feeling I should say something to the girl who'd saved my life. "I don't know whether I–"

"Blessed are the merciful, for they shall obtain mercy."

"Is that… Are you quoting? I can never tell."

She gave me a saddened look. "My parents always said I was too quick to violence. They trained me so I could defend myself if I had to – but I had to love my enemies, pray for those who persecute me. But I liked making the evil suffer. The last thing they said before their kidnapping was that my enjoyment of combat was… unchristian."

"So is that why you didn't… kill Gumdrool?"

She looked away. "I did it because I wasn't going to murder someone in the same room where I sent my parents to Heaven."

If she'd said it in the way you were supposed to, I think I would have understood.

But when you told someone you'd just stabbed your parents as a mercy killing, your voice should quaver.

"Wait – what?"

She picked up the pace. Nervous scientists poked their heads out, saw her advancing upon them, wisely retreated.

Evangeline believed in a God with perfect Upterloading capabilities. Maybe killing wasn't a big whoop for her – she'd just sent her parents to God.

I might have believed that, were it not for the blood on her lips.

"Are you OK?" I asked.

She slammed herself backwards against the wall, slumping down. Then she covered her face with her hands and sobbed.

I patted her shoulder. "That's, uh… A natural reaction to…"

Evangeline scrubbed the tears away with the heels of her palms, knotted her hands in her tangled red hair. She pulled hard enough that I heard her scalp ripping.

"We don't have *time* for this… luxury!" Her words were muffled by sobs. "The guards know our location! I have to… have to rescue you…"

I looked at the scientists peeking out at us through the reinforced glass, wondering whether they could take us. They'd kill us if they could.

"Rescuing would be nice," I said.

I knew I could pull the old military routine, yelling to get on her feet. But ultimately, it'd be the death of her.

Evangeline was tightly wound to begin with; if she didn't acknowledge this hurt now, she never would. She'd bury the death deeper, like a ticking bomb she kept shoveling dirt on in the hopes of tamping it down when it exploded... And it *would* explode later, in a big messy batch of misdirected suicide.

Unless I vented this now, she'd keep seeking out the most dangerous missions – because whenever she stopped dodging bullets, she'd have to start burying her parents all over again. Better to lose yourself in stupid, overblown acts of crazy than face *that* remorse.

I knew, because that's what I'd done when Mom and Dad had left.

So I put my arm around her, glaring death at the scientists. They retreated.

Evangeline shoved me away, but didn't mean it – she could have flung me into the next state. I extended my hands again, and this time she grabbed me, biting my shoulder to hold back her tears.

"You... You did the right thing," I said, stroking her hair awkwardly. "You ended their suffering. And they're, they're in a better place..."

She kissed me.

It wasn't like Peaches' kisses. The one time I'd made out with Peaches, it had been on a rooftop, just before sunrise. Peaches had snuggled closer and closer, nuzzling me, waiting for me to approach. But what if I'd misread the signs? Peaches wasn't kind to those who made unwanted advances.

It was kiss Peaches or go mad. She'd smirked, as if she'd been waiting for me all along, and opened up her soft, soft lips. She kept her tongue at the back of her mouth, rewarding me with tiny snakelike licks, teasing me deeper.

Once I committed, Peaches cut me off. "Look at that beautiful sunrise" was her signal the festivities were over – another test, I knew. Would I be oafish enough to keep pressing her? No. So I agreed it was a nice sunrise, and ignored the throbbing in my crotch that stayed for about a week afterwards.

Peaches was a delicate rose, waiting to be cultivated.

Evangeline was a tiger.

She wrapped her arms around me; our bulletproof vests clunked against each other. She searched my eyes, reading the terror in there as I wondered what I'd done wrong – and then, slowly, she pressed her full, red lips against mine, giving me time to understand as a part of me went *oh*.

Then she kissed me. And *she* kissed *me*, no doubt about that; she grabbed my neck, taking the lead, sliding the tip of her tongue into my mouth.

It was a fierce kiss, one that stole the breath from me. All I could do was sit back while she took what she needed.

But there was one thing Evangeline had in common with Peaches: when she was done, she was done. She broke off the kiss to shove me aside.

"Hey!" I protested – and noticed the three guards rounding the corner, their boots scrambling for traction on the foam-slicked floor.

"Amichai Damrosch," they said, "Set down your weapons and–"

Evangeline shoved herself down the slippery hallway, hooking their ankles with her arms. They toppled, trying to bring their rifles around to bear – she flipped over on her back, stomping on each guard's trigger hand.

The third guard wrestled Evangeline into his sights – and then his kneecap exploded as she shot him. He fell, clutching his ruined leg. She snatched the rifle out of one guard's broken hands and smashed the other in the face with it.

"Wait," the third, remaining guard said. "I–"

She drove the stock into his nose. She checked their necks for pulses, plucked the excess ammunition from their bodies, then extended her hand to me.

I was still sitting down.

I let her pull me to my feet, puffing out my chest to make it seem like… what? Like I would have challenged them to a duel if she hadn't beaten me to it?

"That kiss wasn't… wasn't two becoming one flesh." Evangeline avoided my gaze as she shifted her armor back into place. "You were just there."

I wanted to pull her back to me, foolish though that might be. That had been a lifechanging kiss right there, a kiss that promised whole other worlds of kissitude.

But I also understood the grief that kiss had sprung from.

I adjusted some meaningless settings on the IceBreaker; I didn't want to look her in the eyes. I liked her too much to see regret there.

She jerked her chin towards the guards. "They had orders to capture, not kill. That made it easier."

"For *you*."

Was that a grin? I couldn't tell.

We bolted for the front door, which was blocked by a heap of corpses, all shot dead in mid-brawl. Six guards were sandwiched in a crowd of ragged prisoners, bloody hands still wrapped around the guards' throats.

They were riddled with bullets, guards and prisoners alike – and I understood what had happened.

The server had been designed to withstand almost any outside assault. Yet the principles that made it defensible –

two reinforced doors – meant that it was equally easy to keep people trapped inside. The guards had found themselves in the tenuous position of needing to track down the escaping NeoChristians before they got too far – a difficult thing when the remaining prisoners pressed themselves against the doors, ready to bash your skull in with a rock when you poked your head out.

The six guards had been the sacrifice squad sent ahead to draw out the prisoners, while the rest of them stayed down the hallway and shot at everything.

Nobody on either side'd had an ounce of hesitation; their bodies were disposable, their memories already preserved. I noted the uniforms on the dead soldiers had epaulets; the officers had usurped the privilege of sacrifice.

I threw up.

"Why are you sick?" Evangeline asked, puzzled. "Is it the sight of blood?"

"They all died for me." I wiped my mouth. "Some to keep me in, others to get me out, but if it wasn't for me... They'd all be alive."

I laughed. Everyone, NeoChristians and guards alike, were convinced they were going to a better place. They'd thrown their lives away willingly.

That shouldn't bother me, but it did.

I staggered past the bodies, headed for the courtyard. Evangeline hauled me back as a hail of bullets ricocheted off the entryway. "It's *him*!" someone cried. "Suppression fire only! Don't let them out!"

"All my brethren are with God," Evangeline said, doubling back.

It took me a moment to realize she meant *dead*. "How do you know?"

"Because the courtyard still has gunmen in it."

"Too true," Wickliffe said. "Time to give up, Amichai."

194 THE UPLOADED

The monitors embedded in the hallways flickered on. Wickliffe-faces turned to face us as the remaining guards – some limping – emerged from the interior hallways, rifles ready. They had the cautious look of hospital orderlies surrounding a pony.

Wickliffe looked wise, unruffled, sympathetic – just the kind of man you'd want to surrender to.

"I've examined your Shrives, Amichai." His voice was filled with admiration, tinged with regret. "And I know what you're thinking now."

"You don't know me."

"I do. You're thinking if you go out in a blaze of glory, you'll live on as a memory."

I felt like a cold breeze had blown straight through me. What else did he know about me?

"I'm not some backwater orphanage administrator, Amichai," Wickliffe said. "I created the Upterlife. I've spent years protecting the entire *world*, and you? You're a momentary concern, I agree – but don't overestimate yourself."

He chuckled. "Now, the Supreme Court session where they decided whether the postmortemed had the right to vote? Now, *that's* a moment to give me nightmares. You, my dear boy, are an error that will be corrected. Once you're gone, not even your parents will miss you. Not that they do now..."

If a bodiless man could punch me in the heart...

"I'm sorry, Amichai. We're on the same side – I wish you could understand how much I admire you. The fact that your parents ignore you isn't your fault – it's proof of how badly your parents have been corrupted. You? You're everything I want the living to be – bold, moral, intellectually curious. Not to flatter you overmuch, but... I see too much of myself in you."

I moved to protect Evangeline. "So let us go."

"In a better world, I could. But you're in my way."

"Of doing evil!"

"Such a small perspective, Amichai. A *young* perspective. After five hundred years, you come to understand what works. This brainmeddling is unpleasant, but it *will* work in time."

"Don't give me the old 'ends justify the means' speech…"

"You know who tells you the ends don't justify the means? People who mean nothing and end poorly. Trust me, Amichai. I haven't changed. I created the most peaceful society this world has ever known – and if I say a few living brains is the cost for paradise, then *that is the cost.*"

"You're not dissecting *brains!*" I said. "You're torturing *people.*"

"If I could use lab rats, I would. But that's how the real world works, Amichai. It feeds you constant choices between moral compromise or destruction – and there's never a third way out. That's why I created the Upterlife – I wanted a place where all the choices were good…"

"Don't talk to me about choices – you're trying to take away our choices…"

"I won't debate. But you don't have to void. Surrender, and I'll ensure your last Shrive – the ignorant one – gets to the Upterlife."

"I thought the dead got to vote on who got in," I said.

"They'll welcome you with open arms once I announce you died quashing a branch operation in Little Venice." He gave me his kindly old man's smile. "Peaches was right; noble sacrifice is a tale the dead always love to hear."

"Stop talking about her like you know her."

"But I do, Amichai. I know everyone who's Shrived. Better than they know themselves."

"So what am I thinking now?"

"You're thinking of Therapy."

Evangeline gave me a confused look. My face must have

given me away, though, because Wickliffe nodded sagely.

"This time, Amichai, the pony lives. I know you respect your NeoChristian friend, there – it's a little deeper than that, actually, but we won't go into that now – and you'd never surrender unless you knew she was safe. So she'll be safe. We'll lock her in a prison, and you have my word she will *not* be – how do my scientists so clumsily put it? – doggified."

"Unacceptable." Evangeline cocked her rifle. The guards at the end of the hallway raised their weapons.

"Amichai." Wickliffe spoke quickly, his voice low and urgent, "My simulations show you both have a 78 percent chance of voiding. We can't subdue Evangeline without killing her. You have to talk her out of it – it's the only way to protect your sister…"

I turned to Evangeline, who glanced between the guards on the inside of the server, the guards on the outside of the server, and me. Would I betray her?

If Wickliffe got ahold of my recent brainscans, he'd know the path we took here. That would make tracking Dare and Peaches down among Little Venice's ruins that much easier – he'd capture them before they could make it back to tell the living. And then the NeoChristians would keep getting brainfried until he discovered how to mold the living to his needs.

The servers won't be any fun for me without my little brother there.

"Do you believe in things beyond death?" I asked Evangeline.

"…what? Of course I do."

"Then say a prayer for my sister."

She pulled down her armor to press one palm against the black cross tattooed on her breastbone, then touched her fingers to my lips. It felt intimate, a benediction.

I turned to Wickliffe. Exultant. Triumphant. Embracing my

insanity.

"You lie like a politician, Wickliffe!" I cried. "You've got a horde of NeoChristian prisoners on the run – and my friends with video evidence. If *one* of them testifies to what you're doing, you're dead. You wouldn't be trying so hard to get my brain unless you thought I knew something you didn't. You can't kid a kidder, man – you're shitting e-bricks. Oh, you're gonna remember my name."

"As someone who brought down civilization!" he spluttered.

"You built it on our backs. Let it tumble."

The guards outside the server shouted in panic. I said a prayer to no one in particular, hoping Peaches and Dare had made it out safe.

Then I said a final prayer for Izzy.

"Fire," I said.

A roar blew down the corridor.

Things moved very quickly after that.

23: 500 FEET AND RISING

Being shot should be painful, I thought. I expected bullets punching through muscle. Instead, I felt weightless, a leaf in the wind...

...at least until my shoulder slammed into a door that had flown open. I *was* being carried along in the wind. I grabbed at the doorway as the guards were blown away from me, rifles flying from their hands.

It was like someone had dropped a tornado into the hallway.

My ears popped from the pressure differential. Someone yelled – Evangeline? – and the wind reversed course. I was sucked back towards the server's entryway, my hands clawing at the floor, until I slammed into what felt like a wall of metal spikes.

"Get in!" someone said. Peaches? It couldn't be. I turned to look...

...and there was Peaches, waving at me from the cockpit of a military spirocopter. The spirocopter hovered outside the entryway, bristling with stiff metal miniturbines – each quivering in minute computerized adjustments, sucking in air and shoving it out through supercharged jets. It looked like a tapdancing millipede, but it kept the spirocopter perfectly in place.

Bullets spanged off the cockpit glass. Dr Hsiang flinched,

looking distinctly unhappy in the copilot's seat – which was no wonder, because Dare had a gun pressed against her neck.

Peaches pulled the spirocopter's doors open and hauled me inside.

"*How are you...?*" I shouted, looking up at the narrow gap above us. The four collapsed buildings teetered overhead, leaving us with what looked like a chimney's width for escape. "You can't fly!"

"It's self-correcting!" Peaches said happily, vaulting into the pilot's seat.

As if to illustrate, she yanked the throttle straight back just as Evangeline leapt in. The copter whirled madly up the sliver of space between the collapsed buildings and the server, a dandelion seed caught in a storm. Peaches veered too close to a wall; safety jets shoved us back to center with a roar of airfoils.

Peaches drummed on the steering wheel with her palms, laughing like this was the time of her life. Me? I'd never flown before, and discovered I hated it.

I wondered what Peaches' parents would think of her if they saw her giggling, her freshly shaved head still bleeding, steering a hijacked military copter.

I looked down. The soldiers had piled out into the courtyard to take potshots at us, picking their way among the dead NeoChristians.

We popped out of the gap between the four collapsed buildings like a cork, but moving too slow to escape an aerial pursuit. This thing was built to carry tons of prefabbed steel beams; speed had been a secondary design concern.

"*Where to?*" Peaches yelled, the merry shout she used to announce that the drinks were on her.

"*Southeast.*" Evangeline steadied herself against Peaches' chair to peer out the front window. "*I have brethren in Passaic.*"

Peaches seemed to register Evangeline's presence for the

first time. She shot me a quick look, as if to ask, *who brought in the yokel?* but then shrugged amiably: *whatever it takes to save your life, babe.* She punched directions into the navcomputer.

Evangeline slapped her hand away.

"You want to broadcast where we're headed?" Evangeline shouted, rolling her eyes. "Don't give our landing coordinates to their GPSes. Fly manually. That direction."

Peaches' good mood evaporated.

Well, they're off to a fine friendship, I thought. But we had to follow Evangeline's lead; she was the only one who'd never Shrived. How could I outwit someone who knew everything I'd ever thought up until two days ago?

Despite the turbulence, Dare's gun was still pressed to Dr Hsiang's neck. "There's no need for that," Dr Hsiang said, so calmly she might have been discussing the weather. "We're in the same boat, now. I shan't do anything rash."

"How in the void did you get the spirocopter?" I asked Dare.

"They'd blocked off the exits," Dare explained, not taking his eyes off the good doctor. "So Peaches figured if we couldn't go out, we'd go up. And guess who we ran into on the roof?" He waggled the gun.

"I'm not your enemy," Hsiang said. "I'm an employee."

"The doctor here was *frantic* to get out." Dare laughed. "She's got no ticket to the Upterlife unless this project succeeds. So this gun was quite the incentive."

"I gave you administrative access to this spirocopter…" Hsiang said.

"You would have betrayed us in a heartbeat. And I suspect you're already engineering your escape from us…"

"Good on you," I said, slapping Dare's back. The infuriated gaze he directed at Peaches spoke of the argument they'd had over whether to come back for me… and how badly Dare had lost.

Who could blame him for wanting to leave me behind? I'd lied to him, manipulated him, put his sister in danger... everything I'd done in the last two days looked more like an enemy than a friend.

"...thank you anyway," I said, my mouth dry.

I wondered how long Peaches would retain control of the copter. If it was automated enough to avoid crashing, it was automated enough to be remote-piloted. Once Wickliffe rescinded Hsiang's access, he'd fly us back.

I checked the IceBreaker, which was down to a 17 percent charge; all my frequency-scanning and camera-blasting had sucked the batteries dry. I flipped through the program stack, seeing if there was anything to get me root access to a spirocopter, doubting even Mama Alex was that prescient.

Still, even if I got root, what then? We'd never make it to Passaic. President Wickliffe had access to every camera. We'd be visible the moment we flew over a populated area.

Evangeline stabbed herself in the arm.

Peaches whirled around in her pilot's seat. "What the...?"

Evangeline sliced deep into her bicep, extracting a grape-sized chip.

Peaches and Dare gave me a dropjawed stare as if to say, *you brought her in here?*

"A fine idea," said Dr Hsiang. "I'd forgotten about the tracking implants."

Evangeline examined it with the bland expression of someone who'd found an ant on their shoulder, then flicked the tracking chip out the window.

"You NeoChristians are *hardcore*," I said. She smiled.

"Doesn't that hurt?" Peaches asked, looking a little green around the gills.

Evangeline shrugged. "Others have suffered much more for me."

"Who suffered for... oh. That guy, right? Your cross-guy."

With evident effort, Evangeline swallowed back a retort. "Yes. Him."

"I've got nothing against your kind, you know." Peaches spoke slowly, as if Evangeline might have trouble understanding her. "I think if you want to worship a fish or two pieces of wood or whatever, you go right ahead."

Mercifully, a military spirocopter whizzed up over the horizon, roaring over the Roosevelt River to twirl to a stop over the branch server. It dipped down so fast I thought it had lost power, dropping into the space between the four buildings.

"That's unusual," Hsiang said, adjusting her glasses. "He should be bringing in the erasure team, not calling for a pickup."

There was a blinding flash, then a rumble we heard even over the turbine jets.

The military spirocopter popped out of the top of the collapsed buildings, outracing the stream of flame erupting from its belly. The four buildings swayed drunkenly, then crumbled inwards in a gout of fire.

"Well, that's good news," said Dr Hsiang cheerfully. "He's called the erasure team! He's afraid we might get away!"

The military copter's turbines changed angles to zoom straight towards us, chewing up the space in between. Its guns glowed a deep green.

"...that's not so good," Dr Hsiang admitted, as the spirocopter roared into range.

24: GREENWICH VILLAGE, AT A SPEEDY CLIP

"Turn away!"

Peaches had been looking back at the enemy spirocopter. I caught her attention just as dazer lights swept the cabin, making us all woozy.

"They want us alive," Evangeline muttered. "That's something."

"You haven't Shrived in a few days, and you have recording devices," Dr Hsiang said. "President Wickliffe hates unknowns."

The copter banked to one side to get a better shot at us. Peaches angled straight down, dropping into the gap between Greenwich Village brownstones.

Webs of laundry lines strung between the apartment complexes snapped against our windshield. Our turbine wash sent gales of underwear and socks soaring high into the sky, then fluttering back down into the gardens like a rain of smallclothes. The "Live Local, Die Global" initiatives had forced the Village to abandon cars for ponies – so they'd repurposed the asphalt, planting long strips of squash and soybeans in old wheel ruts. The people in the streets cursed, flinging rocks.

"If they want to shoot us down, they'll have to take out

Greenwich Village to do it," she muttered.

"They just might," Dare said. "The LifeGuard's never loved the Village…"

Peaches zipped around Greenwich's winding streets, making wild lefts and rights to confuse them – but we all knew she couldn't *lose* them. Once Wickliffe called in more copters, we were dead.

"Dare, my earputer's out of juice – give me yours!" I shouted. It was hard to concentrate among the flicker of dazers and Peaches' chaotic steering.

"Do you have an actual escape plan this time?" he asked. But he handed it over.

I copied Dare's raw footage into the IceBreaker – the Naked Crazies, the NeoChristians being reprogrammed, Peaches' capture. Sadly, Wickliffe's voice had some interference shield that prevented recording – whenever he spoke, it sounded like a rusty trombone.

Yet the scientists' comments were clear, the implications damning.

More rocks thunked off the side of the spirocopter as the locals on the rooftops flung rubbish at us. The ones who weren't chucking coral flipped the bird at us.

"The locals think it's a raid," Dr Hsiang observed. "That could prove interesting."

The enemy spirocopter roared overhead, catching another round of jeers from the crowd. I spotted a familiar figure hanging off its side, pointing at us and yelling orders: Gumdrool.

So *that* was who they'd picked up. Wickliffe must have hired Gumdrool to hunt us down.

"Why did we trust that asshole?" Dare asked bitterly. "Oh, that's right; you said he'd be good *for my career.*"

Peaches banked around a corner, where foil tents had been set up in the middle of an intersection: an illegal marketspace.

Black marketeers, clad in thick silk hoods and shiny silver buckles, ran out of the tents to see what the commotion was about, their faces obscured so no camera could identify them.

"Black Hoods?" Dare yelped. "This is going from bad to worse."

The spirocopter's whoosh sent the tents' entryways fluttering open, revealing panicked locals. They ran. If your black market bust showed up on *Sins of the Flesh*, kiss your Upterlife goodbye.

The Black Hoods would sell you almost anything inside those cameraproofed tents. Sometimes they sold camera-jamming equipment, but more often it was serious stuff – slow poisons to send your loved ones to paradise, illicit gene treatments for better looks. And they had weaponry to protect themselves.

I pointed at the market's center. "Land there in five minutes," I told Peaches. "Until then keep circling around the block, but stay within half a mile."

"You aren't getting *closer* to the Black Hoods–" Dare yelled – but then Peaches hurled the spirocopter into a twirling reversal that nearly made Dare toss his cookies.

Another enemy spirocopter shot past us, flying directly over the Black Hoods. The Hoods tinkered with a large contraption on the ground, swearing and thumping it. The device convulsed and coughed out a needlelike missile, sucking debris behind it as it flew; the missile arched into the sky, following the spirocopter inexorably like a hi-tech mosquito.

When the missile made contact, the spirocopter went up in an impossibly bright burst of light, raining fist-sized fragments down onto the pavement.

"I'm flying *closer* to the guys with weaponry," Peaches said through gritted teeth. "Yes, this seems wise."

Two other spirocopters popped up on the horizon. The

Black Hoods barked orders at their tents, which collapsed into small silver boxes the size of clothing chests. They had heavy-duty defenses to ward off the first wave of LifeGuard incursions, but even they had to retreat from a coordinated government assault.

Meanwhile, I was seeding files, using the last of the IceBreaker's battery charge to find all the cameras in the area and commandeer them. The cameras at the edge of range winked out of signal as Peaches careened down the street, but the readout showed roughly fifteen hundred cameras in the block.

"This is Amichai Damrosch," I said, talking into Dare's earputer-cam, speaking loud enough to be heard over the copter's noise. "You might remember me from such films as 'that hospital pony-smuggling.' Now I've got even better footage – something every living boy and girl in the world needs to see! Copy this immediately, remix it, share it on every network you can find – because if you don't listen to this today, *you will not care tomorrow*. They will take the ability to care *away* from you."

I made fifteen hundred different copies of Dare's footage, filling each with randomized pauses and static, so the file signatures on each copy would be different. If Wickliffe wanted to scrub the files, he'd have to track them down manually.

"To the ghosts," I continued, "You are nothing more than a resource to be mined. Your free will is an obstruction. They want to mold you into more obedient servants. Until you're dead, *they do not think you are human*."

Peaches made a hard left. The two other spirocopters sailed overhead, homing in on us. Peaches made a quick figure-eight around a statue, looping back to the flash market.

"This is what the ghosts do. This is why you can never trust them. This is why you need to revolt now – before they erase the idea of revolution forever!"

I almost stopped recording, then added:

"Sorry, sis."

I thumbed the "Broadcast" button.

The three spirocopters closed in, their dazers glowing green.

"Land there," I said, pointing to a vacated spot in the market.

"You're messing with the *Black Hoods?*" Dare squealed.

"Ignore Amichai," Evangeline barked. She gripped Peaches' shoulder hard. "Fly to Passaic. Escape while we have the chance."

When Peaches didn't budge, Evangeline leaned over to slap Peaches' hands off the throttle. She was shocked when Peaches clung tight.

"We need to get this message out," I said, thumbing the "Broadcast" button on the IceBreaker. "I've uploaded the footage to every camera in range. They'll emergency-broadcast to every earputer within *their* range for as long as the IceBreaker's controlling them. Which means we need to stay put for as long as we can, to ensure that the word gets out. It's our best chance for letting the world know what Wickliffe's up to."

"And us?" Dare asked.

"We hope the Black Hoods recognize us as friendlies, and occupy Gumdrool's attention for a few moments longer."

"So we *are* voiding ourselves to save the world," Dare said – and though he was still furious at me, he nodded in grim agreement. "Because if we don't tell people now, they'll doggify other folks, enslave the living, and they'll *never stop...*"

I clasped Dare's hand, feeling that swell of brotherhood again.

"Don't touch me," Dare snapped. "We could have planned this better if you hadn't had to show off! If you'd just told me what was happening, then maybe we wouldn't *have* to void!"

"*No!*" Dr Hsiang shouted, snatching the gun away from Dare. She took aim at Peaches, holding the gun well out of Evangeline's reach. "I refuse to be your sacrificial lamb. Take off, Ms Khan-Tien."

I had to credit Peaches; the copter never wavered as it spiraled down towards the flash marketplace. Evangeline weighed the options, trying to figure out how to safely disarm Hsiang.

"I assure you," Hsiang said, watching as Peaches kept the control stick in a steady descent. "I will shoot, if you don't escape."

"I believe you," Peaches said serenely. "This is worth it."

Hsiang shrugged and fired.

Blood splattered across the windshield.

Dare went for the gun as Hsiang pulled the trigger three more times. Peaches' scream turned into a sucking gurgle.

"You bitch!" Dare shrieked. "I'll fucking kill you!"

Dare wrestled the gun out of her hands, punched Hsiang in the face over and over again–

Evangeline grabbed at the copter's controls, but it was too late; we were off balance, smashing into a brownstone. The Black Hoods below us dove for cover as the copter crashed into the dirt, spraying asphalt everywhere.

I fought my way back to consciousness, but the darkness threatened to drown me. The last thing I remembered before passing out was Gumdrool, hanging off the edge of a spirocopter, blasting the last of the Black Hood resistance as he made his way towards us. And Dare, weeping next to Peaches, screaming for help.

My eyes unfocused. Then: darkness.

PART III: COME TO JESUS

25: PARALYZED PASSENGERS ON PERILOUS PILGRIMAGES

"… him to," a voice said.

I wasn't awakened so much as switched on. I stared at bright spotlights embedded in a brushed-metal ceiling, trying to remember who I was. Last I knew, I'd been in a crashing spirocopter, trying to save New York, while Peaches–

Peaches.

Peaches had been shot.

I leapt off the bed – or tried to. I ordered my legs to *get up, get up*; they ignored me. I felt the weight of scratchy blankets resting on my chest, my lungs breathing – but aside from autonomic impulses, my body didn't respond. My eyes stared straight up into a blinding light, watering from the pain, dumb cameras I could no longer control.

Something had disconnected my brain from my body.

"Let him blink," a familiar voice said. "A man should be comfortable in his last moments."

The sound of a technician pressing buttons. Blurs of blue-suited men – LifeGuards – moving at my vision's edge. The scrape of a chair, pulled up next to the bed.

Gumdrool leaned in.

Really not good.

Gumdrool looked grim, carrying the sad nobility of a doctor

about to deliver bad news. His eyes were still blackened from where Evangeline had punched him.

He cleared his throat, silencing the men around him.

"Would you gentlemen give me some alone time with Mr Damrosch?" he asked.

The scuffle of boots. The hiss of a door opening; sunwarmed air whooshed in, ruffling Gumdrool's hair. The constant rattle of the bedframe told me we'd been moved to a monorail.

"Meat-death is a terrible punishment." Gumdrool spoke gravely, pinching the bridge of his nose. "Delivered to only the lowliest of criminals. Despite what you may think, I loathe killing.

"I tried to warn you, Amichai – but you're the lowliest of criminals now."

I should have broken out in a cold sweat. But my body didn't react, even though inside I shrieked.

"Not an effective criminal, it's true," Gumdrool continued. "We shut down your little broadcast, Amichai. We've got people eradicating the seed files you tried to spread. And soon, at our new facility in Lacona Springs, we'll manufacture the devices to encourage the living to fix this wretched world. You kicked up so much trouble, Amichai... and all you managed was to get Peaches shot."

Looking into Gumdrool's twisted compassion, I *felt* like a lowly criminal. If I got Peaches killed for a cause, the least I could do was win.

"It's ironic," he continued. "I needed you to get me my big break. And you did! Your security breach made Mr Wickliffe agree He needs better eyes on the ground." A dreamy smile crossed Gumdrool's face. "He's put me in charge of his most critical project. *Me. I'm* heading up security at Lacona Springs..."

He blinked, seeming to notice me again, and looked grave.

"I... must admit I owe you."

Would he set me free?

"Mr Wickliffe," Gumdrool said thickly, "believes you can be *converted*. Mr Wickliffe hopes to convince you to become a more amenable citizen. No mind control, no incentives – He believes a heart-to-heart *chat* will convince you. Whereas I believe…"

Gumdrool swallowed.

"*I* believe Mr Wickliffe is irrationally fond of you."

As Gumdrool's brow furrowed, I realized that no. I wouldn't live.

"He's taken too many risks to get you back on His side already. So… I'll pronounce judgment upon you to save Him. There'll be an error. A glitch in your paralysis program. It won't hurt!" he assured me. "But… your death will remove a bad temptation from a good man."

He closed his eyes, nodded. "Yes. It's the right thing to do."

Gumdrool leaned in close. "But I promise you, Amichai: I will watch over your sister like the imaginary angels of old. She wanted to be a LifeGuard. She understood her duty. And with my guidance, she *will* get into the Upterlife. That's a good last thought to cling to, I think. That you saved your sister."

He coughed, embarrassed, and stood up. *No, no, no*, I thought, *I can't die like this–*

"Yes," he whispered. "This is the right thing."

His hand reached for the switch–

"I-i-i-ian!"

Wickliffe's voice blared over the speakers – but it skipped like a corrupted music file. Gumdrool's heels clicked as he snapped to attention.

"Sir?" Gumdrool sounded as horrified as I felt. Wickliffe had always been the world's voice of reason, his words comforting us during unimaginable tragedies… even when they were tragedies he himself caused. Hearing those comforting tones chopped up into slurred computer damage felt as though the universe itself had gone mad.

"Thuh- thh- thuh- theeeeeere is a *security* bre-e-each," Wickliffe continued. "They're d*ooooi*ng something to me, I-i-ian! I've traced the SIGnal to the rear of the mmmmonorail! Geh-het the g-g-g-guards into the last car!"

"Are you OK, sir?"

"Get the g-g-guards into the car! Uh-uh-all of them!"

A strange relief flooded Gumdrool's chiseled face as he removed his hand from my life-support controls. Then he ran out. I heard other doors opening, the rattle-and-bang as the monorail roared down the track, feet scuffling as people ran past me to the back, screaming, *"Get to the signal! Go! Go!"*

The door slammed shut. A tingle skittered across my body.

My fingers twitched.

I could move again.

What was happening?

I sat up, dizzied; I'd been motionless for so long, my muscles cramped from the sudden exertion. Sensations flooded back in: my bloody nose throbbed from Gumdrool's rifle butt, my chest ached from where the spirocopter's backwash had smashed me into a door, my stitches stung.

…stitches? The medtechs had sewn up my coral gashes. They'd also dressed me in a flimsy medical gown.

I clambered to my feet, clutching a rail for support, looking for something I could use to assault Gumdrool when he came back. I stood in a windowless hospital room roughly the size of a subway car. Equipment hung off every square inch of wallspace – medicine cabinets, EKG machines, spray-on disinfectants. The bed-slash-operating-table had been placed in the room's center, presumably so soldiers could walk around it as they made their way up and down the monorail.

The IceBreaker rested in a tray nearby. I grabbed it, grateful to have my old tools back.

"Ah- ah- Amichai?"

Wickliffe looked down at me from a monitor. He wore a monocle now, squinching Wickliffe's solemn expression into a mischievous half-wink.

"Guh-get to the back door," Wickliffe told me. "I think-think-think you want to whuh- watch this."

I staggered over to the oval door at the monorail's rear. I'd never been on a monorail, but I knew how they worked from TV shows – you levered open one door, almost like an airlock, then stepped out onto a platform between cars.

Except the trailing car's door was locked, trapping the guards inside. Gumdrool banged a rifle butt against the window, mad to escape. The rest of the LifeGuard looked on, puzzled, waiting for Gumdrool's orders.

When Gumdrool saw me, he screamed red-faced threats – threats I couldn't hear. I gave him a shy little wave.

He grabbed a bigger gun, blasted the door off its hinges. But by then, there had been a quite satisfying *clack* as Gumdrool's segment of the monorail decoupled, then rolled to a stop.

The last I saw of Gumdrool was his guards holding him back as he tried to leap out after me.

"That dude is a total *ass!*- assmunch," said Wickliffe.

"Now that's a fine sight to see," I muttered – and then stood, astonished, as the monorail pulled away further, revealing an endless canopy of vibrant green forests rolling underneath us at a hundred-miles-per-hour blur.

I'd never travelled this fast before. I'd never seen the wilderness up close. Void, I'd never even set foot outside of New York – and here I was up on an unsettlingly high rail, zooming towards an unknown location, on a monorail piloted by a glitchy Wickliffe.

"Who are you?" I asked. "What's going on?"

"Nuh- nuh- no time for explanations, Amichai!" Wickliffe was as merry as a game show host. "We must es- es- escape before Wickliffe cuh- catches up with us. After all, we're on a mmmonorail, it's nnnnot like we can lose them. Gggget Dr Hsiang. We're technozombies, Amichai; we neeeeeed her brains!"

"Where are we going?"

"Boston."

"There is no Boston. You killed Boston."

"Nnnnot me," he said sternly. "You huh- huh- have ffffriends there, Amichai, huh- hiding in the ruins. They have fuh- firepower aplenty, but lack knnnnowledge! If there's a weakness in Wickliffe's factories, it lies- *lies!*- lies within Duh- Doctor Hsiang's brains. Shuh- she headed up the project. Shuh- she's the k- key to our victory. If she dies, then Wwwwwickliffe wins."

"You're not Wickliffe?"

"Not these days." He winked out – literally *winked* out, squinting one eye before the screen flickered into blackness.

The monorail shook, picking up speed. I grabbed at the walls for support; I'd never moved faster than a pony ride before. I couldn't even see New York; we must have left the city behind.

I thumbed the "door open" button and clambered out onto the narrow platform between cars, watching the ground shoot by beneath my feet. One slip, and I'd die forever.

I hauled myself into the next car with gratitude; it was another medical car, the floor clotted with blood.

Dr Hsiang lay on a cot. Dare had done a number on her after she'd shot Peaches; her nose had been mashed into her eyes, her features stitched together with black thread. Worse, her chest bulged in ugly ways; she must have been hurled through the window when the plane crashed.

She breathed thanks to mechanical help, but her wax-white skin told me she hadn't long to live.

I heard a clack, and looked down:

Dare was unplugging Dr Hsiang's life support machines.

"*Dare!*" I yanked him back. He wriggled in my grasp.

"Dare, you can't kill her. We need Dr Hsiang alive!"

"I know that." He looked wounded. "I'm moving her to the front of the monorail. That crazy Wickliffe-thing told me to move Peaches first, but I... I couldn't bear to look at her..."

The relief was so sudden, it stole my breath. "So Peaches is...?"

"Alive. But she's in bad shape." He knelt again, meticulously disconnecting Dr Hsiang's rebreathers before plugging them into a battery – something I'd have noticed if I'd taken the time to look.

"...Dare, I am *so sorry.*"

"Peaches keeps making choices to bail you out," Dare whispered. "I think you should take a good look at what those choices do, Amichai."

I fled to the next car. I should have stayed with Dare and talked it through, explaining how I didn't mean to hurt anyone...

Yet when I saw Dare, helping save the woman who'd shot his sister, I realized Dare knew a lot more about sacrifice than I did.

I made my way into the next car, and saw Peaches.

26: SOARING TOWARDS STURDIER HEAVENS

Watching Peaches' cut-up body breathe was somehow worse than a corpse's stillness. I held my own breath each time her chest rose, her lungs assisted by the ventilator. She was barely taking in oxygen; the last of her life could slip out at any moment.

Peaches had always worn short shirts tied tight under her breasts to show off her flat belly. That kissable stomach was now carved full of flaps, tubes, and wires. They'd strapped her to a metal backbrace; I could see the incisions curving back to where they'd operated on her spine.

I didn't cry. Grief felt like the worst of indulgences. Instead, I knelt by her bed and started figuring out how to unhook the machines.

The far door hissed open.

Evangeline walked in, dressed in the same skimpy medical gown we all wore.

She jerked to a stop at the sight of Peaches, rattled. Which struck me as weird: she believed in an all-powerful skybeard who Shrived everyone up to Heaven. Blood sure as void hadn't bothered her when she'd seen her dead friends back at the branch server. Why would this surgical recovery room get to her?

Evangeline unhooked a briefcase-sized battery from the

wall. "I'm told this is the spare power. I'm unfamiliar with the rest of the technology."

"It's got diagrams. We can figure this out." Of course, if I got it wrong then Peaches would die on the spot, but hey...

"Good." Evangeline rose, squeezed her hands together, then headed for the doorway.

"Hey! A little help here?"

Her hand hesitated at the door switch, then she clutched her fists and nodded. "Of course." She untangled the wires, crouching hip-by-hip with me as we leaned in to examine the connecting cables, keeping her eyes averted from Peaches.

"I'll help get... Peaches... ready for transport," she said. "Then I must go."

"Like, *go* go?"

"One should walk not in the counsel of the wicked, and you're... a sinful people. Though I'm... I had hoped to help you repent." She shook her head; a lock of red hair dropped across a blushing cheek.

"Where will you go? I mean, your parents, they're..."

"Dead," Evangeline finished. "As is my clan. I must admit, Amichai, I don't have good options. I've heard rumors of NeoChristian enclaves in the Appalachians. I could try to make my way back to them, I suppose, but they're hard to track down – and even if I found them, they might not welcome me." She drew in a breath through her nose, steeling herself. "I've made do with worse."

"So stay." I grabbed her. "We need all the help we can get."

"*No*, Amichai!" She slapped me away – then sighed. "It's not... I'm honored, Amichai. You have a great heart for an unbeliever. But..." She glanced at Peaches, tormented. "You love her."

"What?"

Her green eyes went wide. "I never would have kissed you if I'd known you had a lover, Amichai. *Intent* was sin enough. I shouldn't have–"

"...Amichai?"

Peaches gurgled around the plastic tube in her throat. I leapt to my feet to comfort Peaches, trying to ignore Evangeline's stricken look.

"It's OK, Peaches." I tried to sound confident. "We're getting you to safety."

She clutched my hand, her grip even weaker than Izzy's. "Did we... did we get the word out?"

"...now's not the time to talk about that..."

"No." Peaches struggled to get up, arms flailing; her legs remained motionless. "The living are depending on us..."

"We have to get you somewhere safe."

"*No.*" Even in an anesthetic daze, Peaches' will was strong as titanium. "We have to *stop Wickliffe.*"

The monorail jerked to a stop.

"What's happening?" Peaches tugged the intubator out. The monitors on the wall flickered on, showing the monocled Wickliffe, dressed in a conductor's uniform.

"Luh-luh-last stop!" he cried. "Yyyyyour ride has arrived. Tuh-tuh-to the front of the monorail, children!"

Dare pushed Dr Hsiang's bed in, and the three of us pushed the beds up into a cargo railcar.

A high wind poured through the wide door on the railcar's side, where the ponies would normally be led up to unload whatever cargo the monorails had delivered. Except we hadn't stopped at a platform; the monorail had halted between stations, motionless yards above the forest floor.

A spirocopter, festooned with crudely painted crosses, hovered outside the cargo door. Its jets kicked up a miniature hurricane as automated computer controls kept it locked into position next to the entryway.

A group of sour-looking women wearing long woolen shirts loaded crates into the copter's holding bay. Their shirts flapped madly in the copter's breeze. They had machine guns slung over their backs, glaring balefully at us with the hard look of women ready to kill – which made sense when I saw the blue marks of inked crosses tattooed across their necks and foreheads.

"*NeoChristians?*" Dare spluttered.

"Yyyyyou're luh-lucky you kids led a rescue effort to suh-save them at the buh-branch server," the Wickliffe-conductor said. "Uh-uh-otherwise they'd have let you rot."

"NeoChristians have spirocopters?" Peaches asked.

"You think we ride horses?" Evangeline stood straighter in her brethren's presence. "We use computers, weapons, programs – same as you. The difference is, we don't pretend programs are people." She thumped her cross tattoo. "And we don't *worship* them."

"No one worships Wickliffe," Dare shot back.

"No. You just elect a piece of *code* to serve as your leader."

Dare spat out an argument – but the NeoChristians ignored him, wheeled Peaches and Dr Hsiang up a ramp into the spirocopter's belly, then shoved the rest of us in at gunpoint. The copter was covered in a shifting camouflage green, the sides blurring with color as its illusion-engines mirrored the treetops below.

The copter eased back a bit once we were all on board, putting some distance between itself and the railway as its pilot waited for orders.

"Burn it," a leathery, white-haired woman said.

"Huh-huh-hey!" Wickliffe spoke from a computer tablet, urging Dare to lift the screen into view. "There's no nuh-need to duh-*destroy* the monorail… tuh-technology is guh-getting harder to replace…"

"Need? No." The old woman grinned; each of her yellowed teeth had tiny crosses engraved into the surface, like scrimshaw. "Still. Explosions bring us closer to God."

The NeoChristians whooped as the spirocopter lurched away, arcing up over the vast forest. Someone offered the old woman a red button; she stabbed it gleefully. The monorail detonated in a thunderclap, the long curve of the rail collapsing, the burning cars tumbling down.

"Explosions also remove evidence," the old woman said. "They discourage pursuit. All sorts of benefits in explosions, really."

"Thuh-that was *gratuitous!*" Wickliffe said. Dare looked miserable, blindly pushing Wickliffe's tablet towards the NeoChristians. "Thuh-they wouldn't have fuh-found you! Ah-ah-I'm *shielding* you! Thuh-that's why I got you the spirocopter!"

"The program expects *gratitude?*" The old woman snatched the tablet away.

"I eh-eh-expect you to act ruh-*rationally!* Thuh-thuh-that explosion almost damaged the copter! Huh-how will you bring our mutual friends to Boston in-*in!*-in a downed ship?"

The old woman tapped her etched teeth contemplatively with the tablet. "Ah. Then you will really not like what I have to tell you next."

"Wwwhat's that?"

"We don't obey machines who pretend to be people."

She Frisbeed the tablet out the door. It tumbled forwards the fir trees hundreds of feet below.

"*No!*" I yelled. "That – Wickliffe – thing – is right! We need to get Dr Hsiang to Boston! We need–"

My words dried in my throat as the NeoChristians leaned in to listen to me. I wore nothing but a flapping gown over my scrawny ass. They could fling me out the door after the tablet, and there was nothing I could do to stop them.

The old woman pulled my gown aside to press her fingertips to my throat, touching the bare flesh where every NeoChristian got their first cross tattoo.

"We must discover what your soul is made of," she whispered. "Everything else can wait."

27: BOUND BY RELIGION AND LUST

As prisons go, the NeoChristian enclave was top notch. They didn't lock us in a room; they let us wander in the woods around their compound.

Hey, if the city kids wanted to run into the forest and die of exposure, they'd let us.

I wanted to kidnap Dr Hsiang to Boston. Boston was a slim lead – a rumor, given to me by a possibly insane program that wore Wickliffe's face – but if there was someone who could stop this "brainwash the living" plan, we needed to get Dr Hsiang there soon before she breathed her last.

The NeoChristians seemed to understand our urgency, meeting it with kindness. The compound was more like a caravan than a permanent outpost. Each of the fifteen NeoChristian families had their own transport methods – mostly stolen spirocopters and hovercrafts, but a few had offroad dirtbikes. They'd built a temporary city in the forest, convening so their pastors could determine how best to judge Peaches, Dare, and me.

The compound bustled with activity, everyone pitching in to help. They'd strung camo net over the trees so the satellites wouldn't spot them. Nobody rested from sunup to nightfall; people tended the fires, tuned spirocopters, taught krav maga classes, cleaned carcasses, gave lessons in stitching wounds.

And guns, guns galore – people fieldstripping them,

testfiring them into targets, picking off squirrels, debating the merits of various models.

But more importantly, there were rehabilitation lessons. Lots of the NeoChristians were missing limbs, had been half-blinded by shrapnel; a few pushed themselves around in wheelchairs. The sight was baffling. You didn't see injured people in New York, mainly because any wound that affected your productivity gave you a free ticket to the Upterlife. But here, the injured sought out the injured – trading coping techniques, building elaborate mechanisms to help them get around better, consoling and strengthening.

All the while, drones buzzed by overhead, sweeping the woods – but we had a million trees to hide under.

A small group held vigil outside the medical tent they'd built for Dr Hsiang and Peaches, where NeoChristian physicians tried to repair the damage to Peaches' spine.

The NeoChristians cried to the Lord to save these sinners, taking shifts to pray.

I remembered the New York doctor treating Izzy with all the compassion a mechanic showed a stuck valve. Why bother treating her pain? She'd be OK when she died, so who cared?

Whereas for the NeoChristians, crazy as they were, there was something at *stake* here. If Peaches died, she'd go to Hell.

These were the same NeoChristians who wanted to kill everyone in the Upterlife.

I pondered that, and my head spun; the NeoChristians could kill a man one moment and weep for him the next, and void knew how to judge someone like that.

Maybe they were evil when they hurt you and good when they helped you. Yet that felt too relative. Because Wickliffe, with all his angst, seemed to feel he was doing the right thing, too. And here *I* was, standing among people who'd had no problems planting bombs to kill people like me, and if there was a clear morality to any of this then I was lost as surely as if I'd walked out into those deep woods.

I needed to get away.

Dare dozed on the other side of the surgical tent. The portable operating room was just wide enough for two doctors to work on a single patient. The tent's whoosh of filtered air sounded like lungs. If you tuned out the prayer susurrations, you could make out surgeons muttering their strategies to fix Peaches' spine.

If anyone could, it was the NeoChristians. Always on the run, they had no time for leisurely recuperations. It was rumored the NeoChristians had miracle techniques to get people up and walking in days.

Still. Surgery was dangerous. Germs had evolved past most of our antibiotics. More people died from postsurgical infection than the actual surgery. Dead doctors hadn't bothered to devise new antibacterials; why waste technology on the living?

If Peaches died, she wouldn't get uploaded.

I couldn't quite comprehend that... and neither could Dare.

"Hey," I said to him.

Dare groaned and leaned back against the tent, as if dealing with me was just one more burden to manage.

I held up my palms in surrender. "I'll leave you alone if you want. I didn't want you to... to think I didn't want to be here."

He scrubbed his forehead with the back of his arm. "...void it, Amichai. You really screwed up."

I thought of all the NeoChristians suffering in Wickliffe's laboratories, all the living who'd be brainwashed. "...I don't know that I *did* screw up. This is... it's bigger than any of us."

"Maybe you didn't." He glanced at his feet. "But she's a big price to pay to save the world, you know?"

"I do."

"I'm not selfish, Amichai. We have to stop Wickliffe. But…
you lied to me."

"So did Peaches."

"She's family."

Two painful words dismissed years of friendship as neatly
as an amputation.

"So what are we?"

"Stuck. I could have been at home, Shriving, blissfully
ignorant. Instead, I'm sacrificing the people I love to do the
right thing – and I probably *would* have done that, but I never
had a choice *not* to. I gotta resent you for that. I have to."

"So should I… should I ask the NeoChristians to separate
us?"

"It's too important not to be allies," Dare sighed. "But if I
look at you too much now, I might punch you."

I was crazy-concerned about Peaches. But so was Dare.
The least I could do was to let his vigil take priority.

I shuffled away. He called after me. "Hey."

"What?"

"You get points for giving me space." Dare shook his head.
"Not a lot. But a few."

I didn't want to be surrounded by NeoChristians, so I walked
off. I'd seen pictures of forests, but nobody'd mentioned the
uneven ground or how slippery dead leaves could be or how
bugs buzzed in your face. The NeoChristians had dressed me
in a woolen robe; it caught on every branch.

I sat on a rotted log, perched next to a ditch of burbling
water. The birds sang bird songs for no good reason.

I wanted to run into the woods, let the trees swallow me
up.

"You look a little goggle-eyed, city boy." I jumped; I hadn't
heard Evangeline approach. I almost told her to leave me
alone – until I saw how she shivered with trepidation.

"All this green's a little shocking," I replied. "I thought the whole world was like New York."

She smirked. "Every New Yorker does."

She sat next to me. Suddenly I was ravenous for her touch. I could see from the careful way she sat on the log, putting a calculated space between our hips, that she wanted me, too.

That goddamned kiss. That one kiss back at the branch server told us how good more kisses would feel, how perfect her palms would feel on the small of my back, and all that felt like a betrayal when Peaches' life still hung in the balance.

Evangeline kicked rocks into the creek. I wanted to ask her if she'd ever kissed anyone before. I didn't think she had. That would explain her nervousness; to a virgin mercenary, kisses were scarier than gunfire. But asking would lead to a line of questioning that would do us no good.

"I don't know how to do this," I sighed.

"Do what?"

"Stop Wickliffe. He's got literally all the power in the world..."

"A man once took down the largest empire the world had ever seen just by saying the right words." She flattened her hand against the cross tattoo between her breasts, and I realized she was discussing her skybeard. "It's not about strength, Amichai. It's about philosophy. Wake up enough people, and you'll win."

"But didn't..." I struggled to remember her skybeard's name. "Didn't Christ end badly?"

"We all end badly, Amichai. That's why there's a Heaven."

It made me uncomfortable, the way every conversation with Evangeline spiraled back to her belief.

"So what comes next?" I asked. "The pastors talk among themselves, and... do they call us in for questioning?"

Evangeline shrugged. "I have no idea. They're not my elders."

"They're not your people?"

She grimaced. "I had my sect, they have theirs; we only talk during emergencies. Frankly, this is the largest NeoChristian gathering I can remember. You must be important."

I whistled. "You guys talk more to God than you do each other."

Evangeline saw my distaste and gave me a sad, knowing grin.

"We *can't* be close, Amichai. When Wickliffe captures one of us, he copies our brains and knows everything we do. So we trade goods, share tactics, but in an age of persecution we don't share information that could betray us. You confide in God, your parents, and your husband, in that order... and no one else. We usually get married at thirteen just to have someone to talk to."

I did a doubletake. "Wait. You should have been married – what, four years ago?"

That shy smile again. "I figured I'd be a warrior for Christ. A machine-gun nun. By the time I was old enough to desire... company... everyone else had married."

Void, no wonder she trembled. When Evangeline had stabbed her parents, she'd killed the last people she could talk to.

I wanted to kiss her for confiding in me.

That felt slimy, wanting to make out with Evangeline while Peaches fought for her life, but that was death for you: when it brushed against you, you burned to touch life. It's why Peaches had kissed me in the pigeon room and why Evangeline had kissed me in the branch server and it's why I wanted to kiss Evangeline now.

One kiss could erase our fears.

I didn't move. Which felt unfair. Peaches made out scandalously with whoever she pleased, and always returned to me like nothing had happened.

Why couldn't I kiss a girl?

But kissing meant nothing to Peaches. Kissing Evangeline would have been a promise that I'd be there for her – and I wanted to make that promise, because this lonely girl deserved someone to confide in. Yet part of my heart would always be with Peaches, and I didn't think "sharing" was much on Evangeline's agenda.

Evangeline's green eyes told me everything we both wanted, and couldn't have.

So we trembled, our fingers close to each other, watching the water churn. Feeling the beat of all we left unsaid.

Refusing to look away.

28: OUTSIDE THE OPERATING ROOM

Evangeline and I spent hours in the woods not kissing, waiting for the pastors to call us in. Eventually we attended training classes to stave off the inevitable makeout sessions.

Evangeline told me cross-training was the traditional NeoChristian way of socializing. At first I thought she meant they, like, lifted crosses – but she actually meant that NeoChristians learned as many skills as they could.

So they taught me their songs, which were beautiful as long as I ignored all the references to their Big Skybeard. They taught me how to weave a proper camouflage net so I wouldn't show up on infrared scans.

They tried to teach me hand-to-hand combat, at least until I got knocked out by a ten year-old. And I threw up when they put a gun in my hand; too many memories of bullets punching through Peaches' spine.

I didn't stop. I craved distraction. My thoughts kept returning to Gumdrool, in that factory in Lacuna Springs, overseeing the manufacture of brainwashing machines. My thoughts kept returning to Izzy – what had they told her about me? Did she know I was alive? Was Gumdrool interrogating her right now?

I pushed the thoughts away by learning how to skin rabbits.

The NeoChristians never asked how I felt. They never asked how I knew the girl in the tent. They never asked what I did

in the woods with Evangeline. They prayed instead of talking.
It seemed bleak.

Dare slept outside Peaches' tent. Dr Hsiang had her own
tent, where concerned NeoChristian paramedics rushed in,
carrying donated blood.

Which meant Evangeline and I slept alone.

She cried when she slept. Her fingers flexed and clutched,
flexed and clutched, as she dreamed endlessly of stabbing her
parents.

After the third night, I couldn't watch her any more. I crept
over to stroke her hair.

She headbutted my face.

"…Amichai?"

Of *course* a tightly-wound fighter would react badly to an
unexpected touch.

"I was just–" I wiped blood from my nose, "– trying to
comfort you–"

"Jesus' courage." She swept me up in an embrace. "Will I
hurt *everything* I love?"

Love? I thought – but then the tent door was pulled open by
the old woman with the engraved teeth. She cocked an eyebrow
at my bleeding nose – but in what I'd come to realize was the
NeoChristian style, she refused to investigate the matter.

"The last pastor has arrived," she told us. "Let's show your
merit, boy."

The pastor – her name was Mara – led us through the woods
to a large clearing, where NeoChristian guards patrolled the
edges with RPGs. Thirty elders spread out across the woods in
a semicircle, facing inwards – though not all the elders were
old. A few of the younger elders sat in tanklike wheelchairs,
their mangled limbs proof of the lessons they'd learned. Their
tattooed faces, lit by a bonfire, each had the haggard look of
knowing a single bad decision could doom your family.

Mara led me into the center of an impromptu stage.

Two guards stopped Evangeline, looking at her with disdain; she acquiesced with slumped shoulders. The other NeoChristians sniffed, ignoring her pointedly.

I felt the trickle of blood dribbling from my nose, my dirty robe, my uncombed hair. As the NeoChristians peered in to examine me, I realized how mad I looked.

Mara had purposely stacked the deck against me.

One on one, that might have intimidated me – but I was born to perform for audiences.

"So this is the boy who's inspired riots in New York City," said a massive man, his biceps engraved with images of a bearded Christ. *Riots?* I wondered. "He looked bigger in the videos."

"His *heart* is large," a Mexican woman retorted. "This boy rescued us from Wickliffe. You place too much emphasis on physical strength."

"Willpower alone won't stop Wickliffe's troops."

"*Pastors*," Mara declared. "You've seen this boy's videos. You've heard the fate of the heretics. Does anyone question the severity of the threat?"

Crucifix necklaces rattled as everyone shook their heads.

"So my videos got out?" I asked. "Did they go nationwide?"

"The videos themselves have become contraband, carried on encrypted hard drives. The unbelievers are asking questions."

"That's good, isn't it?"

"What's good for unbelievers is rarely good for us." A murmur of assent. "We want to know why Wickliffe summoned us to help you, when you are Wickliffe's enemy."

I'd wondered that myself. Fortunately, I'd had time to piece together a theory. "Wickliffe didn't summon you."

"Then who did?"

"Wick*cleft*."

The mobile elders rose to their feet, demanding

explanations. Mara gave me a disgusted glare. "We are not a game show, Amichai. You will provide full explanations without the drama."

"Stick me in front of a crowd, and I'm a drama-generating machine," I replied. "And I know because Wickliffe himself implied it back at the branch server. *I could split my consciousness off*, he'd said. Which meant that at one point, he *had* copied himself – which makes sense. As president, if you had the ability to create multiple copies of yourself to investigate problems, why wouldn't you? Who would you trust more than yourself?"

"A soul cannot be *copied*." Mara's lips wrinkled in disgust.

"A program can. Whatever you think Wickliffe is now, he designed the Upterlife. He'd be able to make infinite copies of himself. But he *didn't* do that to aid his brain-altering project… Which implies copying yourself has its downsides."

"And you think…"

"One of Wickliffe's copies went renegade."

The elders nodded. Good. I had to convince them to get Dr Hsiang to Boston soon.

"A man is the sum of his decisions," I continued. "And *this* Wickliffe copy, separated from the Wickliffe we know and loathe, experienced different things. He got out of sync with his main personality, started fighting himself. That's Wickcleft – a *literal* ghost in the machine. He's got all of Wickliffe-prime's knowledge – and he's *on our side*."

I rocked back on my heels and waited for the applause.

Instead, the NeoChristians looked troubled.

"So the same program that thought us little more than cattle is now helping us?" Mara asked.

"N… no!" I protested. "It's a *different* man – a different program! A program repelled by Wickliffe's beliefs!"

"That doesn't mean it's on 'our side.'" The pastors grunted assent. "It means this Wickcleft construct will take risks to help *you*, Amichai. Yet this program contains a logic that, in one circumstance, calculated NeoChristian lives were worth experimenting on. Who's to say it will not do so again?"

"*I* say!" I countered. "I think what drove Wickcleft to rebellion is the way Wickliffe hurt your people!"

"The Wickliffe program has been executing us for centuries."

"And the Wickcleft has to be at *least* that old! Copying yourself would be one of the first things *I'd* have tried."

"But you do not know."

"Neither do you!"

"What we *do* know is the Wickcleft construct has already demonstrated a potential for betrayal. *This* is who you ask us to ally with? We do not find your words reassuring."

"They don't *have* to be reassuring!" I shot back. "Wickliffe is planning to *rewrite* you. Next time he captures one of you, he won't just know your plans – he'll send you back as a saboteur! If he gets his way, Wickliffe will *wipe the faith from your brains*. So how picky do you want to be about your allies?"

The response from the crowd was more mixed. Mara looked around uncomfortably, losing a fight she'd expected to win handily.

"Look," I told them. "You took Wickcleft's spirocopter. How do you know that's not filled with spyware?"

Mara snorted. "We had our best people scan it from jets to OS."

"Then that's what you do with Wickcleft!" My exasperation played well with the NeoChristian audience; their prayers were loud, their faith was loud.

I paced circles around the bonfire. "I'm not saying to trust him; *I* don't trust him. If he is what we think he is, then he – it – is a greater gift than any spirocopter. Use it. Use it *carefully*. Because we can't afford to turn down any weapon to fight Wickliffe."

Shouts of approval. A handful of NeoChristians thrust their fists in the air.

"So we should investigate our potential allies, should we?" Mara asked.

I sensed the danger in her question, but didn't have a way around it. "Yes."

"My brethren in Christ." Mara stepped before me, taking center stage. "I know how frustrating it has been, sneaking and skulking, feeling as though this tribulation would never end. Yes, this scrawny wastrel has done more to wound Wickliffe than generations of our work. I understand why you'd want to follow him into battle."

...*battle?* I thought.

"But scrape the surface, and you'll find another sinner."

The pastors grumbled... but heard her out.

Mara knelt before me. "Do you believe in our cause, Amichai?"

"I believe in overthrowing the ghosts."

"You know that's not the same thing."

"Would that distinction have mattered if I'd died trying to save your people from Wickliffe?"

"It's quite noble that you're willing to sacrifice yourself, Amichai," she admitted. "But you didn't, did you? Who died getting the word out?"

"... your people."

"You're good at getting people to sacrifice themselves for you, Amichai. You give people certainty where there is doubt. Yet you only have certainty because you haven't thought this through."

"That's not true. I vowed to bring that bastard down when I saw *your people* in chains."

"I'm sure you did. But your error, Amichai, is thinking the programs are human. Even as simulations, their circumstances don't reflect mortal concerns. They don't eat. They don't sleep. They don't *require* anything. They are designed to be inhuman."

I thought of Mom and Dad, leaving Izzy and me to struggle while they played games. "Don't be ridiculous. They have our brain patterns. Even if they're not ensouled – whatever that is – they *act* like people."

"Like people who share none of our concerns. You believe that if you alerted them to the danger, these programs would call a halt to Wickliffe's reign. But no. At first they'd pretend to be horrified... and then they'd accept the cost."

"That's not true. They're people. With *consciences*."

The pastors growled; what I'd said was clearly not a popular argument among the NeoChristians. "Do they, Amichai? We've seen how willing they are to kill us."

"That's because you *bomb* them!"

"We bomb programs, Amichai. We've taken great pains to avoid killing the living."

I winced, thinking of how easily they would have shot Izzy if she'd ever graduated from the Academy. "I guess the LifeGuard aren't human?"

"They are tragic zealots. They favor suicidal maneuvers, seeking self-immolating glory. No, we've always aimed our weapons at the servers... And for that, we've been slaughtered. The programs *will* move to defend themselves. If the living riot, and the programs' only hope for survival is brainwashing the living into compliance, then what conclusion do you think they will reach?"

"They won't... The ghosts, they... they used to *be* us!"

"Whatever they were, they are parasites now."

"No. There must be another way."

"There *is* no other way, Amichai. The Upterlife schema are spread across the globe, redundant, backed up a thousand times over. Our only choice is to destroy the Upterlife. *That's* why the heretics died for you. They'd hoped you'd guide your people to tear down this monstrosity!"

"That would kill the dead too. I can't allow that."

"So you'll let our people die for you?"

"Yes – no! There are people *in* those servers. We can reason with them–"

"And if you can't?"

I slumped. "…The living. I'd side with the living."

Mara arched her eyebrow. "And your sister?"

"What *about* Izzy?"

"She'll die, too, if this goes the way it must. You're good at getting others to sacrifice themselves – our people, the Korean girl, the rioters in New York. You'll even sacrifice yourself. But can you condemn your sister to the void?"

"That's not fair! You're making an–"

Mara pulled herself up to her full height. "If it comes down to you or the world, will you let Izzy die?"

"I don't know! I can't–"

"You see?" Mara whirled to face the pastors, who stood grim-faced, a jury ready to convict. "He lacks faith! And without faith, he lacks the conviction to lead the battle to tear down this false Heaven. Oh, my brethren, he claims he'll lead you into battle… yet when the time comes, *this boy will fail you.*"

"*Bullshit!*" A voice rang loud and pristine from the other side of the clearing.

Peaches.

Mara flinched. Dare, puffing, pushed Peaches' wheelchair down the path to the gathering.

But Peaches didn't look like a girl in a wheelchair; she looked like a queen on a throne.

"A fine appeal to terrible emotions." Peaches crossed her arms. "Now let me make you the counterproposal."

29: PEACHES ON THE PODIUM

"Here's what I think you need to do." Peaches gestured for poor, sweating Dare to push her closer to the pastors. "Forget Amichai. You already know Wickliffe plans to manufacture mindslavers in Lacuna Springs. *I* think you need to capture that technology, then reprogram the living."

"To do what?" Mara asked.

"To make everyone in the world NeoChristian."

The crowd spluttered. Guards moved in, then paused, unwilling to haul off a postoperative patient in a wheelchair. She'd counted on that, I was sure.

"You've got Dr Hsiang's knowledge right here!" Peaches shouted, her voice ragged. "With a little research, you could rewrite every living mind to worship God in the purest fashion!"

The pastors stepped forward, furious. Mara held them back.

"Brainwashing," Mara replied loftily, "is not faith. Faith comes from *choice*."

"Really?" Peaches raised an eyebrow. "Then what choices have you given Amichai?"

"What?"

"This meeting's not about whether you should fight Wickliffe – you know you have to. That's why you gathered here. This meeting is all about whether you can trust Amichai."

She slapped her immobile legs. "Well, *I* trusted him. Because he's too noble to compromise and too stupid to lie. That's the kind of man you'd better protect, because he'll get his ass killed.

"For years, Amichai's been told that the servers are heaven and you NeoChristians are the devil – and despite that, he risked his life to save Evangeline, refused to kill the crazies in the warrens, and *went back* to free your prisoners.

"Amichai has done nothing but good for your people, more good than I would have done... and you're rejecting him because he's not willing to burn it all down *four days* after he's discovered the downside to the Upterlife?"

The pastors glanced away, shamed. Mara looked furious, but stayed silent; Peaches had outplayed her.

"If Amichai is not a good person..." Peaches bit her lip to stop the hitch in her voice. "Then no one is. And you might as well break into Lacuna Springs. Because if all it takes for you to write someone off is for them to *doubt* you, well... you're *gonna* have to brainwash everyone."

She slumped forward in her chair. I knew Peaches well enough to know a mic drop when I saw one. Applause erupted.

Peaches made a subtle gesture; Dare pushed her back to the settlement. A small crowd of pastors followed, offering to help Peaches.

Though I couldn't see her face, I knew Peaches was smiling.

30: WHAT GROWS FROM THE KILLING FIELDS

Dare had wedged his arms into the canvas straps attached to the spirocopter's loading bay wall. He looked like a drooling marionette as he tried to catch some sleep on the way to Boston; his legs flopped as the copter bounced through the crosswinds.

The NeoChristian family who'd offered us a ride in their spirocopter gave him admiring glances. He'd refused to sleep until Peaches got safely loaded.

Dare napped, unconscious – but he was in the same copter with me. Progress.

I sat wedged between Dr Hsiang and Peaches, wrinkling my nose at the stench of pus rising from Hsiang's body. She lolled on a portable surgical table, muttering in delirium. The veins on her chest had swollen dark black; postsurgical infection had taken root.

Even in a morphine-induced sleep, she looked terrified. Each breath edged her closer to meat-death. And though she'd tried to kill me, I couldn't wish the void upon anyone.

And then there was Peaches...

"Amichai." Peaches' voice brought tears to my eyes. "Amichai, look at me."

"I can't–"

She grabbed my chin, forcing me to look at her in her wheelchair. Her legs were strapped, motionless, into the footrests.

How could she be smiling?

"I'll never walk again, Amichai." Her words were gentle as a hug. "I'm a paraplegic."

"Don't say that! These NeoChristians are, they're… they're battlefield doctors. Back in New York, there's–"

"Zero interest," Peaches finished. "They hadn't figured out how to regrow nerves by the time Wickliffe invented the Upterlife, and nobody was much interested after that."

"We'll find a way–"

"We'll find a way to bring down Wickliffe, stop the dead from using the mindslavers, bring joy back to the living – and then, if we have time, maybe we fix my legs."

I scrubbed my face, my cheeks raw. "How can you be so *cavalier* about this?"

"Because I made the decision." She moved the treads on her chair experimentally, wincing from her wounds. "I thought I'd die forever when I got shot. I get to keep breathing. Losing my legs is a small price to pay."

"…I don't know if I could be grateful for that."

Peaches shook her head. "You don't understand, Amichai. Neither does Dare. But… when I looked down that gun barrel, it answered a question I'd wondered my whole life: if it came down to it, did I *really* believe in the cause? I talked big, but… I was a spoiled rich kid. Maybe my relatives were right. Maybe everyone toes the line." She chuckled. "I didn't."

"And now you'll never toe anything again."

"My scars are life." Peaches pulled up a woolen sleeve to reveal her puckered, tongue-red Bubbler scars. "They remind me how fragile my body is. They remind me to get shit done before everything breaks down."

"So you're… driven?"

"I've got maybe sixty years left. When Hsiang trained the gun on me, I had six seconds." She sagged back in the chair, a cryptic smile blossoming across her face. "I made each one count."

"You just seem so... at peace with all of this."

She gripped her thighs hard enough to leave marks. "Oh, I'm angry. Angrier than you could ever imagine. But my anger runs cold, Amichai. Every day I give into despair is a day I'm not making Wickliffe pay for his sins." Her face darkened. "And I'm going to shut down his server personally."

"I get that." I looked back towards Dare's sleeping form, jiggling in the canvas. "Now can you explain that to him?"

She looked away, exasperated. "Dare's always run from his problems."

"Dare's no coward."

"He won't run from *my* problems. He's loyal." Peaches pulled up her robe to slap her stitches, trying to stop the fresh itching without breaking open the wounds. "He's changed both my bandages and my bedpans. It's not easy for him to look at my sutures, but he does it. For all his specialized bravery, though... he's not a risk taker. He can't understand that I chose to sacrifice myself for a cause; to him, everything that happened in Little Venice was you, thrusting me into danger...

"And speaking of thrusting," she said, muffling a giggle, "It doesn't help that he's seen how hot you are for that Evangeline girl."

I jerked as though she'd kicked me. She winked, happy to have the drop on me.

"...I'm not trying to hide her from you..."

"*That's* obvious. You two sneaking into the woods, her looking after you with those big green puppydog eyes... She flinches like I've whipped her every time I make eye contact. Have you kissed her?"

"Of course not!"

"Oh, Amichai." She patted my hand. "Why hold back? Me? You know I'll dance with anyone." She frowned down at her wheelchair. "Well... maybe not now. But this won't stop me from flirting. And I'm no hypocrite. So have fun."

Peaches telling me to go kiss Evangeline mixed me up. I wanted to kiss Evangeline, but I wanted to kiss Peaches, too.

"...I don't know if Evangeline's a good girl to 'have fun' with."

"Nonsense." Peaches swatted my objections away like mosquitoes. "It's all in the setup. Just make it clear you'll only kiss her on the dance floor, metaphorically speaking. I made out with tons of boys at the Blackout Parties."

"Yeah, but you're special."

She leaned in closer. She smelled of blood and disinfectant. Yet a hint of that musky Peaches scent wafted up from below – a promise Peaches would be all right again.

"Don't talk to me about special," she purred. "Do you know how many boys I brought up to the rooftop to kiss, alone, by the sunset?"

"...no."

"One."

She glanced over at Dare to make sure he was still asleep, then pulled me down into a long, slow kiss.

We could have kissed forever... until we heard NeoChristians laughing at us. Peaches pulled away reluctantly, staring out the windshield towards Boston.

"We have a long fight ahead, Amichai. But when it's all over... I'll be waiting for you, on that rooftop."

We held hands, feeling an uncertain future rush towards us. The spirocopter banked in a wide arc towards another endless forest.

The pilot leaned back, smirking – it was Ximena, the Mexican woman who'd stood up for me at yesterday's pastor meeting. She steered her copter the same way she led her family: confidently moving forwards, never looking back.

"Wouldn't believe it from the newscasts, would you?" she asked.

I started to say I didn't know what "it" was when I realized that forest was Boston.

The only signs the woods below had once been one of America's greatest cities were the humped dinosaur-like skeletons of collapsed skyscrapers in the trees. Clusters of pines had erupted through the organic girders in contorted boughs, fusing into beautiful wood-and-bone sculptures. Flocks of birds chased each other through the mazes.

"How did the skyscrapers fall?" I asked. "Little Venice is a nightmare of growing coral. Why…"

"They stopped seeding the clouds here," Dare said, leaning out of the copter to admire the beauty. "The skyscrapers starved. Nature took over."

"God reclaims everything," Ximena said serenely. Her family caressed their tattoos for emphasis.

"But Boston…" I stammered. "They *razed* it. They seeded the clouds with herbicides so the rebels couldn't grow food…"

"That was fifty years ago," Ximena chuckled. "A short time for a computer program, a long time for nature. They show you bloodsoaked footage taken hours after the Culling so you won't investigate. But give a city fifty summers of growth, and…"

"It's beautiful," Peaches said.

Dr Hsiang gripped my shoulder. "…I killed you, didn't I?"

"Can someone put this bitch down?" Peaches asked.

"Give her any more painkillers and we risk killing her," Ximena's son Facundo said. "The poor woman's body is reaching her end."

"Isn't she your enemy?"

"Perhaps. But it stains the soul to *rejoice* at damning someone."

I tried to process that mixture of kindness and superstition. Hsiang grabbed me like she was drowning.

"I didn't mean to kill you!" she cried. "You got in the way, that's all. Mr Wickliffe would have killed us all..."

"Yes, yes, that's fine," I said, too weirded to answer properly.

"He's *got* to forgive me. He has to let me Shriiiiive..."

She sobbed, moaning how she didn't want to die, how she had to get to the Upterlife, how she'd been promised paradise...

I pushed her away. I wanted her to be dignified in her last hours – but her muddled confusion reminded me that I was a leaking sack of chemicals, one injury away from raving incoherency.

"Step away from the bitch, Amichai," Peaches said. "If she dies, she dies."

"If she dies, we lose our last edge on Wickliffe."

"Why do you think I haven't stabbed her?" Peaches snorted, looking at Hsiang with disdain. Hsiang's delirium made me want to lecture Peaches that not even our worst enemies deserved meat-death... but Hsiang *was* our worst enemy, and Peaches thought otherwise.

"Prep for landing." Ximena dipped the copter down. The suburbs around Boston had been taken over by federal troops when the Culling had started, then abandoned afterwards when people didn't want to live near a graveyard half a million deep.

"Shouldn't there be garrisons?" Dare asked, pointing down at some overgrown troop bases. "To shoot looters?"

"There were." Ximena deftly threaded the copter into a grove of trees. "Guess the Bubbler hit."

Peaches unconsciously traced the Bubbler-scars on her shoulders; Dare wrapped a blanket around her. "I heard the Bubbler was less fatal out here."

"Killed nine out of ten in New York, where they pack 'em

tight. Still got four out of ten out in the sticks. Left Wickliffe short on living troops. And there's not enough metal left in the planet to build drone armies the way he used to. He kept his victory symbol secure as long as he could... but the Wickliffe-program's pulled out enough for us set up shop."

"The 'Live Local, Die Global' initiatives shut down most travel anyway," Peaches said. "Most people see the world through video. Guess who controls the video?"

Ximena brought the copter to a halt in a landfill, seagulls scattering at our approach. Or maybe they scattered at the stench the jets kicked up, as the miniature whirlwinds knocked over garbage heaps, unleashing the slimy fester of microenvironments.

"Did we have to land here?" I asked.

"Secret entrance is around here, according to the Wickcleft."

Mara settled the copter into a crevice between two great stacks of rubbish. The spirojets kicked up splatters of composted muck. Everyone's face got spattered with sewage-scented compost, and it got no better when Dare puked and the jets flung vomit into the air.

The NeoChristians stormed out of the copter in brisk formation, setting up a guard perimeter around the landing site. Evangeline slunk out afterwards, clutching her rifle like a teddy bear.

She looked *shamed* to be here. Ximena's NeoChristians worked around her, accepting her help without acknowledgment.

We unloaded everyone, which got tricky when Dr Hsiang started bellowing deranged apologies to President Wickliffe and we had to gag her. Peaches rolled down the landing ramp, but her wheelchair's tanklike treads spun in the mushy soil, forcing Ximena's sons to carry her.

"Where do we go from here?" I asked.

"The Wickcleft told us of a tunnel," Ximena said. She

was stoic, but her tanned face was turning green from the smell. Which was, in its own way, comforting; if hardcore NeoChristians couldn't tolerate the landfill, it was doubtful that anyone else would follow us.

Searching turned up an old, dark highway tunnel cut into a cliff face. The cracked pavement of the entryway was barely big enough to push Peaches through.

The smell dissipated as we pushed deeper into darkness. Mara lit a torch.

"Don't you have flashlights?" Peaches asked. "You know, actually *good* options for fighting the darkness?"

"Why use precious electricity when trees grow for free?"

I'd never seen anyone shut Peaches up before.

We rounded a corner. Dare made a happy "ooh!" noise.

"It's the Big Dig!"

"...What?"

"A big engineering project from centuries ago. They had to dig a freeway underneath a living city – and void, what a fiasco." It was good to see Dare's old love of architecture surging to the fore. "The Dig didn't stretch out this far into the suburbs, but I bet some people found ways to interconnect with it over the years. Secret military tunnels, or maybe rebel projects..."

Dare lectured about the Big Dig's political challenges; it almost felt like old times. Except it wasn't a conversation – Dare was so lost in reverie, he would have talked to a stump.

Still. Progress.

It might have been an enjoyable trip if not for Dr Hsiang, who'd begun coughing up a tarry foulness. She raved, begging a stonefaced Peaches for forgiveness, asking over and over again why we wouldn't let her Shrive.

"I followed orders!" she wailed. "I was loyal! I'm *not* the lowliest of criminals, I'm *not*..."

She *was* loyal. But Wickliffe was only loyal to his own needs.

We broke for dinner, then slept in the chill tunnel. The mothers nursed their babies while Dare helped Peaches pee.

When it came time to eat, Evangeline took a strip of pemmican before retreating, nervous as a squirrel. Peaches waved her over to eat with us; Evangeline shook her head.

"Is she OK?" I whispered.

Ximena shrugged. "Who can tell, with heretics?"

"What do you mean, 'heretic'?"

Ximena nibbled her jerky. "She didn't…? Well, she might not discuss her faith with an unbeliever. I don't suppose it much matters to *you*."

"What matters?"

"Theology." She stiffened. "Ah, but I do not pass on gossip." And of course, I could not get another word out of her.

In the morning, we trudged on again. By early afternoon, we saw the literal light at the end of the tunnel.

This light, however, had several men with guns guarding it.

"Stand down!" they cried – but Ximena's family already had their rifles out.

"*You* stand down." Ximena sounded quite reasonable for someone ready to pull the trigger. "You invited us."

The two factions faced off, one cloaked in shadow from the light spilling in through the entrance.

Then a familiar voice:

"All right, you knuckleheads – she's right. We asked 'em here." And a lanky black woman with beaded dreadlocks walked out to greet us, her robed body festooned with gaudy necklaces:

Mama Alex.

The leader of the Boston rebels.

Of *course* the leader of the Boston rebels.

"Mama!" I cried – but she pushed me aside. "Void below, girl," she muttered, scrutinizing Peaches' wounds. "That wheelchair permanent or temporary?"

"Permanent."

Mama Alex clenched and unclenched her fists in rage, then bent down to kiss Peaches' forehead. "You'll be all right," she whispered, mostly to assure herself. "Your strength's never been in your legs."

Peaches lit up, radiant, a smile to please Mama Alex. Mama Alex smacked her lips. "…Yeah, you'll be fine."

She glanced around the gathering. "Amichai, you make the right enemies – but hoo boy, do you make 'em big. Dare, I'm still surprised these two dragged your timid ass into this mess, but good for them; you're the most useful."

Dare beamed.

Mama whistled low, hands on hips, looking at the seventeen tattooed soldiers. "I didn't expect y'all to bring a NeoChristian strike team. But if anyone could bridge gaps, it's Amichai and Peaches. I mean, *we've* never exactly called you folks allies."

"I wouldn't start now," Ximena said… with a grin that made everyone ease up.

"That's all y'all, except for the dying woman." She bent over Dr Hsiang, who'd taken to swatting imaginary spiders. "She the one carrying Wickliffe's secrets?"

"And also the one who shot me," Peaches replied.

The hatred in Mama Alex's smile terrified me. "Well, then," she said. "We'll suck her brains out through a straw."

31: THE SLAUGHTERHOUSE OF CONSCIOUSNESS

The tunnel led out to an overgrown forest – or at least it *looked* like more woods. When you squinted, you could just make out the remnants of what had once been a busy downtown; vines snaked around rusted lampposts, crumbled coral buildings slumping against trees, buckled sidewalk-chunks poking out of clay soil. Dapples of sunlight reflected off the solar-panel canopies strung overhead.

Workers in dirty outfits climbed trees to adjust the panels, taking voltage readings and comparing them. They sounded thrilled to work.

And why not? They'd escaped Wickliffe.

I smelled a rich stew, a thick meaty scent that made my stomach growl. They *cooked* here, not like the gray gruel back at the Orphanage. Ximena and the other NeoChristians sniffed hungrily.

Mama Alex grabbed a worker. "Get these NeoChristians a nice meal. Y'all bringing more friends with you?"

"If we feel safe," Ximena allowed.

Mama Alex brayed laughter. "This is the farthest place from safe! Eat up. We'll be back." Then, to Dare and me: "You two, pick up Doctor Dyin' there. Red-haired girl! Push Peaches, some of the road's all buckled."

Evangeline separated from the other NeoChristians, looking profoundly grateful – even as she kept a stiff-armed distance as she pushed Peaches over the cracked streets. "How did you know I was Amichai's friend?" she asked.

"I didn't. You looked too miserable to be left behind."

Mama Alex marched us towards a sprawling metropolis of shining silver and glass. This chrome-plated temple was engulfed by the forest, but stood unbowed by the weight of nature.

"That's a *mall*," Dare said reverently.

"Wow," I said. "They *did* build them impressive."

Dare blinked. "You know what a mall is? Most got torn down in the 'Live Local, Die Global' initiatives before we were born…"

"Of course I know what a mall is. You *told* me."

Dare looked confused. "I thought you were just humoring me when I yammered on about architectural history…"

"Nope."

Dare waited for me to follow that up with something stupid.

For once I kept my mouth shut.

Mama Alex led us up a long flight of shallow stairs, then through a row of green-glass doors, then across a wide plaza of gold-speckled tiles. Dare took it in breathlessly as we strode through a huge open space, with looping staircases to connect the levels, the walkways circling around one great courtyard, everything lit by sunlight falling through broad glass panes overhead.

In that courtyard stood a towering server, three stories high.

The rebels' server was a ramshackle stack of CPUs and hard drives, like luggage piled too high, with weldscars on its case and wires sticking out and air conditioners bolted on. The tin Shrive helmet attached to its base rattled and hummed.

Dare and I both let out low whistles.

Dare doubtlessly appreciated the chamber that held the branch server – but to me, that server was a glorious finger in Wickliffe's eye. The Boston rebels had assembled it from scavenged parts, knitting it together with modified software: proof the living could accomplish great things.

"It's a small one," Mama Alex allowed, slapping it proudly. "Room for maybe two hundred brains. We call it the Brain Trust. Ever since Boston died, we've been uploading New York's cleverest minds to help us with our revolution. It's theoretically a big advantage against Wickliffe."

"...theoretically?" Evangeline asked.

Mama Alex seemed to notice Evangeline again. She squinted. "Go run an errand. This won't be pretty."

"But I don't..."

"I see scared in your eyes, and this is gonna friction your principles something fierce. I'm not mad, but I will be if you stay and fuck this up. Skedaddle. Come back when we call you."

Evangeline looked to me for confirmation; I shrugged, unsure what would happen next.

"Nice girl," Mama Alex allowed after Evangeline had left. "Needs a shepherd. I got my own flock to tend."

She rummaged around in a sack until she found a needle filled with a clear fluid. She gestured for Dare to pull Dr Hsiang underneath the Shrive helmet – then plunged the needle into Hsiang's throat. Pus squirted from Hsiang's infected wounds. Dare shrieked, and so did Hsiang.

Mama Alex knelt down.

"Now. We're gonna take everything you know," Mama Alex said. "This isn't closed-source technology, with Wickliffe's safeguards; this is jailbroken. Our people will sift through your every memory. We'll watch your every orgasm, your every shit – and when we're done, we'll all know what a pathetic sack of wetness you were."

Dr Hsiang shivered. "Will I live?"

Mama Alex sucked her teeth. "You're pretty far gone. You might wind up as mangled as those brainburned NeoChristians."

"I... I can't die. I'll do... I'll do anything. Just – don't let it all end..."

Mama Alex turned to me. "We're going deep with this one, Amichai. Most brainscans retain the foggy memories, the opinions slurred by pride. But our goal today isn't fidelity – it's extracting information."

Dr Hsiang clutched the hem of Mama's dress. "Please... save me..."

Mama looked at me sourly as if to ask, *You see the shit we have to put up with?* Then she slammed the Shrive helmet down over Hsiang's head. Hsiang convulsed as the server ripped her memories away – not a pleasant Shrive, but a brutal neural interrogation.

Hsiang shrieked garbled conversations. She relived old experiences so intensely that she tried to walk, ripping her stitches. Then Hsiang fell catatonic under the Shrive hood.

Mama Alex fished out a knife and sliced Hsiang's throat.

I'd seen more emotion from butchers slaughtering pigs.

I looked at the green nodes lighting up around the Shrive hood. "Did we get her?"

"Most of her." Mama Alex knelt to mop up the blood with a rag.

"What would have happened if she'd refused?"

Mama Alex gave me a look that hovered somewhere between pity and respect.

"Oh, Amichai. I'm glad you didn't ask that before." She blotted Hsiang's neck, flung the rag in a corner crusted with old bloodstains.

I looked at Dr Hsiang's body. I should have been shocked, outraged, stunned. But I was getting too used to bodies.

"Bring me to Wickcleft," I said. "It's time to plan our next move."

32: DONNING THE CAPE

"You call him Wickcleft, huh?" Mama Alex hooked up a monitor to the rattling branch server after Dare had hauled Dr Hsiang's body away. "That's a clever name. We call him Good Walter. You figure out his secret on your own?"

"He's a copy."

Mama Alex bit back a grin. "Situational analysis! From Amichai Damrosch! Wonders never cease."

"But what was Wickcleft splintered off to accomplish? What was his goal?"

"Void if *he* knows." Mama Alex balanced the monitor on a wooden crate, then aimed an old gooseneck camera at us. "Wickliffe's hunted Good Walter through all the servers in the world. Good Walter – Wickcleft – only survived by storing memories anywhere he could, and now he can't remember where he left them all."

"So he's fragmented."

"No," Mama Alex said. "He kept his heart intact."

She flicked Wickcleft on.

Wickcleft shimmered onscreen, still in top hat and monocle, pleased to see us. The real Wickliffe had been dry, hollow, resentful – but Wickcleft looked avuncular, the uncle who'd slip you a beer at Thanksgiving.

"The b-b-brave warriors return!" he cried, flinging his artificial arms wide open. "P-p-peaches, Dare, *and* Amichai.

I ffffeared you were duh-duh-dead. But nevvvvver write off *true heroes*!"

I blushed. Having the president shower praise upon you was intoxicating.

"I need all the information we have," I said.

"Ah-ah-I'll give you what I can. Alas, Duh-Doctor Hsiang will tuh-take a whuh-whuh-while to reassemble. What do you nnneed to know?"

I looked up at the Brain Trust. "Shouldn't the council be talking to us as well?"

"Thuh-these old geezers?" He made a fluttering gesture with his hands. "Thuh-they're the buh-best theorists in the wwwworld, but thuh-they don't get out mmmuch. The ruh-real world is fuh-ful of uglinesses, bad data, uncertainties. The human mind cuh-cuh-craves certainty, so they cuh-come to prefer the fantasy..."

"And you get out because...?"

"*My* sympathies lie with the lllllliving."

"So you'll help us stop Wickliffe?"

"I-i-I will. But I think *he* muh-means well..."

Dare scrubbed Hsiang's blood off his hands. "After all that bastard's done to us, you still think Wickliffe has good *intentions?*"

"I admit the evidence is suh-slim. iiiiiiiI don't know whuh-why I'm doing this." His screen fuzzed with distress. "I remember whuh-working on the Buh-Bubbler, but I can't keep my memories together... *Why have I turned so evil?*"

Watching him mourn his parallel self was like watching my own mourning for Wickliffe – the sadness of seeing someone who'd once done good, but now had degenerated into incomprehensible wickedness.

"I trust you." I pressed my palm against the screen.

"He's gotten better at thinking ahead," Mama Alex observed to Peaches, "But the boy's still a slave to his instincts."

"The last time this boy went against his instincts, he lied to his best friend and teamed up with Gumdrool."

"And also g-g-generated this huh-handy little political fiasco." Wickcleft stepped backwards to fling a newscast towards the screen. Two dead newscasters, their sculpted faces poreless, flashed porcelain smiles as they discussed the day's events.

"If President Wickliffe can't stop a pony, can he govern?" asked the lady newscaster. "That's what living voters are asking right now."

Footage of my hospital pony-race flashed on the screen as the guy newscaster took over.

"Amichai Damrosch, a Mortal-Shriving teen, has gone viral with his madcap pony escape – in a video that's garnered over four billion hits thanks to a boost from *Sins of the Flesh*. But his latest video, which alleges President Wickliffe is researching forbidden brainwashing techniques, is forcing our leader to answer some hard questions."

Dare's footage of Evangeline's parents being reprogrammed in the branch server played while I spoke. "To the ghosts," I roared, sounding far more confident than I'd felt when we'd fled from the LifeGuard. "You are nothing more than a resource to be mined. Your free will is an obstruction. They want to mold you into more obedient servants. Until you're dead, *they do not think you are human.*"

"It got out!" Peaches squeed.

"But Gumdrool told me he'd shut that signal down." If the state channel had aired my video, then it had gotten so popular that Wickliffe had given up trying to suppress it. "Did you get the word out, Wickcleft?"

"I helped," Wickcleft said sadly. "But whuh- whuh- wait for it."

The newslady looked saddened as the screen cut to a huge demonstration in New York. The living gathered in Central

Farm, doing the pony dance from the Blackout Party. Some even rode ponies, exchanging high-fives. They bellowed demands to see "The Pony Boy! The Pony Boy!" before spirocopters flew over to disperse them.

"The video has caused living riots in several cities, holding up rollouts of the much-desired Upterlife scent upgrades."

"They're upset because their simulated world doesn't *smell* better?" Dare asked.

"The duh-duh-dead are always sc-sc-scavenging your world to im-im-improve their own."

"President Wickliffe says it's clear the living are unwilling to be rational, since the video makers have acknowledged it's a fake," the newscaster continued.

"*What?*" Peaches yelled, almost leaping out of her chair.

The screen showed Dare and me standing penitently before the 82nd Street Orphanage, the autumn wind whipping through our hair.

"After my pony video got record ratings on the dead's most popular TV show—" A popup ad for *Sins of the Flesh* appeared next to my tear-stained cheeks "—I wanted to see if I could generate a sequel that garnered even bigger market share."

"Amichai talked me into designing a fake branch server," Dare said. "Then we faked a movie."

"We thought no one would believe young teens like us…"

"*That's not even how I talk!*" I spluttered, as my parents appeared on screen to explain what a troublesome child I'd always been. "'Teens like us'? 'Market share'? That thing talks like Wickliffe!"

"It's the s-s-same technology that generates our onscreen images," Wickcleft apologized. "Wickliffe cuh-cuh-could fake perfect confessions if he could get at your s-s-saved Shrives, but even he can't do that. Only people who nuh-nuh-know you well could tell the difference."

"The Blackout Parties." Peaches looked frantic. "*They*

know. They're telling people, right? Nobody's believing this bullshit, right?"

"Most of the duh-duh-dead believe it," Wickcleft said mournfully. "They're the ones with the power."

"And the living?"

"They're buh-buh-bitching, muh-mostly. They're angry, but they duh-don't know how tuh-tuh-to bring Wickliffe down."

"We'll help them," Dare said. "We'll make a plan. We'll show them how to fight."

"You're too small to lead a revolution." Peaches' assured voice shut down all debate. "*All* of us are too small. Wickliffe can void an ordinary person at will. If he can void anyone, then why should anyone else risk their eternal life?

"...No." Peaches savored the thought as it came to her, a wicked grin lifting the corners of her mouth. "What we need is a Robin Hood, a Batman, someone who flouts the system. You need someone flashy, good on camera, audacious. You need someone who Wickliffe can throw everything at and *still* fail."

"...That's kinda what I did," I said.

"That's why your video's resonated, Amichai. The living don't need a kid; they need a mad, pony-riding, spirocopter-hijacking *supervillain*. Can you do that?"

I tried on that idea for size.

"...do I get to wear a cape?"

33: ENTERING CHEAT CODES AT MAMA ALEX'S COMPUTER DOJO

The Upterlife had thousands of servers dedicated to reconstructing the information from uploaded meat-brains. Our refuge had one, hacked-together server. It'd be ten days before Dr Hsiang could talk to us again.

Wickliffe was doubtlessly analyzing Dr Hsiang's research now, working hard to perfect the mindslavers. But until we heard from Hsiang, we had nothing to do but sit on our heels.

Might as well learn to program.

The rebels lived inside the mall, taking refuge in old convenience stores. They were mostly wiry technosavants like me. You'd find them perched in the oddest of places, hanging high in the mall windows as they reprogrammed the camouflage nets, soldering together new servers from smuggled-in parts. They were grease-stained and exhausted and still somehow excited from the mere act of *creation*.

The NeoChristians and the rebels had one thing in common: when they weren't learning, they were teaching.

Mama Alex was no exception. She'd set up two computers for Dare and me in an old delivery dock.

"*I did it!*" I cried.

I leapt up to do a triumphant booty-dance. Dare had chained together an elaborate set of helper modules – so complex I couldn't figure how they worked – but he abandoned his work to look over what I'd done.

"…that's *cheating!*" he cried. Dare stared at Mama Alex like she was a bribed referee. "Amichai didn't construct a series of anonymized proxy servers to the internet!"

Mama Alex squeezed Dare's shoulder affectionately. Dare had taken to programming with a surprising ferocity – and prodigious talent. In the old days, Mama Alex told us, programming used to consist of writing code. These days it was about chaining existing modules together in weird ways. If you wanted your computer to understand spoken English, you hooked up the module that knew how to listen to sounds and fed the data from *that* into a module that translated sounds into English words, then fed the words from *that* into an English grammar parser module and a dictionary module, et voila! A program that could transcribe English.

And just like with buildings, Dare could envision huge structures in his head. He'd spend hours in a daze, linking complex webs of modules together, getting them to do things that even Mama Alex whistled at.

I'd programmed, too, but had missed lessons when I snuck off to check on Evangeline – which Dare resented me for. Plus, honestly, linking together modules was kinda the boring part.

"'A series of anonymized proxy servers'?" I tried to laugh it off. "Look at you talking now! Dare, you didn't want me to show you how to mute your grandparents!"

He grimaced. "Maybe you read the instructions then. You sure as void don't now."

"Then why do I have an untraceable internet connection and you don't?"

"*Because you hacked into Mama Alex's computer!*" Dare chucked his keyboard at Mama Alex's feet.

"That's code!" I said loftily. "It's running, is it not?"

"Zero knowledge of protocol. Zero knowledge of the underlying principles of the net. Zero *grace*."

"One hundred percent results."

"You used only four modules! One to listen to the noises from Mama Alex's keyboard, another to track the unique sound of each keypress, a third module to map the frequency of each keypress to the most common letters in the English language…"

"…and a fourth that mapped my keyboard sounds into a stream of every letter I typed." Mama Alex sniffed as she scanned my paltry linking code. "You didn't even feed the output through an analyzer, Amichai. You just manually scanned through everything I typed in until you stumbled upon my login credentials."

"…but I *am* on the internet." I gave her the puppydog eyes. "And there's no safer connection than yours – am I right, Mama Alex?"

She cuffed me upside the head. "You are so full of shit you squeak. I *left* that option open for you. What would you have done if I'd used trifactor authentication?"

"Uh…"

"Do you even know what trifactor authentication *is*?"

"Uh…"

"You *see*?" Dare paced in outraged circles. "Void, Amichai, I used to think you were a techno*God*. Yet I've spent weeks learning to program while *you* waste time creating animated videos of yourself! You're making *selfies* while people die!"

"Selfies are part of my plan!"

"OK, zip it," Mama Alex said. "This difference in philosophy illustrates the difference between a *programmer* and a *hacker*." She hugged Dare, squeezing his rage-trembles away. "Dare, I'm gonna need you to maintain the branch server when I'm gone – you understand how all this hardware fits together. All Amichai can do is break things;

you have a special talent for building."

Dare stuck his tongue out at me. He looked quite surprised when Mama Alex poked it back in.

"Now, when y'all were trapped in the branch server," she continued, "did you want someone who could build things… or someone to break shit?"

"But if Amichai–"

"Talk to Amichai, not me."

He hauled his gaze upwards. "If you'd thought through things more, maybe we wouldn't have needed to break *out*." His shoulders tensed as he thought of Peaches. "You want to lead a revolution, Chai. But you can't improvise a government overthrow."

"And you can't overthrow a government without a little improv." Mama shoved us together. "You're two halves, boys – creation and destruction. You need to work as one." She heaved herself to her feet with a groan. "So hug it out."

She left.

Dare did not look like a man who wanted a hug.

"Look…" I ventured. "You know I'm sorry…"

"I have accepted the fact of your apology." He turned away, sounding regretful. "You know what it was like living at the mortuary? With all my relatives watching?"

"I know you got yelled at."

"I didn't know what praise sounded like." He massaged his wrists. "I was stupid, I was clumsy, I was a disgrace. My barber aunts would count the stray hairs left out of place after I'd combed, my tailor uncles would yell at me for the way I buttoned my shirt."

"They were just voices, man."

He stiffened. "No. Amichai. They were the only people I'd ever loved. I measured myself by them. So when they told me I was worthless, why wouldn't I believe them?"

"You had Peaches…"

"Peaches tried to introduce me around. She got past her self-hatred by getting everyone to love her. I never managed that. Because inside of me, I…" He punched his chest. "There was *nothing*. I'd imagine flower gardens and mansions and ballparks, all empty. Because my fondest dream was a beautiful room where I did not exist. When I got free time in the Upterlife trialrooms, I recreated those empty spaces, and hated myself for wasting time."

"*No!*"

Dare cocked his head, puzzled by my denial.

"You loved making those spaces, Dare. It's all you did when you moved in with me."

Dare goggle-eyed at me, then strangled a laugh. "You… you don't even *remember*, do you?"

"Remember what?"

He shoved his face into his palms. "How the void did you ever call me your friend, Amichai? Did you even *notice* what you did to me?"

I longed to lie, but I'd done enough of that.

"…No."

He leveled a steely gaze at me. "I. Voiding. Hated. Creating things, Amichai. I should have been tending to our clients' rose cottages, or repairing the building's cameras, or something else my great-greats would have approved of. Instead, I made toy rooms. Childish. But I couldn't stop.

"My great-greats saw, of course. So I moved to the orphanage, because maybe I'd be alone and worthless and making fake rooms, but at least no one would *yell* at me for it. And you…"

He scrubbed tears from his cheeks. "How does that work, Amichai? How can someone change your whole life and be *so voiding oblivious?*"

"Dare, I… what'd I *do?*"

He slumped to the floor. "You peeked at my buildings. And

you called them beautiful."

I froze.

"That was – is – the first time *anyone* said anything nice about me. You were a stranger, but... I made another building to see if you'd like it." He closed his eyes, smiling. "You did."

"Dare, I–"

"*Shut up.* For once in your voiding life, Amichai, just shut up. That praise changed everything. The next time Peaches hauled me off to a party, I showed off my designs... And for the first time, I felt like someone worth talking to.

"By the time you got to know me, yeah, I liked being an architect. People liked *me* as an architect. So I thought maybe... that's the one thing that made me worthwhile.

"Then you told me I was shit."

The words hit like bullets. I finally understood what I'd stolen from Dare, why Dare had been so eager to kill himself in Little Venice.

Dare had wanted his Upterlife self to never know the pain of my betrayal.

I laid my palms flat upon the floor, surrendering.

"...I don't even deserve your punishment, man. That'd make you my keeper. I don't know what to do. I just don't want to make it worse for you."

He massaged the bridge of his nose. Then he tapped my hand – not quite affectionately, but like someone who longed to be affectionate.

"Void take you, Amichai. You're so fucking stupid. But just when everybody's going to kill you, you get one thing right."

"Isn't that enough?"

"No." He pounded the floor in frustration. "You look good on camera, so New York is all 'Oh, Amichai, let us believe in you,' but... everything you've done is predicated upon you *not feeling guilty.*"

I stayed silent, giving him space.

"That's not good enough," he said. "Not when you're leading a revolution. Peaches sacrifices herself? Fine, her self-esteem is fuelled by rebellion. Evangeline dies? Fine, she's a warrior for her skybeard. The LifeGuard, void, we all know how eager *they* are to punch their ticket to the Upterlife.

"But what happens when you need unwilling people to die? I was *raised* by the dead, Amichai. They don't let go of *anything*. And let me tell you: we won't make progress until every last one of them is *erased*."

The only sound in the room was my breathing.

"There must be a better way," I said.

"That's not an answer."

I pulled my legs under me. "No. That *is* my answer. There's a better way, and we'll find it."

"Void, Amichai, isn't what we've been through *proof* you can't save everybody? And yet you're still...!"

Dare was so frustrated, I could see this argument would lead to blows if it continued. He grabbed his keyboard, staring at his development environment, trying to lose himself in code.

"...So where do we go from here?" I asked.

"We fight Wickliffe." Dare fired up his programming project, weaving interdependent modules together. "And hope *one* of us finds the strength to do the right thing."

34: ISABELLA DAMROSCH'S CYBERWAR

I had a live internet connection, and no best friend. Yet I had to share my triumph with *someone*.

I paced the mall and found skinny New York rebels teaching NeoChristians how to improve their solar panels' efficiency, found NeoChristians leading shooting classes… but found no Evangeline. She'd made herself scarce since we'd arrived at the rebel camp.

But I also found a bunch of NeoChristians and rebels repairing the road, making it more wheelchair-friendly. That was Peaches' influence; even when she wasn't around, she was still matchmaking the two factions together.

Peaches. *She'd* want to watch the news with me.

She was easy to track down; NeoChristians and nerds alike crouched around her wheelchair, hooking it up to a beefier motor. She propelled it forward with a squeal of delight, running over a handsome black kid's toes – an atypically clumsy move for Peaches. But when she squeezed his arm, I knew the contact was no accident.

I thought of Evangeline, and swallowed frustration.

"Got a second?"

She reoriented her wheelchair at me, and smiled. I'd watched her flirt with a thousand boys, and *that* smile was mine alone. I hoped it was the genuine Peaches.

"For you? Always." Her technicians looked disappointed

at being abandoned – until she wheeled herself backwards to showcase me. "You boys know Amichai, don't you?"

They stepped forward as one, fighting to clasp my hand.

"The Pony Boy." They oozed so much reverence it wigged me out.

"We saw you fighting," said one.

"We saw you *winning*," said another.

"You fought for my brethren," said a third boy, his throat a blotchy red from his first cross tattoo. "It's an honor."

"Now, now, Amichai clearly has important business with me," Peaches told them, preening. "Otherwise he would *never* have interrupted my first test run. Would you mind gifting us some privacy?"

They skedaddled. I blushed as Peaches drove in happy laps around me.

"Look what they did, Amichai! I can practically bulldoze my way across cracked pavement now!"

"And I, uh…" I held out the tablet. "I got an internet connection."

She grabbed it. Her girlish joy evaporated, replaced with the satisfied smirk of business-Peaches. "At last. *News*. I have been *so* needing to hear the outside world."

"I thought you would have charmed a boy into feeding you some signal."

"Mama Alex told me I couldn't get access until you did. She thought I'd encourage you."

"You let her get in your way?"

"Oh, Amichai." She patted my cheek. "You *don't* cross Mama Alex. Now let's see how the revolution's coming…"

She loaded her news aggregators: Opinion polls. Riots. Votes. Ponies. Seas of protesting people in every city, demanding to see me, the *real* me.

"Wow," I said. "People are getting pony tattoos. They're spraypainting ponies on walls. Is that… is that a pony

Mohawk?"

"You're a symbol, yes, yes," Peaches muttered. "LifeGuard reports Blackout Party attendance has doubled, which means it's quadrupled. Folks keep drowning in Little Venice, searching for the collapsed server. But... nobody's stopped Shriving. And Wickliffe's been dropping heavy reminders that even if all the living voted against him, the dead would *still* outnumber them. So the living..."

"...aren't sure what to do," I finished.

She wheeled backwards, placing a disappointed gap between us. "We need to give them a plan, Amichai."

"I don't *have* one! Evangeline says it's about getting the people on your side, but... they're *on* my side! And Wickliffe has all the technology and the armies and the weapons..."

Peaches hooked her index finger into my collar, pulled me down to kiss me. As usual, my entire body shorted out.

"...better?"

"That didn't teach me how to win."

She gave me an indulgent purr. "The same way you always win, Amichai. You *cheat*. You cheat *magnificently*."

The word "cheating" reminded me of Evangeline's snuggles.

"I didn't come here to ask you to help me plot," I admitted.

"Oh?"

"I thought you might want to see how Izzy is doing."

Peaches touched her fingertips to her mouth, shocked and shamed. "...yes. Yes, I do."

"Then let's pull up her videostream. And – whoah. Her account's shut down?"

"That makes sense. They don't want her talking to the public. Search for her name, though."

"There's..." I swallowed. "Sixty *million* videos with Izzy in it... mostly news reports referencing her as my sister, but..."

"Never look at the front page for the *good* information." Peaches clicked deep into the search results. "Drill past the obvious hits, and most of these are the same video. Very few hits on each. I suspect people are mass-uploading that video illegally, and then the video's being taken down as fast as the dead can yank access..."

"So my sister's video has triggered a *cyberwar?*"

"Let's watch this one quick before it disappears."

The video was purposely glitchy, with hitches and bursts of static and random blocks of color popping onscreen so the automated content-scanners couldn't flag it. But...

It was still my sister.

Seeing Izzy, even sick in the hospital, was like getting hugged and gutpunched at the same time. I was flooded with memories of Izzy and I chatting late at night in our respective orphanages – me endlessly complaining, Izzy endlessly reassuring me that things would get better...

But Izzy had squeezed herself into her LifeGuard uniform. I knew it no longer fit her properly, not after the plague had warped her body – and no one but me knew the effort it took her to sit up straight, like a soldier, so she'd look good on camera.

"People have been asking me about my brother for a long time," she said. "Mostly, they've been asking if I'd arrest him."

She exhaled a long breath, signaling that this was going to be difficult to talk about.

"Anyone who knew me at the Academy knew that when my superiors asked about my brother, I gave the politic answer: *only the dead can decide who's guilty.* But my fellow cadets also knew what I told them informally: *If my stupid brother steps out of line, I will be the first to arrest his dumb ass.*"

She thumped the breast of her uniform in a half-salute, blinking back proud tears.

"I would have graduated top of my class if the Bubbler hadn't taken the LifeGuard from me. Because I *believed.* I was proud of my fellow cadets, proud of the way they had signed up to keep the living safe. It was an *honor* to stand by the side of such noble guardians.

"But...

"My brother doesn't lie to me. Not about anything important. And that video where he claims it was all faked? That's not the way he talks. I *know* my brother, I..."

Izzy ran her hands through her hair, clearly deciding whether she was going to actually say what she was thinking.

"I believe in Amichai Damrosch."

She gazed into the camera, as if daring anyone to contradict her.

"I believe that my brother discovered something horrible that Wickliffe is planning. Something to brainwash us. Don't get me wrong, I am still immensely proud of the living – I pledged myself to protect them when I put on this uniform.

"But I am no longer proud of the dead. I believe in my brother. I believe in his cause. And I believe that any LifeGuard member who pledged themselves to the service of the living has to examine this evidence that Amichai has provided. They have to..."

There was a knock on the door.

"Gotta go." She leaned over to turn off the camera.

Peaches pounded her armrests enthusiastically. "Did your sister just try to tell the LifeGuard to rebel? Oh my sweet void, I have never been prouder."

I wanted to feel the warm glow of family pride, but all I could think of was that knock on the door. What happened after that? Why didn't she rerecord her video?

"Her main account's shut down," I said, typing frantically. "But we had a backdoor account we shared, just in case Beldon tried to close off our nightly chats..."

"Look," Peaches said. "There's a new video with no hits. Set to family-only credentials."

I hit play. The screen filled with grainy shadows – a late-night video post.

Izzy looked haggard, as if she'd been woken from a bad dream.

"I'm being shipped off," she said. "I knew they'd assign me to factory work, but... they're relocating me before my physical therapy is complete. The nurses say that's... unusual." Her eyes glanced off camera, seeking permission to speak.

"...They're telling me this project is vital to the Upterlife. They tell me... No, fuck it! I won't sucker him in! You give them hell, Amichai! You fight! I believe in you! I–"

"That's enough." A familiar face leaned in:

Gumdrool.

He gave me the shit-eating grin of a poker player with a royal flush, and the video went dark.

I dropped the tablet.

"Lacona Springs," I said. "That's where he's taking her. We head to Lacona Springs, and we–"

Peaches grabbed my arm. "We will *not*."

"He's bringing her to Lacona Springs to experiment on! *My sister is in danger!*"

"Tell that to Dare, why don't you?"

As I looked down at Peaches' wheelchair, the stirring argument I'd been about to give lost all traction.

"Look," Peaches continued. "Gumdrool could have deleted that post. Instead, he uploaded it. Why? Because he wants *you*. He wants you bullrushing him, so he can capture you. He's playing the only card he has to get you. Like it or not, that card is Izzy."

"But my sister..."

"...may have to void, Amichai. Same as all of us."

"But she didn't sign up for the cause!"

"Watch that video again," Peaches said. "She did."

35: AT THE FOOD COURT, WATCHING NEOCHRISTIANS BEAT UP NEOPHYTES

I wasn't sure how to rescue Izzy, so I retreated to the food court to ponder my next move. A NeoChristian family had heaped soil over the tiles there to teach karate.

I'd thought their martial arts would be flashy, movie-style throws. But the NeoChristians were brutally efficient: a kick to the crotch, stiff fingers in the throat, dirt kicked in your eye.

I watched them, pretending every blow was to Gumdrool's face.

The rebels took their beatings with enthusiasm. They all shared my fearlessness: screwing up meant you'd learned something interesting. Though in their case, "interesting" often meant a smashed eyebrow.

They waved me over, inviting me to join in their reindeer games. But if I started punching people now, I'd never stop. Not a good attitude to bring to a sparring session.

Mama Alex sat down next to me. Her knees cracked as she eased herself onto the bench. "Good to find you here."

"In the food court?"

"In the compound. I had Ximena's family ready to hunt you down if you took off after Izzy." She cleared her throat. "...I mighta told 'em to rough you up a little."

I chuckled. "It's good to watch them playing, isn't it? NeoChristians and unbelievers together?"

She sucked air through her teeth. "Won't last."

"Doesn't seem like that thought bothers you."

"Everything good comes with an expiration date, Amichai." She smiled as a NeoChristian took a knee to the forehead from a one-armed stringy housewife. "See that girl? Josie's her name. Lost her girlfriend in a LifeGuard attack in Poughkeepsie. Wickliffe's thugs voided her lover, then shot her as she tried to escape. Left her to die in a ditch. Gangrene took her arm. She staves off the grief by fighting harder."

My sister was in trouble, maybe brainscrambled by Gumdrool... but at least she was alive.

Josie's girlfriend had been erased from history.

I shivered. Josie might be meat-dead tomorrow. Maybe at my orders. And I wanted to imagine Josie and her girlfriend happy somewhere together, rewarded for all this bravery instead of being meat in a grave.

The NeoChristian Upterlife still seemed childish. But now I understood the appeal.

"The NeoChristians aren't our friends, Amichai." Mama Alex chewed a stalk of grass. "They got too much stock invested in that skybeard of theirs to stay permanent allies. But right now? I got two hundred people missing lost friends and lost limbs. They're looking straight into the void, and they ain't flinching. The NeoChristians are the only other people left on the planet who know what it's like to lose – *really* lose – a loved one.

"So we're bonded by a common enemy, and a common fear. But some day, there'll be a funeral for someone they both loved, and you'll see what happens when one draws comfort from thinking the dead are in the clouds, and the other thinks the dead are in the ground."

I thought about Evangeline. Our friendship. Our maybe

more-than-friendship.

"No," I retorted. "We have more in common than that."

One of Mama Alex's silver amulets buzzed. "Th-th-*that's* what I like about him!" said Wickcleft, from Mama Alex's bosom. "Tuh-tell him something's impossible, and he-*he!*-he digs right in! Luh-like me, when I faced down duh-death!"

"Maybe the world woulda been better if you hadn't been so damn stubborn," Mama Alex picked up the pendant between two long fingers, twirled it. "Wisdom comes from knowin' when to give up."

"Nnnnnonsense," Wickcleft riposted, with a well-worn sense of banter. "Idealism forges paradise. You knnnnnnow that."

"Really? I 'know' that?" She swooped the pendant around dramatically, as if to show Wickcleft the whole world. "Then why ain't we livin' in paradise?"

"Duh-don't confuse an en-en-engineering problem with a fuh-fuh-flaw in my philosophy. The Upterlife juh-juh-just needs some adjustments, is all."

"You carry him around with you?" I peered at the pendant – which was studded with not rubies, but camera lenses.

"We're partners. Walk with me, Amichai, walk with me."

She got up – producing another old-lady groan – and led me outside the mall. NeoChristians and rebels alike were patching up the NeoChristian ships.

Then an alarm sounded. Everyone fell silent as a missile-drone whooshed overhead. They stared at the sky, hoping the camo nets held, imagining what would happen if that bomb found them. It'd blow them to wet meat-scraps.

I trembled, hostage to my body's fears.

"Nobody wants to die, Amichai," Mama Alex said. "But I can't say death is bad."

I thought of the bullets ripping through Peaches' belly. I thought of Evangeline, plunging her knife into her parents' hearts. I thought of Hsiang, raving as her dysfunctioning body messily shut down. "How can death *not* be bad?"

"Everything has a time." Her voice was as soft and implacable as water. "You know people like me weren't allowed to eat at the same table as you, right?"

"That was centuries ago."

"You know boys like Dare used to be beaten for liking other boys?"

"Also in the past."

"And girls like Peaches used to be called sluts?"

"Not anymore."

"And genetic engineering used to be seen as an insult to God?"

"Genetic engineering's *still* not allowed."

"Yeah," she said. "Because the people who grew up believing genetically modified kids were abominations *never died*."

She held her sea-gray gaze on me, letting her point settle in.

"Thing is, Amichai," she continued, "people don't change all that much. But the most virulent racists died off, and the new kids grew up with more black and Latino and Asian friends, and the world got a shade better. Not perfect – occasionally some freshfaced asshole raised on yesterday's thoughts would squirm into power for a time – but *better*.

"We never could have won if we had to face down all our enemies in their prime, Amichai. We just *outlived* 'em.

"You're right to call 'em ghosts, Amichai. They *haunt* us. Every baby could be gene-engineered disease-free. Except the old-guard dead think genetic engineering's a violation of nature, and they're still around. And that opinion is *not going away*. Their old, bigoted culture gives new kids an excuse to be assholes.

"You might hate death. But we've come to fetishize

eternity – like hanging around forever is an unquestionable good. Death? It's got its downsides, Amichai. But it sure clears away the underbrush."

"You say that," I ventured. "But nobody *wants* to die."

"Oh ho-ho-ho!" Wickcleft was unsettlingly jolly. "Ask her, Amichai. Shuh-shuh-she's been offered a puh-place in our branch server. We've carved out spuh-space for one woman's muh-magnificent mind. And guess what shuh-she's said?"

"You can Shrive," I spluttered, "and you're *turning it down?*"

"I got a lot of wisdom to teach," she demurred. "I've also got a lot of preconceptions. Like I said, everything good comes with an expiration date."

"You can't void. We need you…"

She shrugged, somehow making the gesture eloquent. "We got a hundred seventy-eight people living in the Brain Trust. They're smart people… But creative as a rock. Wickcleft thinks it's some subtle flaw in the compression techniques used to store minds; *I* think old people get set in their ways. I trust the Trust to analyze technical specs, but devising creative solutions?" She squeezed my shoulder. "That's up to living boys like you."

I blushed. "Thank you."

"But it doesn't have to *be* you."

"What?"

Mama Alex knelt before me, her knees cracking like ice on a winter pond. "Amichai, you stumbled into becoming the man people want to follow. But you don't have to lead this revolution. We can put you somewhere safe. 'Cause if Wickliffe goes after you with everything he's got… he'll get you."

He'll get you.

My own death became a reality. In Mama Alex's arms, in this hollow quiet after the missile had missed us, I felt my body's fragility. My consciousness was a weak current trickled through organic mush. A poke with a sharp stick here, and my systems splattered apart.

It wouldn't be difficult to take me down.

"Even if you win," Mama Alex continued, "the NeoChristians are right: it's got to be shut down. I don't see the dead relinquishing power. And we can't stuff 'em in a box and ignore 'em; they control the electronic world. If you take this job, your *best* case is the worst choice a human being's ever had to make: voiding every person in the Upterlife."

"No." The word surged out, reflexive – but I felt the rightness of it, shaping a world that needed to be.

"Amichai, you can't just–"

"No, Mama. I talked about this with Dare. There's got to be some way to reconcile their needs with ours. I mean – void, I don't even know how to stop Wickliffe, but… Killing people is never the solution. If you tell me that's my choice, then *I refuse*."

Mama Alex looked as though I'd struck her. Applause emanated from the speaker around her neck.

"I tuh-tuh-*told* you!" Wickcleft roared. "Juh-just like me! Luh-look reality in the eye and *deny* it, Amichai! That's how men make power!"

"I'm sorry, Mama." I pulled her into a hug. She felt like a bag of sticks, terrifyingly thin.

I wasn't sorry. I felt connected to the billions of lives who'd be enslaved if I failed. Humanity as I understood it would cease to exist.

I also felt a connection to the trillions of lives in the Upterlife servers – shortsighted idiots, greedy, but still deserving of life. If we destroyed the Upterlife servers, then humanity as I understood it would *also* cease to exist.

What did one life matter, weighed against that? Even my own?

"Nuh-nuh-never mind her." Wickcleft's voice buzzed

against my sternum. "Whuh-whuh-what gifts do we have for the mmmman who will guh-give his life for the people?"

"This isn't a *game show*, Mr Wickliffe."

"Suh-sorry," Wickcleft apologized. "Buh-but Amichai, you have nnnnno idea how muh-many favors I had to c-c-call in to get this guh-gift for you – Buh-Black Hoods, fuh-farmers, wwwwageslavers, and it was all duh-doubly difficult thanks to that Guh-guh-Gumdrool *thug* crossing swords with me..."

"What are you *talking* about?"

"Shuh-show him."

Mama Alex took me by the hand. All the other rebels seemed attuned to some great secret I knew nothing of; their heads turned, then they found excuses to walk behind us. Within minutes, we led a procession of whispering fans – and by the time Mama Alex led me to the old cargo storage containers, the whole enclave surrounded me.

Mama Alex unlocked the container.

The door creaked open.

The hot scent of hay and shit wafted out.

It was dim; strangled sunlight-slivers flickered through rusted holes. But inside, slumped and low-eared, stood a familiar silhouette:

"Therapy!"

Her ears perked as she saw me – and then she launched herself forward, bowling me over, snuffling that soft nose all over my face.

A cheer went up as she licked my nose. "They came to see you ride, Ah-ah-Amichai! So ruh-*ride*!" The rebels surged forward, lifted me up, deposited me on a confused Therapy's back.

"The Pony Boy!" they cried, exultant. "The Pony Boy!"

Therapy craned around to look at me, as if to ask, *Are you sure this is OK?* I wobbled on her back; I'd never actually ridden her, or any horse. The crowd seemed convinced I was an awesome rider, though.

I knotted my hands in her mane. "Come on, Therapy," I whispered. "Let's have an adventure."

Therapy leapt *over* the crowd, a ten-foot high soaring leap. She pumped her legs, bringing us looping in a thunderous circle around the mall, Therapy whinnying in delight, our muscles moving as one as the world blurred into one great swell of movement, going fast and nowhere all at the same time with the crowd whooping and everything contracting to a beautiful certainty of this movement, this motion, this grace.

And you know what?

I *was* an awesome pony-rider, much to my surprise.

36: HANDS, WHERE THEY SHOULDN'T BE

"She's so beautiful," Evangeline murmured, stroking Therapy's nose; Therapy leaned into her touch. I loved the way Evangeline's tangled red hair looked against Therapy's sandy fur, but loved the blissful smile back on Evangeline's face more.

"Not as beautiful as she once was." I pulled back Therapy's mane to reveal a metal bolt implanted in her skull.

"An autobridle." Evangeline examined it. "Shuts down her higher functions when desired, right? Ensures she never can pose a threat?"

"I like threats." I got out the IceBreaker, synced it to the autobridle's signal; there was a pop, then a thin stream of gray smoke streamed out. Therapy shook her head, a dog shaking free of a leash.

"You're good now, girl." Therapy blinked and took off, running out for another exultant loop around the mall.

"You sure that's wise?" Evangeline asked. "You may need to rein her in at some point."

"I need to rein *you* in. I can't find you during the day. You only come at night, and I'm always asleep when you sneak in."

Evangeline had taken to sliding into my arms after I'd

drifted off. She pressed her body against mine, nuzzling my neck as though she was terrified to believe in my existence.

It wasn't sexual – but it wasn't *a*sexual, either. Evangeline's body held a terrible, trembling tension, vibrating towards a decision. Sometimes she sobbed, biting my shoulder. Other times she rubbed her body against mine, her breath warm against my ear, straining against some urge neither of us quite wanted to name.

"I'm sorry," she apologized – and looked away. That disturbed me. I remembered the Evangeline of the Wickliffe Orphanage, the Evangeline in the prison yard, and both those Evangelines had stared at me until their green eyes swallowed me up.

"You don't have to be *sorry*. It shouldn't take a pony to lure you out. If you can't talk to me, at least talk to another NeoChristian…"

Her laugh was bitter as coffee. "They don't talk to outsiders."

"I know you have to confess to someone."

"They'd just tell me I'd sinned."

"Is it us? Should I not be kissing you?"

"*I'm* kissing *you*."

She was right. I didn't dare trespass into whatever hurt she had, so I'd let her take the initiative. Every kiss had been her idea… though it had taken all my strength not to slide my palms up her stomach.

"You don't even *believe* in sin. Why do I think I can talk to you…?"

I reached out, took her hand. Her calloused fingers in mine felt more intimate than the makeout sessions. "Because I want to listen?"

She leaned over, kissed the spot beneath my ear.

"I don't know if I can fight any more, Amichai," she said, resting her head on my shoulder.

"OK." This was good. This was her working through

things. This was certainly not a beautiful girl pressing her body against mine. "...is it because of... of... your parents?"

"Have you ever watched anyone you love die?"

Peaches, I thought, flashing back to that moment I was sure Peaches had died – and shook it off, remembering that Evangeline needed me to listen to her right now. I felt guilty, thinking of Peaches, but... Peaches had told me to kiss other girls. Peaches was kissing other boys.

Who was I betraying?

I cleared my throat. "I watched my parents die, from the Bubbler. It was... I would have done anything to save them from that."

"I had to kill them." She was talking about her parents, of course.

"You did."

She licked her lips. "They... they told me death was a reason to rejoice. My parents were going to *Heaven*, Amichai. Casting off these mortal shackles. But instead, they just looked... pained."

I had no idea what to say. How could she have thought meat-death was glorious?

How could she ever have believed in God?

"I tried not to let it affect me," she said. "So I got in the spirocopter, barking orders, back in combat. I'd been *trained* for combat. But when Peaches got shot and the copter crashed, I saw... I saw my mother's eyes. Her empty hope. And... oh, God, Amichai, I was afraid."

"We're all afraid."

She stiffened, pulling away. "*We* are not. *We* fight for the Lord. But there's a poison in my soul, Amichai. For the first time, I... I value this life."

"Why wouldn't you value your life?"

She shoved me away hard enough I tumbled ass-backwards.

"Because I need to value my *soul!*" She thrust her shaking

hands out at me. "I can't load bullets like *this*! And what am I, if not a warrior? How can I be perfect and complete, lacking in nothing, when I quail in the face of danger? What... What should I fight for, if not for the Lord?"

I laughed.

She slapped me hard enough to rattle my teeth.

"How *dare* you minimize my pain!"

"No, no." I held up my hands. "I'm not... ow, *crap* that hurts."

"I should break your jaw. Of all people, *you* should understand. Your people are dying in riots; you set them aflame, and now you must find out what it means to lead them. How can you steer them to safe havens without something to aim for? Faith *matters*, Amichai."

"It's not your faith I laughed at. It's just... Peaches would never talk like that."

She flinched, hugging herself. "I'm sorry. I don't mean to intrude on your... your relationships..."

Was there another possible way I could screw this conversation up?

"No! It's... That's why you're special, Evangeline. You never hide your feelings. Sharing is a special kind of bravery."

She bit her pink lip, suppressing a smile, and oh void how much I wanted to kiss her.

"So how do you *deal* with it? That... emptiness?"

"I've got one life. I'd better spend it right."

She squinted from behind a tangle of hair. "You're not scared?"

"Not scared enough to stop, no. I know what I need to do. I may not know how to do it, but..."

"Then what scares you enough to stop?"

"...Everyone else." Now I trembled. "If I void myself, that's my choice. But Izzy? Dare? My decisions keep fucking them over."

"And Peaches. You... you yell about her in the night sometimes. You flinch in time to the gunshots."

"That's... I'll be fine. Let me worry about you."

"Why? Why do you keep digging for my weaknesses?"

"Because you matter, Evangeline. When I saw you in the Orphanage, you were a... a warrior saint. Strong, and beautiful, and... I was so glad I rescued you."

"You didn't. *I* rescued me. I always rescue me."

"That was even hotter."

Not my wisest phrasing. But my feelings spilled out in a waterfall of words–

"And then you came back to save me from Gumdrool. And it hurts. It hurts to to think maybe... I screwed you up somehow... because, I mean, you're amazing, and..."

She kissed me. Kissed so hard all the barriers shattered, and my hands slid under her woolen shirt, and she touched me in all the ways I'd been aching for.

Things got very physical.

37: IN DEEP

Eight words you don't want to hear when falling asleep with a beautiful woman:

"Now we are one in the Lord's eyes."

38: FRANTIC EXPLANATIONS FOR TERRIBLE DECISIONS

Evangeline clung to me, her face wreathed in a blissful smile, sleepily pulling me back whenever I moved.

I didn't want to go. But I wasn't sure I could stay.

I shouldn't have done that. I'd heard religious people viewed sex as something sacred. And I liked Evangeline, cared for her, but... one in the Lord's eyes?

I didn't believe in the Lord. And I wasn't sure I believed in being one in anyone's eyes.

She knew something was wrong when she woke.

"Did we..." She curled away from me. "Was that bad?"

"No, no, it was good. *Really* good. It's just..."

She grabbed for her clothes, blushing. I tugged her back.

"Listen! That was wonderful! But... what was it to you?"

She snorted. "Less than it was to you, evidently."

"That doesn't make it *nothing*. I just... you know I'm not a 'Lord' kind of guy, Evangeline."

She yanked her boots on. "I am aware you are an unbeliever, yes."

"Look, that was a mistake. Not because... it was bad... but we should have talked. About what that sort of thing means to you. Because I don't know how it is for NeoChristians..."

"It's a bond for life."

"...yeah," I admitted. "That wasn't that."

She went cold. It was the look she'd given the guards at the branch server before she'd destroyed them.

Then she punched a tree.

I moved to pull her back. She elbowed me in the chest.

"Void it, Evangeline!" I huffed, clutching my bruised sternum. "We have to talk–"

"Shut up, Amichai." She ripped a strip of robe to bandage herself. "I don't know what that was for me, either. If I had faith, I would have... have resisted you. The works of the flesh are evident. Yet I used you to not think about death for a while and..." She whirled on me. "But it would have nice to have had you *want* me for life, you understand?"

"I–"

I strangled my immediate reaction, which was to assure her of *course* I wanted her for life. Because I didn't. I wanted to know her, but all this Jesus stuff scared the void out of me, and I wasn't sure we were compatible and oh void I hoped Peaches was going to be as cool with this as she said she would.

"Evangeline." I tried to make a sentence grow out of the end of that word, failed. "Evangeline, I–"

"*There* you are."

Therapy stepped through the underbrush, leading a grim-faced Mama Alex. Mama Alex cruised to a stop as she noted me, still naked, talking to a blotchy-faced NeoChristian in hastily donned clothing – but she closed her eyes and shook her head, as though she had expected no better.

"The Brain Trust's got Hsiang's online," she said. "Time for a war council."

"*Now?*"

"Did the clock stop ticking? Your attendance is mandatory, Pony Boy. And, uh... Evangeline, is it?"

Evangeline couldn't look Mama Alex in the eye. "...Evangeline."

"Be there, too."

39: WATCHING COMMERCIALS FOR THE APOCALYPSE

By the time Evangeline and I shuffled up to the Brain Trust, there were at least three hundred rebels and NeoChristians seated across the mall's levels, playing in a big drum circle.

That would have been awesome if the drum circle hadn't dribbled to a stop when I walked in, announcing my entrance.

Between my matted Jewfro and Evangeline's tangle of wild Irish hair, it was blazingly apparent what had happened. I searched for Peaches, trying to indicate via silent gesture that this wasn't what it seemed, which, OK, it was what it seemed, but perhaps more explanation would calm this out...

...and Peaches was fine. She stopped talking to a set of strapping young boys to look me over: a new respect for me blossomed across her face.

Dare, however, looked ready to strangle me.

Wickcleft flickered onto the screens, rapping his cane on his simulated floor. "All-*all!*-all right, children. Dr Hsiang has been assimilated into our luh-luh-lovely little microculture, and... shuh-she's mostly intact. Say huh-huh-hello, Doctor."

Dr Hsiang crept onscreen. Her features had slackened, like a stroke patient.

"HHhhhhhhaaaaa," she said. It took me a second to figure out that meant *hi*.

Wickcleft pushed her gently aside. "Nice girl, but if shuh-shuh-she's going to debrief you, it'll take all duh-duh-day. And you thought I-*I!*-I was bad!"

Laughter from the crowd... or at least from the rebels. The NeoChristians scowled.

Evangeline squinted, suspicious of me for treating a program like a human. I wondered what she'd think about me wanting to win the love of my parents, whether she'd even think of Izzy *as* my sister once Izzy uploaded.

Sleeping with her seemed like an increasingly poor decision.

Wickcleft noted their coldness, bowed. "In deference to our allies, I shall luh-luh-let the living deliver the nnnnnnews."

Mama Alex stepped forward. "Hsiang doesn't know much. Wickliffe's been tweaking the mindslavers for a long time. If he'd been willing to spring for new hardware, he could have rolled them out years ago – except, for some reason, he wants to do it all through Shrive helmets. Which aren't really designed to *alter* brains so much as read them."

Josie, the one-armed girl, held up her hand. "Why wouldn't he just roll out new Shrive helmets? Ones with brainmelting technology built right in?"

"Good question. First off, the dead hate spending cash on *this* world. He couldn't acknowledge brainwashing was his goal, so Congress would block the budget."

"And the other reason is?"

"Secrecy. Way easier to slip in mindslavers through a firmware update."

The rebels muttered. The idea of waking up one morning, Shriving, and being silently coopted...

"And finally, Wickliffe's... reluctant. If it was up to Hsiang, she'd have rolled out a halfassed version already, but Wickliffe... he has a real distaste for this. He won't do it until he's positive it won't harm the living."

"Thuh- thuh- that's m- me!" Wickcleft said. "I- I!- I *told* you I loved the luh- living!"

He took in the hatred in the NeoChristian eyes, the disgust on the rebels' faces.

"...Orrrrrrr I did, at one point," he added.

"I wouldn't be too proud of yourself," Mama Alex said. "Bad Walter's made his next move."

Wickcleft flickered away, replaced by a sleek onyx headpiece that rotated on the screen like jewelry. It dripped raw technolust.

"In a world with fewer living," a basso voice boomed out, "We must maximize each life."

Cut to a pan across the devastated farmlands of the Midwest, the putrefying coral of New York City.

"The physical world decays," the announcer continued. "Farmers who don't know what blight looks like, rain-battered circuit boards with no trained hands to repair them, sickened coral with no living medics to tend it."

The focus snapped back to the crown, now descending like a UFO to land on a rapturous living woman's temples. *"It's time to reclaim life."*

A zoom pan through complex circuitry. "The Mother Mentor is civilization's best hope to keep the Upterlife working. The Mother Mentor reads your mind to train you in lessons customized to make sense to you as if you had learned it yourself. Every concept will be explained instinctively, so you're guaranteed to remember it! You'll learn a lifetime's lessons in weeks!"

Cut to rich, vegetable-laden farmlands tilled by hale, satisfied living men. Cut to straight-backed living women fixing sickened skyscrapers. Cut to a living teenager diagnosing a circuitboard, then *repairing* it.

My breath caught in my throat. Every rebel in the room leaned forward, drawn by the pull of honest work, yearning for *agency*.

"The Mother Mentor will be rolled out on a test basis to select individuals!" boomed the voice. "Those found eligible will be put down at age forty – a just reward for a life well spent. Apply today!"

The commercial faded... and we slumped forward like marionettes with cut strings.

"It's fiendish," Peaches murmured. "The ambitious living will want it because it'll give them choices. The unambitious will want it for the premature death..."

"Are you *insane?*" Evangeline asked. "No one will try it! They saw Amichai telling them Wickliffe is trying to *erase their mind!*"

"They also saw Amichai apologize for faking it," Peaches told her. "Admittedly, a lot of the living won't bite. But dying at forty is a *huge* incentive. And Wickliffe... maybe he doesn't need everyone to try it. We don't know what he's trying to change living minds to *think*. He never told Hsiang that."

"Convenient, that."

"I-*I!*-I always did puh-play it close to the vest," Wickcleft admitted sheepishly.

"If we can get our hands on one," Mama Alex said, "We can reverse-engineer it. We can find the parts that rewrite brains, and we can release that information to the world. Anyone with a copy of a Mother Mentor can verify Wickliffe's treachery."

"The Buh-buh-brain Trust has broken into everyyyy access center they kuh-can get. Huge numbers of technical suh-suh-supplies have been rerouted to one puh-puh-particular factory. Our guh-guess is that's where they'll muh-muh-mass produce the Mother Mentors."

"Lacona Springs," I said.

"Jeezum crow," said Mama Alex. "That Gumdrool boy is trying to lure you in there *fierce*."

"Good thing I've got a plan to stop him."

40: THE TIMES SQUARE DOG AND PONY SHOW (BUT MOSTLY PONY)

If you were in Times Square on a Monday morning, you either had a lucrative dead sponsor or were trying to find one.

Times Square was one of New York City's biggest marketplaces. The "Live Local, Die Global" initiatives had ensured most things were made within walking distance of your home – seamstresses sewed clothing, rooftop farmers grew food, furniture growers tended hydroponic tanks that sprouted hard-coral chairs. No sense spending valuable energy carting those things in from factories miles away.

But there were always things only big industry could produce. That's what came whizzing in on the monorails. The living couldn't afford the good stuff, naturally, but the dead needed living men to pick up the canisters of roach and rat-kill, living hands to repair their properties, living minds to troubleshoot the cameras that served as their eyes to this filthy world.

So Times Square teemed with hungry employees. There were no merchants – all the negotiating was done online, from dead to dead – but there were stacks of lumber, barrels of nails, pallets of computer servers wrapped in clear plastic, bolts of fabric, girders for the new waves of Upterlife servers, rolls of cable, refrigerated fruits brought in as gifts for the most faithful living servants, tubs of wifi antennae, rows of earputers strung on fishing line, vats of clips and fasteners and door hinges.

And winding among the merchandise were sweat-stained living workers, toting crates and scanning in the latest shipments, all with that glazed look of distraction as the dead barked orders into their ears. Times Square was motion and money.

We'd planned on getting caught, of course.

The LifeGuard patrols cocked their heads, noting an alert generated by the dead who'd made it their hobby of keeping track of arrivals: one hundred new people, folks typically not seen in this area.

Then, a few minutes later, when the dead had run the new arrivals' faces through the recognizer software and realized none of them had Shrived in over a year, the *real* alerts went out.

We watched ourselves on the huge monitors placed over Times Square. Once, Times Square had been festooned with house-sized signs to advertise old sodas, or movies, or whatever else the moldy oldies spent cash on. Now, those monitors showed images of the Square itself, directing people to pick up their goods.

Standard operating procedure for protestors was to "kettle" them. You quietly called in LifeGuard to seal off as many exits as you could, then stampeded protestors into a corner.

Difficult in a place as big as Times Square.

Our Brain Trust had told us they knew trouble was coming. They'd intercepted memos showing how Gumdrool had gotten the funds to station superfast LifeGuard squads in specially equipped supersonic spirocopters all over New York State, ready to respond to any threat within half an hour.

Oh, Gumdrool. You always did think ahead.

So our new faces kept trickling in, one at a time, as

LifeGuard forces from all across New York state relocated to just outside Times Square. You wouldn't have noticed anything particularly amiss in the usual commerce-crazy hubbub, unless you noticed the tense cops.

A record-scratch. The shipping announcements on the overhead speakers cut off, replaced by a mournful version of the national anthem.

Everyone looked up. Wickliffe's voice boomed overhead, reciting the speech he'd made all those years ago:

The Upterlife offers eternal life, boundless liberty, and infinite happiness. Black or white, rich or poor, zealot or atheist; all should pass through, but for the lowliest of criminals. And if you do not allow this, then this country is not free, and this server is not paradise.

A LifeGuard clamped his hand on Josie's good shoulder. "Ma'am, you'll have to–"

And Josie's clothes exploded in a fine powder, covering everyone within ten yards in dusty irritant.

As did every other rebel's clothes.

That had been a particularly nice trick the Brain Trust had developed a while back – a complex chemical compound that, when triggered, burst open in a crossbreed between a super-itching powder and a chemical fog. Some LifeGuards tugged gas masks onto their face – but fine fiberglass particles dug in underneath, turned their cheeks caustic, made them rip the masks off.

Some popped dazers. The smoke diffused the light into ineffectiveness.

That's when I appeared on the screens above them, mounted on Therapy, who in turn stood on a pile of crates. It was a beautiful image: me holding a spear in one hand, the American flag on its end rippling magnificently.

"All should pass through!" I cried. "Except for the NeoChristians, who Wickliffe has decided are lab rats! Except for the whistleblowers, who Wickliffe has condemned as criminals!"

I paused dramatically. "Except for you! Who won't make it to the Upterlife because he will rewrite your minds!"

All across New York State, alerts popped up: "AMICHAI DAMROSCH SIGHTED".

"Wickliffe has given up on the living!" I looked quite noble as the LifeGuard struggled through the crowd to get at me. "He's sold you out to the ghosts! He wants to tell you that you can't fight back – but the ghosts can't exist without our labor!

"Wickliffe wants you believe you can't fight the power. But trust me." I took a moment to pat Therapy's flank. "If a mere pony can baffle them…"

The civilians in the square ran riot, knocking down the guards. The LifeGuard battled back to their feet, hunting down the rebels. It wasn't hard – all the rebels were naked except for me. The guards shouted "Get the Pony Boy!" And then…

They heard the low rumble of incoming hooves.

And I will tell you: if there is a sight more glorious than the cops' widening eyes when they see a herd of genetically engineered superponies bearing down upon them, *I do not know what that is.*

Oh, it had taken pretty much all our resources, hacking every autobridle in Central Park to get the ponies to make a break for it simultaneously. Hacking the autobridles to navigate the ponies to each of our fallen rebels was a tricky thing algorithmically but…

…just in case, each naked person *was* equipped with a bundle of tasty carrots.

The ponies thundered through Times Square, causing havoc, knocking over the dead's precious merchandise, trampling the LifeGuard as they heroically hurled themselves underfoot.

I, however, stood my ground, having leapt onto a forklift. The cops let the others go to concentrate their efforts on me, looking overhead for guidance, making their way through the thick fog.

"You can fight the Upterlife!" I cried exultantly as the rebels staged their preplanned escape, darting down into old subway tunnels. "Don't believe what you see on Sins of the Flesh – Wickliffe will create CGI versions of me to spout lies! But I promise! I have never ever in my life created a CGI version of me to fool anyone!"

The LifeGuard had finally fought their way to the forklift I stood on. Except, as they wiped their watering eyes, they discovered I wasn't there. They looked down at real life, but doublechecked the screens.

I looked down at them.

"*Well,*" I winked, "*maybe once.*"

Just like at the branch server, the living trusted readouts over their sad little meat-eyes. My onscreen image gave a little wave and flickered out of existence, leaving cops from all across the state to blink in confusion.

Meanwhile, I was two hundred miles away, waiting for the generators to explode at Lacona Springs.

41: IN AMBULANCES, ROCKETING TOWARDS EXPLOSIONS

The hazmat uniform I wore was three sizes too big and stank of BO. We were crouched in an ambulance a couple of miles of down the road from the Lacona Springs factory, which had been built right next to one of the colossal geothermal springs that helped power New York State. Made sense; the chip factory sucked down monstrous amounts of electricity. Steam hissed out from vast pipes, blotting out the sky, causing iron-scented drizzles that fogged the windshield.

"Dare," Mama Alex asked. "How long would you say before Ximena inserts the package?"

"About ten minutes ago."

"If." Mama scowled at floor. It was close packed in the ambulance, with Darc, me, Evangeline, Mama Alex, and Facundo our driver. We all felt the tension.

If something had gone wrong with Ximena, we'd never know. If we were even close to on-schedule, she was crawling through rock a hundred yards underground – but highbeam communications strong enough to penetrate that much slate and granite would have given our position away.

The Times Square distraction was going on as we spoke; it was scheduled to reach its height when the maximum number of LifeGuards had been diverted. If Ximena didn't finish in time, they'd regroup and converge on our position at supersonic speeds.

We shivered in the electric ambulance, hoping she hadn't boiled herself in the tunnels.

"How will we know when she's successful?" I asked.

Mama Alex glared at the steam plumes. "We'll know."

"Ugh. My facemask has flopped over again. Evangeline, could you..."

Evangeline knotted the back of my suit to pull it tight. She looked pale, but had demanded to come along – and I didn't feel right, telling her to stay home. Mainly because she no longer *had* a home.

"I recognize we are low on materials," she muttered. "But you'd think getting a properly fitted suit would be doable."

"You'd think," Mama agreed cheerfully. "But these hazmat suits are chipcoded to the factory. Normally, they'd do a retina scan and all sorts of other bioconfirmations before letting us in the front gate, but I'm betting they'll skip a few steps once the explosions start and us helpful emergency technicians show up. Still, without the embedded chiptags to verify our access, we'd set off an alarm the second we stepped over the doorway."

"So where'd you get them?"

"Bribed the real technicians with a tailored norovirus," Mama Alex said. "Gives you runny noses and sporadic vomiting, but otherwise you feel fine. They're relaxing in their home, happy for the day off. When you work at *these* factories, you *never* get a day off."

"Why not just kill them?" Dare asked.

"Couple of people out sick, they figure something's going around. Couple of people turn up dead..."

"Wait a minute," I said, making a clumsy timeout with wobbling, misfit gloves. "Won't that void them anyway? When they Shrive, and the dead figure out they were slacking?"

"No," Mama Alex said. "Almost everybody's faked a day off. Almost every technician's made a profit from selling something illegal to friend. Humans are creative. Even the Upterlife can't kill crime."

"But... they'll Shrive Criminal once the dead know what they did... they'll get barred forever..."

She tapped my faceplate affectionately. "Oh, Amichai," she sighed fondly. "You think the dead judge you according to some legal system?"

"I kinda thought law had something to do with it, yeah."

"If it did, nobody would make it in!" She laughed. "No, Amichai, they tell you it's the lowliest of criminals who don't get in – but really, that whole Mortal/Venal/Liminal is a good ol' boy system. They don't consult the lawyers; void, even the Upterlife doesn't have that kind of processing power, asking the dead to play jury to every living human's life.

"Naw, it's all *gut feel*. They get a sense of you; all they care about is, 'Would I want this guy living next door to me?' Everybody's called in fake-sick. Everybody's taken a bribe. Long as you do most of your job and don't stick your head up too much, you can get away with spectacularly petty crimes."

"But *I* Shrived Mortal..."

"Yeah, well, you did something big and splashy. If you'd stolen painkillers for Izzy, nobody would have looked at you sideways. I made charts."

"...charts?"

"They broadcast the names of the voided. Look those people's histories up, and you can assemble pretty reliable profiles of what crimes are acceptable. And I can tell you: the dead? They don't mind if you call in sick. Those technicians–"

The mountains echoed with the muffled sound of an implosion, then the sound of metal creaking. Steam and shrapnel jetted into the air – shrapnel that, since I could see it from miles away, had to be the size of dumpsters. The smokestacks juddered, toppling. Sirens blared.

"– are probably fucked," Mama Alex admitted, wincing. "Come on, soldiers, let's roll."

But our driver Facundo – Ximena's son, a man seemingly made entirely of muscle and beard – had already stomped on the accelerator. We roared down the access road to the factory.

We zoomed towards the steam gouts. The windshield fogged over, then imploded as a chunk of twisted metal smashed through the window, shattering Facundo's left forearm. He cursed and punched the broken windshield down.

Without the windshield to buffer the noises, the wildcat sounds of metal tearing itself apart flooded through the ambulance. Superheated steam rolled in off the dirt access road, hot enough to make us sweat inside our hazmat uniforms. We drove blind, with two misty feet of visibility.

There was a *bang* as something heavy bounced off the roof, leaving a deep dent in the ceiling. Turbines the size of football fields chewed themselves to shreds, spinning off-kilter as superheated steam from the earth's core rushed up and around them in a lungmelting hurricane.

Normally, that energy would be used to make electricity. But Ximena had slowly piloted a small drilling device underground, drilling through rock at an achingly low speed to insert bombs. It had taken her several days to bore a yard-wide tunnel through half a mile of bedrock, but she'd cleared a path to the pipes driven deep into the earth. Then, at great risk, she'd crawled through the tunnels to carefully liquid-patch in a shunt that could be used to pop explosives into. If the shunt had gone wrong, she would have been boiled alive.

Now those explosives had rocketed up to the surface and were going off, their detonations magnified according to Brain Trust calculations.

Though I knew this was our plan, it still seemed unwise to

drive towards the collapsing smokestacks.

Dare was hyperventilating. He'd always hated risks. Yet he wasn't backing down. That made me proud to know him, even though he went out of his way to avoid me.

Peaches said it was because Dare didn't understand her. Though Dare had thought I'd talked Peaches into getting herself shot, he had come to terms with the fact the shooting had ultimately been Peaches' choice. But "humiliating" Peaches by carrying on with that stupid NeoChristian had been the final straw. Our relationship status had been ratcheted back to "tenuous allies."

"Keep fighting the good fight," I told him.

He looked grateful for the distraction, pathetic as it was. Facundo jerked around a curve.

Evangeline was hunched down next to me, head lowered like a horse ready to bolt at the start of a race. She too hyperventilated, but this had the staccato sound of an athlete trying to psych herself up.

Evangeline had not come to me again to snuggle.

I'd like to say neither Dare nor Evangeline had spoken to me... But we'd needed to plan our attack on Lacona Springs. We'd spent our days in stiff strategy meetings, both Dare and Evangeline shoving aside their evident distaste for me to hash out the best approach.

It was awkward, painful, and it was all worse because we had to *look* like a team. This was being filmed; if we survived, we'd edit it into a story and broadcast it. Acting insufficiently heroic during this mission might shatter Pony Boy's nascent mythology.

"*Chingada!*" Facundo shouted, clutching his injured arm as the ambulance smashed through a wooden barrier. We skidded to a stop before a guard house seated in front of a concrete loading dock, steam curling around us. The great, mountain-hugging curve of an inbound monorail track had been crushed beneath a toppled smokestack.

We ran up the steps to the admittance area, leaping over the boiled-red bodies of security guards sprawled on the steps. They'd either come out to gawk at the explosions, or gone out to fix something; regardless, they'd been blistered to death.

Behind that was the chip factory's industrial bulk, a dirty gray box several stories high, its roof obscured by the web of power cables that fed into it. Sludgy trickles of bacterial waste dribbled down the sides.

Izzy was in there somewhere.

A handful of still-living security guards had retreated to the processing center's interior; they held cool rags to their mouths as they ushered us in through the doors. The lobby was shadowed, the camera monitors dimmed – as we'd expected. The Upterlife servers had their own power supplies – the dead wouldn't risk someone pulling their plug. But since the living's needs weren't as essential, the East Coast was mostly powered by this single plant. All nonessential devices in New England were experiencing some serious brownouts – including a lot of cameras. The dead could still talk to each other, but we'd fogged their view of the living.

We made for the inner doors, headed for the biochip factory's inner sanctum. The guards grabbed our arms.

"Remove your suits. Mr Drumgoole says all employees are to be face-scanned before entry."

"Void, man," Dare said. "We've got minutes before this place blows! We need to fix it!"

"Mr Drumgoole was quite clear," the lead guard replied, looking shaken. "He just called us." He reached for my hazmat hood–

I smashed him in the nose with my rifle.

In a movie, the guard would have gone down like a sack of potatoes. Instead, I bloodied his face. He screamed for help as he grappled with me; the other guards went for their earputers.

Mama Alex shot first.

The guard above me took Mama Alex's bullet to the neck, feathering blood across the retinal scanners. Evangeline shook her head, as if waking from a dream – then unloaded her rifle on full auto. She wailed as she walked the gunfire across the guards' chests, a cry of almost orgasmic relief.

Followed by an embarrassed silence.

Mama Alex batted me across the forehead. "Why didn't you shoot the bastard?"

The crosses on Facundo's cheeks contorted with disgust. "Why did *you* shoot *them?*" he bellowed. "You just condemned those poor souls to damnation!"

Dare knelt to search the bodies. "They wanted to die; we needed them to be dead. That's a good deal."

"Murder is *never* good!" Facundo glared at Evangeline as though she should have known better. "We could have knocked them out."

"First off," said Mama Alex in a firm voice, "I *told* you we might need to take some people out."

"That phrasing," Facundo said darkly, "is ambiguous."

"Second, the only reason Wickliffe hasn't exterminated us is because his troops turn ordinary battles into suicide missions. If his minions didn't fling themselves into death at the first bad excuse, we'd have *zero* hope of overthrowing Wickliffe." Mama Alex walked down the row to finish off the survivors, punctuating each sentence with a life-ending gunshot. "Now, these good little guards got their Upterlife, we got to live – and if your skybeard has a problem with that, well, we'll take the hit. *We* killed. *Your* hands are clean."

The guards, choking on their last breath, didn't look victorious; they looked horrified. The dream was eternal life, but this shredded-meat reality was awful to witness...

"So," Mama Alex finished. "Feel like wasting *another* minute?"

Facundo scowled; I wasn't convinced, either. But we were both in too deep to argue.

When did I start agreeing with terrorists?

Who were *the terrorists?*

Dare got the door open using the dead guards' credentials, and we charged through onto the white-tiled floor of the employee locker room. Long rows of biohazard suits hung down, their rips poorly patched. Walls and suits alike were covered in moldy fuzz.

We grabbed some plastic bags to cover our guns before moving on to the white room airlock chamber. The door hissed shut as caustic chemicals sprayed over us.

The wait seemed endless, but the Brain Trust had assured us it was an impassable chokepoint. There was simply no way to bypass the mandatory sterilization procedures before entering the biocrystal matrices' delicate workings. With Gumdrool on the alert, we knew the LifeGuard's transport ships were evacuating Times Square, redirected to Lacona Springs minutes after the explosion. Once they arrived in force, we'd never escape.

Bad enough. But the seething silence between Mama Alex and Facundo portended greater schisms to come.

"So," Dare asked, "you *still* think revealing yourself as a CGI trick was a good idea?"

Was Dare needling me? But no; he shivered with fear. We might all void in the next twenty minutes, and he was trying to rekindle the old banter we'd once shared.

"Peaches told you, Dare: I'm a supervillain. Supervillains telegraph all their best tricks."

I'd argued we needed to explain the trick when the distraction ended, just so the punters would get how very clever I was. The hero had to not just defeat, but *outwit* his enemies. Dare had countered that the explanation would also explain things to our enemy.

Gumdrool had known we were coming. Had I clued him in?

"...maybe I should have kept my mouth shut," I allowed.

"Silence was never your strong suit."

We were still on camera, our earputers filming everything for later broadcast. It might have even looked good to someone on the outside; Dare and I had honed our banter from the good old days, back when we'd run around New York dressed up like ninjas.

Yet Dare drummed his fingers against his gun barrel, disappointed; we'd spoken the old words to summon good feelings, and they'd failed.

Dare had often questioned my sanity in our Blackout Party videos, a ha-ha joke for our audience. Now his questioning was barbed: *Did your grandstanding just get us killed, Amichai?*

We stared at the airlock. With Gumdrool alerted, that door might open to reveal a firing squad. Tomorrow's newscast might have first-person footage of our deaths.

The door creaked open.

42: THE CHIP RECLAMATION FACTORY

There were no firing squads. There were no employees, either.

There was an ominous lack of anyone.

We smelled the lowtide stench of decaying biomatter. Flashing red emergency lights illuminated a long industrial hallway barely wide enough for two skinny workers to work elbow-to-elbow. We squeezed in, bumping along the creches lining each wall – aquariums holding the bacteria that assembled computer chips from waste material.

In the old days, I was told, they dug metal out of the ground and pressed it into computer chips. But the Earth's crust had been looted by past generations, leaving us to recycle what we could from antiquated machinery.

The racks above the long rows of crèches had old motherboards scavenged from waste dumps, each protected by a pane of sterile glass. The racks stretched out for city blocks, crawling slurries of brown goo in a hyperbaric environment – the bacteria that teased out the scant molecules of yttrium and scandium, ferried them down the antfarm pane of the crèche and into the organic chip assemblers.

In the glass mangers of the creche, crusted barnacle-like formations served as microscopic mazes, where the bacteria laid the chips' electronic pathways out one slow layer at a time.

The small maze mirrored the massive factory maze. You couldn't make bacteria work fast, so instead they'd built half a million crèches online to work in parallel. Long pipes gurgled overhead, ferrying nutrients. Panels glowed with readouts, regulating the temperature, monitoring the bacterial stock for mutations. Water burbled underneath our feet, an artificial stream running below slotted steel catwalks to carry away waste materials.

Dare slowed to a halt. "I'd memorized the plans," he murmured. "But it's breathtaking in real life…"

"This one?" Mama Alex tapped on a nutrient pipe.

Dare squinted, following that pipe's path among conduit-clogged intersections. He pointed in various directions, determining where it ended up, then nodded affirmation to Mama Alex.

"It *is* amazing," Mama Alex acknowledged, getting a blowtorch to cut a hole in the pipe; thin red goo splattered into the wastestream. "We were shortsighted enough to destroy our planet, then smart enough to solve the problems our stupidity caused. That's human history for you."

We were on the factory's growth side. On the assembly side, the workers – glorified slave labor – would take the chips grown here to build the Mother Mentors. Still, the hallways should have been choked with people harvesting chips, adjusting chemical balances, resupplying motherboards.

"Where is everyone?" I asked.

Mama Alex stopped to squeeze my shoulder. "Gumdrool must have called them back."

"But we–"

"We got ten minutes less than we planned before the LifeGuard arrives. Our priority is to find a working Mother Mentor." She softened. "I promise you, Amichai. We'll find Izzy if we can. But…"

"…Izzy's never been guaranteed."

"Your sister's the hook. Gumdrool's jiggling her in the water."

I thought of Izzy in Gumdrool's hands and tried not to vomit.

Mama Alex took out a pressurized canister, wedged it into the nutrient pipe, stuffed a wad of selfsealing plastic into the gap to stem the leak. "T minus twelve, I think," she said. "Organics don't follow set schedules. Dare, get us to the supply rooms."

We ran through the endless creches, the glass panes turning dark as Mama Alex's injection did its work. Evangeline led the charge with her gun at the ready, Facundo in obvious pain but clutching his revolver in his good hand.

No one intercepted us.

We arrived at another sterilization chamber, losing another two minutes as it cycled, then emerged near a vast warehouse near a loading dock. The warehouse had a corner stacked with hat-sized Mother Mentor boxes – a stack the size of a house. That seemed large until I examined the rest of the warehouse, and realized they intended to fill these empty spaces with thousands of Mother Mentors.

Still no guards.

Evangeline and Facundo took up guard positions as Mama Alex and Dare pulled out sample Mother Mentors from the stacks, tested them for evidence of Wickliffe's mindslaver technology. If we came this far to find Wickliffe only had slave-linked certain Mother Mentors – or worse, had none at all – then our whole plan was ruined.

"Open up an encrypted channel to Peaches," Mama Alex said. "Send her whatever data we get as we get it, just in case we get interrupted."

I found a monitoring station, broke out the IceBreaker to hack it. The security here was top notch – Gumdrool must have overseen it – but I'd spent the last few weeks being taught secop subversion by Mama Alex.

"They've withdrawn the employees to the break areas," I said. "I've located Izzy. She's not that far away."

She's also supposedly alone, I didn't say. Even I didn't believe that.

"Facundo, you go with Amichai," Mama Alex said. "You're down to one hand anyway. Evangeline, you stay here, and–"

"No."

"What?"

Evangeline's face was resolute. "I'm not afraid," she said. "I am *not* afraid."

"What's that have to do with anything?"

"He hurt me." She bit her lip until it bled. "Gumdrool. He hurt my people." Evangeline seemed to sense this wasn't enough, so she jerked her chin reluctantly towards me and added: "We've worked together before."

But she didn't look at me.

Mama Alex opened her mouth to argue, then looked terribly sad. "All right. Facundo, you're better suited to guard the main mission anyway. Amichai, you…" She shook her head, the beads in her hair rattling. "I'd tell you to retreat if it got too bad. But you wouldn't listen anyway, would you?"

"I'd feel bad about ignoring you…"

She hugged me tight. "We have ensured you have every chance to rescue Izzy. But our tech docs *not* make you invulnerable. Or indispensable. I love you, Amichai, but I will leave your ass behind if I have to. My concern is these Mother Mentors."

"Then why let me go at all?"

"Because if you can rescue her, the footage will go megaviral."

We fled. Evangeline cracked her knuckles eagerly. I imagined all the nights she'd sat up, thinking about her parents driven insane by the experiments Gumdrool loved, thinking of Gumdrool's abuse at the Orphanage – turning Gumdrool into the face of everything wrong with the world.

A face she could finally punch.

Her bloodlust unnerved me. I was all for beating the crap out of Gumdrool, but the eager way she'd shot those guards demonstrated how different we were.

I wondered if she was eager to punch Gumdrool because she couldn't punch me.

We arrived at the cafeteria where Izzy was supposedly holed up. There were swinging access doors; through the grimy windows I saw stained coral benches and dispensers on the walls that dripped sludge-nutrients into bowls. I checked the IceBreaker; the cameras that monitored this area were in brownout.

I instructed the IceBreaker to redirect the ventilators.

Then I saw Izzy.

Even bound to a wheelchair piloted by Gumdrool, she was still the most beautiful sight I'd ever seen. Her wide brown eyes were cataracted, her arms covered with sores and ringworm; she'd picked up the inevitable array of biochip infections.

Izzy cried out: "Why did you come, you idiot? Of course it's a trap!"

Those were the most beautiful words I'd ever heard.

Up until now, I'd been unable to consider the inevitable – that Gumdrool had mindslavered my sister into a drooling, compliant worker.

But she struggled in Gumdrool's grip like a woman possessed.

"I know." I walked forward, trying to swagger for the cameras. Gumdrool had dressed for the press as well, wearing an olive-green general's outfit, his broad chest dangling with medals. "Gumdrool. You've been stationed here for weeks, waiting for me to arrive. Why didn't you pick us off at the entryway?"

"Because I want you alive." Troops stepped out of the kitchen, aiming tasers at us. "My men will execute the rest of your crew. They're too dangerous." He patted Izzy's head as she struggled. "You, however... you won't dare shoot with Isabella in danger."

He smirked. "Honestly, Amichai, I'm surprised it's taken you this long to get here. I'd mentioned Lacona Springs twice in our last conversation. How many hints do I need to leave?"

"I thought you'd planned to void me on the monorail."

"I intended to." A wrinkle of concern appeared on his forehead. "But I've learned never to underestimate you, Amichai. After the branch server fiasco, I instituted my own rule: always have contingency plans when dealing with Amichai Damrosch."

"Funny," I replied, just as the ventilators in the room began to hiss. "I have the same rule with you."

Clouds of black acid billowed into the room.

43: BRUTAL LESSONS ONLY A MOTHER COULD PROVIDE

The Brain Trust knew that destroying a chipmaking factory was trivial. The bacteria only managed to do their jobs due to a specialized environment. Raising the temperature ten degrees would destroy the biomass.

However, the Brain Trust had an idea buried deep in its archives: a tailored virus that wouldn't just destroy the bacteria, but cause them to disintegrate into toxic gas. From there, it was a matter of redirecting the gas vents to the proper places – tricky, but doable if you had an IceBreaker, Mama Alex's supervision, and Dare to chart out the quickest ways to redirect the gas.

The look on Gumdrool's face as his troops choked? Priceless.

They fired tasers at me before collapsing, doing their obligatory duty before succumbing to the death threat. But we'd altered the hazmat suits; the rubberized fabric dispersed the current.

But honestly? This toxic gas would be fatal in time, but initially it was no worse than pepper spray – blinding, painful, but a devoted man could fight for a few minutes more to get to safety.

If his minions didn't fling themselves into death at the first bad excuse, Mama Alex had said, we'd have zero hope of overthrowing Wickliffe.

And, as expected, Gumdrool's handpicked troops clasped their hands over their eyes and fell to the floor, writhing and eager for death.

Gumdrool grabbed a napkin, clasped it over his mouth. Though his eyes were nearly swollen shut, he stepped forward – the only opponent in this room eager to live. "Damrosch," he gurgled. "This won't stop me–"

Evangeline punched him in the throat.

Or tried to.

Gumdrool moved with fluid grace, anticipating Evangeline's move. He swatted her punch away with his free hand, aimed a kick at her groin.

Evangeline moved backwards, shifting to a defensive posture. I was no martial arts expert... but had Gumdrool been this good last time?

Gumdrool's chortle told me just how much better he'd gotten.

"The Mother Mentor can teach you things *horrifically* fast." He circled around Evangeline, coughing as he reached for a rebreather at his waist. "It programs in the correct muscle memories, makes you hyperaware of your stance. And after this NeoChristian bitch took me out, I've spent the last month having it improve my martial arts..."

He exploded at her, a flurry of kicks and left-hand punches so quick I couldn't even track them. Evangeline's years of training weren't enough to anticipate Gumdrool – he broke past her defenses, slipping in a knee to the gut, landing a blow to the jaw. She tried to muster a counterattack, but the hazmat suit weighed her down.

And this is him one-handed, half-choking on gas...

"We knew we might lose this facility!" he crowed, stepping around Izzy's wheelchair to backhand Evangeline. She scurried away from Gumdrool, panicked. "I don't know

where you've gotten this new biotechnology, Amichai, but...
One factory to get you was a small cost. We've got hundreds
of facilities. And when we're done, every LifeGuard will be
trained as extensively as I am–"

He unholstered his truncheon. Evangeline wept, nearly
begging – she'd lost her parents, lost her faith, lost her battle...

"*No!*" I screamed, and launched myself at Gumdrool.

He shattered my right shoulder.

I bit my tongue, thinking this is all on camera, how will it
look if Pony Boy screams in his last moments?

He adjusted the rebreather over his mouth and nose –
then stepped on Evangeline's neck. Something popped. She
wriggled, muttering fragmented prayers.

"Now, little NeoChristian." He bore his weight down. "I
hope there *is* a God. I want to send you to Hell..."

Peaches' voice rattled over my earputer speakers.

"If you kill her," Peaches told Gumdrool, "we'll blow up
the plant."

44: THE PURITY TEST

Gumdrool didn't remove his boot from Evangeline's neck – but he did pause, staring in my direction with a strange courtesy. Gumdrool had always held respect for Peaches.

That was good. We had no way to blow the plant. But Gumdrool didn't know that.

"You should know by now that I do not fear death, Ms Khan-Tien."

"No," Peaches said in a hoarse whisper – so hoarse that I realized how terrified she was for my safety. "You fear *failure*."

Evangeline struggled. Gumdrool bore down.

"Wickliffe despises you," Peaches continued. "He's not even supervising you, because he hates knowing he has to use someone like you. He wants Amichai instead."

Gumdrool's wounded flinch signaled just how on-target Peaches was. Wickcleft had been my champion back at the rebel base. Whereas Wickliffe had disdained Gumdrool from the moment they met; things had apparently not improved since Gumdrool had become Wickliffe's righthand man.

"If Amichai gets voided, Wickliffe – your hero – will forever regret that he relied on you."

Gumdrool slumped.

"You hit hard, Ms Khan-Tien," he admitted. "Mr Wickliffe, he… he *drinks*. All the pleasures the Upterlife has to offer, and he crawls back into his father's bottle.

"And when he drinks, he… becomes abusive. He tells me that people like me made the Upterlife a shithole. He calls me a murdering thug, laments how he has to rely on savages like me. And I stand there. Listening. Because he *orders* me to. Every day, I accomplish more for this man than *thousands* of these greedy eternity-seekers…" He swept his hands to encompass the dying troopers. "And all the while he longs for Amichai, Amichai, Amichai."

"So give it up," Peaches said. "You don't have to work for him."

His handsome face crumpled into a bitter smirk. "But I do, Ms Khan-Tien. His relentless adoration of Mr Damrosch is just one of many errors Mr Wickliffe makes – he's so loath to use the mindslavers, I practically had to blackmail him into authorizing the Mother Mentor program. And…"

The gas swirled as he contemplated Peaches' question.

"If I leave," he asked, "who will be pure?"

"No. If there is a way to save the future generations who would void without our technology, I will take it. Wickliffe needs me to make the choices that he will not. If I void, it is for a good cause."

"Ian," Peaches protested, her bluff sagging at the edges. "If you brainwash the living, you're not actually putting those people *into* the servers…"

But he'd stopped listening. That sinuous grin blossomed across his face; you could see cities burning in his eyes.

"As people with no future at all," he continued. "I believe you value lives more than I do. Amichai, are you OK knowing your sister will be dead forever? Or better yet, your NeoChristian companion?"

He ground his bootheel on Evangeline's neck. She cried out in terror – the wail of a woman who'd betrayed God, and now would face eternal torment…

"Stop!" I said. "I'll be your prisoner."

Gumdrool smiled.

45: PREPARING TO SAY GOODBYE

Gumdrool strode ahead, speaking into his earputer. "I have him."

He was near-blinded from the gas, his vision so uncertain he placed a hand on his freshly summoned LifeGuard troops to ensure he didn't stumble.

"Yes, Mr Wickliffe. Him *and* the NeoChristian girl. No, I haven't heard back from the other troops yet, but – I got you your prize. I'll... yes, I know. Communications are spotty everywhere, sir. I don't know where they got the firepower to take out the geothermal plant, but we'll wring that from Damrosch's mind..."

The troops dragged us towards the spirocopter on the loading dock. As a combatant, Evangeline had been drugged to drooling; as a noncombatant with a shattered arm, I'd been given enough painkillers to keep walking.

My only consolation was that they were wheeling Izzy alongside me. Even though they'd hooked her up to an oxygen tank, she was still hacking up a lung. The chipfarm infections had made her sensitive to the toxic gas.

"At least we're together, brother," Izzy coughed. "Together till the end..."

"I don't know if talking to Damrosch now is a good idea, sir," Gumdrool continued. "We're... hello? Sir, I... I can't hear... The..." He removed his earputer, shook it angrily. "I *told* Him we needed to bulk up the infrastructure. We've been neglecting the living side of things so long, we're paying that price..."

He wiped tears from his eyes. "The biohazard was a clever ruse, Amichai. I warned him you'd come at us sideways. 'You should gene-engineer us all,' I told Him. 'Make us as strong as Amichai's beloved ponies, so he'll stand no chance against us.' But no. He's terrified of progress. 'One genetic experiment gone wrong,' He keeps repeating, 'And you wind up with another Bubbler...'"

"So what now?" I asked.

"We haul you back to an area with full power, and Wickliffe talks to you."

"No mindslavery?"

"Mr Wickliffe believes he can convince you using mere *words*."

I tried to imagine what words would make me buy into Wickliffe's scheme...

...but stopped when I saw Mama Alex and Dare standing before Gumdrool's spirocopter.

Dare was bruised but unbroken, standing tall, the wind whipping through his hair. Mama Alex held out her hands, wearing nothing but a thin tie dyed dress.

Gumdrool waved his troops to a halt. "Thought you'd have been killed."

"My guards got killed," she replied. "Scary business. So I decided I don't wanna void yet."

Gumdrool spat phlegm to one side, clearing his throat. "Drug her, search her, get her in the copter."

The guards raised their trankguns. She smirked. "You keep calling me an old woman. You know what you should ask?"

"What?"

"How'd she get to be so old, when she's always flinging herself in death's teeth?"

The beads in her hair flickered. The room filled with a throbbing light that hurt my head. Gumdrool and his guards toppled over, convulsing.

"You carry dazers in your *braids*?" I asked, delighted.

Mama Alex didn't look delighted; she looked grim. "Also a garrote in my dreadlocks, a hacking card embedded in my shoe sole, and five other tricks I'll never tell anybody about. Come on, Amichai, help me load Gumdrool into the copter."

"Just cut his throat!" said Dare.

"We can't," Mama Alex sighed. "Gumdrool told Wickliffe that Amichai is on the way. If Wickliffe doesn't see this ship taking off soon, he'll know we escaped. He'll flood this area with troops... and he'll catch you." She closed her eyes, breathed through her nostrils. "No, we need to crash this ship. Make Wickliffe think everyone voided."

"OK." I fired up the IceBreaker to plot a course for crashing.

"You..." She put her hand over my IceBreaker. "You don't understand. That ship is trifactor-secured – it won't take off unless it registers Gumdrool's brainwaves inside. And it's autopiloted via satellite."

"So how do we crash it?"

"Someone's gotta be inside when it goes down. Smash the satellite feed, then crash it hard enough they won't be able to count the bodies in the wreckage."

I'd survived one copter crash, but that had been from thirty feet up – and it had killed one person and crippled another. I imagined a drop from a mile up, crashing into the hard rock of a mountainside – and shuddered at that terrible, bone-shattering death.

Who would do it? Dare, Mama Alex, or me?

Then I realized: Mama Alex had already made that decision.

Dare seized her, pulled her back from the spirocopter's cockpit. "*No! I'll* pilot it! I will *not* allow you to–"

"Dare," Mama Alex said gravely. "Look at me."

Lights strobed.

Dare collapsed onto cold concrete.

"Wish we had more time to argue," Mama Alex said, dragging Gumdrool into the spirocopter. "Facundo'll be back soon with a vehicle. You take everyone and get the void out of town."

"Mama, I–"

"Don't make me daze you, too, Amichai," she said. "There's troops inbound from all over New York state."

"But why's it have to be *you?*"

She knelt down. "Because everything good comes with an expiration date, Amichai. Everyone else who could do this is either too incapacitated or too necessary. I don't want to void, but... This is a better death than lots of people get."

"I can't–"

She pulled me into one final hug.

"We've got no other choice, Amichai. I've... It's not like I *want* to do this. But..." She swallowed. "But don't you give up. Peaches and Dare, they'll do what's necessary to keep the revolution running. Your job is to *dream.*"

"Dream of what?"

Mama Alex held me at arm's length. "I think the dead are beyond saving. But you – you're *stupid* stubborn, just like Wickliffe. You won't give up on anyone. Peaches and Dare would just erase everyone, and so would I, but..."

She gripped my shoulders hard. "You find a way to save everybody."

"I will, Mama."

"Or die trying?"

"Or die trying."

She stood up, dismissing me, staring into the spirocopter's cockpit. She brushed her dreadlocks back.

"I'm gonna die, trying." The tiniest of smiles crept across her face.

I barely remember Mama Alex climbing into the spirocopter, though we have her final moments on film. I don't remember Facundo screeching up in a stolen electric transitcar, the troops landing hot on our heels, the gunfire, the bursting through barriers, stealing new getaway vehicles, losing the LifeGuard in the mountains.

Grief will erase your memories. Your brain gets overloaded. It just… stops recording.

But I *do* remember watching that spirocopter arc high up into the air, becoming a small dot hovering over high mountain peaks. I remember seeing its smooth flightpath wobble, the copter spinning, plummeting, dropping.

I remember watching that little copter, and imagining the strength it must have taken Mama Alex to keep the throttle down as the rocks rushed up at her. I imagined her hand steady on the controls.

I like to think she met the void with a quiet dignity. I like to think she felt nothing but peace, serenity, and certainty in her final moments.

I know that's not true.

But I like to think it.

46: GOODBYE

I'd never have made it through Mama Alex's funeral if it wasn't for Izzy.

Izzy was in bad shape, exhausted by having worked eighteen-hour days in a virus-laden hellhole. She kept dozing off midsentence. But I held her, so grateful to have her. We hugged each other tight – not *too* tight, given her ringwormed arms and the cast on my broken shoulder.

"Everyone saw your adventures in the branch server," Izzy told me. "It was *scary*, how fast that video spread. You'd get jailed for uploading it, but people copied it to memory sticks. People held showings at Blackout Parties. I got *thousands* of emails, asking if you were for real."

"What'd you say?"

"I told 'em you were a real pain in my butt."

Our laughter felt like lancing a wound. We hadn't been on the same page in so long.

"Then I saw you apologizing." The puzzlement on her face reflected the concern she must have had back then. "I got a stiff videocall from you where you apologized for not dropping by, but... the *words* were wrong. It was like hearing a bad cover band do Amichai's Greatest Hits. And I thought, *your stupid brother smuggled a pony in here to cheer you up. He wouldn't just abandon you.* But the alternative – that the government was faking your identity – it sounded..."

"...crazy."

"This whole thing sounds insane if you haven't lived it." Izzy's laugh dissolved into wet coughs. "Then Ian reassigned me to the chip manufacturing plant – and sweet void, he did *not* believe that hostages should have a vacation. He put me to work, gave me lectures on the glories of the Upterlife, made me stagger up and down those corridors taking samples until I passed out..."

"Oh, sweetie." I stroked her hair while she coughed again. It had been bad enough watching the Brain Trust probe her, forcing her through Shrive after Shrive to sift her thoughts for evidence of tampering – but seeing her newfound lung infections told me how badly I'd failed her.

"They never taught us about those working conditions at the Academy. And – void, Amichai, all I could think about was killing everyone who put me there. Anyone who'd condemn another human to that existence deserves to void." She bit a stubby fingernail, daring me to contradict her.

I didn't. Though I didn't agree. Having watched Mama Alex plunge into oblivion, the idea of erasing billions more sickened me.

If you take this job, Mama Alex had said, your best case is the worst choice a human being's ever had to make.

"We'll never Shrive again, will we?" Izzy asked, heartbroken. "We'll never meet up with Mom and Dad, we'll never grow baby phoenixes with them, we'll never reunite our family. We'll just... void."

I wanted to tell her that wasn't true. But lying to make her feel better was a Mom and Dad move. So I held her hand, the way I'd done in the hospital, in what seemed so long ago.

"...yeah. We'll... we'll die a meat-death."

"Oh void." She squeezed my hand hard. "The lack of the Upterlife – it's a physical ache. Like an *addiction*. I feel like this could all make sense if I could just listen to Mom and Dad for a while longer – to hear them tell me about the glorious voyages that await me..."

Izzy gazed at the dead monitors embedded in the mall walls. Even after the torture she'd been through, she *still* wanted Mom and Dad to tell her everything would be all right. Whereas I wanted Mama Alex to flicker back onscreen to say hello, she made it, things are great here on the other side.

Neither of us could imagine someone just... vanishing.

"Teach me to program, Amichai." Izzy clenched misshapen fists. "I need to make something good with the time I have left."

I'd watched a few Criminal meat-funerals out of morbid curiosity. They were embarrassing afterthoughts. The unShrived burials had been like flushing a toilet – ditch the waste and pretend the accident hadn't happened.

Mama Alex's death made us angry.

So Mama Alex's funeral was dangerous.

We made a pyre, even though there was no body left to burn. We masked the blaze as best we could, but maybe satellite photos could pick up our heat signature through the masking curtains. Maybe overhead drones would notice the movement of our dancing.

Wickliffe had killed our Mama. We were too mad for tactics.

People drank too much and pissed in the bonfires. They shattered bottles and vowed vengeance on Wickliffe. They danced, they screamed, they cut their hair.

And after the rage dissipated, they told stories, trying to keep her alive by sharing memories.

Mama Alex was always harsh, and always helpful. She'd helped get this one kid off drugs by locking him in a room until he went clean. She'd helped another by assigning her increasingly difficult programming tasks to distract her from her addiction. She was brutally efficient, dispensing custom-tailored solutions to problems...

But lots of kids also told stories of the time Mama Alex had made them hot cocoa and hugged them.

We all agreed: she had the best hugs.

There were more rebels at the funeral than I remembered. They spread out across the four mall levels, dangling their feet over the sides, standing next to the NeoChristians pressing in. People had seen my videos. There was an underground railroad of techies trickling into Boston's promised land.

Peaches, clad in black wool, steered her chair next to the Brain Trust.

"...so she told me that our alliance would fall apart at the first funeral," Peaches said. "Did she say that to you?"

A ripple of murmurs. Apparently, Mama Alex had had that conversation with just about everyone.

"I... I think she was warning us." Peaches wrung her hands. "She knew. And she wanted us to consider how ridiculous it would be for us NeoChristians and atheists to... to sunder right now. Because she, she..."

Peaches thumped the Brain Trust's scarred metal casing.

"She *won*! We have the Mother Mentors! We killed Gumdrool! The world thinks Amichai is dead! All that for a single casualty! This feels like loss, but I assure you... it's victory."

She hung her head. "All the same. If we start thinking a life is worth a cost, then... then we're Wickliffe."

Wickcleft bowed his head, shamed by his parallel self.

"Mama Alex, she... she told me forest fires seemed tragic, but secretly made the world better. That the flames that burned the old trees cleared brush to let young saplings grow twice as fast."

Peaches eased her joystick to the left, twirling her chair in a slow circle, meeting the eyes of every single person in that gallery.

"Mama Alex thought you were worth burning for," Peaches told them.

•••

I stumbled into Dare after the funeral. He was making out with a young black guy, guzzling home-brewed booze between sloppy kisses. I didn't notice him at first; there were a lot of makeout sessions that night.

But Dare called after me, belligerent, drunk: "Where *you* going, Pony Boy?"

Dare's lover, sensing trouble, slipped away. Dare swaggered up.

"So you gave in to guilt. *Again.*"

"I didn't–"

"You surrendered."

"It's not like I wasn't looking for an escape…"

"You gave up."

"He called her bluff, Dare. And…" I felt the bones in my broken shoulder grind. "He'd *won*. I couldn't stop him."

"And if we *could* have blown up the factory? Would it have made a difference?"

I studied my shoes.

"I *told* you you'd make stupid choices," Dare spat. "You're perfectly fine watching my sister get shot, and yet the second someone hurts that NeoChristian bitch, *you surrender!* You handed over your precious brain and everything you know about Boston! Mama Alex had to go back to *rescue* your sad ass!"

"Mama Alex thought rescuing Izzy was a worthy risk."

"That's because Mama Alex was a *real* mother. You killed her. You crippled my sister. You're destroying everything I love… and if it was all for the cause, I could *deal* with that! You want… you want this phony Upterlife paradise, where *everybody* gets saved!" He flailed. "You'll do anything to avoid getting people killed, but that just makes *more* slaughter!"

He flung his bottle at me.

"No wonder Therapy's your symbol." He bumped my bad shoulder as he pushed past me. "A crazy pony stampeding through a hospital. *Clueless.*"

•••

I found Evangeline in the woods. She stared up at the sky, hands laced over her belly.

She was positioned like a corpse.

I carefully eased myself onto the ground down beside her, my broken shoulder aching.

I stared at the sky. The sky where Mama Alex had died.

"...You couldn't have done anything," I said.

Her voice was monotone. "That's not the point."

"What is?"

"When I threatened to kill him at the branch server, he embraced death. But... when he threatened me... I cried. I would have begged, if you hadn't jumped in." She swallowed. "Gumdrool – Drumgoole – has more faith than I do."

She turned to look at me. "You took that faith from me, Amichai."

"How did I–"

"If I'd walked away from you, I'd be dead and in Heaven, and everything would be OK. But I'm still here. Sinning. Sinning *all the time*. Not a moment goes by I don't wish we'd both died in that crash."

"You want me to void?"

"I want you to be in Heaven, Amichai." She gripped my hand. "But you don't believe in the Second Coming. You lay with women who aren't your wife. You... Argh." She scrubbed her face with balled fists. "Your beliefs make things complicated, Amichai. I keep thinking that I can only save myself by converting you..."

I tried not to back away. "Even if your God existed, I... I don't think he'd like me much."

"It's not about belief, Amichai. Do you know why my people reject me?"

"Ximena said you were a heretic..."

"We call ourselves *Eibonites*. My people were a fragment of a fragment. Wickliffe targeted my sect because he knew no one would protect us. Ximena's people – all the rest – they believe Christ was God's son, born without sin, without sex – a neuter passed down from the Heavens to die for our sins."

I didn't want to tell her how batshit that sounded. "And you believe?"

"That Christ was an ordinary man, born of man and woman. When He placed Himself on that cross, Christ had no more guarantee of eternity than any of us have *right now*; He was scared, and confused, and uncertain whether this was the right thing to do. Yet He had the faith and the courage to sacrifice His life rather than cease His good works. Then, on the cross, when He had suffered more completely for His brother than any man before Him, God escorted Christ up to Heaven as a beacon to light the way for others. Christ wasn't the Chosen One; He was the one who chose Himself. And nobody wants to hear that, because everyone's waiting for a sign."

"So what does *that* mean?"

"It means if you do enough good works, then we *both* die saved, and we'll go to Heaven together."

"I don't believe that."

"You will. You *have* to, Amichai. Or I'll go mad."

You are mad, I thought, but couldn't say it. Something in her needed to believe the world was like a bank – you deposited in kindness and got it all back in the end.

I'd seen Mama Alex. She'd spread kindness.

She got no reward.

"I want to," I said, the words summing up everything – I want to bridge the gulf between the dead and the living. I want Mama Alex's sacrifice to mean something. I want you not to hurt.

Yet those three words told her just how much I couldn't do any of that.

"Stay with me." Evangeline turned away from me,

clutching herself. "Stay near. I don't know why your presence is a comfort, but it is."

I rested my palm on her ribcage – a promise. "I will."

She drifted into sleep.

Peaches wheeled up nearby. Her wheelchair rocked, spinning in the woods' soft loam, but her freshly upgraded treads gave her traction.

Her face was stark with grief.

"Amichai," she said – softly enough to not wake Evangeline, but firm. "I need you."

I lifted my hand away from Evangeline, feeling both betrayals – betraying Evangeline for stepping away, betraying Peaches for having let her witness such an intimate touch. "Evangeline's in bad shape."

Peaches held her gaze on me, letting me hear myself, and with each passing second the words felt dumber, less defensible.

And still I refused to take them back.

Peaches leaned forward, her eyes glimmering with moonlight and unspilled tears. "I... I know she doesn't want to be alone." Peaches' voice was tender as a sunburn. "But I... I can't spend the night by myself. Not after Mama Alex. I'd normally dance until I forgot, but..."

She hung her hair down until it brushed her withered thighs.

"I need someone to spend the night with me, Amichai. And it has to be you." She swallowed. "No. That's wrong. I *want* it to be you. But if you say no, I'll... I'll find someone else. He won't be as good, and he won't be as kind, but... I'm feeling like when Mama Alex left, she took everything good with her, and if I spend the night staring at the ceiling I'll find a knife and slit my wrists. And I *will* find someone to distract me before I get that stupid. I'm hoping, *begging*, that will be you.

"So please, Amichai." She reached out to me, fluidly inviting me to a dance. "Come with me."

I remembered all the nights I'd spent aching for her. I wanted to reach back – but Gumdrool had broken my good arm.

To take Peaches' hand would have meant stepping away from Evangeline.

"I want that more than you could ever know."

"Then come."

"She…" I couldn't bring myself to say Evangeline's name, not in front of Peaches, not now. "If she wakes up alone, she'll find a knife, too. And she's got no one."

Peaches straightened up, tying her hair back into a bun. "Is that how you decide who gets you, Amichai? Whoever needs you most?"

I had no words.

"…It's a good decision." Each taut word Peaches spoke was like a fist to my gut. "You protect everyone that way, Amichai. Except yourself."

She gave me a sarcastic salute, then turned around, wheels churning in the soil. If she'd stormed off, her leaving would have been mercifully quick. Instead, she plowed her way through the muck inch by inch, giving me all the time in the world to regret my decision.

I lay next to Evangeline, not daring to touch her. I watched Evangeline's chest rise and fall in the night, staying awake, making sure I would be there if she needed me.

My shoulder ached. I imagined what Peaches was doing. Imagined it with every boy I'd seen in the camp: every kiss, every soft gasp, every touch. And in the crux of that moment, entwined with some new lover, Peaches would moan and forget about her legs, forget about Wickliffe, forget about Mama Alex…

…forget about me.

I lay next to Evangeline, and not one person in the world knew I was there.

47: LOST IN THE MOTHER MENTOR'S LOVING THOUGHTS

I held the Mother Mentor's black plastic crown over my head. "Are you *sure* this is a good idea?"

Dare and Izzy kept their distance, as if it might explode at any moment.

"We've eye- *eye!*-isolated the mmmmindslaver hardware and removed it," Wickcleft assured me. "The buh- beast is defanged."

That technology touching my temples still squicked me out. "You realize I'd feel much more comfortable with this if you weren't glitch-stammering when you said spoke."

"Huh- huh- had to choose between retaining intact verbal centers or my muh- muh- moral structures," Wickcleft shot back. "Buh- buh- besides, with Mmmmama Alex gone, whuh- we've lost our best technician. Call this uh- uh- a necessary risk. If whuh- whuh- we can make you as good at hacking as Gumdrool was at fie- fie- fighting, then we've guh- got a *monster* on our hands."

I grinned. "I like being a monster."

"So put it on."

I lowered the Mother Mentor onto my head. Little servos gripped my skull. The world vanished, replaced with a mosaic of tiny screens. I felt embraced by a helpful presence, one eager as a dog to please. I thought *oh, that help screen looks interesting* and the help screen zoomed up eagerly to meet me–

Crap, we're still gesturing at computers, Amichai, Peaches had said. Why doesn't your earputer read your mind?

I wondered what it knew about the Upterlife; tutorials spun out before I finished the thought, starting with childish explanations of the communications protocols Mama Alex had taught me. Each tutorial zoomed towards me and shivered for a moment, then obligingly whisked itself away when it became apparent I understood it already. More tutorials zipped into view, each increasingly complex, until seventeen tutorials shuddered to a halt – knowledge hovering at the limits of my comprehension.

How would you break into someone's consciousness on the Upterlife? I wondered. A friendly helperbot explained how the collective memories of a stored mind were used to generate a unique passkey. In other words, a memory could only be added, changed, or retrieved if someone had access to all your *previous* memories. The Mother Mentor's explanation made perfect sense to me: the only person who had access to your information was, by definition, you.

Breaking in was impossible. Each memory you added made you more unique, made the passkey increasingly impossible to fake.

So how do people in the Upterlife interface with other stored consciousnesses? I wondered – and tutorials unfolded themselves to demonstrate all the ways one stored consciousness sent requests to another: textstreams, audio files, images, skin-simulators, and of course the subconscious dreamstream used to feed people's Shrives into each brain for judgment.

It was like I'd explained it to myself: clear, simple, digestible. I wondered if there was a way to feed a tainted image to someone's consciousness, to trick it into writing malicious data – and the Mother Mentor taught me all the methods of the visual APIs the Upterlife supported. Wickliffe had ensured images had to be sanitized to match strict inputs before they would be accepted – but maybe the auditory channels were–

Izzy giggled and took the Mother Mentor off my head. "Having a good time?" she asked.

My head spun. Those lessons had been like nailing two pieces of wood together and realizing you could use those principles to build a skyscraper. The implications of everything I *could* do set my mind reeling.

"That was *amazing*." I made a weak grab for the Mentor. "Give it back, I gotta… Wait, why is it so bright out?"

"It's noon, Amichai," Izzy giggled. "You've spent four hours in there."

Judging from Dare's vacant stare, the Mother Mentor on his head, and the way his fingers twitched on an imaginary keyboard, time passed differently when you learned at an accelerated rate.

"Yuh-you just cuh-compressed six weeks of learning into a mmmorning," Wickcleft said. "Guh- get some air, kid."

"But I–"

"Don't hog the Mentor, Amichai." Izzy cradled the black plastic crown. "All I've been thinking is how great it would be to play games with Mom and Dad in the Upterlife these days – and learning to program is the ultimate game, isn't it?"

"So you've just been watching me for the past four hours?"

"Not quite." A broad, wet nose pressed against my neck. "But Therapy's ready to play with someone new."

Therapy pranced around the mall, Peaches strapped to her back. I sat in a corner, almost hidden from sight, as everyone in the mall cheered. Peaches' retinue of smitten helpers had tinkered up a specialized saddle Peaches could tie her legs to, and the first trial run had been a success.

Peaches clopped around, mock-knighting the rebels

and NeoChristians who'd helped her. It was a good tactic; playacting as their leader set her up as the next Mama Alex, and the praise raised spirits.

Still, my stomach turned sour. She'd spent the night with one of them. *At least* one of them.

"Shuh- shuh- she needs to gladhand, you know," Wickcleft told me, flickering onto a monitor next to me. "Puh-politicking is puh-part of her job. Duh-doesn't mean she's stopped caring for you, Amichai."

"She hasn't talked to me since... since that night."

"And the NnnneoChristian girl?"

"Not her, either." Facundo had convinced his mother Ximena to take Evangeline under her wing. Evangeline had avoided me, instead helping Ximena's family with whatever task was at hand. She sang prayers so plaintively she threatened to overwhelm their gospel chorus.

"Thuh-that's understandable, too," Wickcleft said. "Whuh-when someone falls off the Guh-God wagon, they-*they!*-they huh-have to surround themselves with like-*like!*-likeminded people to get back on again."

"But why does she *need* a skybeard?"

Wickcleft shrugged. "I nuh-never believed in God, Amichai. I just built one."

Therapy started a game of tag with the rebels. They whooped and hollered as Therapy made twenty-foot leaps from floor to floor, a blur of movement. I doubt the geneticists who'd cooked Therapy up had envisioned their pony becoming the queen of Dodge-'Em, but no one managed to touch my girl.

Peaches clung to Therapy's mane, determined not to be thrown off.

"So you found the mindslaver tech," I said. "What message is your evil twin trying to burn into our brains?"

Wickcleft polished his monocle.

"I duh-duh-don't know," he finally admitted.

"How can you not know? He's you!"

"He is nuh-nuh-not *me!*" He massaged his temples in frustration, almost facepalming. "I wouldn't do *any* of this! And yuh-yet…I'm muh-muh-*missing* something, Amichai."

"But the message?" I insisted. "That must be obvious, right?"

"The Buh- Buh- Brain Trust thought it would be a simple order, like OBEY THE DEAD. Buh-but no. They perfected *that* uh-overt brainwashing a *long* time ago. What other me wants to do is an insidiously cuh-cuh-complex change, huh-heavily encrypted.

"And until we fuh-figure out what opinions huh-he's trying to uh-alter," Wickcleft continued, "we huh-have to sssstay in hiding! We can't bring you buh-back from the dead to have you suh-suh-say, 'Citizens! There is evil *stuff* in the Mother Mentors! Buh-but we don't know whuh-what their message is.'"

"But he *is* trying to brainwash us."

"Buh-buh-brainwash? Nuhnot quite. This is more like a gentle rrrrrinse. He- *he!*-he's making subtle changes to people's minds – very luh-long term…"

I frowned. "You sound OK with that, though."

"Nuh-no! Even suh-subtle manipulation of muh-memories mmmmmakes my gut churn. And it should mmmmake *him* sick, too!" Wickliffe yanked his tie off, slumpcd to sit down on a virtual sidewalk. "I spent *so* much time fighting puh-politicians, Amichai. Do you nuh-know how many whuh-wanted to install backdoor fuh-filters to ensure loyalty? And thuh-that was… it *offended* me. It wasn't *you* in the servers if they altered you. I mean, I wanted my fuh-fuh-father to quit drinking – but if I'd *stripped* his alcoholism away… well, he wouldn't have been my fuh-father, don't you see? You cuh-can't force puh-people to change."

I hadn't realized how badly I'd needed to hear Wickliffe,

any Wickliffe, say those words.

"So I told China, and the USA, and... and, well, every country. They *all* wanted to 'fix' people. I told them to guh-guh-go hang themselves. Then I muh-made my Upterlife so much better they huh-*had* to come to me. Thuh- hat's why I worked twenty-hour days, cuh-constantly making the Up-*Up!*-Upterlife's servers the finest. Because if I didn't, some scuh-scumbag would put puh-parodies up on the internet and call them *people*."

That was all true. That was Wickliffe's mystique. After the government bureaucrats had uploaded their consciousnesses, they'd defected to reveal what draconian plans their governments had *wanted* to implement – and as a result, people came to trust Wickliffe more than any set of laws. He'd gotten elected president *because* he'd safeguarded eternity.

"So huh-huh-how did I come to betray myself, Amichai?" Wickcleft materialized a bottle of scotch in his hand, gazed at it longingly, then smashed it into the gutter. "That duh-drives me mad."

"Would it help distract you if I asked you to help me hack the Upterlife?"

Wickcleft gave me the indulgent laugh you gave a kid when he said he'd be an astronaut when he grew up.

"Yuh- you can try. Buh-buh-but I locked those up tight."

"Surely the president could..."

"Nuh-never hand your uh-enemy a weapon you wouldn't whuh-want used on yourself, Amichai," Wickleft chided. "I duh-didn't know I'd become president. I designed the entire suh-system so that no one, and I mean *no one*, could read your mind. Nuh-not even me. And no one could change your mind unless yuh-you desired it. Thuh-that's baked in. Once you're uploaded, yuh-yuh- our memories are your own."

"Wait – Wickliffe told me he'd read my Shrive... He predicted what I wanted..."

"A lie to thuh-throw you off. Wuh-we are just *very good* at suh-sizing people up. Uh-especially when wwwwwwe can pull up your luh-life's history."

"But surely a security flaw could let me read someone's..."

"Nuh- not many left at this point. I've puh-puh-patched them all. I vuh-verified every snippet of code before it was chuh-checked in..."

"So there's no workaround?"

"I'd say no, but... yuh-yuh-you *do* surprise me." His admiration warmed me. "You have a whuh-way of coming at people from unexpected angles."

"I think I can turn this all around. If I can just talk to the dead..."

Wickcleft steepled his fingers, intrigued. "You think *talking* will solve this?"

"Well, it's all I'm good at."

He laughed, invigorated by the challenge. "Vuh-very well, Amichai Damrosch. I will huh-help you hunt for security fuh- fuh- flaws in my programs. I'll huh-hook up with the Mmmmother Mentors to teach you uh-uh-all my secrets. So you can have a chuh-*chat*."

A tension unknotted in my chest. "Thank you, sir."

I looked at Peaches, who'd unstrapped herself from Therapy. Therapy nuzzled her neck, and she laughed in delight... Until she saw me.

She asked one of her rebel suitors to help her back into her wheelchair, turning away.

"Whuh-what will you tuh-teach Isabella?"

It was a crude politician's distraction. But Wickcleft had reminded me that whatever happened with Peaches, I still had Izzy.

"Gonna do it the way Mama Alex taught me," I said. "She's gonna hack her own internet connection."

"Tradition," Wickcleft murmured. "I lllllike it."

48: ACTS OF SUBTLE SABOTAGE

"You broke it," Wickcleft whispered.

I sat next to the Brain Trust, staring at the testbed software that we'd been battering for... well, I didn't know how long. You lost track of time in the Mother Mentor. Days. Probably weeks.

But inside that testbed was a complete working copy of Wickliffe's Upterlife software, holding every safeguard the Upterlife had to offer. I'd spent days proposing methods to sneak past the various defensive measures, with Wickcleft telling me how *that* wouldn't work, *that* wouldn't work, *that* can't work.

After assaulting the Upterlife from a thousand different angles, I'd finally found a crack to wriggle through.

Wickleft's image flickered across every monitor on the Brain Trust server, doing a looping cha-cha with himself. "You did it!" he cried. "You thought of something I hadn't!"

I removed the Shrive helmet and checked the miniUpterlife for the third time. The vulnerability was still there.

"I did it," I told him, and Wickcleft echoed *"Yes, you did it!"* and Dare, distracted, took off his Mother Mentor.

"You did what?"

I held out the Upterlife readings to him. If anyone could prove me wrong, it was Dare. With Mama Alex gone, he'd spent twenty-hour days in the Mother Mentor learning how to maintain the Brain Trust. Between that and his architectural superpower, he'd become the enclave's acknowledged master of Upterlife hardware.

Dare flicked through the result sets. He checked each indicator off, verifying this wasn't a false signal.

He whistled low as he confirmed the exploit.

"That is a *gigantic* vulnerability," Dare said. I drank in his approval. "Now how do we weaponize this glitch?"

"I've got just the ticket." I turned to Izzy, who muttered to herself beneath a Mother Mentor hood. "Hey, Izzy – look what I did!"

She didn't respond. I checked her feeds; she'd finally cracked a connection open to the internet.

I felt a warm glow of triumph. My sister, who'd once yelled at me for talking to Mama Alex, was now a badass illegal programmer. The moment I'd broken into the Upterlife, *she'd* cracked her first connection – a wonderfully symmetrical victory.

Why hadn't she told me?

I dropped into her line, seeing who she was talking to.

Mom and Dad crowded the camera, looking concerned.

"You shouldn't feel *guilty*, love," Mom reassured her. "We saw what Amichai did on the news – blowing up that factory, disrupting Times Square–"

"He's a terrorist, Izzy," Dad said. "Endangering billions of dead citizens. The news told us he'd voided, but Mr Drumgoole told us not to believe that until we saw the body…"

Izzy flailed her hands, confused. "Amichai's not… a terrorist, Dad! *You're* the terrorists. You're enslaving the living to… wait. Why did I call you? Why would I risk that–?"

Mom pressed her palm flat against the screen. "It's for the best, Izzy. We've been waiting for your call. Mr Drumgoole gave us a program that's traced your signal. Just sit tight. Everything will be over soon."

Izzy ripped the Mother Mentor from her head, horrified. She focused woozily on me, her eyes dilated–

"Amichai, I'm... I don't know why I... I *had* to call, I missed them *so bumper*, every day I creosote biotic *syntax*–"

She fell backwards to the floor, her teeth chattering as she went into a seizure.

I grabbed her, remembering what Gumdrool told me:

I instituted my own rule: always have contingency plans when dealing with Amichai Damrosch.

Dare helped me get Izzy to a safe position, screaming at Wickcleft: "I thought you guys brainscanned her!"

Wickcleft pulled up images of Izzy's brainwaves, doublechecking them. "Whuh-we *did*! Dr Hsiang chuh-checked her scans personally! I duh-duh-don't understand..."

"I do," I said, seething.

"Huh-how?"

"Gumdrool didn't alter. He *amplified*. Izzy was always close to Mom and Dad – Gumdrool piggybacked on an existing concern. He left the rest of her brain pristine – but when she got a chance to talk to them, she was *driven* to call." I grimaced as I wiped drool off Izzy's chin. "It's those 'subtle changes' you were talking about."

"I've uh-uh-alerted the camp that it's tuh- tuh- time to evacuate," Wickcleft said. "Fuh- fortunately, we have suh-suh- security measures that–"

A hollow boom fired overhead. The glass in the mall rafters shattered, raining down; the Brain Trust's monitors fizzled and dimmed. Wickcleft's image flickered into darkness.

Dare and I ducked for cover, huddling as the glass shards splintered on the tile floor. Above us, we saw cloudy contrails etching their way across the sky – incoming warships.

"I guess Wickliffe was ready to strike," Dare said.

49: ONE WISE CHOICE, AND ONE UNWISE ONE

I caught Dare by the sleeve before he ran off.

"You need to help me get Izzy to safety!"

"No," Dare snapped. "*You* need to get Izzy to safety, then send in some help. *I* need to get up to the solar panels and restore power, so we can wipe the Brain Trust server."

Distracted by Izzy's seizure, I hadn't thought that far. The Brain Trust was darkened – not *quite* offline, saved by emergency power sources, but as offline as complex Upterlife software could get without corrupting itself. It jutted up, big as a rocket, too large to move.

Dare shook off my grip. "We can't move the hardware. Wickliffe's troops are incoming. They *will* get their hands on this server. Which means they *will* find the back door you discovered. If we don't destroy this, we've lost our last advantage."

"But... Wickcleft's in there." I thought how proud Wickcleft had been of me. "And... all the other rebels–"

"They'd give their lives to stop Wickliffe. Will you let them?"

Dare gave me a flinty, merciless look, his gaze sending a clear message: *Will you finally make the hard sacrifices, Amichai?*

I had no choice. Only Dare, who knew the mall's layout better than anyone alive, had a chance of getting the server up online again to start its selfdestruct sequences.

"...Go."

Dare gave me a sarcastic salute and bolted.

I needed to get Izzy to a medic. She was emaciated after her time in the factory – but I was no bodybuilder, and my broken shoulder wasn't helping. I grabbed her by her wrist and hauled backwards, dragging her across the tile floor, yelling for help. But there was none. I heard commotion from outside. The contrails above were getting larger, the skies filling with explosions as people brought our antiaircraft defenses back online – but Wickliffe's troops would be here any minute.

I heaved her backwards, my good arm practically popping out of its socket. I did a crabwalk with my feet to brush the broken glass away before hauling her back another yard or two. The troops were incoming, terrified the LifeGuard would rappel down through the broken ceiling to scoop me and Izzy up...

"Come on."

Evangeline tossed Izzy over her shoulder. I should have been overjoyed to see her, but Evangeline had the disgust of a woman shoveling out a stable.

"You've got to tell... your people," I huffed. "We need firepower. We need... need you... to get to the server, protect it until we–"

Evangeline's nose wrinkled. "That will not happen, Amichai."

"But Wickcleft – he–"

Evangeline almost flung Izzy to the floor in exasperation. "Amichai, my people will not sacrifice themselves to save *a program*. I know you think this Wickcleft is a person – but it's a tricked-up Turing test. There is no *soul* there! I think it's *disgusting* how you expect humans to sacrifice their lives for this... this *playtoy* you've befriended!"

"Holy crap," I whispered. "Are you jealous?"

I really should not have said that.

Evangeline stalked off. She kept her gaze fixed on the wide multiple-doored exit, where people ferried supplies to the spirocopters, directed by Peaches.

"I offered myself to you," she said bitterly. "And you pledged yourself to a glorified *tutorial*."

I felt my last hopes for Evangeline plummet into an abyss. Wickcleft was my friend – but to her, Wickcleft was a *thing*. For Evangeline, treating Wickcleft as though he deserved social niceties was every bit as crazy as her God was to me.

We could never cross that gulf.

"Not only is that not fair, it's not why I'm concerned. I've found a–"

"Found a *what?*"

"...a... thing," I finished, stumbling to a stop just before I screwed everything up.

I was in a NeoChristian bind: if I told Evangeline about the Upterlife exploit, and she got captured, then Wickliffe would scan her brain. Wickliffe wouldn't know the precise nature of the security hole, but he could lock down the Upterlife until he tracked it down.

"Your people need to hold the line until Dare gets through," I told her. "You have to trust me."

"I'm thin on trust with you."

"It's... I can't share the details. Not now." I tapped my temple, waved at the incoming ships. "You should *understand*."

She softened. That, at least, we had in common now – that fear that everything we knew would be used against us. She pressed her fingertips to the cross on her throat. "Is it necessary for... to end this, Amichai? Have you learned something that can stop the Wickliffe program?"

It's Wickliffe, not a program! I thought.

Instead, I nodded.

Evangeline kicked open the doors to the mall, exposing the overgrown courtyard. Peaches whirred back and forth in her wheelchair, directing traffic, as rebels and NeoChristians alike evacuated the area – carrying the wounded away, hauling equipment, getting blown apart by the stray missile that made it past our defenses. Overhead, you could see the gleaming outline of the incoming ships, the heatshields blackened from descending from orbit, parachutes jerking out to slow them to a stop.

Evangeline handed Izzy off to Facundo, then fished a loop of black wire out from her belt – a loop studded with silver crosses. She wrapped it around my neck with the care of an explosives engineer applying detcord. Then she pressed a black metal canister with a red button into my hand.

"Click it twice to enable it," she explained, tugging on the canister to show me how it connected to my neck with a wire. "Once you activate it, you have to keep a constant pressure on the button. If it's untouched for thirty seconds, it explodes, presenting your body as a living sacrifice by blowing out the carotid artery. You bleed unconscious in under a minute, unrecoverable brain death in three." She grinned. "It's an old NeoChristian trick to keep secrets."

"You are…" I looked down at the button. "You are the *weirdest* girl I ever dated."

"That's over, Amichai." She made the sign of the cross over her lips, then touched her fingers to my forehead. "Facundo and Ximena, they've shown me my way back to God. Iron sharpens iron, and you have blunted my edge. It turns out in the aftermath of great tragedy…" She blushed. "Many do foolish things in their grief."

The hard wall of NeoChristian faith rose between us. We might have been able to forge a friendship in another time, but she had fundamental beliefs she was unwilling to question – and I had mine.

"Now, I think… I think you mean well," Evangeline continued. "But my people – they fear that as long as you worship the servers, you'll come around to the Wickliffe program's view…"

"But can *we* be allies? You and me?"

"I will fight for you." She glanced nervously at the sky. "I'll see who else will." And she broke away, waving NeoChristian soldiers over to listen to her.

Her hesitation was gone, replaced by a beautiful certainty as she directed her fellow believers to intercept Wickliffe's troops. Like me, she'd sacrifice everything for principle.

I'd been drawn to her confidence. I still was. But I was drawn for all the wrong reasons.

And in truth? I loved someone else.

Peaches steered herself next to me.

"Amichai! Where's Dare?"

"Inside." I ran my fingers along the silver crosses, felt the tiny wads of explosives behind them. "He's gone to destroy the servers before Wickliffe gets his hands on them. Stay still, I'm going to try something."

I fired up the IceBreaker, grateful it still functioned. Mama Alex had shielded it from whatever electrical malfuckery Wickliffe had rained down upon us. I trickled a charge into Peaches' earputer, wrote files to her shared drive.

"There," I said. "I've just passed you the back door to the Upterlife."

"What the *void*, Amichai? Why would you give this to me when Wickliffe could capture us at any moment?"

"Because you're the only person I trust." I knelt down, getting face to face with her. "And you'll leave as soon as I'm done talking. Listen, Peaches, I'm sorry–"

Peaches' chest hitched; she clasped her hands over her heart. "Are you finally choosing me, Amichai Damrosch?"

"I can't," I told her. "You don't let people choose you. All I can do is apologize and hope you choose me."

She gripped her armrests. "Why do you say the perfect thing only half the time?"

She grabbed me by the back of the neck, bringing me so close I could smell the perfume on her. I trembled at her touch;

I hadn't realized how badly I'd needed to feel her again.

"...so you're not mad?" I asked.

"Furious. I found another boy that night. He was gorgeous, with big thick muscles and long blond hair. He got me through." She chewed her lip, contemplating. "So did others. But none of them were you. You stupid, shortsighted, bullheaded *idiot*."

She yanked me down into a kiss; all my nerves shorted out. If I'd ever been foolish enough to think only Evangeline could kiss with passion, Peaches made those NeoChristian kisses look like fizzled matches.

Peaches was fireworks.

Peaches was forgiving me.

Peaches was love.

Gunfire started up. Wickliffe's troops landed on the mall roof, looking more like robots than men – encased in airtight uniforms, smoke-glassed helmets, prepared for any dazzlers or biohazardous gas. Thick green teargas permeated the woods. The NeoChristians laid down suppressing fire, making the LifeGuard scramble for cover, but soon enough Wickliffe's troops would turn this courtyard into a killing zone.

"You were the one I always trusted," Peaches told me, kissing me between sentences. "You respected my limits even when I made them arbitrary. So when my world tilts sideways, I cling to you. Any questions?"

"No, ma'am. Now get out, and take that Upterlife vulnerability with you." I doubleclicked the red button and sprinted back towards the mall.

"*Amichai!*" Peaches leapt halfway out of her wheelchair as a rebel guard dragged her back to the last of the spirocopters. "*Where are you going?*"

"To rescue Dare!"

With the memory of her kiss still on my mouth, I had never felt better in my life.

50: DARE, UP SO HIGH IT BREAKS MY HEART

I booked for the mall's upper levels, my thumb mashed on the dead-man's button. I was betting Wickliffe's forces would head straight for the server, which had to be visible from the sky once all the glass had shattered. They'd be focused on retrieval – why take captives when you could extract far more information from an Upterlife server?

NeoChristians charged past me, ready to play hit-and-run with the incoming troops. Ready to distract Wickliffe's men so I could get Dare out.

Because Dare's skills were way more important than mine.

Dare was right: we couldn't afford to hand over the Brain Trust's secrets to Wickliffe. But our best-case scenario ended with the Brain Trust selfdestructing – and if that happened, our rebellion had lost Mama Alex, the Brain Trust, and possibly Wickliffe. All of our technological expertise, gone.

The only person I knew who could build another Upterlife server was Dare. *All Amichai can do is break things*, Mama Alex had said to Dare; *you have a special talent for building*.

The Pony Rebellion had only gotten this far thanks to our technological edge. Without Mama Alex or the Brain Trust, Dare was our last hope for building a future. If I had to sacrifice my life to get Dare to safety, well, that was a solid exchange.

Fortunately, I had a plan to get both of us out. I wished I could text him a message, let him know I was coming, except Wickliffe had depowered our earputers...

I raced up to the fourth floor, near the shattered glass ceiling, approaching the edge of the wide walkways that looped around the Brain Trust's server stack. Bullets shattered the concrete below me. The NeoChristians had lined up on the lower levels to fire down into the courtyard, while the LifeGuard fired back with much heavier weaponry that punched through the tile floor.

The LifeGuard's armored suits were airtight, hermetically sealed so no one could gas them. But that came with its own dangers.

I flung myself into an old pharmacy and fired up the IceBreaker.

The IceBreaker scanned the area, bombarding me with information about the LifeGuard's military-grade encrypted broadcasts. The suits had to communicate with each other, which gave me a vector of attack.

Fortunately, I'd spent the last weeks being trained in decryption methods by Wickcleft himself. I flooded the air with quiet login attempts, hunting for access to their armor.

I remembered to mash down the dead-man's button before it blew my head off, then bit back a curse. The LifeGuard's high-level communications were brainencrypted – as secure as a man's thought patterns. I'd expected no less. But there had to be lower-level maintenance protocols I could hijack...

That's when a voice drove all thoughts of programming from my head:

"Don't waste your fire on these NeoChristians!" Gumdrool said.

...Gumdrool said.

"Their weaponry can't hurt you! Get those emergency generators working!"

Yes. That was my enemy – my dead enemy – speaking. It was madness, peeking over the edge of that walkway, where troops could put a bullet in my brain. But I had to see him...

...and sure enough, Gumdrool was there. Not a copy – Gumdrool, in the flesh. *Preening.*

How had he survived?

But survived he had. He barked out orders on a megaphone, having removed his faceplate. It was a show intended to demoralize the NeoChristians – if he was serious about tactics, he would have communicated to his men over their encrypted frequencies.

Worse, his show was working. Armored men dragged a glowing generator up to the Brain Trust server. The NeoChristians' bullets sparked off the LifeGuard's black shiny exosuits without leaving a mark. Gumdrool was right: there *was* no sense in fighting, and the NeoChristians weren't eager to protect a collection of programs anyway. My defenders withdrew.

Then I heard a rattle from above.

Nestled between two girders, high off the floor, Dare tinkered with a solar panel. I don't know how he got that high up; I could see no access panels. He might as well have been Spider-Man.

Wickliffe's men, distracted by the firefight, hadn't seen him yet. Dare stuck his tongue out between his lips as he reconnected wires, trying to...

...I didn't know what he was trying to do. That was why we needed Dare. I'd studied the Upterlife's vulnerabilities, but Dare had trained himself for Upterlife maintenance and repair. I had no idea what Wickliffe had done to disable the Brain Trust's selfdestruct routines, nor how Dare intended to bring them back up online.

Everything depended on Dare. If I could get root access to the armored suits, I could buy him time...

He looked down, verifying the LifeGuard hadn't spotted him – then scowled when he saw me. I realized how things looked:

It looked like I'd endangered the mission to rescue him.

I gesticulated, touching my neck, holding up the button

to demonstrate how they'd never capture my secret from me – but there was no good way to get all this across without alerting Wickliffe's troops. *I handed the Upterlife exploit to Peaches! I wanted to yell. If they capture me, the rebels still have the loophole! Now we need to get you out, so you can rebuild our defenses!*

You irresponsible asshole, Dare mouthed, then returned to rewiring the panels.

Test protocols found, my IceBreaker informed me. *Breach?*

A whir filled the room as the Brain Trust server hummed back to life. Gumdrool took out a black-and-gold projector from a carrying case, and knelt reverently before flicking it on.

A holographic image of President Wickliffe appeared.

"Come out, little splinter." Wickliffe squinted sourly at the Brain Trust with bloodshot eyes, looking as though he'd stumbled into the room after a months-long bender. "I'm not putting any portion of my code into that server, so let us communicate across the air like men."

The monitors across the Brain Trust server flickered on, each showing Wickcleft crouched behind a shot-up wall, waving a small white flag. "Congrat-t-tulations," he said sourly. "Yuh-yuh-you got me. And uh-uh-all it took was one brainwashed girl."

President Wickliffe sucked in his hollowed cheeks. "That… it wasn't my idea." He glanced at Gumdrool. "But sacrifices must be made. If Damrosch hadn't forced my hand…"

"Yuh-yuh-you can't excuse delegating your duh-duh-dirt to thugs like Gumdrool. I'm ashamed to say I whuh-whuh-was you. What happened to the boy who cuh-cuh-conquered death?"

"You don't know what it's like!" Wickliffe roared.

Wickcleft raised an eyebrow.

"Very well," President Wickliffe cracked his knuckles. "The sole reason you don't agree with me, little splinter, is because you don't know how bad it's gotten. So here. Let me send you my memories…"

Wickcleft's eyes rolled in their sockets, revolving to show streams of numbers as Wickliffe flooded him with information. Dare froze in mid wiring, sweat dripping from his brow, realizing he was too late:

Wickliffe was synchronizing with Wickcleft.

I checked my IceBreaker – it was still working to crack the test protocols, which had been properly locked down by Wickliffe himself. But Wickcleft had taught me how to *un*lock them, given time.

Assuming Wickcleft wouldn't be our enemy when all this was done…

Wickcleft staggered back, his face wrinkled with despair. "That can't be true."

President Wickliffe looked serene. "Check my work."

"No, no… I can see your projections are correct," Wickcleft said. His stutter had vanished, which filled me with horror. "And they match up with my old memories. Yet we could…"

President Wickliffe looked saddened, sympathetic. "No. We tried that."

"Of course. But then there's always…"

"I checked that, and *that's* a nonstarter. And before you go there, no, that won't work either."

"Oh, the options are so *slim!*" Wickcleft cried, clutching his head. "It's all going to fail – going to fail horribly…"

"So you see what I had to do?" President Wickliffe asked, leaning closer. "You see why it's *necessary?*"

Wickcleft eyed President Wickliffe, seeming to view him in a different light. Then he leaned down to brush his hands on his pants before straightening to meet the president's hungry gaze.

"No, Walter." Wickcleft spoke with the gravity of a doctor pronouncing an incurable illness. "I don't know when you lost the last of your morality, what divergent event made you think this plan was OK, but… there are some lines you can never cross."

President Wickliffe tore his gaze away from his splinter self, clasping eyes on the armored soldiers in the room – looking for sympathy.

All he found were people who'd obey him.

I felt a little bad for him, truth be told. He'd just voiced his concerns to the only person in the world who should understand him... and been rejected.

President Wickliffe removed a glimmering bottle from his vest pocket, the scotch inside it glistening with holographic light. He bit out the cork, swigged the entire bottle in one act of supreme self-hatred, then tossed the bottle aside.

"Break in," Wickliffe commanded. "Take everything he knows."

The server exploded.

It wasn't a fiery burst – a series of explosive bolts placed at strategic locations on the Brain Trust detonated one by one down its teetering stack. Wickcleft's resigned stare turned to a fistpumping "yes!" just before the monitors imploded, the server tumbling down in chunks around them, storage devices bursting in midair.

Dare could have hidden. Nobody would have known where the selfdestruct signal had come from.

Yet there he was, high in the crook of the girders, waving frantically.

At me.

Run, you idiot, he mouthed. You have the key to defeating Wickliffe, this all falls apart without you–

"Something's moving in the girders! *Fire!*"

When I fall asleep, I dream of an alternate universe. One where I'd learned a little more from Wickcleft, or where the IceBreaker had had more power, or where President Wickliffe's encryption routines were weaker. Some universe where I was five seconds quicker.

But I wasn't. So I got to watch Dare's first shock of pain, the bits of Dare spattering against the ceiling as Gumdrool's soldiers shot him to pieces.

And *still* he waved at me to run. He was revolted by my weakness, the way I'd betray my cause to save him. He didn't know I'd passed on the information to Peaches. He didn't know how much I valued his skills, and poor Dare could never believe that he was worthy on his own.

As far as Dare knew, I'd devised a plan to break into the Upterlife – and then abandoned that plan rather than let an old friend die.

He killed himself so I'd never have the chance to rescue him.

He gripped onto the girders for a moment, blood pouring onto the tile below. He gave me one final, disappointed look.

Then he dropped out of sight.

I never saw his body hit the floor, because that's when the IceBreaker chimed: *Access granted*.

Flush self-contained breathing tanks, I commanded to all suits in the area. Lock suit. Begin testing cycle.

The suits hissed as they emptied their tanks. The soldiers took a breath, realized there was no oxygen left, and thumbed the "faceplate release" buttons on their suits' UI. But their suits had gone into verification mode and wouldn't respond to feedback until the testing cycle was complete. Maybe they'd suffocate before it finished.

It was uncharitable, perhaps, but I hoped they did.

"Damrosch!" I heard from below – Gumdrool's voice. Of course he was OK. Of course he'd taken his faceplate off to talk to the NeoChristians.

Of *course* he'd survive.

"Damrosch, I know that's you! I am coming for you! I will end your menace once and for all!"

I didn't listen to the rest. I headed for the exit, mashing the dead-man's switch for another thirty seconds of life.

51: MY BEST GUMDROOL IMPRESSION

Now, I've avoided telling this story from Gumdrool's perspective because, well, I'm not him. But forgive me if I slip into Gumdrool's head for a moment, because it's been a hard day.

Hi. I'm Gumdrool. I'm a big bully who justifies meanness by saying the Upterlife will make everything better. And I'm about to be the meanest guy ever.

See, I have my enemy Amichai trapped near a mall. He's neutralized my squadron, but I've scraped together enough LifeGuards to form a bully squad.

He's cornered. After this, I drag him back to another secret enclave, scrub his mind, and make him lie to the world. All I have to do is break into this metal shipping container, and I win at life.

"Mama Alex told me you'd defeat me." If I make him mad enough, maybe he'll try to bum-rush me – and I like gloating anyway. "Just before I strangled the bitch. Turns out those dazers don't work well when you're half-blind from gas – and she really didn't plan on me coming to prematurely.

"I used to feel sorry for you, Amichai. And then I remember how the people of New York rioted when we told them you died – cities all around the globe, refusing to work for the Upterlife because of some callow boy.

"Alas. You've taught me to hate. I've brought four men

354

with me, ready to wrestle you down. So do the rational thing, Amichai: Surrender."

Amichai yells back: "I've been in this situation before, Gumdrool! You've seen the footage. A smart man wouldn't stand in my way."

My ears redden. They always get red when I'm angry.

"All right, then. LifeGuard! Break down that door in three… two…"

I motion them to go on two. I always go on two, no matter what I tell you. But as they rush the shipping container, there's a whinny as the doors burst outwards to meet them.

Amichai charges out on a Sleipnir pony.

"It can't be," I mutter. "It can't be the same pony…"

My jaw hangs open in disbelief as the pony – yes, the same pony – charges at me, lowering its head to trample me. Panicked, I dive to one side into a pile of pony poop, shrieking get him, get him – but nobody dares fire because they might kill Amichai, and I told them we needed him alive.

Amichai hugs his pony with his good arm, his legs tied to its sides, vanishing into the woods. I regret all my life's choices and wish that anything in the world loved me as much as Amichai's pony loves him. But nothing does, because I am a heartless jerk.

Then I spit out pony poop.

My crosscountry ride remains a literal blur for me. I have the IceBreaker recordings, but we jounced around so much that not even its blur-compensators could clean up the footage.

I remember dashing through the woods, lashed to Therapy's back. I remember Therapy leaping over the heads of inbound troops. I remember Therapy juking left and right as though she was born to dodge gunfire, picking her way among volleys of dazers and tasers and I'm pretty sure a couple of spirocopters at one point.

I passed out sometimes. My broken shoulder was *not* meant to take evasive maneuvers, and I was being whipped back and forth like a bronco rider. It's a miracle I kept pressing the dead-man's switch, or else my neck would have exploded.

My IceBreaker ran out of power, leaving us without a map. But Therapy charged ahead at breakneck speeds, seeming to know our destination.

And void bless her, that little pony escaped the craziest ambushes – and *every time* she sideswiped Wickliffe's army, she looked back at me with this little satisfied smirk: *See what I did there?*

Finally, I looked across the water to see the familiar outline of New York's skyscrapers.

"You," I said, hugging Therapy with one arm. "Are the best pony in the whole wide world." I rested my cheek against her neck, feeling a deep and encompassing love.

I took a moment to appreciate this final moment of peace.

PART IV: TIME'S UP

52: IN A RAGGED ROOM WITH A STRANGE BOUQUET

"Wake up," said a familiar voice. "You gotta help us out, Amichai."

Tiny beads dragged across my forehead, rattling like –

– dreadlocks.

"...Mama Alex?" I asked hopefully.

"No." Peaches gave me a sad smile. She'd knotted beads into her hairstyle as tribute. And like Mama Alex, she now had strands of gray in her lush black tresses.

She was only seventeen, and already she had gray hairs.

"You slept for two days," she told me. "It's time to wake up."

Peaches gave me a hug. I'd have hugged back, except the right side of my torso was in a plaster cast.

I tried to sit up, failed. I was in a low-rent apartment, nicely kept – a swept floor, a clean table with a bouquet of flowers, spotted curtains on the windows. Just enough to let me know the residents didn't have money, but they did have pride.

I scanned for cameras; there were none, just empty sockets in the walls. Those weren't flowers on the table – they were eyestalk cameras, rooted from the walls and twisted together in a bouquet.

I was betting there were lots of camera bouquets around

Greenwich Village these days.

I felt a tightness at my throat. I touched the crosses, with their explosives. "You didn't remove the detcord?" I spluttered, feeling for the red button, realizing Peaches had taped it down.

"No time." She shook her head. "No experience in defusing neckbombs. We lost a *lot* of people escaping that last assault, Amichai. We've got a hard drive full of supertechnology stolen from the Brain Trust, but few people with the expertise to implement the Brain Trust's ideas. We're breathing fumes."

"It's OK, Peaches. I've got this."

"Your plan, Amichai," Peaches said, soft and urgent. "I've been assembling the necessary technology to work your exploit. I read your notes. But…"

"But?"

"It's a… a *nice* plan. Very trusting. But…"

She whipped the curtains open. Smoke rose from all over Greenwich Village; some buildings were burnt pyres. I couldn't make out much of New York's skyline through the narrow window – but I could count twenty patrolling spirocopters from here.

I wanted to blast them all.

I looked down. The streets, once full of gardens, were choked with rubbled chokepoints, so the LifeGuard couldn't squeeze tanks in here. People scurried from building to building, dashing like rats before the spirocopters could get a bead on them.

There were also soft heaps of dirt in the gardens: fresh burial mounds.

Only the golden towers of the Upterlife servers remained intact – the sole thing neither side could bring themselves to damage.

Peaches whisked the curtain shut.

"I have fought the government to a standstill," Peaches said proudly. "I kept the lines open so Wickliffe couldn't cut the signal and do his dirty work – though void knows he's tried. Whatever he does, he'll do it with the world watching. And he's been reluctant to firebomb Greenwich Village – voiding that many innocents would be a PR disaster."

"Why?"

"'Cause according to him, you made all this up. We're innocent fools who bought into stupid propaganda. And they *have* to stick to that story. It's a script – Mama Alex told me the same thing happened to her family in Boston. They pretend we're misguided, so they look compassionate and we look like violent idiots. Meanwhile, they bombard the Upterlife with fake news stories about us tearing up Upterlife servers, telling everyone how we want to void the postmortemed, so when he eventually slaughters us all it'll look like he had no choice..."

I leaned forward. "Does anyone believe him?"

"The LifeGuard's been suppressing riots everywhere. Polls show the living no longer trust the dead. But..."

"...they remember Boston."

"And Topeka and Leeds and Beijing and Avignon. Everyone has a Boston nearby."

"So we get..."

"Lots of sympathy." She ran her hand through her hair, exasperated. "Well, no, that's not actually true; Evangeline brought some NeoChristian firepower with her. And we've got tons of help from locals – Greenwich Village's in full rebellion. But if the rest of the world was willing to help, it probably wouldn't be up to me to run this operation. They're sitting back – they figure if we make a show of it, then they can revolt. If we get squished like a cockroach, well, then better a tainted Upterlife than no Upterlife at all."

"So... when will Wickliffe attack?"

Peaches rolled away, staring out the window. "He's *been*

attacking. He sends tanks, I've got rebels with tankbuster mines. He tries nanoswarms, we break 'em up with Brain Trust nanoviruses. He sends drones, we fuzz his targeting systems. And every time I think about giving up, I think about Mama Alex." Her face darkened. "And when that fails, I think about Dare.

"But defense isn't offense. We've got a day, maybe two, before Wickliffe decides it's safe to enter the 'make an example' phase.

"So I'm out of options." She wheeled back around to face me. "If you're wrong, and your plan fails, you will void everyone in Greenwich Village. And so I ask you: do you think your words will make *any* difference?"

"I think words are the *only* things that make a difference. And this?" I brandished the IceBreaker that held my plan. "It's not just words."

"Then what is it?"

"It's how we'll rewrite the rules of the Upterlife."

Peaches grinned.

53: GRASPING HANDS AND DESPERATE HEARTS

Word had gotten out that I was back – and the apartment complex was crammed with people. Rebels clogged the hallways, eager to get their hands on me.

They didn't need to touch me for long; a quick handshake, a pat on the back, a tap on my cast. They needed to believe I was real. Once they'd confirmed that I was indeed the Pony Boy, they broke out in broad grins. And they cheered when I told them that yes, everything in the videos *was* true, and would they help me exterminate those fucking ghosts?

I knew what my presence meant to them: Wickliffe had thrown everything he'd had at me, and I was still fighting. That meant they could fight, too. Their lives may be null and void, but their sacrifice would matter.

Dare would matter. Mama Alex would matter. Wickcleft would matter. I would ram their names straight down Wickliffe's throat.

"Everyone on the rooftops," I told them. "*Everyone*. Do it at dusk; it'll be more dramatic that way. Your job's to counteract whatever they come up with to get us to run. We need to stay put."

"What if they firebomb the buildings?" a half-starved Greenwich Village rebel asked me.

Everyone knew we didn't have enough countermeasures to stop a full-on Wickliffe onslaught. His actual question was, *should we prepare to void?*

"Won't matter by the time we're done," I told him. "This is a coup. Come nightfall, they won't have one single hold on us."

"What about us?" Evangeline asked, blocking my way. Rumor was she'd left the spirocopters behind to fight her way to a safe haven in the mountains. Her single cross tattoo was now a reddened ring of delicately inked sergeant's crosses, half-hidden by the bazooka strapped across her back.

"What *about* you?"

Ximena and Facundo and the rest of the NeoChristians crossed their arms, stepping behind Evangeline to form a wall. "What happens if we win, Amichai?"

"You've earned your place at the table," I told them. The Boston rebels nodded, having fought side-by-side with the NeoChristians. But the New York rebels made gurgles of dissent – not quite contradicting me, but evidently nervous about working with tattooed barbarians. They shuffled their feet, eyeing my necklace of crosses – nobody'd had time to defuse Evangeline's suicide switch, but to the newer rebels it must have looked like a declaration of faith.

Evangeline jerked her chin towards the nervous New Yorkers, as though they proved her point. "You don't dare alienate us when you need us. But tomorrow? Would you betray the Son of Man with a kiss?"

This was the fracture point Mama Alex had foreseen. And Evangeline refused to let me give her private reassurances, forcing me to make all my promises before an audience.

I'd intended to, anyway.

"If we win, I'll get your people their own land. We'll find a space where you don't have to listen to any orders from the dead. If you keep your peace, we'll keep ours."

A NeoChristian I'd never met before yelled, "How do we know you'll keep your word?"

"Because I kept my word when I rescued your people from the branch server," I said. "I don't care who you worship. *Everyone* deserves a good life."

I wished that had been met with a better response from the NeoChristians. But Evangeline, who'd somehow become the bridge between her people and mine, nodded as if that was good enough.

She tugged a knife from a sheath, carved a cross into my cast.

"You don't believe," she said. "It was foolish of me to think that you might believe. But... not everyone who cries 'Lord, Lord' will enter the kingdom of Heaven, yet the one who does the will of the Lord will pass. You do the will of the Lord, Amichai, whether you intend it or no."

"So... you'll protect the rooftops?"

"We've brought extra firepower for the Tribulation." She slapped her bazooka.

Her enthusiasm was frightening. She was *eager* to die. Her faith had made her deadly.

More proof we'd never really been suited for each other.

54: IN THE IZZY-PRISON

Izzy was stashed deep in the underground warrens, at Peaches' request. It was probably safer that way; lots of people had died in Wickliffe's onslaught, and the rebels were hot for vengeance. Most folks understood that what happened wasn't really Izzy's fault, but...

People had a tendency to beat up whoever was within arm's reach when they couldn't get a shot at the *real* villains. And though Izzy hadn't been responsible for her actions, she *had* given away our position. Maybe she was still a danger.

Nobody wanted to be friends with someone like that. Even I was a little nervous going to see her.

Therapy nickered. She knew something was up. But I wanted both Izzy and Therapy out of harm's way; besides, Therapy had always comforted Izzy.

My palms sweated the whole trip down. How much of my sister was left?

I tied Therapy to a post – she could snap any rope, but she'd come to accept my tether as a request to stay put for a while. I nodded to the two security guards, who unlocked the doors to a small green room.

Izzy was curled in a corner, hugging her knees, rocking back and forth. Her unwashed hair hung over her face like a greasy curtain. They'd rounded up some old paper books for her to occupy her time – but she ignored them. Instead, she muttered apologies over and over again to Dare, to Wickcleft, to everyone who'd died in the raid.

"Hey," I said.

She flung herself into my arms, weeping.

"I'm not me," she whispered.

"No, Izzy." I squeezed her shoulders for emphasis. "This is *you*. A little pinched at the edges, but... mostly you."

She burst into tears. "I called them. I'd *still* call them, Amichai. That's why they had to take away my electronics and lock me down here. It's... an instilled madness. I wake up, and I itch to see Mom's face, I crave Dad's voice – the only thought that makes me happy is the idea of being with them some day in the Upterlife. I hate them, but... even now, I'd call them because I need them, I *need* them..."

"That'll fade," I told her – but her quivering need made me itch.

She saw my reluctance, reached out to caress my cheek.

"I held myself together when Mom and Dad left us," she said. "I didn't cry when the Bubbler hit. I kept going when they kicked me out of the LifeGuard Academy. I prided myself on my strength, Amichai – and yet they *broke* me. They broke me *so easily*. I've got this implanted addiction that affects everything I do – and with the Brain Trust and Wickcleft gone, there's no way to fix it..."

"I can stop it from happening to anyone ever again."

"You're going to kill them all?" Izzy asked, fearful. "You're going to topple the Upterlife?"

"I'm just going to change some rules, Izzy," I muttered, repeating the words again elsewhere. "Some really... fundamental rules, I think."

"What's that, sweetie?" Peaches asked, looking up from her earputer. She was coordinating hackers all over Greenwich Village – getting cameras into place, fixing inactive Shrive Points, making sure we had backup power.

"...Nothing," I said. She smiled, kissed me on the cheek, returned to her preparations. I stroked the wires of the detcord locked around my throat; once activated, the NeoChristians had designed it to be impossible to remove. We had bigger problems to solve. Yet whenever I swallowed, I felt cold silver and warm explosives pressing against my neck.

Peaches made my plan work, but I could tell from the way she chewed her lip she wasn't sold on it. Only she knew what was supposed to happen. Everyone else trusted me blindly, partially because we needed to surprise Wickliffe, partially because we had no other choice.

It was me, or get Bostonized.

And I was fine with that. Dare had asked how I expected to lead a revolution without getting blood on my hands... And he was right. I had to accept that innocents could die.

I just hoped I wouldn't void the Upterlife in the process.

"Whatever I do *has* to be an improvement," I'd told Izzy. "Sometimes, all you can do is smash things with a hammer and hope to rebuild them better."

"You can't take the Upterlife away from me!" Izzy cried.

I stood, shocked by how broken down she was. Izzy had screamed at me, she'd demanded, but she'd never begged. And beg she did; she fell to her knees, grabbed clumsily at my shirt, cried...

"Without the Upterlife, what do I *have?*" she yelled. "Parents who left me! An aborted career cut short by plague! A kidnapping and a brainwashing! Everyone *hates* me – I'm the traitor who got everyone killed at Boston! And if I die... *this is all I got!*"

Was that desperation Izzy's natural fears, or Gumdrool's amplified urges?

Our brains were such fragile things. A stroke could undo decades of learning, the right pills could drive you mad or soothe you. Who's to say Izzy wouldn't have panicked anyway? She'd always been a Liminal Shrive, right up to the moment of her rebellion – and even then she had still believed the LifeGuard would follow suit if they only knew her.

Revolution was an option for her, not an inevitability.

"Without the Upterlife," she said, her words dissolving into sobs, "everything that's happened to me is *random*, and *cruel*, and *stupid*. You can't take that away from me! There has to be *some* reward for what I've been through!"

I muttered some vague reassurances, because I *wasn't* sure what I was going to do would leave the Upterlife intact. And in that moment, I wanted to toe the line, get my sister the eternity she needed – I'd seen how welcoming Wickcleft had been. Maybe if I defected, I could change Wickliffe's system from within, preserve the status quo so Izzy's life wouldn't be a brutal series of cruelties, but the prelude to a peaceful forever...

All I had to do was pretend a few thousand NeoChristians and billions of brainwashed kids were a necessary sacrifice.

"It's time to leave, Mr Damrosch," a guard had told us. Izzy had grabbed my arm.

"*Please*," she'd begged. "You can't knock it all down, Amichai! You can't void them all, we need the Upterlife – I need my parents – I need more time to make things right–"

Was that Izzy's panic, or Gumdrool's tampering? Or both?

How could we ever know who we really were?

As I marched up the stairs to the rooftops, a hundred people filing obediently behind me, I heard the *clack* of Izzy's doors closing forever. I stopped by the entrance to the blacktopped roof, closing my eyes – trying to convince myself this plan would not only work, but was *right*.

I helped haul Peaches' wheelchair through the doorway. She squeezed my hand. I'd seen many Peaches in my day – efficient bureaucrat Peaches, furious out-of-control Peaches, placating-crazy-people Peaches, Blackout Party Peaches.

This Peaches, however, looked at me with concern, caring, love; a look that said, *if you need to call this off, I will never blame you.*

That was, I think, the real Peaches.

I cupped her cheek. "We should probably have, you know, done the sex thing. When we had the time."

She pulled me close. "*You* were the idiot who scheduled the revolution for tonight." She kissed me for as long as I wanted, and a little more. And when we were done, she added, "But I have some time in my schedule for you tomorrow."

She didn't, as it turned out.

55: SHOWDOWN

I'm pretty sure the roof was hot enough to make me dizzy. I can see the wavering tar fumes in the video footage; my stomach must have churned, because I kept biting my lip in what I'm pretty sure was an attempt to keep from fainting.

What's clear is that everyone filed past me to sit on the coralline ledges, hanging their battered feet off the edge.

The sunset lit up Greenwich Village's roofs with the golden shine of a Liminal Shrive. On each roof, people walked out to stare at a sky filled with spirocopters, then perched on the edge – each one shove away from falling.

They all carried Shrive Points, dragging cables behind them. Peaches had burned our last technological miracles to splice our wiring into diamond-hard Upterlife cable, but she'd managed it – and extended our network to cover Greenwich Village, despite burned-out buildings and scarce supplies.

The spirocopters, bellies filled with LifeGuard soldiers, buzzed overhead in attempts to scare us off. These were military copters, their turbojets intermingled with guns and gasjets and void knew what else. A few flickered dazers experimentally, but Peaches waved a hand and counterfrequency signals lit the sky.

The spirocopters swooped in from all horizons, descending in greater numbers, preparing for the onslaught.

That's when the booming noises sounded across the rooftops.

Every time I see the footage, I think it's gunfire. That noise must be gunfire. Then Peaches wheels around to bump me, and yanks me to my feet, then hauls herself up into my arms. You can see the surprise on my face as I realize what she's doing:

She's dancing.

They're drumming.

The rest of Greenwich Village rises to their feet.

In our final moments left alive, we do what only the living can do.

I am never prouder of Greenwich Village than I am in that moment.

Peaches is dancing with me, one last time, and I know it's because that's what she does when she's nervous – but she's not letting go as everyone else sways and exchanges partners. Her legs dangle, her toes scuffing against the roof, but it is beautiful because she's mine. I'm hers.

This is our anthem. Our defiance.

Four spirocopters break formation and buzz the rooftops, their turbojets' backwash almost strong enough to shove us off the roof. But they keep a wary distance, fearful of our countermeasures.

Then I realize: they're afraid of me.

Sure enough, Gumdrool's leaning out of a spirocopter's door, pointing at me and barking orders. Guns swivel into position, bathing me in targeting reticles.

I reach down to touch my IceBreaker, verifying that it's still tethered through the Shrive links to the Upterlife servers. I could have just queried the connection mentally... But I wanted to touch it. I know that.

The copters swoop into position. The Greenwich rebels continue to dance, as at least a hundred army vehicles cordon off Greenwich Village.

Peaches squeezes my hand.

"Showtime," she says.

Lights flicker on; Wickliffe stands as tall as an Upterlife server, his holographic image knitted together by several copter projectors working in conjunction. He's clad in a somber black suit, his glimmering feet stretching down to tread on fresh graves.

Gumdrool stands in a copter jittering inside Wickliffe's torso – as though he were Wickliffe's stilted heart.

"Amichai Damrosch," Wickliffe booms. "Will you admit to your monstrous lies?"

I check the IceBreaker. Sure enough, all the wireless signals in the area are flooded out by the copters' jamming shrieks – it's like a thousand people yelling to shout down a single person's conversation. Every camera in the area goes dim – except for Wickliffe's. He'll edit the footage to look good later.

The copter's gunports fire up, ready to kill.

"*Shrive*," I say into the IceBreaker. My word booms across the Village, loud as Wickliffe's. There's a rattle and clank as everyone lies upon the tarmac, puts on the helmets, starts the Shrive sequence.

Peaches kisses my cheek before she goes under. The NeoChristians patrol among the Shriving thousands, brandishing bazookas to ward off the LifeGuards.

Wickliffe looks down, perplexed, trying not to go offscript. "Are they... Are they confessing their crimes?"

"Not *their* crimes, no," I say, looking up defiantly at Wickliffe and his copters. "Don't you feel it? I'd think you of *all* people would feel it."

"Feel what? I–" He pats his chest, as though he'd forgotten a pen, then looks down at me in horror. "Oh, no."

Void help me, I can see it clear as day in the footage: I began to *strut*.

"I know your problem, Wickliffe. Let me spell it out for you: you made the Upterlife *too* good, didn't you?"

Wickliffe flickers out of meat-space to stop my Upterlife onslaught – but it's too late.

The poison's in the well.

Wouldn't stop me from monologuing, of course. You can't be a good supervillain without a good monologue.

"You had to make it workfree to get everyone onboard, back in the day. You sold the afterlife like it was the best show ever, making it *so* good everyone would write their local politicians to pass whatever law they could to get access to it. You needed perfect reviews – so you used every neurological trick you could find, pushing our pleasure centers, making the games so good they'd lure anyone with the slightest trace of imagination...

"But how could you protect yourself when you were a ghost? I mean, you're nothing more than a signal bouncing around a circuit; what happened if the government cut funding to the Upterlife? Or the public's sentiment soured on consciousness uploading?

"So you made your big error: you gave the dead real-world political power. You pushed through measures to let the postmortemed vote... and put them into a cost-free playground.

"Centuries later, the dead outnumbered the living fifteen to one. Not many of them voted... but not many of them *had* to, with numbers like that. The Upterlife had the votes to push through any foolish measure it wanted... Even if those measures caused real-world riots."

The copters shift into position. Gumdrool's shouting, "Take Damrosch down before he talks more heresy!"

And Wickliffe flickers back into life, his hands spread wide as though he were calling a runner safe at second base: "NO ONE SHOOT! ALL GUNS DOWN NOW!"

The rebels groan, returning to consciousness.

Wickliffe points an accusing finger at me. It quivers. "You did this," he says. "You *did* this."

"That's what *Sins of the Flesh* was, wasn't it?" I ask. "It was your last-ditch attempt to get the ghosts interested in the living. All the smart people had flitted away into your games! The only people who paid attention to the living world were the most tedious, incompetent bottom of the barrel *scrapers*. So you tried to lure the competent back to real life. You offered fabulous prizes, turning our antics into tawdry entertainment, all so a handful might pay *any* attention to what was going on outside the servers."

"They were drifting," he pled. Even now, it's terrifying to see that face, so familiar, broken and begging. "I made the games too addictive. The postmortemed have gone mad in isolation, Amichai. They don't have to eat, to work, to breathe – they've forgotten what it's like to *suffer*. They think they can do anything to the living as long as they threaten to take away your Upterlife. A few generations from now, that won't work. You'll revolt and tear down the servers, and *everything will be gone*.

"Amichai," he begs. "I'm on *your side*."

"If you were on our side, you'd hold them *accountable!*" I yell.

"It's the only way." Wickliffe falls to his knees. "I've tried to hack their archived brains, Amichai! I've tried political changes! The only way the Upterlife can survive into future generations is to change the living."

"That's your plan, isn't it? If you can change our minds *before* we upload, programming us to love the physical world, then every living person who dies will serve your agenda in the Upterlife! Oh, it'll take a few generations before your new waves of brainwashed uploads outnumber the stubborn ghosts already in there – but you think long term, don't you?

And I'm betting once you get your hands on our meat-brains, we'll be *very* devoted to voting in your interests..."

"I'm not playing politics," Wickliffe pleads. "The Upterlife is sick. It's lost touch with reality – I need to tweak your minds before you get in there, make you strong enough to not lose yourself in simple pleasures, amplify your interest in the real world so it survives into your postmortemed existence... It'll make things better for *all* the living..."

The folks on the rooftops yell at Wickliffe, raining garbage down upon him. Rubble tumbles through his flickering body, bouncing off the spirocopters.

"We're not your slaves!" they cry. "Life is choices!"

"Once you remold us to make the Upterlife cozy," I ask, "then where's it stop? Do you start tweaking us to eat the foods you want? To sacrifice ourselves for your future?" I shake my head. "You won't stop. You *haven't* stopped. And Lord knows you've already tried to hack the Upterlife to suit your agenda–"

"It's a *good* agenda!" he roars. "It's *what you want!* I'm trying to build the life you *asked for!*"

"Not like this," I say. "Not like this."

I turn as something flutters inside Wickliffe's chest. It's Gumdrool, waving something at me, holding his fist high in triumph. I squint, trying to make out what it is:

A button. A big red...

He pushes it.

My throat pops.

Peaches screams as Gumdrool's remote detonator, somehow tuned to my necklace, goes off. He could have just shot me, but that's not Gumdrool's style: he wanted me to know he'd hacked my technology.

The NeoChristians see my blood dribbling onto the rooftop. They bring their rifles up to shoot Gumdrool, but I wave them off; I want Gumdrool to know exactly what hit him.

Gumdrool looks at me through Wickliffe's ghostly chest with a fierce pride: *I got you, you sonuvabitch.*

"You fool!" Wickliffe yells. "You just proved his point!"

"I disproved it, sir," Gumdrool replies proudly, his voice emanating from the copter's speakers. "These scum won't make the Upterlife. So let's void the unworthy and go back to fixing the system."

"You don't understand! He hacked the voting system!"

"...what?"

Gumdrool looks up. Night has fallen. Everyone in Greenwich Village holds up their Shrive Points, revealing their final judgments:

A thousand points of gold.

Every one of the Greenwich Village rebels has Shrived Liminal.

"How can that–" Gumdrool looks around, refusing to believe in the results he's seeing. "The *dead* decide if you get in! They all get to vote! He can't override the collective wisdom!"

I'm too busy clutching my tattered throat to explain things. But Peaches, as usual, is ahead of everyone.

"No," she says, looking at me with sad admiration. "But he can change the collective wisdom."

It was, I think, my most elegant workaround. Could I hack into the brains of the dead? Wickliffe tried for years and couldn't manage it. Could I hack the results of a single person's Shrive? No.

But with every Shrive, a copy of our brains was sent to the dead's subconscious for judgment.

What if I made my case directly to the dead's subconscious?

Maybe I amplified it. Maybe I sent more data than I should have – you know, tons of spicy footage and decrypted code of everything Wickliffe had said to me and all of Wickliffe's interactions with Gumdrool, popping into the subconscious of a quarter-trillion brains like an infomercial from hell.

And when all of Greenwich Village Shrived, it beamed one gigantic message into the minds of the dead.

Was it mind control? Absolutely not. Wickliffe's safeguards ensured I couldn't send false messages:

Only things I believed to be.

Listen, I said. Here's the proof Wickliffe has been trying to hack your brains for years. Now he wants to hack ours.

We want to live. We want to eat delicious food, make love to our partners, make something good of our lives. But we refuse to enter the Upterlife with compromised thought-patterns. We would sooner void now than live in an uncertain paradise, not knowing whether we are truly ourselves. We would sooner disappear than be compromised.

If you think we're wrong, void us.

If you think our cause is just, let us in.

"The dead just voted," I cough through what's left of my larynx, staggering to the rooftop's edge. "They think you're full of it."

"You can't *do* this!" Gumdrool screams. "If the living can die at will, then – then nobody will be left to run the servers!"

It's not about strength, Evangeline had told me. It's about philosophy. Wake up enough people, and you'll win.

Didn't Christ end badly? I'd asked.

We all end badly, Amichai.

In the footage, I can see myself whispering. My lips are white from blood loss. Nobody knows what I'm saying, not even me.

I wish I knew what I'd said.

"Yaw... Your choice," I gurgle, a herculean effort. "Your... policies have given everyone a... a guilt-free ticket to the Upterlife. So maybe... you should make this world better... for the living." I raise a hand, too slowly, to point at Wickliffe. "Start... by getting rid of him."

"*No!*" Gumdrool shouts, beet-red. "The Upterlife can't let in traitors like you! The Upterlife needs the pure! The dutiful! The committed!"

"One way to find out," I whisper, giving him a bloodtoothed grin that will be emblazoned across every newscast for months to come.

Then I tumble off the ledge to smash onto the broken pavement below.

56: THE UPTERLIFE

Not that I remember any of that.

I lay down for my final Shrive, nervous whether this would work. Peaches had to put my Shrive helmet on for me, because of my injured arm.

I took off my Shrive helmet with both hands.

I looked down, confused. My arm had healed. How had that happened…?

…oh.

Even when you're braced for it, it's a shock to find you're dead. But my body felt nothing; my simulated body only released simulations of unpleasant hormones into my simulated bloodstream if I wanted.

While we can enable stress reactions, the world hummed, *studies have shown it's best to remove physical reaction factors from transitional space.* A variety of "Welcome to the Upterlife" tutorials flitted into view, offering to bring me up to speed.

Mother Mentor technology. The dead had had supertutorials all along.

I batted the helpscreens away. The room was a perfect white square in a vast emptiness, the walls made out of shimmering diamond. It glowed – my eyes felt like they should water, but they didn't. My eyes wouldn't water here without my authorization.

I punched the wall. Small displays popped into view,

registering the simulated damage they could inflict, the level of pain this would have caused in the outside world – then offered a variety of body customizations, from superhuman strength to synesthesia.

"That's…" I said, then fell quiet as I listened to the sound of my voice. It was as clear as life.

A bell chimed. Would you like to watch video footage of the events between your most recent Shrive and your mortality? a tutorial asked. Many find it provides a feeling of closure.

Peaches, I thought, panicked. *Greenwich Village*. They had to know my plan had worked – and more importantly, they had to know not to all jump off the roof now that I'd won, because if they did then we lost our leverage.

It occurred to me I might have escaped the void, only to be trapped in rusting servers as the living committed mass suicide.

I put my hands to my temples – *simulated hands to simulated temples* – and scanned for the IceBreaker. I'd attuned it to my brain patterns, which hopefully translated properly into the Upterlife – so now the IceBreaker, hardwired to the Upterlife servers, should respond to my command.

I focused. My brain snaked along the invisible wires threaded through the Upterlife – and I reeled. My mind brushed across billions of brains, all linked by the same subconscious pool, suggesting an astonishing array of wonderlands. My parents had stayed with the stupidly childish dungeon-crawls, but there were places far more interesting: inversion zones and fifth-dimensional crawlspaces and worlds where silicon was the primary organic chemical…

With an effort, I activated my IceBreaker.

Screams flooded through the microphones. "Peaches!" I yelled through the IceBreaker's speaker. "It worked! I'm here! What's happening?"

"A… Amichai?" Peaches said, first hesitant, then thrilled.

"Amichai! You mad bastard, you did it!"

"Why are people screaming?"

"You... you started a rain of bodies, Amichai. It's... I can see you on the ground." I realized how hard this was for her – even though she knew I'd uploaded, she'd just seen the man she loved splatter across Bleecker Street. "You're buried under corpses. The streets are..." She squealed as an explosion erupted over the mic, followed by falling debris.

Oh no. I'd stashed the IceBreaker under the ledge, out of sight, but that meant my cameras couldn't get a good view of the action – and all I *had* was cameras, I was a ghost...

"Peaches, tell our people not to jump! Use the NeoChristians to hold them back if you have to. We've gotta use this as leverage to make some changes, or Wickliffe is right – everything will collapse. The Upterlife's worth fighting for – just not his way."

Please, Izzy had begged. You can't knock it all down, Amichai...

"It's not that," Peaches said. "And don't lecture me, I just saw you die."

"OK. The real world's a trauma circus: got it. What's happening?"

"Gumdrool jumped before you were halfway down. He splattered. Then the LifeGuard in the copters went diving out after him, seeing a clear path to the Upterlife. The 'copters are crashing, Amichai–"

"*You.*"

I whirled around.

Gumdrool stood at the far end of the cube. He was breathing heavily. *He'd* enabled shock reactions.

"*You do not belong here.*" Gumdrool walked towards me, cracking his knuckles.

"*I* don't? How'd *you* make it in?!" But the dead loved devotion to duty, and Gumdrool had been nothing if not faithful to the Upterlife. Even his suicide at the end was designed to prove me wrong. He'd probably gotten in by the skin of his teeth, but–

I ducked as he swung. Diamond shattered behind me. He'd enabled superhuman strength.

I wondered how to activate mine; a swarm of tutorial-screens blocked my vision. I scrambled backwards.

"I will splinter your bones," Gumdrool swore. "Then I will erase you from the Upterlife, because you do not deserve this paradise, and I'll tell Wickliffe I solved his problems, and *I'll* be the hero! Not you! Me! *I'm* the only one who ever cared about the Upterlife, Damrosch! Me!"

– wait a minute –

"Quite right," I said. "Take your shot."

He cocked his head, confused. Then swung.

As his fist barreled towards me, a dialog box appeared:

Injurious physical contact initiated by Ian Montgomery Drumgoole at 8:13 p.m.:

Accept for this session

Accept for this injury

Accept all injurious physical contact options for this session

MORE OPTIONS

DECLINE ALL, I chose, and Gumdrool's fist swung through my head as though he'd punched a cloud.

"We're in the Upterlife, you idiot," I told him. "You think it'd be Heaven for me if you got to beat me up all the time?"

"I'll find some other way to stop you," he said. "I'll–"

"You'll do nothing." I pulled up a long list of interaction allowances for Ian Montgomery Drumgoole. "We're both immortal now. You have no way to trap me, or imprison me, or even interact with me if I don't desire it. That's a special hell for you, isn't it? Knowing I'll be dismantling Wickliffe's legacy… And all you can do is listen to me on the news."

"But I–"

"Oh, dear." I stabbed at the list merrily, narrowing our potential interactions. "Maybe if you'd stayed in the real world, you could have done something. Tortured Peaches. Kidnapped my sister again. Shot up a school full of orphans. But here, in the greatest technological achievement known to man? Why, it appears you have been reduced to a ghost."

I blocked him from visual cues. He disappeared from sight, though I heard his bellows of rage as he tried to tear my throat out.

"This is what you wanted, Ian," I told him. "You got your Upterlife. Don't blame *me* if it wasn't what you signed up for."

"I *will* find a way to stop you, Damrosch! I'll make you pay for–"

"You'll forgive me," I said serenely. "In a century or two."

I pressed the "BLOCK" button, and Gumdrool left my Upterlife forever.

I savored the moment. Then I tuned back into the IceBreaker.

"Peaches! I've got some political maneuvering to do. Can you hold off on broadcasting what we've learned until I can get a better solution?"

"Absolutely," she said. "But Amichai – Gumdrool's the only one who made it. All the other LifeGuard, they just – just voided…"

"Yeah." I felt a pang of sympathy. They'd flung themselves out of copters because they were eager for death; they hadn't realized Gumdrool's pure intentions saved him. They were selfish suicides. And they were gone.

A lot more would be going soon, I realized. A lot of real death was going to hit the world.

I hoped that was a necessary sacrifice.

57: CONVERSATIONS WITH CRIMINALS III

Wickliffe's Upterlife home was surprisingly unassuming – a dingy apartment, old enough to be made of wood and paint. The only sign of his immense wealth was the abundance of plastic, which impressed me until I realized Wickliffe had grown up in an era where plastic was common as wood.

At first, I thought the dinginess was because Wickliffe didn't spend a lot of time here. Then I looked out the back window and saw the tombstone with the bouquet of dandelions, and realized where we were:

The apartment where his father had strangled his mother.

This was the place where, alone and grieving, Wickliffe had vowed to defeat death.

Wickliffe looked shrunken, cadaverous; he sat at a scarred table, drinking from a bottle of cheap scotch. He didn't look up.

"So what are your terms?" he asked.

"It doesn't matter," I told him. "You just got the quickest impeachment in history."

He took another drink. "And you're going to do what, exactly, with all these newfound votes?"

"Form a new government."

"One all-living, I suppose?"

That was a sentiment popular in the living world – *no more ghost politicians.*

Yet it was chilling – you never realized how easily people ignored a videoscreen until you were dead. I'd suggested things to the emergency council Peaches had assembled – but they'd ignored my image to turn to the flesh-and-blood human next to them. I could clear my voice to regain their attention… but I wondered how much of that came from the fact I'd just saved their world.

I wondered whether anyone would listen to me after a century or two.

"Not by a long shot," I said, more confident than I felt. "But the dead vote for the dead, and we all know it. So they'll get to vote their representatives into the postmortemed chamber only. The dead will control forty percent of Congress, the living sixty percent. They've still got a say – just not the *final* say."

"What else?" Wickliffe asked, his eyes bleary and bemused. "You won't stop there, of course."

"Higher taxes on dead-owned property. Heftier taxes for each living generation they've existed through, until the eldest postmortemed are taxed at 90 percent. The goal is to free up resources for the living."

"Because we've got everything we need right here." Somehow, his words felt like a sly joke.

"The Upterlife *is* a paradise, sir." I never understood why I said "sir" to him. Except maybe that I was in his shoes now, and they were a lot heavier than I thought they'd be.

He rose, creakily, from his chair. "They won't like that. The postmortemed crave their power. But they have to take what you're offering, don't they? You woke them up to the fact that they couldn't keep building their paradise on the backs of the living."

I straightened with pride. "Voiding straight I did, sir."

He poked me in the chest, a low-level interaction I'd preauthorized. "You couldn't have done it without me. Remember that."

I wanted to contradict him, but in a way he was right. None of this would have been possible without his dreadful experiments. If he needed to convince himself it had been the right thing to do, then so be it.

"And me?" he asked.

"You'll be assigned to prison branch. You didn't build a mechanism to purge consciousnesses from the Upterlife–"

"I think ahead."

"– so we confine you in a small Branch in Kansas. Low-memory. Separated from the main network." Not many managed to commit crimes in the Upterlife – embezzlement was your best option – but once in a while, someone would leave aside more exciting virtual heists to pull off an actual accounting shenanigan. "Your life's going to be very boring, I'm afraid."

"Hrm." He squinted knowingly. "Well, I suppose it's what you must do now that you've vilified me. Want me to tell you what these new taxes will do in the long run? What damage this sloppy bicameral legislature will cause in a century or two? Oh, I've foreseen all the possibilities."

"I'd like to know."

He shook his head. "No. That's *my* secret."

"If you're bargaining for a better sentence–"

"No." He looked at me with pity. "Thing is, Amichai, if you live long enough you'll find out there are no good answers. If I tell you what will happen, you'll find another course that looks good now, and *that* will backfire in a century or two. You're smart enough to topple me – but nobody's smart enough to fix things forever." He stared at the bottle as though it were his only friend, took a good long pull, coughed up hot booze.

"'One experiment gone wrong, and we wind up with another Bubbler," Gumdrool had said.

"Sir," I asked. "Was the Bubbler a virus that got released prematurely? Was that...how you'd planned to flood the Upterlife with newly brainwashed activists?"

He turned from me to stare at his mother's tombstone. "I'll let you make your own mistakes." He took another drink. "Just so you can see how far good intentions get you."

58: SIX MONTHS LATER

I'd reenabled my simulated body's shock trauma, activating the adrenaline rushes and blood sugar crashes – all the little things that made triumphs sweeter.

"We got the votes?" I asked Peaches, my heart in my throat.

Peaches slapped her hand against the monitor in a virtual high-five. "We got the votes, Amichai. Our new government structure is complete. You've got forty percent of the power, I've got sixty."

I slapped my hand against the screen. It was as close as we could get to touching each other these days. Not that we tried much; Peaches was always a physical girl, and I hadn't expected her to stay faithful to someone she couldn't dance with. Neither of us discussed it.

This time, however, we left our hands touching the monitors – hers to real glass, mine to simulated.

The tabloids hinted she'd moved on to other physical pursuits. Some of the pictures were nice – she'd created the sport of wheelchair offroading, and people would clear the floor for her at formal gatherings to let her waltz with a variety of partners.

I wanted to ask her how often she thought of our final kiss – but no matter what her answer was, it wouldn't have made me feel better.

I pulled my hand back. "So it's 'you' and 'me' now, is it?"

She had the decency to look shocked. "No, I mean –
we're a *team*, Amichai. I work the living, you work the dead.
Together, we accomplish miracles."

Neither of us were politicians – me because I had no
interest in running for office, Peaches because she was too
young to hold official power. Still, a word from us could
topple institutions.

"You know we're together." She looked sad. "Right?"

"...Yeah." I forced a smile to my face. "And we're rocking
the worldchanging, right?"

She brightened. "We are *killing* the worldchanging."

She was right to be jubilant. I'd been worried that opening
up a loophole for the living to step into the Upterlife would
cause mass suicides... Though as it turns out, once you offer
challenges that *mean* something, the living step up. Tell
them they might choose their own careers and own their
own businesses – and suddenly, the American living were
completely revitalized.

(The foreign governments had their own legislative
hurdles. There were heated calls to our diplomats, warning
us we were setting a bad example. And when those calls got
forwarded to us, Peaches told them, "We're your future. Get
on board or be left behind.")

But we had so much to do. Peaches struggled to find
materials – we'd mined the planet dry, so the rare earth metals
she needed to forward her technological agenda had to come
from *somewhere*. And that somewhere was us. The Upterlife
would have shortages – but when I saw the videos of factories
being retooled to create Mother Mentors for orphanages, I
thought shortages were a small price to pay.

Me, I was tasked with revitalizing the Upterlife's
infrastructure – a position many said was more powerful
than any politician. Wickliffe's whole "subconscious vote"
schemata had worked back when the Upterlife was a lot less

forgiving about their neighbors' crimes, but my engineered Liminal Shrive had shown a system rife for exploitation.

I was devising a complete overhaul dedicated to fighting what the press now called "Good Ol' Boy syndrome," wherein the dead would subconsciously authorize anyone like themselves. This overhaul would take years: it had to be foolproof enough not to exclude based on human error, scalable enough to judge trillions of votes, and above all secure against sneaky bastards like me trying to exploit it.

There were protests, of course. *The Upterlife is a fundamental human right!* people shouted, flooding my inbox with billions of emails. I explained the Upterlife was still going to be open to everyone – we just needed to make entry a little less dependent on who *liked* you.

I tried not to think too hard about how Gumdrool's agenda and mine overlapped.

Still. It'd be insanely great, given time. The one thing I had in surplus was time.

"She's OK, isn't she?" I asked Peaches.

"For the thousandth time, Amichai, Izzy's fine."

"But she won't *talk* to me!"

"She's trying to wean off the urge to call her parents. Any connection to the Upterlife, well… it's reinforcing bad habits, is all. She's going through a detox process. She'll come around."

"That's what you said about Dare."

She flinched guiltily. "And I was… kind of right…"

"The scurvy architect prances along the rim of Saturn!"

Peaches winced, then cut the connection before Dare saw her. She'd told me a thousand times that I should force Dare to pass a knock protocol before he could enter my private spaces… But I couldn't deny Dare anything.

He walked down my mansion's curved stairway, wearing flipflops and swim trunks, trailing his fingers along the carved mahogany railing. He'd designed my mansion himself, telling me, "A man of your caliber can't live in a dingy apartment."

I looked up at Dare – except it wasn't Dare. Not the worn and beaten Dare who'd died back in Paradise. This Dare was offensively smooth of scars.

The government had decided Dare's Criminal status was unfair, and so had uploaded Dare from his last Shrive Point. A point hours before he'd even gone to the Blackout Party where we'd met Gumdrool.

"You don't need the passphrases any more," I told him.

"They're still *fun*, Amichai." He had a beach towel draped over one shoulder, a fizzing drink in his hand. "How're those NeoChristians coming along?"

"Pretty good. They're a little worried about being reservationed to death down in New Mexico – but the Native Americans didn't have half the firepower the NeoChristians've built up."

Evangeline was wielding political firepower, too, but she refused to talk to me; to her, my existence was a mockery of my memory. She would only talk to Peaches, and (I'm told) lectured Peaches on the foolishness of treating "the Amichai program" like a human being...

Dare nodded. "Good, good. Listen, I was gonna do a walkthrough of the new Harmony Center – a literal walkthrough. I've designed it, the plans are ready, but I have no idea how it looks from the inside. And I figured, *why not make it fun*? So I've got some hot bartenders lined up, the best DJs, let's hold a party in the place. Whaddaya say?"

I grimaced. "It's kind of informal for a serious project, don't you think? And besides, I'm working on the specs for this new morality-checking architecture..."

He set his drink down. "Look. Would it be easier if I stopped dropping by?"

I swallowed back guilt. "No, no, I'm always happy to... to

see you. You're my best friend."

"I have this weird definition of 'friend.' One where friends actually, you know, spend time together."

"It's not you," I lied. "Ask my family. I'm not returning my Mom and Dad's calls either..."

He chuckled. "I blocked all my ancestors. That's when I knew this was heaven."

"I... I wanna hang out with you, Dare. But I need to spamproof the Shrive channels, and the current servers need to be optimized now that we're not building new ones..."

He grabbed my shoulder – an interaction I'd also authorized. "You think I'm not working hard on my career, man? I am. But we've got so much to do, this work will crush you if you don't escape once in a while. If you don't enjoy the Upterlife, you'll become the next Wickliffe."

"I just–"

"Amichai." He grabbed my chin, forced me to look him in the eyes – eyes too trusting to be Dare. "I watched the footage. I saw what happened. I know what you did... and it's OK. I'm *here*."

You're not the same, I wanted to say. I'd watched the footage of my own death a thousand times, always wondering what I'd muttered to myself. What if I'd had some last-minute revelation about things that I'd lost?

Was I me?

This Dare found it easy to forgive me because he'd never lived through my betrayal – but the Dare back at that final assault on the mall, the *real* Dare, had looked at me with disappointment. Such unflinching disappointment.

This is the sacrifice I make for future Dare, he'd said. He'll never even know I did it.

"...I've got a project meeting in an hour. Maybe I'll stop by after that?"

Dare sighed. "You gotta get over your posttraumatic

transition syndrome, man. I did."

He had less trauma to transition past – but I didn't say that. Because this Dare was happy, and... that's what Dare would have wanted. Right?

"You better stop by," he said. "You'd watch me build meaningless bullshit all the time back at the orphanage – and when I get a chance to design the new Capitol building, you ghost out on me? You gotta see the work I'm doing, Amichai! I'm collaborating with living artists, creating the new look for our new nation – and it's gonna be built. Living people will bring my work into reality – and Peaches will get to wheel through *my* building. This is everything I've ever dreamed of, man."

It was everything I'd ever dreamed of, too – at least back when I'd been alive. The idea that the dead could work with the living to create something new was something that would never have happened before the revolution.

You set them aflame, Evangeline whispered. Now you find out what it means to lead them.

"I'll stop by," I told him. "I promise."

Dare closed the door behind him. I turned back to the screens, watching the living, making sure they were OK.

Watching. Endlessly watching.

ACKNOWLEDGMENTS

Welcome to the book I never should have written. If I'd understood just how challenging this novel would be when I started the first draft back in 2011, I would have realized that I wasn't talented enough to write it.

Because honestly? I'd created a fascinating world to explore, but there's a huge challenge in explaining to people, "Yo, he wants to murder his sister – but when there's an actual Heaven you can point to, murder's a wonderful gift!" Screw it up, and you're lost in the Sea of Mucky Infodumps.

Which is, I suppose, the glory of ignorance – you lean *way* over the side of the horse, grabbing for brass rings that saner people would pass up. And you either level up as an artist to become worthy of the Impossible Project, or you fall face down in a pile of pony poop.

And oh *man* did I level up here. I'm glad I did. Every once in a while, somebody who'd beta-read a version of this would corner me at a con to ask, "So what happened to that crazy electronic afterlife book you wrote? I still think about that story sometimes." And I was like, "It's not ready yet."

I got it ready by swelling *herculean muscles* as an artist. This book made me *swole*. Thanks, book!

Yet the lengthy development of this manuscript *does* present a problem: if you've read my 'Mancer trilogy – *Flex*, *The Flux*, and *Fix* – you'll know that I thanked every beta-reader personally, marking their unique contributions. Which isn't possible here, because this novel outlasted two laptops, each taking my archived emails crashing down with them. I don't have a record of everyone who gave me critique, except I know it was a lot of people over a lengthy development process. So I'd love to thank everyone who beta-read this for me in the early stages - but your emails are lost to history. So if I see you at a convention, buttonhole me to say, "Hey, you sonuvabitch, I gave you good critique for *The Uploaded*", and I will apologize meekly and say yes, yes, of course you did, let me buy you a beer. (Please: do not abuse this loophole to extract free drinks from me. I'm generally happy to buy my friends a beer without faked emotional blackmail.)

But the people I *do* have remaining records of critique for are Daniel Starr, EF Kelley, Miranda Suri, Keffy Kehrli, Amy Sundberg, Kat Howard, Erin Cashier, Morgan Dempsey, Nayad Monroe, Paul Berger, Erin Cashier, Sarah Gailey, Cassandra Khaw, Rebecca Galo, and Jeremiah Fargo – all of whose critiques made this better, and most of whom will probably be surprised to realize how little this book has in common with That Thing They Read In 2012.

I also must thank all the people who helped me in my Clarion Write-a-Thon – the fine people who donated money to my Clarion Science Fiction and Fantasy Writers' Workshop fundraiser and, in return, got to see me live-write an early draft of this novel. Their feedback, chapter-by-chapter, gave me hope.

I know I have to thank my agent, Evan Gregory, for giving me some of the most valuable advice: ensuring that the third act of my books answer the questions I raised in the first two-thirds. That gentle nudge let me rewrite the last third to become something more fitting. So if you read an early live-written draft and you thought you knew where this was going, *sucker*! You've been *hogswoggled*, thanks to the efforts of one Mr Gregory!

Also thanks to my, uh, best friend Angie, who refused to read the first draft. Angie likes strong beginnings. The first draft had a crappy beginning, so Angie got bored and walked away, which is often the best critique an honest friend can give you. She likes the new beginning, so if you don't like it, you can corner Angie at a bar and say, "Hey, why weren't you meaner to Ferrett?"

And while we're at it, I should acknowledge the influence of one Jennifer Melchert, who may or may not be insulted when I say she's been kiiiiind of an inspiration for certain parts of Peaches' personality.

And much thanky-juice to Marna Carney, who made a magnificent effort to do a last-minute sensitivity read even though artificially inflated deadlines were approaching and she had honest-to-God tornados to wrangle. Also thanks to Shakira Searle, who also helped me with some of the trickier bits of handling the bits involving Izzy and Peaches. If you can have someone cuddle you while they critique you, I recommend it. (Also thanks to Aileen, Kalita, and Laura, who may have generously donated snuggle time.)

Thanks to God. Seriously. My heart's with the NeoChristians, guys – and any time I stumble on a book's progress, I ask, "So, Big Fella, if you've got anything in particular You want me to say, please, help me to say it better." That's gotten me through a lot of blocks. If you're not getting your story written the way you want, maybe try some prayer.

(Or you could try listening to Rise Against's "Re-Education (Through Labor)" over 300 times like I did, making it the unofficial theme song for *The Uploaded*. But that hard-rock shout of rebellion is probably less applicable to your tale than mine.)

And thanks to everyone at the monstrously efficient company of the mighty Angry Robot – Marc Gascoigne,

Michael Underwood, temporary Robot pal Simon Spanton-Walker, Paul Simpson, Nick Tyler, and Penny Reeve made this book not only better, but, you know, *possible*.

And finally, as we approach the end of the novel, if y'all wanna see what I'm up to, you can hit up my personal blog at *www.theferrett.com* – that's two "R"s, two "T"s – or just follow me on Twitter as *@Ferretthimself*. I yammer a lot. Some people even consider this a bonus.

But those who've followed me through several books know where my acknowledgments always end. Because there's only one woman who's consistently hugged me when I was on the verge of giving up writing. There's only one woman who's calmly endured my panicky frenzies when I'm not quite sure how to fix this book but I know I *have* to. There's only one woman who, back in those crazy days of 2008, said, "Sure, take six weeks off and pay several thousand dollars to go to the Clarion Writers' Workshop even though you've spent fifteen years selling precisely bupkiss – because I want you to follow your dreams."

I dream of being a writer. But I also dream of being the best damn husband in the world to my wife, Gini, because damn if she hasn't been a far better wife to me than I (or any man) have ever deserved.

I love you, Gini.

Arf.

Ferrett Steinmetz
April 2017

ABOUT THE AUTHOR

Ferrett Steinmetz is a graduate of both the Clarion Writers' Workshop and Viable Paradise, and has been nominated for the Nebula Award, for which he remains stoked. Ferrett has a moderately popular blog, *The Watchtower of Destruction*, wherein he talks about bad puns, relationships, politics, videogames, and more bad puns. As well as the acclaimed 'Mancer trilogy – *Flex, The Flux* and *Fix* – he's written four computer books, including the still-popular-after-all-these-years *Wicked Cool PHP*. He lives in Cleveland with his wife, who he couldn't imagine living without.

theferrett.com/ferrettworks • *twitter.com/ferretthimself*